Lexi James

AND THE

Council of Girlfriends

Lexi James

AND THE

Council of Girlfriends

MELISSA JACOBS

AVON
TRADE

An Imprint of HarperCollins*Publishers*

HarperCollins books may be purchased for education, business, or sales promotional use. For information please write: Special Markets Department, HarperCollins Publishers Inc., 10 East 53rd Street, New York, NY 10022.

FIRST EDITION

Designed by Elizabeth M. Glover

Library of Congress Cataloging-in-Publication Data

Jacobs, Melissa.
    Lexi James and the council of girlfriends / by Melissa Jacobs.
        p. cm.
ISBN 0-06-074398-0 (alk. paper)
1. Young women—Fiction. 2. Volunteer workers in social service—Fiction.
3. Commitment (Psychology)—Fiction. 4. Female friendship—Fiction.
5. Older Jews—Fiction.   I. Title: Lexi James and the council of girlfriends.   II. Title.

PS3610.A35646L498 2005
813'.6—dc22   2004016377

05 06 07 08 09 JTC/RRD 10 9 8 7 6 5 4 3 2 1

For my mommy

Acknowledgments

Big hugs, much love and tremendous thanks to:

My brother Dave, for the support he gave.

Maury Z. Levy, the first to say,
"You'll be a good writer some day."

Betsy Amster, fairy godmother,
agent and editor like no other.

The Avon Ladies:
Lucia Macro and Selina McLemore.
Book takers. Dream makers. It's you I adore!

Kammie Gormezano, my Special K,
for believing in me all the way.

The divine Dr. Monica Duvall.
I couldn't have a better friend on call.

Mom, for her hope, joy and love.
Daddy, who guides me from above.

Sorority League Leadership Conference
Irvine Auditorium, University of Pennsylvania
September 1990

"Your generation reaps the benefits of the generations which came before you. When I graduated from this university in the 1960s, my diploma was from the College of Women. From that time to this, women have broken ceilings and soared to the skies. Your generation has seen the first female justice of the Supreme Court, the first female astronaut to go into space, and the first female to run a Fortune 500 company.

"And so it is with great hope that I look out into this audience and see the next generation of women. You have more choices today than any women in any country. You can continue your education. You can get married. You can have children. You can launch your career. You can work in politics, medicine, or business.

"These are your choices. Make them wisely."

Taking the lollipop out of my mouth, I lean toward my friend Monica and ask, "So what exactly are we supposed to do?"

This is the night before the day of my wedding. The wedding I canceled.

My best friends and I are commemorating the nonwedding by drinking champagne at the Ritz-Carlton Philadelphia. We call ourselves the Council of Girlfriends.

We the COG are reclining on the tapestried lounges and brocaded settees in the hotel's bar, which is full of Oriental rugs, statuary, silver, gold, and pizzazz. An ornate crystal chandelier hangs above the center of the rotunda. Marble columns lead to a skylight, through which we see the starry night.

"To the Council of Girlfriends." Grace raises her champagne glass.

"To us," Ellie says.

"¡Salud!" Lola shouts.

"To friendship," I add.

The four flutes meet in the middle of the table. The crystal glasses sparkle and the gold champagne shimmers. Carefully, we move our flutes together until they clink. Each of us moves a flute to her mouth and I sip slowly, looking at my friends through the barrel of my flute.

"I love you girls," I tell them.

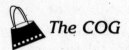 *The COG*

These are not just any girls, and not just any friends. I have girlfriends, and then I have the Council of Girlfriends. My very best friends. Friends? Family. Sisters. I am an only child, and my parents separated before I could speak. I haven't seen a whole lot of them since. But the Council of Girlfriends knows the details of my life. I talk to them almost every day.

Talk? We don't just talk. We debate, debrief, advise, justify, rectify, and argue about our lives. It comforts me to know that these women will call me if three days pass without me calling them. We know everything about one another. Food allergies, favorite TV shows, bra sizes, first boyfriends, and every heartbreak since. Because we know so much about each other, we act as an advisory board for life decisions big and small. I like having a committee to which I am responsible for my actions.

On our way out of the Ritz, I spot George Larrabie at the reception desk. Is that George? He's wearing a trench coat and a hat, but it is George, the president of Liberty Bank, a client of The Gold Group, of which I am the executive vice president. "Come say hello with me," I tell the COG.

"Wonderful to see you, George," I greet him with a big PR smile and offer my hand for him to shake.

"Oh, Lexi," George stammers as he shakes my hand. "Funny running into you here."

Funny? Why? George smiles and looks guilty. I glance at the twenty-something woman standing next to George. Is she his wife? Do I care? No.

I introduce the Council of Girlfriends. "This is Lola Bravia," I begin. George gives Lola a long look, which is not surprising. Lola is an exotic, voluptuous Latina with dramatic eye make-up and expensive, colorful clothing and jewelry.

"I've seen your TV show," George says. Lola owns one of the hottest restaurants in Philadelphia and hosts her own local TV cooking show. "I love to eat at your restaurant."

"*Muchas gracias.*" Lola bows her head.

"This is Ellie Archer," I continue.

"Ellie Archer," George murmurs. "The name sounds familiar."

"She writes for *Vanity Fair,* the *New Yorker,* and sometimes for *Philadelphia* magazine," I explain.

"Oh, yes," George says. "I read your story about the upsurge in teenage volunteerism. It inspired my daughter." George looks guilty again. "You may have changed lives."

Ellie flashes her huge brown eyes and tugs at her shoulder length, brown hair. She raises one of her perfectly arched, Audrey Hepburn eyebrows and gestures to Grace. "Grace is the one who changes lives," she says.

"Hi," Grace smiles at George and extends her hand. "I'm Grace Harte." Grace is a Gwyneth-esque WASP with long blond hair and blue eyes. Grace is beautiful, even in the scrubs she wears as an RN at Philadelphia Hospital.

And me? I can't be as sexy as Lola, or my male clients would be all over me. I can't be as sophisticated as Ellie, because my female clients would resent me. I can't be as carelessly beautiful as Grace, because I'm not beautiful.

I have to work at being attractive. My brunette bob is straightened every week, my nails are manicured every other week, and my eyebrows are waxed every two weeks. My makeup changes seasonally. I don't own shoes shorter than two inches. It takes a lot of work to look this natural.

George doesn't introduce the woman standing with him, so I smile and say, "I'll speak with you soon, George. Enjoy the rest of your evening."

 ## Plan M

Later that night, I stare out my window and think about my life. I had a plan. I did. Actually? I've had several plans. This? Where I am now? This was not my plan.

Plan A was this: Do well enough in high school to get into a good college. Graduate. Get a job. Work hard. Move up the corporate ladder. Make enough money to buy nice clothes, rent a nice apartment, and pay off my student loans.

Ta da. I've done all that. I accomplished Plan A before I turned twenty-eight years old. I moved on to Plan B. Which was this: Make more money. Rent a fabulous apartment. Travel. Save. Make more money. Be financially independent. I completed Plan B when I was thirty-one and a half years old.

Then I went on to Plan C. Really, it was Plan M: Marriage. I am thirty-three years old. I was thirty-two when Ron Anderson proposed marriage. Ron wanted Plan M and the real Plan C: Children. Neither plan was of my choosing, but they seemed to be the alpha woman things to do. I mean, what kind of woman wouldn't want to marry an attractive, successful lawyer and bear his children?

Too late—as in, after I said yes—I realized that I didn't want

6

to have Ron's children. Of course, I didn't want to marry Ron, either. So that worked out well.

I broke the engagement three months ago, after we ordered the invitations but before we mailed them. It was the right thing to do. I think. But now, tonight, sitting here alone in my apartment on what would've been the night before my wedding, I can't help but reconsider my plans and my decisions.

What if I decide, in a few years, that I really do want a baby? I mean, I'm an excellent aunt to other people's kids. What if I miss my chance at maternity? I can't wait forever to have kids. Maybe there is a big countdown clock in my uterus. I thought it was only halftime. Maybe I'm in the third quarter. Maybe I have only a two-minute time-out before the fourth quarter. Maybe it's time for a Hail Mary.

I tend to get neurotic after I see the COG. They—and by they, I mean Grace and Lola—make me feel that I am a Mistress of the Universe who missed the right exit and took a wrong turn on the highway of life. Why do Grace and Lola make me feel this way? Grace is a stereotypical thirty-one-year-old who wants marriage and children. Grace is sure that Michael, her boyfriend of four years, will propose. Any day now. Maybe tomorrow. Or the next day.

Lola divorced her adulterous husband and will never trust another man with her heart. However, she thinks Grace, Ellie, and I should get married. Hey, it might work out for us. Lola thinks we should give marriage a whirl. She believes that being divorced is better than never having been married.

God bless Ellie. She is my comrade in the single world. Ellie is confidently going about the business of auditioning lovers for the role of Husband. She is not worried about the time clock. As far as I know.

And then there is Mia Rose. The fifth member of the Council of Girlfriends. She's not around much. Not anymore. Mia is married to Michael Rose and has a lovely life in the Jersey suburbs with their two young sons. Mia got it right.

I have not gotten it right. Not yet. I look at my clock and see that it is 12:03 AM. Here it is. The day I was to be married. Did I do the right thing by ending the engagement? Why do I keep questioning myself? Self-doubt is a new thing for me. I have always known who I am. Now I'm wondering who I've become.

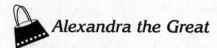 ## Alexandra the Great

You're being ridiculous, I tell myself as I get into bed. You know who you are.

I am Alexandra James. I have friends, a career, money, clothes, shoes, and a swanky apartment on Rittenhouse Square, the poshest address in Philadelphia. I even have a comfy, cozy, royal, queen-size bed and sheets with a three-hundred-fifty thread count. Of everything I own, my aunt Emma is proudest of my sheets' obese thread count. "You haven't made it," she told me, "until your sheets have at least a three-hundred thread count."

So I guess I've made it. I pay my own bills, take out my own trash, and fix my own toilet, or pay someone to do it. I can take care of myself. I don't need a man. I do need a penis, however. Penises are good to have around. I am quite fond of them.

 ## I'm Fine

On the morning of the day I was to be married, I turn off my alarm clock, get out of bed, and stretch. And smile, as though someone is watching me. "See?" I say out loud. "I'm fine."

After that midnight wallow, I am determined to be happy and show everyone that I am happy. Might as well start practicing while it's just me and God in the apartment.

"I'm fine," I tell my loofah in the shower.

Before I pick out my clothes, I turn on my TV. "Good morning, Diane!" I gush. "Good morning, Charlie! How are you today? You're fine? Me too! What's that, Charlie? Yes. I was supposed to be married today. What, Diane? Oh, no. I'm fine. Really. I'm better off this way."

Turning to my closet, I tell myself, "Let's wear something sophisticated, shall we? How about this beige pant suit? Perfect! Does the chocolate silk blouse go underneath? Yes, it sure does. And how about this leopard print neckerchief? Grr. Fabulous. With the chocolate leather boots? Pearl drop earrings? Excellent. A spritz of Chanel No. 5? Don't mind if I do."

Looking in the mirror, I say, "Really, Lexi. You're fine."

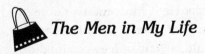 ## The Men in My Life

"Morning, Miss Lexi."

"Good morning, John," I greet my doorman. Over the past several years, John has been the most consistent man in my life.

John sits behind the mahogany reception desk and doesn't move to open the door. "Now, Miss Lexi," he says.

"Yes?"

"You lost the date again, Miss Lexi," John says, looking at me as if I've flunked spelling.

"I know perfectly well what the date is. It's January thirty-first." Thinking he is going to comment on my nonwedding day, I brace myself for John's doorman wisdom. Of course John knows about my broken engagement. He knows almost everything about my life.

"You got to leave me tip money for the grocery boy," John says.

"Oh." On the last day of every month, Rittenhouse Grocer delivers my standing order for dry goods. I don't have time to shop for toilet paper and the like. Why should I, if I can pay someone to do it for me? Anyway, I have an aversion to supermarkets.

"Here's five dollars, John. Thank you." The store bills me, but I leave tip money with John for the delivery guy.

"Now, you got any dry cleaning coming in?" John asks.

"No."

"Any packages? Anything else?"

"Nope."

My life would not run smoothly without Doorman John. I hate when he takes his vacation. He is more than a doorman, and I tip him an enormous amount to take care of me as best he can. I like to think John would be fond of me even if I didn't give him three hundred dollars every Christmas and twenties when I need something extra. Maybe John doesn't like me at all. Maybe he's just doing his job. Maybe he thinks I'm nuts. Maybe I am.

*   *   *

"Good morning, Lexi."

"Morning, Patrick."

"Grande latte to go?"

"Yes, please." Patrick works at my favorite coffee shop. It's the opposite direction from my office, but I like to walk through Rittenhouse Square every morning. In Philadelphia, we have five squares, remnants of William Penn's plan for a "green countrie town." Rittenhouse Square is an urban park, two blocks long and two blocks wide. Trees, benches, statues, landscaped flower beds, and a reflecting pool make Rittenhouse Square as beautiful as Place des Vosges, its Parisian cousin. Cafés and high-rise, high-end apartment buildings circle the Square, and if that wasn't Mr. Penn's original intention, well, he might not mind.

Café Oz sits on the Square's southwest corner, and Patrick has been working the morning shift for as long as I've been coming here. He's very well spoken and has only one noticeable tattoo. I considered hiring him. But then who would make my morning latte?

"Good morning, Veep." Veep is slingo for my title at The Gold Group.

"Good morning, Low Man." Low Man on the Totem Pole is also a title at The Gold Group. The current Low Man is Mike DiBuono, and he is actually a junior account executive, but as the newest hiree, he has to answer the phones and sit at the reception desk. I refuse to have an automaton answer the phones. And anyway, it's motivation for the newbies to move up the ranks of the company.

"Veep? You've already had a few phone calls." Low Man

Mike hands me pink slips of paper. "It's 9:18 AM. I was beginning to worry about you."

"I'm fine."

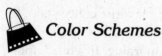 ## Color Schemes

I love my office. The brown leather couch sits in front of a glass coffee table. Awards and work-related photos hang on salmon-colored walls. Instead of a desk, I have an old-fashioned writing table. My chair is a Louis Quinze high-backed chair, not a drab thing with wheels. The truth is that I bought the chair for twenty-five dollars at an estate auction, but no one knows that.

In the corner sits an armoire that began life as a catalog-issue storage closet, but was reborn via a can of varnish and a rag. The pièce de résistance is on the floor. It's a leopard-print area rug, which stretches from my desk to the coffee table to the door. A rug like that would give my Amex an erection, which is why the rug is not a rug but a bedspread I found in the consignment shop my mother manages.

The best part of my office is the wall of windows. The Gold Group is on the twenty-fourth floor of Executive Tower, and my wall of windows affords me a view of downtown Philadelphia. The city looks like a peaceful village from this height, especially at night.

I'm standing in front of my wall of windows thinking about the wedding invitations when Low Man on the Totem Pole buzzes my intercom. "Veep, your mother is on line five."

"Please tell her I'm at lunch."

"Lexi, it's 10:30 AM."

"Then please tell her that I'm in a meeting."

I pick up my thought where I left it, which was trying to re-member the wording of the invitation. My parents are now married to other people, and I remember haggling with myself over the order in which their names appeared.

"Veep?" Low Man buzzes.

"Yes?"

"Grace Harte is on line seven for you."

"I'm in a meeting." What did the invitation say? *Mr. & Mrs. James and Mr. & Mrs. Northstein* . . . No, that wasn't it.

My intercom buzzes again. "Lexi?" Low Man asks quietly.

"Yes?"

"Lola Bravia is on the phone. Are you in a meeting?"

"Yes, thank you." *Leo & Mary Ann James and Gloria & Howard Northstein invite you to* . . . No. That wasn't it either.

"Lexi?" Low Man calls hesitantly through the intercom.

"Yes?"

"Lola says she got up at this *loca* hour to make sure you are feeling okay and she doesn't believe that you're in a meeting, and even if you are, you should pick up the phone and at least say hello to her."

Loca hour? It's 11 AM. "Mike," I say calmly. "Tell her that you couldn't disturb me but you'll transmit her eloquent message."

"Okay," Mike singsongs.

I try to visualize the invitations. They were creamy taupe with chocolate ink and a satin border topped with a pale pink bow.

"Veep?"

I grit my teeth and pray for patience. "What, Low Man?"

"There's a delivery for you. A basket of gourmet junk food."

"Put it in the kitchenette for the staff."

"Dontcha want to know who sent it?"

"Open the card and tell me."

Not hesitating a minute to literally tear into my life, Low Man rips at the envelope. Through the intercom, I hear him sigh. " 'Thinking of you today. Love, Mia.' How sweet. Why today, Veep? It's not your birthday. Is it an anniversary of some kind?"

"No," I thunder into the intercom, all patience lost. "It's nothing"

Sitting on my couch, I wish my friends would let me forget what today is. Was. Would've been. Isn't. My intercom buzzes again. Low Man clears his throat. "Lexi?"

"Low Man," I say firmly. "You obviously can't take a hint. Please hold my calls until I tell you otherwise."

Over the intercom, a voice says, "Tell her to stop being a bitch."

"Uh, Lexi? Miss Ellie Archer is here to see you."

The Therapeutic Properties of Butterscotch Krimpets

"You forget that I'm a journalist," Ellie greets me when I meet her in The Gold Group lobby. "I want to know what's happening? I go to the source." Ellie smirks and sticks out her tongue. I roll my eyes at her, even though I'm glad to see her.

Ellie looks very much her shabby chic self, in jeans, black boots, and a long, black wool coat with a long, thin red scarf tied around her neck. Ellie wears a black watch cap that covers half of her face, upon which she isn't wearing any makeup. "You look stunning," I tell her.

Ellie ignores my sarcasm and says, "I brought you a present." She holds out a plastic bag from Wawa, the Pennsylvania chain of convenience stores.

"Gee thanks. Want to go on the roof?"

Ellie follows me up the stairs to the roof of Executive Tower. Officially, the roof is off-limits. Unofficially, I bribed the head maintenance man into giving me a key to the roof door so I could smoke up here, as opposed to down there on the street with the other addicts. Even though I have quit smoking, I still consider the roof a concrete oasis.

"Wow," Ellie says when we emerge from the stairwell onto the roof. "Some view."

"Yeah." Sitting myself on a throne of abandoned bricks, my coat cuddling me in warmth, I reach into the WaWa bag and remove a Diet Dr Pepper and a package of Butterscotch Krimpets, my favorite kind of Tastykake. "This is perfect, Ellie. Thank you." I look down so she doesn't see my tears.

Ellie's not looking at me anyway. "There's the Ben Franklin Bridge." Ellie points to it, as if I haven't driven over Ben my whole life. While Ellie points to landmarks that I have seen from this vantage point many times, I pop open the can of soda and open the Krimpets. At the noise, Ellie comes to sit next to me on the bricks. I take a bite of Krimpet and offer another cake to Ellie.

"I got me mine." Ellie grins like a kid. From her jacket pocket, she pulls a package of Kandy Kakes, the peanut butter and chocolate Tastykakes. We take nibbles of our treats, enjoying every bite of the snack cakes we allow ourselves to eat only in emergencies.

Licking her fingers, Ellie says, "Want to talk?"

"No."

After a few moments, I clear my throat and tell Ellie what has really been on my mind all day. "I hope Ron is okay. This must be a hard day for him, too."

"Yeah," Ellie murmurs.

"I feel sick when I think about the pain I caused him."

Ellie puts her arm around me. I lean my head on her shoulder. We sit quietly, looking at the city.

 ## The Bed-In, Part One

Later, I am in my office reviewing the final details on the promotion for Boudoir, a national chain opening a boutique on Walnut Street. Boudoir sells high-end lingerie for women and men, silk and satin sheets, pillows, candles, lotions, and tasteful sex toys. Boudoir has boutiques in Chicago, Dallas, Miami, San Francisco, and Atlanta.

The Gold Group is organizing a six-city celebration of Boudoir's Philadelphia opening, which happens on Valentine's Day. We are creating a national Bed-In with the ironic tag line "Love is all you need." Boudoir agreed to donate 50 percent of the day's profit to the Planned Parenthood chapters in each city. It was my idea, and it's one of my best.

Executing the idea is Maria Simons, one of The Gold Group's senior account executives. Maria is organizing the twelve-hour kissathon. King-size, tastefully appointed beds will be set up in the middle of every Boudoir. Couples—over the age of eighteen—have registered to keep the bed occupied in fifteen-minute shifts. The couple has to kiss—and just kiss—for the entire fifteen minutes. For each of the six stores, Maria and her team have lined up local sports celebrities, politicians, entertainers, and regular folks. Including gay folks.

Maria expected me to object to her targeting the demographic of which she is a member, but I don't. As long as I know who's screwing me, I don't need to know who anyone else is screwing. Also? Gays have a lot of disposable income.

The press is devouring this. There are still two weeks until the Bed-In, but Maria has early commitment from national morning shows and entertainment shows.

With a smile on my face, I read Maria's Bed-In progress report. She's amazing. The roster of people she has enlisted is impressive. Then I see my name. "Lexi James + ?" I put a line of red ink through that.

 ## The Relentless Romantic

After leaving my office early, which is 5 PM, I return to my building to find that the evening doorman has a pile of stuff for me. Dad sent a bouquet of colorful, nonbridal, flowers. Mom delivered a paper bag filled with aromatherapy candles and bath salts. Lola left carefully packaged food from her restaurant, with instructions on reheating. Grace dropped off her DVDs of the first three seasons of *Buffy the Vampire Slayer*.

They are so good to me. I leave thank-you messages for Mom, Dad, and Lola, then dial Grace's apartment, expecting to leave another message. But Grace picks up on the first ring.

"You're da bomb," I tell her.

"I didn't know which movies you'd like. Are you in the mood for *Buffy*? You don't have to watch the DVDs if you don't want to"

"Gracie, this is perfect," I assure her.

"How are you feeling?" Grace's question has just a shade too much pity.

"I'm fine," I snap. I snap at Grace a lot. Maybe it's because I see her as a little sister. Grace pledged my sorority as a freshman. I was a junior. Despite the age difference—and hazing—we became friends. Our friendship deepened when Grace graduated into the real world. Many Penn grads leave Philadelphia seeking high-paying jobs, but Grace and I are from the area, so we were already home.

Our friendship has withstood the test of time, and my resignation from the I Want To Get Married And Have Kids party. Grace is still a card-carrying member.

"You'll get through this," Grace says with sugar. "You'll find the right man. The man who is perfect for you."

"I know I will," I bark. Be nice! I yell at myself. She means well, despite her relentless romanticism.

"All right, sweetie," Grace coos as if I haven't been a big meanie. "I have the night shift at the hospital, but page me if you need anything."

"Thanks, Gracie," I say quietly.

I hang up the phone and feel bad. Worse than I've felt all day, and there's a long night ahead of me. It's only 5:18 PM. Hey! That's dinnertime at the Home.

The Elder Council of Girlfriends

Every other week or so, I visit the Jewish Geriatric Home on Broad Street. Years ago, Susan Gold-Berg, president of The Gold Group, got guilted into doing pro bono work for the Home's annual fund-raiser. Of course, she passed the buck to me, and, surprisingly, I enjoyed it. I like the feisty women— and the residents are almost exclusively women—I met. They became my adopted *bubbe*s. My grandparents died when I was young. Even if they had lived, I doubt they would've been as entertaining as the Elder Council.

It's 5:45 PM when I get to the Home. Way past dinnertime. The Elder COG is gathered in the recreation room. When Ruth sees me, she puts down her needlepoint and opens her arms for a hug, folding me against her bosom, which is like a shelf of lumpy flesh. "Hello, Lexi. Ach, look at you. A *shayna madela*. So pretty."

"You look older," Sylvia says. This is her way of telling me that it has been too long since I last visited. I am now fluent in Jewish guilt.

"I am older," I tell Sylvia. "Every day."

"All right, Lexi," Ruth says. Ruth is an uber-*bubbe*. She has curled, dyed auburn hair, gigantic glasses, and a gold necklace with a Star of David dangling from the cliff of her bosom. "Tell us about your life. What's new?"

Although I have regaled these women with tales of my life, I'm not surprised that they don't remember today was The Day. Of course I told them about the broken engagement. I tell them the truth about my life, adding some melodrama and deleting seedy details. They love the PG-13 version, re-

19

joicing in my successes and offering Yiddish wisdom to heal my failures.

"Tell us what's going on with you," Sylvia urges. Sylvia refuses to dye her short, angular cap of gray hair. Comfort is paramount to Sylvia, so she wears an interchangeable wardrobe of velour, elasticized pants and zip-up sweatshirts that sometimes match. Sylvia's hearing is spotty, which makes for interesting conversations.

"You don't have to tell us anything, darling," says Esther. Queen Esther, as she is called behind her back, is a beautiful woman with long, blond-gray hair that she brushes and styles every day. Her makeup is always flawless, and she dresses in eclectic but stylish clothes, like lacy blouses and long skirts. It's as if Esther is expecting male visitors. Which she may be.

Esther smiles at me and says, "A real woman knows to keep her secrets."

"*Zash til*, Esther," Sylvia says.

"Don't tell me to shut up." Esther pouts.

"Honestly, there's not much to tell," I say.

"But, *shayna*," Ruth says, "no new boyfriend?"

"Don't start on her about the husband and children thing," Esther warns.

"Your generation waits too long to get married. Oy vey, it's a crisis," Ruth declares.

"My life is not a crisis. Other people might be in crisis, but I'm not a crisis. I'm a noncrisis. I'm an anticrisis."

"Anti-Christ?" Sylvia exclaims. "She's the Anti-Christ?"

"I said," I say, "crisis. Not Christ. In that sentence, there was no Christ."

"There was no Christ? Is that what you said?"

"Are you finally becoming Jewish, dear?" Ruth asks.

"No, I am not becoming Jewish."

"You never know, Lexi," Esther says. "There's still time for you to meet a nice Jewish boy. *Kina hora.*"

"*Kina hora,*" Sylvia and Ruth repeat.

"Don't we have a grandson to fix up with Lexi?" Ruth asks. "Between the three of us?"

"I don't want to be fixed up," I say nicely.

"My grandson Eric would be perfect for you," Sylvia says.

"Didn't Eric get engaged last week?" Esther asks.

"Yeah," Sylvia grunts. "But I don't like her."

I listen to updates on the children and grandchildren of the Elder Council. The news is of marriages, births, and brises. "Someday," Ruth says, "we'll dance at your wedding. *Kina hora.*"

"*Kina hora,*" Sylvia and Esther repeat.

"Someday," I agree skeptically, rising from my chair. I give each woman a hug and a peck on the cheek.

 ## The Fifth Girlfriend

Leaving the Elder Council, I head back to my apartment. As I'm putting away the groceries left by the delivery boy, the phone rings.

"It's Mia," she exhales into the phone. "How are you? I'm checking to see how your day went before I fall asleep."

Looking at the clock, I see that it is 9 PM. "I'm fine," I say for the last time that day. "Thanks for the basket. Very sweet. Loved it." I've learned to speak to Mia in short sentences. I never know when one of her two boys will interrupt the conversation.

"So, this day is over," Mia says. "It passed."

"Yes. How are you, Mia Rose?"

Mia starts to speed talk like David, her six-year-old. He is clearly a bad influence on his mother. "When can I see you? How about tomorrow? Wait, is tomorrow Saturday? Saturdays stink. How about Sunday? Brunch? Oh, poop." Mia talks like a mom. She's eliminated curse words from her vocabulary. "We have a birthday party. You know what? Michael can take the boys. You and I can hang out. Can we? Hang out? Just the two of us?"

"Of course, Mia."

"Great. Come here. Can you?"

"Yes," I answer, and Mia giggles with excitement.

 ## Be Another Vegetable

Although I do not feel like going out on Friday night, I let the COG convince me to go to a gallery opening in Old City. We're going to Artists' House Gallery to see this month's exhibit: Junk Art. Lola is interested in a piece of Junk Art for her restaurant and wants the COG's opinion. It doesn't sound promising.

In a corner of the gallery, we find space to stand and observe. "This is depressing," Grace says, surveying the twenty-somethings in their flirtatious revelry. Gallery openings in Old City are social scenes. They are Events.

"You know what's depressing?" Ellie asks. "Last night, I saw a TV show about mothers in their twenties who delayed careers so they could bear children."

"Does the documentary make it seem like that's a good choice?" I ask.

"Biologically, yes. Women are at their peak childbearing capability in their twenties. Forget about getting an education to get a job to earn enough money to support a family. Or finding the right man to be a good father to the children."

"As if we can just go out and find husbands," I say.

"Men do that all the time," Grace says. "When they decide to get married, boom. They do. Men don't worry about their biological clocks. They just find a younger woman to marry."

"This documentary said it's a biological instinct for men to select young, fertile women as mothers. It seems women our age have passed our expiration dates."

"Like milk," I say. "When you're not sure if it's too old or not. It smells a little off, but you think maybe you can stretch it for one more day. Then you just leave it in your refrigerator because it's too nasty to deal with. Then it wrinkles and curdles and it's too gross to wash down the sink, so you throw the whole carton into the trash."

"I don't want to be milk," Grace says. "I'd like to think of myself as fruit. Something sweet and small. Perhaps something in the berry family."

"I'm a plantain," Lola says.

"Because it's exotic?" Grace asks.

"*Sí*. And because a plantain isn't ready to be used until it is overripe and the peel looks like it's rotten. But that's when it's sweetest inside. You can't use a young, hard, green plantain. You have to be patient and let it mature. Then you can do all kinds of things with it. Mash it. Fry it. Use it as a vegetable, or a dessert, or just as a decoration. That's me. A plantain."

"I would be an onion," Ellie says.

"Yuck," Grace says.

"Because you have to peel away the layers?" I guess.

"Nope. Think about it. Onions are an essential ingredient in cooking. So many recipes start, 'Sauté the onions and garlic in butter.' Actually? I would be a shallot. A shallot is a sophisticated onion. I think it's French."

"I used to think of myself as a tomato," I say.

"Because you're from Jersey?" Lola asks. "I love Jersey tomatoes."

"No. A cherry tomato. A cute little cherry tomato. Tiny, so it's a burst of flavor in one tiny bite. A nice accent to other vegetables. Decorative. And delicious. And healthy."

"Tomato is a good thing to be," Lola says. "It's low-maintenance. You don't have to peel it. No special storage. Just leave it sitting in the sun to ripen. A little salt, and it's ready to eat."

"Now I think I've been sitting in the sun too long." I shrug. "Maybe I passed the point where I was juicy and ripe. Soon my skin will start to wrinkle. Then I'll be a sun-dried tomato."

"Sun-dried tomatoes are good," Lola says. "They are expensive."

"But you only use a little bit at a time because they are so pungent. Pungent. Not cute. Not juicy. And you can't rehydrate a sun-dried tomato. Once the juice is gone, it's gone forever."

"Be another vegetable," Grace tells me. "It's not too late."

 ## The Artist

We decide to circulate instead of standing in the corner like old fogies. Lola approaches a Junk Art sculpture of whisks, spatulas, and other kitchen tools. "Will it fit?" Grace asks. The sculpture is seven feet tall and five feet wide. "I'll make it fit," Lola says. "I love it."

"Glad to hear that," someone says. I peer around the sculpture to see who is talking.

"I'm Jack McKay," the man tells Lola. "Otherwise known as the artist." He offers his hand for her to shake.

The artist is hot. He's about five-ten with blue eyes and dark blond hair that tousles down to his chin. He's wearing a deep purple, velvet, button-down shirt and light blue, distressed jeans. The black cord around his neck holds multicolored beads, and a thick silver ring sits on his right ring finger.

Holy bad boy, Batman.

"And this is my friend Lexi James." Lola gestures to me. She's been introducing the COG while I've been salivating. Stepping around the sculpture, I smile at this Jack McKay man. Man oh man.

"Nice to meet you," I say more throatily than I mean to.

"And you." He smiles.

"Lexi is the best PR person in town," Lola says. "She could really help your career."

I blush. Blush? Me?

"Public relations?" Jack says. He puts his hands in his jean pockets, inadvertently showing me his narrow hips.

"Give him your card," Ellie murmurs. I pull my Tiffany card case from my purse, extract a card, and hand it to Jack. In the act of leaning toward him, I inhale his scent. It's soap. The ultimate, only, true smell of a man.

The COG on Irish Spring

"He is so not going to call me," I tell the COG as we walk backward down Market Street, searching for a cab to hail. "I practically drooled on him. I made an ass of myself." No one disagrees with me.

Lola snags a cab and we pile into it. "It's that smell," I tell them. "That soap smell. It gets me every time."

"Forget cologne," Ellie says. "Soap does it for me."

"Irish Spring is my favorite," Grace says. "I buy it for Michael."

"Brings out their pheremones," Lola says.

We sit quietly in the cab, paying silent homage to Irish Spring.

 ## Sixteen Candles

It's another Saturday night in Philadelphia. In gym clothes stained with dried sweat, I'm sitting on my couch eating tablespoons of Skippy Super Chunk Peanut Butter from its plastic jar and watching *Sixteen Candles* on some obscure cable channel. It's almost over, and this is one of the best endings of any of John Hughes's epics.

Like the good girl she is, Samantha runs back into the church to retrieve her sister's veil. When she comes outside, Sam sees her family piling into their cars. Once again, they have forgotten her. Sam is disappointed, but not surprised. Then the crowd clears and Sam sees Jake standing across the street from the church. He's looking particularly perfect, standing with his hands in his pockets, leaning against his little red sports car. Jake gestures to Sam, and she looks behind her to see who he's pointing at. Sam puts a finger to her chest and mouths, "Me?" "Yeah, you," Jake says. Sam runs down the steps toward Jake's car. He opens the door for her. Sam waves to her ditzy but benevolent father. The next scene is Sam and Jake sitting on the dining room table in Jake's house. Between them is a birthday cake, alight with candles. "Happy birthday, Samantha," Jake says. They lean toward each other, over the cake and candles. They kiss. The credits roll.

Tears roll down my cheeks. I want to call the COG, but Lola and Grace are working and Ellie is on deadline. I call my mommy.

"What's the matter?" she asks, alarmed.

"I don't know, Mom."

"Did something happen? Are you hurt? Why are you crying?"

"I just watched *Sixteen Candles*."

"Again?" Mom groans. "Why do you do that to yourself?"

"It's just so perfect," I snuffle.

"It's a movie, Lexi. About a sixteen-year-old girl."

"I want to be a sixteen-year-old girl," I whine.

"Why?"

"So I can go back and do things differently."

"Lexi. You can't sit around your apartment watching movies from the 1980s and wishing you could start your life over. You weren't such a bundle of joy when you were sixteen. Believe me. I was there."

"I know, Mom."

"Listen, honey. I've been meaning to bring something up with you and now is as good a time as any."

"What?" I sniffle.

"I'm wondering," Mom says slowly, "if you would think it might be a good idea to see a psychiatrist."

In response, I blow my nose. Mom proceeds with caution. "Because, Lexi, it's been, what? Three or four months since you broke up with Ron? And I don't think you have moved your life forward since then. Maybe you're depressed? A little?"

"Yes, I'm depressed. Of course I'm depressed. I'm sitting alone in my apartment eating peanut butter and sobbing over a Molly Ringwald movie."

"Do you think," Mom tries again, "that you are clinically depressed?"

That gives me pause. I stop sniffling. "No," I answer firmly.

"How would you know?" Mom asks gently.

"I know myself. I'm not nuts."

Mom doesn't answer.

"Okay, sometimes I'm a little nuts. Like now, for instance. But that doesn't mean that I'm clinically depressed."

"Maybe you need some help," Mom says. I hear papers shuffling on Mom's end. "I have the name of a great psychiatrist in Philadelphia. I asked around."

"Around?"

"Many of my friends have been in therapy at one time or another, Lexi. Don't worry. I didn't say the referrals were for you. Here it is. See?" Mom is no doubt showing the piece of paper to the phone.

"What's her name?"

"Dr. Franklin. And it's a he, Lex."

"A man is going to help me with my man problems?"

"Try it?" Mom asks. "Just to see what you can get out of the experience."

"Fine."

Mamma Mia

The next morning, I steer Lola's Jaguar roadster toward New Jersey. I don't own a car. Not that I can't afford one. I can't pick one, and when I think I'm close to deciding, I read the buyer agreement, and the commitment to years of car payments scares me. The logical thing to do? Lease a car. That way, my car commitment would have a beginning and an end. Which, I guess, isn't really a commitment. Why should I bother when I can borrow Lola's or Grace's cars?

Anyway, I'm off to see Mia Rose. My friendships with other women whom I met in my early twenties have evaporated, but I hold on to Mia Rose. She was my partner in crime at The Gold Group. We were hired as junior account executives within the same year, and we hit it off immediately. We worked hard and played hard. Then Mia took the Husband, Children, Suburbs exit ramp. Right after her twenty-fifth birthday, Mia married Michael Rose. When she gave birth to David a year later, Mia stopped working at The Gold Group. There was no maternity leave for her; Mia knew she wanted to stay home with her son instead of putting him in day care. When Mia gave birth to Simon, Mia declared herself finished with pregnancies. Michael got a vasectomy, although he doesn't know that we know that but of course we do.

Driving over the river and through the woods of strip malls, I try to remember the last time I saw Mia. We talk on the phone and e-mail, but Grace is the one who actually sees Mia. Grace, Mia, and their Michaels socialize. Ron and I used to join them, but now that I'm single, things have changed. I guess I don't fit into the seating chart.

Mia hugs me into her home. And, oh baby, my nose twitches at my favorite scent. "You made chicken soup?" I ask Mia with sheer joy.

"Yes, I made chicken soup," Mia says in her singsong voice, and I follow her into the bright, clean kitchen.

"And did you make . . . ? I mean, the soup alone is amazing and I appreciate that you took the time to make it, but," I close my eyes and cross my fingers, "did you make matzo balls?"

"Yes."

"And the boys aren't here, so I don't have to share?"

"Right." Mia laughs. "Although, Lexi, you will have to learn to share one of these days."

"Not today."

Mia stands on her stepstool to get soup bowls out of the cupboard. "I sent you the basket, on the, well, what would have been that day. But I thought chicken soup would be even better. Junk food helps. Chicken soup heals."

Leaning over Mia's six-burner stove, I lift the lid of the stockpot. Warm, scented clouds float into my face, and I see the matzo balls, lumpy globes of love, floating happily in the broth. Mia's thoughtfulness touches me deeply, and I smile sadly into the pot. A tear drops from my eye into the soup, adding one more dash of salt.

We sit at Mia's cozy kitchen table. It's a Shaker-style table with light wood topping hunter green legs. A sisal mat lies under the table to catch kids' crumbs. The chairs match the table and have pads with yellow and purple flowers, which match the soup bowls.

Mia tells me about her boys. I adore the Rose boys. David is six and a half. Simon is five. "Baby Sy goes to kindergarten in September," Mia says. "I'm thinking about working part time."

"You're hired."

"Just like that?" Mia laughs. She scoops her shiny black hair behind her ears and tugs at her thick bangs.

"Like I'd let you work at another PR firm? No way. I want you to work at The Gold Group. It will be great."

"Don't you have to ask Susan?" Mia puts her heels on her chair and brings her knees to her chin.

Rolling my eyes, I say, "No, I don't have to ask Susan. I have the authority to hire whomever I need. Susan can't name half our current employees. She'll be glad to have you back. Actually? She probably won't realize you left."

Mia laughs and rises to clear the table. "I've been out of the business world for six years. I have a lot of catching up to do." Mia turns on her espresso machine and takes whole beans out of her freezer. I watch her grind the beans, put them into the machine, brew espresso, steam the milk, and pour the two liquids together, dividing them perfectly, for two perfect cups of café au lait. If Mia can do that, she can do anything. "You'll be fine," I tell her.

"Part-time is okay?"

"Please." I wave my hand at Mia. "I have four baby mammas, all on part-time."

"It would be great to be around grown-ups. Making my own money."

"Wait. I have to pay you?"

"Ha." Mia shakes her head at me. "It will be wonderful to be working with you again, Lex. Like old times."

I shrug. "Not exactly like old times."

"Why not?"

"Now, I'm your boss."

We spend another hour talking about The Gold Group, employees and clients. The phone rings as the February sun sets. It's Michael, and I hear Simon and David hollering to Mia over the phone. "The boys are hopped up on ice cream cake," Mia says when she hangs up the phone. "Michael called to give us fair warning. You might want to skedaddle. This could get ugly."

I don't get out the door soon enough. David and Simon come hurtling into the house, faces and shirts smeared with brown stuff, which is chocolate, dirt, or both. David and Simon charge at me. "Auntie Lex!" David hollers as a war cry. I gave up trying to get the boys to call me Aunt Lexi instead of the dyslexic Auntie Lex.

David hugs my legs while Simon climbs on a chair and throws himself at me. I catch him, and he wraps his arms around my neck. Simon looks up at the ceiling, opens his mouth, and screams, "Kisses!" We kiss cheeks, left, right, left, right.

David is poking my thigh. "Auntie Lex? Wanna know what I learned in school?"

"Yes."

"Okay. Okay. Ready?"

"I'm ready." I look down at David, giving him my full attention.

"*Me llamo David Rose. ¿Cómo está usted? Estoy bien. Gracias.*"

"*¡Perfecto! ¡Muy bien!*"

"Me, me!" Simon pokes my boob. "I know Spanish, too, Auntie Lex."

"*¿Sí? Dígame.* Tell me."

"*Uno, dos, tres, cuatro, cinco, seis.*" Simon pauses to breathe. "*Seis, siete, ocho, new, new,* uh, um. Wait."

Trying to lead him phonetically, I say, "*New-ay?*" Simon claps his dirty hands over my mouth. "Don't tell me, Auntie Lex. I'll find it in my head." Simon starts over, this time finishing correctly with "*nueve, diez.*" I applaud.

"Hi, Lexi," an exhausted Michael says as he kisses my cheek. "It's good to see you," he adds warmly.

Another hour passes and I decline Mia's invitation to stay for dinner. Michael is asleep on the couch, exhausted by the birthday party. The boys are getting cranky, coming down from their sugar high. "I'm leaving before the boys get the shakes," I tell Mia, and she doesn't blame me.

At the front door, Mia hands me a glass jar filled with chicken soup, and a plastic container of matzo balls. "Shhhhh." She holds her finger to her lips and nods to the family room where the boys are playing.

"I love you, Mia Rose." I hug her hard. "Thank you."

"I love you, too, Lexi."

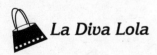

La Diva Lola

Lola's restaurant is between my office and my apartment. It's a weekday dinner hour, which means Lola will be crazy busy, but I pop in a for a quick hello. I'm used to my friendship with

Lola operating on a restaurant schedule. After all, the restaurant was the conduit for our friendship.

In the mid-90s, Lola and her husband, Enrique Castillo, opened a South American bistro on Rittenhouse Square. It quickly became one of Philadelphia's hottest spots. The bistro was decorated in sexy, Latin earth tones of oranges and reds and browns. Being so fabulous, the bistro was called, naturally, Lola. In a short amount of time, Lola and Enrique won national acclaim for the bistro. Lola the woman was the culinary force behind Lola the restaurant. Enrique was the mouthpiece front man.

Two years after the restaurant opened, Lola came to my office at The Gold Group. It was the first time we met. "I need your help," Lola told me.

In person, Lola is more sultry than she appears in photos. She has traditional, straight black hair that she wears below her shoulders. Her skin is café con leche and her eyes are deep brown with flecks of gold. Her body is slim, but solid, with strong arms and legs from working in kitchens all her life.

"What can I do for you?" I asked Lola.

"There's going to be a lot of media attention surrounding me very soon, and I need an expert to make sure the publicity is positive." Lola paused and eyed me warily. I nodded and smiled. "Go on."

Taking a deep breath, Lola said, "I'm divorcing my husband."

"Oh. I'm sorry."

"Don't be. He's a *cuñejo*," Lola spit.

"*Lo siento mucho.*"

"*¿Habla español?*"

"*Un poquito,*" I answered. "I took Spanish in high school and college. *Yo sé* the curses."

"*Que bueno,*" Lola replied. "I'll be using them."

*   *   *

Lola wanted a divorce because Enrique cheated on her. While this may have been par for the course in Latin America—or, heck, in this America—Lola would not stand for it. She wanted a divorce and wanted what was hers: the restaurant.

I proposed a tweaked Hillary strategy for presenting Lola's divorce to the media. It went like this: a wronged woman who tried to stand by her man, but decided to strike out on her own. It would've worked brilliantly, I think.

We never had to use any kind of spin. The fact that Lola hired me was enough to make Enrique agree to a divorce settlement that gave Lola sole ownership of the restaurant. He went back to Argentina, from whence he came.

Once Enrique was gone, Lola's career soared. Lola the restaurant was better than ever. Lola the woman became a media darling in her own right, without a man as her mouthpiece. She had me for that.

When Lola was approached by The Cuisine Channel about creating a television show, mine was the first number she dialed for advice. I worked a great deal for Lola with the television production company. The show is called *Lola!* and Lola is the executive producer, which gives her the creative control she wanted. The Gold Group gets a cut of the show's profits. The show is in reruns, but still scores great ratings.

Now in her late thirties, Lola is constantly asked if she will remarry. The first time a reporter asked her that question, Lola answered, "Why the hell would I?"

I came up with a better answer. "The restaurant and TV show are my children, and I'm a single mother. But for the right man, I would make the time."

*   *   *

Walking into the restaurant, I see Lola chatting with a party of ten. All their attention is focused on Lola as she entertains them with the story of her life. Even if they have read the story in magazines and newspapers, they want to hear Lola tell her At First I Was Afraid, I Was Petrified, Kept Thinking I Could Never Live Without Him By My Side saga.

Leaning against the bar, I watch Lola do her shtick. Her arms wave, she gestures with her eyes, hands, and hips, and punctuates with Spanish and Spanglish phrases. Lola tells her customers the survival story they want to hear. She tells it dramatically, but she tells the truth.

There's another truth, I realize as I watch *mi amiga*. Lola has organized her life so that she will never again be dependent on a man. That's a good thing, I think. Maybe not. I watch Lola, and I wonder if she realizes that her feminism is in direct proportion to her distrust of men.

When Lola sees servers approaching the table with food, she winds up her story and finishes with a grand "*¡Buen provecho!*" Spotting me at the bar, she vibrates toward me on her electric purple wave.

"*¿Qué pasa, amiga?*" Lola asks as she gives me a kiss on each cheek.

"Well, Mom thinks I should see a shrink."

"It can't hurt."

"Can't you just give me your Xanax?"

Lola shakes her head. "Get your own."

Two servers approach with news of some imminent disaster, and I say goodbye to Lola.

"*Buenas noches,*" she says, and I leave.

The Lola & Lexi Show

The next morning, Lola is in a very different mood.

"Señorita Bravia is on line five for you," Low Man on the Totem Pole tells me. I look at my watch. It's 10:15 AM. "What are you doing up at this hour?" I ask Lola. There's no response. "Lola? Are you there?"

"You know I hate speakerphone," she says.

I pick up the handset. "*¿Bueno?*"

"*Sí, amiga. Gracias. Otra cosa.* The guy who answers the phone? I've asked him repeatedly not to call me *señorita*. I'm no *señorita*."

"What do you want Mike to call you? Bitch?"

"How about Lola, like the rest of the world?"

"He's trying to be polite and respectful. I'll tell him to stop immediately."

"*Gracias.* Listen, Lexi. I am nervous about the deal with the publisher."

"Why? I thought our meeting went very well. We should hear back from them in about a month or so."

"I'm nervous. Talk to me."

I have talked Lola through worse situations. It's part of our friendship, and part of my job.

Lola and I have decided that her next career step is a book. Not just a cookbook, but a lifestyle book. This is part of the branding of Lola. I even came up with a title: *Life a la Lola*. The title is purposeful Spanglish.

Lola wants the book published simultaneously in Spanish and English, and this has been a sticking point. The publisher wants the English version to come out first and be successful, then do a Spanish translation. This isn't good enough for Lola. She feels the Latino community will be slighted if the Spanish version is released after the English version. Lola wants what she always wants: everything. Right now.

In the upcoming conference call with the publisher, I will offer a compromise. Lola will forgo the advance money she would normally receive upon signing with the publisher. That money will be put toward the publication of the Spanish edition of the cookbook. Instead of her advance, Lola will receive a higher percentage of royalties on both the English and Spanish books. I know this will pay off; cookbook publishers have yet to target the enormous Latino audience in North or South America.

Lola trusts me, but my wheeling and dealing is making her edgy. She knows I would never jeopardize her career. Not only because she's one of my best friends, but because damaging Lola's career would damage my own career. Lola made me, and I made her.

"I know they will agree," I tell Lola on the phone.

"What if they don't?

"Do you trust me, Lola?"

"*Sí. Siempre.*"

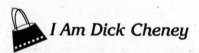 ## I Am Dick Cheney

I have the trust of many people. Like Susan Gold-Berg, who trusts me to run her company.

When I was twenty-one years old and a sparkly graduate from the University of Pennsylvania, Susan Gold hired me as a junior account executive for The Gold Group. Mia was already working for Susan, and she raved about Susan's mentoring skills. It was true. In the beginning, Susan was a wonderful mentor. Then she got married to Stephen Berg and, at the age of thirty-two, Susan fast-tracked her motherhood.

Susan gave birth to Ashley one year after her wedding, and Joshua came along eighteen months later. While Susan was nesting, Mia and I worked late, schmoozed existing clients, landed new clients, and trained hirees. When Mia left for the motherland, she left me to my upward mobility. Susan rewarded me with a senior account executive title, a new office, and a salary bump. That made me happy. For a while.

By the time I met Lola, I was the most senior account executive. Others had been at the company longer, but I was the most ambitious AE. I brought in the big clients. I made the big media hits happen. And I began to really, really resent Susan for not giving me my due. But I didn't want to leave the company. I had too much invested.

With the juicy potential of Lola's TV show, I nudged Susan over the edge and asked her to make me vice president with all the trimmings. Susan was too busy with her children to protest, and I think she was secretly relieved to have someone else look after the company. Susan's priorities had changed. As far as I was concerned, Susan had abandoned her first child—The Gold Group—for her human children. I was the one nurturing The Gold Group as it grew into a respected communications firm. My name became more closely associated with The Gold Group than Susan's. Do I feel remorse about consolidating my power while Susan breastfed?

Nope.

Now I have the title of executive vice president, which is

what I wanted, but sometimes I miss being an account executive. The career is always greener on the other side. Before I was the veep, I had clients for whom I wrote press releases, organized promotional events, and did a lot of media placement. My days were spent speaking with reporters and producers, convincing them to do stories about my clients. I was good at media placement. Now The Gold Group is my client. My time is spent approving other people's work, making sure the company infrastructure is working, pursuing new clients, and solving problems. Sometimes I miss interacting with clients and the media. I like working with people, not paper.

What's the alternative? What would I do? Demote myself?

No. I am happy at The Gold Group, except when Susan is in the office. Now that her children are almost teenagers, they need and want Susan around less and less, so she comes to work to bother us. We don't need her, either, but we can't pout about it. Well, I can. But it doesn't do much good.

The problem is this. When Susan comes into the office, she feels the need to exert her will over at least one matter, in order to keep her authority. No one, including me, cares. We know Susan is president. And we know that I am Dick Cheney.

 ## What's Important

When I hang up with Lola, my intercom buzzes. "Veep?" Low Man calls.

"Yo," I answer, chipper from my conversation with Lola and excited about the prospect of making her publishing deal happen.

"Susan is waiting for you in her office," Mike says.

"What does she want?" I moan. My derision for Susan is not a secret.

"The billable hour reports."

I glance at my day book. "That meeting is tomorrow."

"Susan forgot that she has mommy library duty at Joshua's school tomorrow, so everything that was scheduled for tomorrow is rescheduled for today. I sent an IM."

Looking at my computer, I see Low Man's message. I exhale loudly.

"Tell me about it," Mike says.

Watching the mostly finished reports print from my computer, I wonder what "mommy library duty" is at Joshua Gold-Berg's private day school. Do I really care? No.

Reports in hand, I walk down the hall and around the corner to Susan's office, which is on a diagonal from my office. In other words, our offices are as far apart from each other as possible.

"There you are," Susan greets me.

"Here I am." I smile thinly and hand Susan a copy of the reports. While she peruses them, I remove a pile of papers from the catalog issue chair across from Susan's desk. The debris of Susan's life is piled on every available surface: chairs, sofa, table, filing cabinets, windowsills, desk. Some of those piles have been there since the last century. The only things that change with any frequency are the photos of Susan's children and the displays of their art projects. The current exhibition consists of Ashley's giant lanyard and Joshua's watercolor portrait of his mother. Joshua has accurately captured Susan's perm-gone-wild. The boy might have a future in art.

"The work distribution looks good," Susan says, drawing my attention away from Van Gogh-Berg's portraiture.

"Yes," I agree with Susan. "Everyone is logging the right amount of hours in proportion to their client load. Michelle is spending a little too much time on Quaker Insurance, but that's tricky stuff with a steep learning curve."

"How long has Michelle been working here?"

"Five months." I'm not surprised that Susan doesn't know that.

"She's fine," Susan says to reassure me, although I don't need reassuring.

"Client contract time lines?" Susan requests.

"Fourth page." I watch her scan. I know what she's going to say.

"Some big contracts are almost up for renewal," Susan says. "We need to get on that, or we need to pull in new accounts."

By "we," she means me. "I know that, Susan. I'm the one who compiled the report." I expect some passive-aggressive retort. Instead, Susan smiles widely at me. Uh oh.

"We have a new pro bono account," Susan gushes.

Bracing myself, I ask, "Who?"

With great flair, Susan declares, "The Gold Group will be promoting Camp Cool, the summer camp of choice in the Philadelphia area."

"A camp?"

"It's not just any summer camp," Susan retorts. "It's a very prestigious summer camp to which kids must be accepted. Like college."

"Why does such a prestigious institution need PR?" Susan clears her throat and glares at me. I have finally irritated her.

Usually it doesn't take this long. "Susan, did they ask for representation, or did you volunteer it?"

"I volunteered our services," Susan says through clenched teeth.

"I get. We're representing Camp Cool pro bono so your kids can get accepted."

Susan twists her mouth and doesn't answer. Trying a different tactic, she says, "You're the one who made the policy that everyone should represent a charity account pro bono."

"Yes. They are supposed to do volunteer PR for what's important to them. Not what's important to you." Susan's cell phone rings and she answers it, ending our conversation. Susan's cell rings in the middle of many uncomfortable conversations, and I wonder if she has a panic button under her desk.

As she's talking on the phone, Susan hands me a manila folder with "Camp Cool" written on the tab. She smiles at me. I smile back.

We can't stand each other. Too bad we need each other.

 ## The Fabulous Ellie Archer

Saturday afternoon, the COG is waiting for me inside Lola's restaurant, and the girls are hungry. Lola orders for us. Empanadas, ensalada Lola, pollo con naranja, and arroz con frijoles.

We get a round of mango margaritas. Ellie is telling us about Jesse, her latest conquest.

"I thought we would have a lot in common. He's a graphic artist at a magazine; I write for magazines. The first two weeks of dating was fun. Now? I'm bored."

"It's a good thing you didn't sleep with him," Grace says.

"I slept with him."

"Oh." Grace doesn't try to hide her disapproval.

"The sex isn't good enough to keep him around?" Lola asks.

Ellie thinks while she munches on an empanada. "I'd give him a six for technical and a four for presentation. That makes a combined score of five." She shrugs. "Not high enough marks to make it the finals. Luckily, I'm leaving for two weeks, so breaking off the relationship won't be difficult."

"Where are you going?" I ask.

"I'm flying to Vancouver to cover a dog fashion show."

"How chic," Grace says.

"No, it's awesome," Ellie insists. "The fashion show benefits the Vancouver City Pound, which is the first no-kill shelter in Canada. Last year? Three hundred people attended. I'm telling you, it's an event." Ellie reaches for more salsa verde, then continues. "I'm writing the piece for *Fashion Forward*. They got blasted for putting a model in a fur coat on their cover. This is a little animal-friendly bit to make up for that. Anyway, I'll be in Vancouver for two weeks."

Ellen Archer is in almost constant transition. I am envious of her life. It's a nomadic life, except that Ellie roams from excellent job to excellent job, thereby finding justification for her inability to commit to one occupation, apartment, or city. Or, of course, one man.

What I love most about Ellie is her fearlessness. Part of that is endemic to New Yorkers. Ellie spent a privileged childhood on Central Park. When she graduated from Columbia, Ellie got a job at *Vanity Fair* as an editorial assistant, which is the Lowest Man on the Totem Pole at any magazine. Her ambition and fearlessness got her out from behind a desk and onto the masthead.

The year that Lola filed for divorce and I became VP of The Gold Group, Ellie accepted an offer to be arts and entertainment editor of *Xess*, a new magazine for Gen X women. That's how we met Ellie. I pitched her a story about Lola's triumphant divorce and subsequent success. Lola became Ellie's first cover story at *Xess*. To write the story, Ellie came to Philadelphia, met me, Lola, Grace, and Mia, and fell in love. We fell in love with Ellie. The Council of Girlfriends was formed.

When the economy crumbled in 2001, advertising dollars dried up and *Xess* folded. Casting about for a new home base, Ellie spent a few months with her parents in Palm Beach, then moved to Philadelphia. Turning down offers of staff positions at magazines, Ellie decided to go freelance so she could write about what interested her.

What interests her at the moment is doggie style. Given her career, it is not uncharacteristic of Ellie to spend two weeks in Vancouver covering a Canadian canine catwalk. Still, I miss Ellie whenever she leaves, even if it's just for a few weeks.

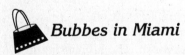 ## Bubbes in Miami

"You'll e-mail, right?" I ask Ellie.

"Of course. And I'll be back before you miss me."

"Maybe you'll meet someone special," Grace says.

"I'll meet lots of special someones." Ellie winks at me.

"*Cuidado, amiga,*" Lola warns.

"I am always careful."

"Do you think we will always be friends?" Grace asks abruptly.

"*Sí, amiga.* We'll always be friends."

I say, "That's right, Gracie. Forty years from now, we'll be *bubbe*s sitting around a pool in Miami. Trying to remember the good old days."

"We'll be in Miami?" Ellie asks. "Good. We'll get to decide the presidential election. Finally, some real power."

"What's a *bubbe*?" Grace asks.

"It's Yiddish for grandmother," I answer.

"Since when do you speak Yiddish?"

"The ladies at the Home speak Yiddish all the time."

"You know," Grace moans, "with all the Spanish and Yiddish floating around here, it's a wonder I understand any of our conversations."

"Just wait until we get to Miami," Lola laughs. "You'll need a translator."

"*Bubbe*, huh? I call my grandmother Nana. I wonder what my grandchildren will call me. Although we have to have kids before we have grandkids, and we're not even close to that."

"I can see it," Lola says. "Gracie, you'll be a famous retired nurse, but you'll consult at Miami General. In fact, there will be a wing named after you. The maternity wing.

"Ellie, you'll be the editor of some famous magazine. But you only fly to New York once a month. The rest of the time, you hang out with us. At my restaurant. My bistro in South Beach. Where the young and beautiful *bubbes* hang out together. And, Lexi? Let's see. You'll retire at fifty and live off your investments."

"That's it? Retired at fifty? What would I do with the rest of my life?"

"You'll finally have time for psychotherapy," Ellie says. It's then that I realize that I haven't told the COG about my upcoming appointment with Dr. Franklin. I didn't not tell them on purpose. Now is not the time to divulge the existence of my mental health care worker. I'll wait until Ellie gets back from her trip.

"Lexi couldn't live in Miami." Ellie laughs. "With the humidity? What would she do about her hair?"

"We'll be wearing wigs by that time," Lola answers.

"Have you heard about the Japanese straight perm?" Grace asks. "It would be perfect for you, Lexi. The procedure takes five hours and, like, five hundred dollars, but your hair stays poker straight permanently. Or at least until new hair grows in, which takes four to six months, depending on how fast it grows."

"That sounds great," Lola says. "You should get that done, Lexi."

"No way. I couldn't do that."

"Why not?" Ellie asks. "You'd save yourself hours of blow drying and hundreds of dollars of products."

"What if I wake up one day and want curly hair?"

"You never wear your hair curly," Grace says.

"It could happen. I could wake up and want curly hair. But I'd be stuck with straight hair. For six months. I can't make that kind of commitment."

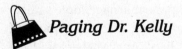 Paging Dr. Kelly

When Ellie leaves, Grace whips out her cell phone. "Excuse me," she says. "I have to find Michael. We're supposed to go to his parents for dinner. I don't know what time he wants to leave." Grace has been with Michael Kelly for four years. She has wanted to marry him for three and a half of those years.

They met at Philadelphia Hospital. Grace was getting her master's in nursing; Michael was finishing his surgical residency. Michael Kelly looks like he should be posing for a Tommy Hilfiger ad instead of cutting up people. If Grace marries Michael, she will become Grace Kelly, a true Philadelphia princess.

The COG is ambivalent about Michael. We like him. We don't love him. We don't love him because he hasn't proposed to Grace. This makes Grace unhappy. We don't want Grace to be unhappy. Grace unhappy makes the COG question Michael's motives, methods, and, occasionally, manhood. But, like the woman herself, the COG is passive-aggressive about its feelings toward Michael.

Grace doesn't push Michael to propose. She nudges him. Although Grace has her own apartment, she spends most nights at Michael's place. Grace figures that Michael will propose eventually. She gives him hints, which he sometimes acknowledges and sometimes ignores. Their parents, meanwhile, are eager for grandchildren. Four Irish Philadelphians waiting for grandkids is like a SWAT team rescuing hostages. They have a goal, a deadline, and an arsenal of guilt at their disposal. This is why Grace loves going to the Kellys' home for dinner.

"I guess Mrs. Kelly will bring up the marriage topic again," Lola says. Grace shrugs, as if there is not a United Nations of Commitment aligned to support her. "And Michael will get pissed off and avoid the subject again," Lola finishes.

"Are you sure you want to marry Michael?" I ask.

"What?" Grace is distracted because the love of her life isn't answering his cell. "Yes, Lexi, of course I'm sure."

"Why?"

"What?"

"Why do want to marry him?"

Grace hangs up her cell and says, "What am I supposed to do? Find someone new? I can't imagine starting over with someone else."

"Shouldn't you say that you want to marry Michael because you love him?" I ask, nicely and quietly.

"Of course I love him," Grace snaps.

"Okay. But you have other options."

"Not all of us have commitment issues." Grace squints at me. "Why don't you just tell the truth, Lexi? You don't like Michael. You don't, either, Lola."

"We never see Michael." I shrug. "I haven't had a meaningful conversation with him this millennium."

Lola crosses her arms in front of her chest and glares at me. "*¿Por qué, Lexi? ¿Por qué?*"

I know what Lola is asking. Why? Why do I always start the same conversation? Trying a different tack, I ask, "How do you want him to propose?"

"You can't tell a man how to propose," Lola says. "It's their last moment in the sun. Men think that the proposal is a grand gesture. Really, it's just a question. Most of the time, men already know the answer. Somehow, this proposing thing has become a big production. The woman is supposed to act surprised and touched and all of that. You have to. It's the last thing men will decide about the relationship. Think about it. Men don't plan weddings. Men don't pick out the invitations or the cake or the reception site. All they have to do is get a tuxedo, and how hard is that? So, what I'm saying is that you have to let them plan the proposal. Give them their last gasp of independence."

"That's harsh," Grace says, and I nod in agreement.

"Yeah, well," Lola says. Grace's cell rings. It's Michael and she waves goodbye to us as she walks to the curb and hails a cab.

"I have to get ready for dinner," Lola says. She stands up and heads for the kitchen doors. I watch her move, her body confident but heavy, as if she is carrying a heavy load. Although Lola is always surrounded by people, sometimes I wonder if she feels very alone.

"*¡Te amo, Lola!*" I call after her.

"I'll call you later," she says over her shoulder.

The COG is adjourned.

 ## Saturday Night Spay Sha

It's 4 PM, which means I have plenty of daylight left to walk to Sang Kee at Ninth and Vine in Chinatown. It's cold, but I'm craving Sang Kee's roasted pork soup. It's not the ordinary soup on the menu. I ask for it specially. No noodle, yes bok choy. It's juicy pieces of spit roasted pork, hand-made dumplings, and garlicky bok choy steamed in delicious broth. The woman at the take out counter knows my face but not my name. I always buy a quart of the same thing. When I walk into Sang Kee, she says, "Spay sha soup? To go? Fie dolla." A bargain.

On the walk back from my Sang Kee pilgrimage, I veer over to Fifteenth and Locust streets to TLA Video. I decide to rent *Unbreakable* and *The Sixth Sense* and wait in line at the counter.

When it's my turn, I hand in the rental stubs. The clerk gets the DVDs and starts typing into his computer. "That's seven dollars," he says. "Don't you need to know my name?" I ask.

"Alexandra James, right?"

"Yes. How do you know that?"

"You've been in here almost every weekend for the past three months. Two DVDs." The clerk smiles. "Usually good choices."

I want to run. And cry. I don't. I hand the money to the clerk. He hands me the DVDs. I go back to my fabulous apartment, eat my spay sha soup, and watch my movies.

 ## Dr. Franklin, Session One

There's nothing like a psychiatrist's office to make you feel nutty. It's unnaturally quiet, as if you are sealed off from the rest of the bad, bad world. It's dim, to soothe the harsh light of the past, present, and future. It's devoid of all aroma, so as not to trigger sense memories. And of course, there's nothing breakable in the waiting room or the inner sanctum.

Dr. Franklin's inner sanctum reminds me of the fifth floor of Van Pelt Library at Penn. Maroon leather sofas with bronze studs, walnut end tables, a worn Oriental carpet, dusty lampshades. And books. And quiet.

I loved the fifth floor, and I feel comfortable in Dr. Franklin's office. The only problem is that I usually fell asleep in Van Pelt. So, you never know. If Dr. Franklin delivers a long diatribe about my childhood, I could start snoring.

Dr. Franklin sits on the maroon leather couch opposite me. As if we are at a cocktail party, ready to exchange pleasantries. He hasn't asked me to lie down and he's not sitting behind me. He's sitting in front of me, looking straight at me. I like that. This is good.

This shrink looks like a shrink. Late fifties. Chinos, olive corduroy jacket, light blue Oxford shirt, and navy knit tie. Cordovan loafers. Bald on top with a bottom rung of dark gray hair. A compensating beard and mustache. John Lennon glasses.

I imagine that Dr. Franklin lives in a quaint Philadelphia suburb, recycles with a vengeance, jogs in black spandex tights, and contributes to the local NPR station. On his oak-paneled wall are diplomas from Temple and Rutgers University. I feel an insidious sense of superiority.

"Let's review your biographical profile," Dr. Franklin begins. He has the form I filled out attached to a blond wood clipboard that doesn't match the walls.

"You are thirty-three years old," Dr. Franklin reads. I nod. "Public relations," he continues. I keep nodding. "Live on Rittenhouse Square. Not married."

"That's my life."

"What brings you here?" Dr. Franklin asks, reaching for a yellow, lined note pad and attaching it to his clipboard.

"Ennui."

"Ennui?"

"A general feeling of discontent."

"I know what ennui means, Lexi. Can you be more specific?"

"A few months ago, I broke an engagement, and since then, I haven't dated. My mom and my friends seem to think I am, like, stuck. I may be stalled on the highway of life, but at least I'm driving a Porsche. You know what I mean?"

"Not really. May I ask a few questions about your family?"

"Sure. But it's not their fault."

Dr. Franklin smiles at me. "We're not here to place blame."

"Well, Doc, if it were their fault, I'd be the first to place the blame on them. That would be easy. If not healthy. Or helpful."

"Are your parents married?"

"Yes."

Dr. Franklin flips to my profile. "Your mother kept her maiden name?"

"No."

"Your mother is Gloria Northstein and your father is Leo James?"

"Yes."

"They are married?"

"Yes, they are married. But not to each other."

"I see," Dr. Franklin says and writes on his yellow pad. "Divorced?"

"Yes," I say. Then, "Well, my father is divorced but not my mother."

"I don't follow you," Dr. Franklin says, somewhat irritated.

"My parents were never married to each other. They lived together. I wasn't an accident, though. They planned to have a child. They just didn't want to get married and succumb to society's expectations. They were protesting something." I shrug. "It was the sixties."

Dr. Franklin nods. "Continue."

"Mom decided that she wanted to settle down. That's how she explained it to me. 'Settle down.' I assume that means she wanted to be monogamous. Dad didn't want that. So, when I was about one year old, they separated. I don't even remember them being together. Anyway, Mom got married when I was three years old. Dad got married when I was ten, and he got divorced when I was fifteen. He got married again when I was twenty-six and he has been married to that woman since then."

"So, you have a stepfather and a stepmother."

"Yes. One of each. A matching set."

"Do you have good relationships with them?" Dr. Franklin wants to know.

"Sure. I know my stepfather better because he's been around longer. He's got tenure. My stepmother is nice, but they got married after I was out of the house, so I don't have a very intimate relationship with her."

"No brothers or sisters?" Dr. Franklin asks. "No half siblings?"

"Nope. Just me."

Dr. Franklin looks at my profile. "You didn't list a religion."

"Technically, I am a daughter of the Church of the Rainbow."

"The what?" Dr. Franklin peers at me through his glasses.

"When I was born, my parents attended the Church of the Rainbow and I was baptized into that order. Thankfully, I have no memory of that. Growing up, I learned about Judaism and Catholicism."

"How's that?"

"Howard, my stepfather, is Jewish. My mom converted to Judaism when she married Howard. But I didn't."

"Why not?"

"I was three years old, Doc."

"Of course," he says. "Then you grew up in a Jewish home?"

"Half."

"Half Jewish?"

"No, no. I half grew up in a Jewish home and half grew up in a Catholic home. Except Mom isn't that Jewish anymore.

She was very into it at the beginning of her marriage. Then she lost interest. Now she's back to her seventies stuff of chanting and the goddess within and all that. I think Mom is actually a polytheist. My father is Catholic. Not too observant. What with the divorces and all. Actually, I had the best of both worlds. Christmas and Chanukah. Every kid's dream come true."

"Of course." Dr. Franklin nods. He looks tired.

 ## The Elder Council's Husbands

"Happy Valentine's Day!" I hand cards and boxes of chocolate to Sylvia, Ruth, and Esther.

"*Gutzel nitupedin*," Sylvia moans.

"Ach, Sylvia. Be nice," Ruth chides. "Look what Lexi brought for us."

"I can't eat sugar," Sylvia mutters. "I have diabetes, in case you forgot."

"I didn't forget, Sylvia. These chocolates are sugar-free. From Mueller's in Reading Terminal. I schlepped all the way to Reading Terminal to buy sugar-free chocolates for you."

"It's four blocks," Sylvia says.

"That's not the point," Ruth interrupts. "Thank you, *shayna*."

"Thank you, Lexi." Esther wraps her bony arms around my neck, enveloping me in a cloud of Shalimar. "I'm expecting a lot of valentines this year," she says.

"Good for you. What about the rest of you?"

"We've had our husbands," Sylvia says, in the same tone as which she says, "I've had my Fibercon."

Sitting on the couch next to Sylvia, I say, "Tell me about your husband."

"His name was Ziggy." Sylvia, Ruth, and Esther turn their heads to the left. They cough, then, in unison, spit over their shoulders.

Not sure what to make of that display, I say, "Ziggy? That's an odd name."

"Back then, everyone had a nickname. His last name was Zigorsky, so it got shortened to Ziggy." When Sylvia says his name, the women again turn their heads and spit over their left shoulders. Then Sylvia continues. "He was the best-looking boy on the block, but the laziest man I ever met. He said my parents had enough money to support us until one of his schemes made us rich. Until then, he wouldn't get a job. Even when he had two kids to support. That's when I took up smoking."

"Smoking? Why?"

"I kept sending him out for cigarettes and hoping he wouldn't come back." She shakes her head sadly. "He always did."

"Oh, Sylvia."

"Finally, I told him that my father's company went bankrupt and there would be no more money. He believed me, and disappeared for two months, then came back to tell me that he was marrying a rich broad in Baltimore. He brought me a box of Winstons and the divorce papers. That was the end of it."

"I'm sorry to hear that story, Sylvia."

"Ach." She waves her hand at me. "It was a long time ago."

"Esther? Were you married?"

"Of course, darling. Three times. Wait. Three times? Yes. That's right. The first was Louie. Oh, I loved him. He was a big, strong boy from the neighborhood. He died of a heart attack four years after we married. I guess he wasn't so strong.

After Louie, I married Larry. Very smart man. A teacher. He loved to drive fast cars. Crashed his car into a tree one night. Maybe he wasn't so smart. Then I met Henry. Henry was the life of every party. Very debonair. Always had a cigarette hanging on his lip. He played cards and danced and sang. Quite a man. Until the cancer took him. I guess the cigarettes weren't such a good idea."

"I'm sorry, Esther."

"What? No. Don't be sorry. They all died quickly. *Kina hora*."

"*Kina hora*," Ruth and Sylvia repeat.

Regretting this trip down husband lane, I turn to Ruth. "What about your husband?"

"Abraham?" Ruth puts down her knitting and looks at me. "Well, let's see. We grew up in the same neighborhood. Got married after high school. Abe went on to college and became a teacher. I stayed home with our three boys. When the boys went to school, I volunteered as a librarian at the school where Abe taught. We had lunch together every day."

Smiling, I take Ruth's hand in mine. "When did he die?"

"He's not dead."

"No? Then where is he?"

"Abe is in a full-care nursing home in Northeast Philadelphia. He has Alzheimer's. Needs constant care. I take a bus up there once a week to see him. He never remembers who I am, so I tell him, 'Abie, it's me. Ruthie. Your wife.' And he'll say, 'A *shayna madela* like you is my wife? I must be a lucky man.' Then I tell him a story from our life. Like, our honeymoon in Niagara Falls. The day our first child was born. Our fiftieth anniversary. Or simple everyday things, like how I made brisket every Friday night, and every Sunday morning he made pancakes. Or that his favorite dish of mine was stuffed cabbage. Or how, after the kids went to bed, we would lay on the couch and watch Johnny Carson. Yeah. I tell him a different story every time I visit." Ruth nods. "Of course, I could tell him the same story every week. He wouldn't know. He doesn't re-member. But I do." Ruth wipes a tear from her eye, and I reach over to take her hand. "Every time I leave, Abie says, '*Ya chuv de lieb*, Ruthie.' That means, 'I love you' in Yiddish. The next week, he has no idea who I am, and we start all over." Ruth pats the back of my hand, then picks up her knitting.

 ### The Bed-In, Part Two

I am having fun at the Bed-In. This is probably because I am not working. Maria Simons and her team of three are execut-ing the event at the Philadelphia Boudoir. Back at the home-stead, three more of Maria's disciples are monitoring Bed-Ins in five other cities. More than half my staff is working the trenches, the blood-and-guts of event coordination. And me? I'm drinking cranberry spritzers with two Eagles, a Flyer, a city councilman, and their wives.

I told Maria to give me an assignment for the day. But by now, she has figured out that this is a test of the Lexi Broad-casting System. This is me giving Maria an opportunity to shine. It's her day. Still, I told her to consider me as staff and give me something to do. Maria asked me to babysit the celebrity guests. I love Maria.

I do, however, have a very good sense of what is going on in Philadelphia, and in the other Bed-Ins. Low Man on the Totem Pole Mike is my eyes and ears in the office. It is he who

will connect any irate store owners or celebrities to the appropriate person at The Gold Group. I check in with Low Man
every half hour. So far, so good. No crises.

As 5 PM approaches, T-time nears. That's television time,
the all important evening news broadcasts. If a cameraman
shows up, you may get a video footage on the 5 PM and/or
6 PM evening news. If you're lucky, and it's a slow news day,
the footage will be rebroadcast at 11 PM. If you're really really
lucky, the footage will be repeated again the next morning
during the 6 AM show.

Getting cameras to events is a game of chance, and publicists hold their breath until at least one cameraman shows up.
However, if you're good, you know how to play the odds. If
you're good, you get a reporter to come with the cameraman.
If you're really good, you convince a reporter to tape a piece in
the afternoon and do a live shot from the event during the
news.

Maria, of course, is lucky and good. And the concept is excellent, if I do say so myself. We have three cameramen ready
to go live, with two taped pieces in the bin. This is a home run,
and it rarely happens.

A cameraman whom I've known for years approaches me.
"Studio wants film of noncelebrities in the bed," he says. "I
don't have the schedule," I tell him, "but give me fifteen seconds and I'll make it happen." I know not to keep cameramen
waiting. Their lives are lived in thirty-second segments. They
don't have much patience.

I haven't seen the schedule for days, truth be told. On the
two-way radios we have rented for the day, I say, "Maria, this is
Lexi." I haven't called her all day, so she responds immediately.

"Go ahead, Lexi."

"NBC-10 News wants to film a noncelebrity. What's the schedule?"

"The Flyer is next, then a civilian. Ron Anderson. Can the cameraman wait fifteen minutes?"

"What's the name on that?"

"Ron Anderson."

"Maria?"

"What?" she asks hurriedly, and I hear people calling her name. I am speechless.

"What, Lexi? What?" Maria is crazed. I let it go. There must be a hundred Ron Andersons in Philadelphia. Or at least more than one.

"Stand by," I tell Maria. The cameraman agrees to wait. "Maria, we're a go for Ron Anderson. See you in fifteen."

What I want to do is search the store for this Ron Anderson. What I have to do is stay with the cameraman and make sure he doesn't get bored or get another call to cover. Ten minutes later, the crowd applauds as the flyer and his wife make it through the fifteen-minute make-out session and dismount the bed. My radio beeps. "Lexi, this is Maria."

"Go ahead, Maria."

"We're ready for NBC-10."

I lead the cameraman to the massive bed, which is made more massive by its three foot platform. Sure enough, in that massive bed is my ex-fiancé. Cuddled next to him is a petite brunette who looks an awful lot like me. Except, of course, that she is clearly on the bright side of thirty. I peg her at twenty-six.

Ron is focusing on Mini Me and the huge countdown time

clock. I know he is strategizing the best way to maintain lip contact for fifteen minutes.

The cameraman puts on his overhead light. Ron looks towards the cameraman, shielding his eyes. I am standing next to the cameraman, but I know Ron can't see me with the light in his eyes. "NBC-10 News," the cameraman says. "All right if we film you for the six and eleven o'clock news?"

"Sure," Ron says, answering for himself and the girl.

"Say your name into the camera, please."

"Ron Anderson."

"And who's the lucky girl?"

"Randi Katchman," Ron says. "My fiancée."

And this is how it comes to be that I stand ten feet from my ex-fiancé while he makes out with his current fiancée for fifteen minutes, and how the entire tri-state area finds out that Ron is engaged to someone who may be my Mini Me, but isn't me.

 ## Mr. Almost Perfect

Ron Anderson and I met at a black-tie fund-raiser for the children's ward of Philadelphia Hospital. Ron is good-looking, smart, and cultured. He's a real estate lawyer with a prestigious firm. Dating Ron was a delight. Ron held open the car door, he refused to go Dutch on dinner, and he called three days in advance to schedule a date.

Ron's politeness extended to sex. He asked me when I wanted it, what I wanted, and where. He brushed his teeth before he kissed me.

Six months into our relationship, Ron discussed marriage

with me. He wanted to have children—two minimum, three maximum—and he thought it would be best to have them at least eighteen months apart. Ron made enough money so I wouldn't have to work while I was bearing children. And he offered me a gorgeous emerald cut diamond ring in a platinum setting with pavé diamonds. I said yes.

Life with Ron would have been easy. I would have had an SUV, a joint checking account, and a partner. Ron would have been a good husband and maybe a great father. This is what most women dream of but few women get. The COG was in awe of Ron. My mother was thrilled—and relieved that I was engaged. And my father? My father said, "He loves you more than you love him. He'll make a good first husband."

That stunned me. The destiny of divorce loomed large enough without Dad invoking it.

I returned the ring to Ron and told him some version of the truth that centered on the real truth that I wasn't ready to get married. Ron said, "Not ready? You're thirty-two years old." As far as he was concerned, that was a ludicrous excuse. He was sure there was something else going on, because he thought that a thirty-two-year-old woman refusing a marriage proposal from someone like him was absurd. Almost everyone agreed with Ron.

I packed his stuff in a box and left it with Doorman John. I never heard from Ron again. I never saw him again, either.

Until now, at the Bed-In, as he makes out with his new fiancée. For some reason, I can't take my eyes off Ron and Randi. Then I feel nauseated from a toxic combination of guilt, fear, and doubt.

As Ron and Randi's fifteen minutes wind down, I snap out of my daze and realize that Ron will see me standing here staring at them. He may be shocked, possibly angry, and definitely embarrassed. I don't want Ron to feel any of those things. He doesn't deserve that. He deserves much better.

I slip past the cameraman and stand behind a display of vibrators.

My phone is ringing when I enter my apartment. My answering machine blinks with messages. I'm sure people want to talk to me about Ron and his new, second fiancée. I'm not ready to talk.

Instead, I change into jammie bottoms and a sweatshirt, and take out a pad of paper and a pen. I start writing.

Dear Ron,

It sounds trite to say that I never meant to hurt you, but in this case it is very true. I still don't know how to explain my actions, but at least I can tell you how I made my decision to end our engagement:

For two hours, I write the letter to Ron that I should have written four months ago. I'll never send this to Ron, but that's okay. I'm not writing it for Ron.

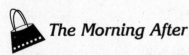 ## The Morning After

"Morning, Miss Lexi," Doorman John greets me the next day.

"Morning, John." Smiling politely, I move to the door. John stands in my way, holding the door shut. He peers at me. "That was Mr. Ron I saw on the news last night?"

"Yes."

John nods slowly. "I didn't know he was engaged to some-one. Else."

"Neither did I, John."

"Awful quick."

"He wants to get married."

The morning after an event is always busy. Reporters call for photographs and spellings and numbers and confirmations. The Bed-In will be a feature story in the Sunday *Inquirer*, and we have postevent follow-up stories in smaller papers. My staff is on the phone with writers all morning. I am not on the phone, but I watch it ring as the COG calls repeatedly and leave voice mails of concern. They called last night, too, and I didn't answer the phone.

Maria comes into my office at 11 AM and closes the door behind her. "I'm ready for you to fire me," she says. I look at her, and she really does think I'm going to fire her.

"Don't be ridiculous," I tell her. "You did an amazing job."

"I put your ex-fiancé and his current fiancée on one of the most watched news channels in the tri-state area."

"You did your job, Maria."

"Honestly, Lex. I didn't realize it was the same Ron Ander-son. I saw the final list, but it didn't occur to me that it would be the same person. I am so sorry."

"Maria? It's fine. Don't make me say it again."

"What can I do to make it up to you?"

"Tell the staff that I'm treating them to lunch. You all did a fabulous job."

"Really?"

"Really."

Things We Don't Say

On Sunday, I face the COG. The COG minus Ellie is having brunch at Rx, a café in University City. Rx is on a tree-lined streetcorner near the University of Pennsylvania, which is between my apartment, Lola's and Grace's. The café is filled with professors, students, and the eclectic residents of West Philadelphia. Rx has two walls of windows, so we can people watch. The food is great, but the owner is an ex-boyfriend of Ellie's, so we try to go there only when she isn't with us.

"I've been calling you for days," Grace says when I slide into my chair.

"Sorry," I say and wave to Greg, the owner.

"We were worried about you," Lola says. "What were you doing?"

"Thinking."

"Without us?"

The waiter comes to take our order. No matter where we eat, we always get the same things. Grace has her WASPy eggs Benedict, I protein-load on eggs and bacon, and Lola loves the multicultural challah French toast. Ellie always gets the special because it's new and exciting. But Ellie isn't here today. I miss her.

Ordering finished, Lola abruptly says, "I want to talk about my TV show. I'm ready for more episodes. I want to approach the network about producing another twenty-two episodes. I've worked up all the ideas. I'm ready."

"Oh" is my flat response.

"Lola, we were talking about Lexi dealing with Ron being engaged. To someone else."

"No, that's okay. I'd be happy to talk about something else."

"Maybe the new episodes can air when the cookbook is released," Lola says.

"That sounds perfect," Grace bubbles. "Smart thinking, Lola. Lexi, you should have thought of that yourself."

I spread my hands on the table. "I didn't think it was an option."

Filming the first twenty-two episodes of Lola's show was a harrowing experience. It was a high point for her career, but a low point for her personal life. The filming took two months of twelve-hour days. Lola, used to being in command of her restaurant, had a difficult time relinquishing control to her director, producers, and the network. There were battles over set decor, plate presentation, and what cooking steps needed to be cut from episodes. As the hours, days, and months progressed, Lola became exhausted and depressed. Saying she had no part of herself to spare, she ended a six-month relationship with a successful businessman who adored her. At the end of filming, Lola retreated to her parents' house in Miami for two weeks. She came back with a prescription for Xanax.

I don't remind Lola of this, because she obviously doesn't need reminding. Instead, I gently ask, "Lola, are you sure you want to do this again?"

"Yes," she answers firmly.

I sit and look at Lola, wearing worry on my face. Grace looks at me with something approaching disgust. "Lexi, why are you so negative about everything? If Lola says she wants to do this, then I'm sure she can do it."

"Okay. I'll make the calls." I don't say any of my concerns. Instead, I change the subject. "So, Gracie. Tell us about last week's dinner at the Kellys. How many times did Mrs. Kelly bring up the M word?"

"Zero times," Grace says. "She didn't say anything about marriage."

"That's a change of pace," Lola says.

"Yes," Grace chirps. I look at her. She's beaming. "What are you so happy about?"

"I'm convinced that a proposal is imminent," Grace answers. Lola picks up her coffee mug and stares into it as if it's a Magic 8 Ball. I investigate the contents of the sugar caddy. "What?" Grace asks us. "What?"

"Nothing," Lola answers for both of us. We are quiet for a few moments.

But I have to ask. "What makes you think a proposal is imminent?" Lola rolls her eyes. Now I've started the M conversation. I've gone and ruined brunch. Again.

"Exactly because Mrs. Kelly didn't bring up the issue," Grace explains. "For the past two years, every time I see her, she raises the M issue. Not last Sunday. Why not? The only reason I can think of is that Michael told her that he is going to propose very soon. So she backed off." Grace ping-pongs her head from me to Lola. "Doesn't that make sense?" she asks us.

I watch Lola nod. I think Lola is punking out.

"Gracie," I begin, and Lola kicks me under the table. I move away from her legs and start again. "Gracie, honey." Why not? I'm already in the doghouse. "I don't think you should put that much stock in what Mrs. Kelly says. Or, in this case, what she doesn't say."

"You, Lexi James, are so negative," Grace says. She flips her blond hair over her shoulder with one hand. With the other hand, she picks up her coffee mug and holds it in front of her face. Grace blows furiously into the mug, although the coffee isn't hot.

The thing is, Grace doesn't drink coffee. Well, she drinks Frappuccinos and those bastardizations. She doesn't drink regular coffee. And yet, every Sunday, Grace ends up with a mug full of coffee in front of her because she doesn't say, "No, thanks," when the waiter starts to pour coffee into her mug. She doesn't say anything, so she ends up with a full mug of coffee that she doesn't want.

"Gracie, there's a difference between being negative and being realistic."

"Should I take relationship advice from you?" Grace asks meanly.

"*Chicas,*" Lola reprimands us, and we sit quietly as the waiter puts plates of food in front of us.

 BYOB

"Beware," Low Man warns as I step out of the elevator.

"Of?"

"Today is BYOB."

BYOB is Gold Group code for Bring Your Own Brat, and it applies to any day when the Gold-Berg children have to be in the office because their school is closed and Susan forgot to find a sitter.

BYOB is aimed not at the kids, but at Susan. It's less about what she brings to the office, and more about what she doesn't bring. No books, no games, no food, no nothing. Instead of bringing things to occupy Joshua and Ashley's time, Susan lets the kids have the run of the office and expects everyone to accommodate them. Usually, I end up spending the day with the kids so my staff can work.

Into the lobby comes a five-foot creature dressed in a white T-shirt, baggy jeans, and a Sixers jersey adorned with the number three and the name IVERSON. A white bandana covers his wavy brown hair, and earphones wrap around the back of his head. This is Joshua Gold-Berg.

"Look," I tell Low Man. "A thuglet."

Over the music blaring into his cranium, Joshua hollers, "Yo, Lexi. Wassup?" Raising an eyebrow, I shake my head. "I don't think so, Joshua."

Joshua drops his eleven-year-old bravado and comes toward me with his arms open wide. "Hello, Lexi," he says with a smile. I hug him and hold his face still while I plant a kiss on his chubby cheek, leaving a lipstick mark that he promptly wipes off with his sleeve.

"To what do we owe the honor of your presence, Mr. Gold-Berg?"

"Presidents' Day. Mom forgot to get a sitter."

"And your sister?"

"In your office," Joshua answers.

"Is that right?" I take Joshua's hand and lead him down the hall to my office. "Lexi," he moans, "don't hold my hand. I'm too old for that."

"I'm not," I tell him. "Humor me."

Halfway down the hall, I see the bottom half of Susan's body protruding from my office. "Ashley," she is saying, "I did not give you permission to come in here. Ashley? Ashley? Listen to me. Ashley? You must learn to respect other people's things."

"That'll work," Joshua whispers and rolls his eyes. I smile, even though I shouldn't encourage Joshua's disrespect of his mother.

"Good morning," I say to Susan's rear. She pops her head out of the doorway and looks guilty. "What's going on, Susan?"

She clears her throat. "Ashley wanted to play office, so she came in here. Although I did not give her permission. Did I, Ashley? No. I did not." Susan steps aside and I look into my office. Her brown curls framing her pale face, Ashley sits at my desk writing on a legal pad. She's done no damage. It's really no big deal, but Susan escalates everything to Code Orange.

"Good morning, Ashley," I say cheerily as I enter my office.

"Good morning, Miss Lexi," she bubbles. Ashley has taken to calling me that since her ballet and piano teachers insist on being called Miss Amanda and Miss Laura. I don't know why Ashley has added the prefix to my name. I have nothing to teach this girl.

"Can I be your assistant today, Miss Lexi? Please? Puhleez? Puhleez?" Ashley is so used to Susan saying no that she begs for things even before she gets an answer. Ashley loves playing "assistant," which involves her making photocopies, doing data entry, and taking care other tasks Low Man usually does, except Ashley does them in my office.

"Did your mother give you permission to be in my office?"

"Yes," Ashley lies. Susan huffs from behind me. "No," Ashley admits.

"Did I give you permission?"

"No." Ashley rises, looking ashamed. I see that her body has grown since I've last seen her. I can't believe how fast Ashley's face is changing from a child's to a preteen's. If the acne fairy stays away, Ashley will have a creamy complexion, big brown eyes, and lots of curlicue curls. She will be very cute.

Now she hangs her head and walks to her mother while I sit in my chair. "Ashley?"

"Yeah?"

"Just like you do at home, we have rules in this office. One of them is that we don't touch each other's things or go into offices without permission. I bet you don't like it when Joshua goes into your room when you're not home and borrows your CDs without asking."

"That's right," Susan chimes in. "Very good, Lexi. Good example."

"I'm sorry, Miss Lexi."

"I accept your apology. And? I'll make you a deal. I'll be in a meeting until ten o'clock. I'm going to give you some work to do, and if you do that well, you can be my assistant for the rest of the day."

"Okay." Ashley claps her hands. "What work?"

I buzz my intercom. "Mister Mike?"

No one answers.

"Hello? Mister Mike?"

"Are you talking to me?" Low Man asks.

"Yes."

"Oh. You threw me off with the 'Mister.' What's up?"

"Did you finish that one-hundred-piece mailing?"

"No. The envelopes need to be stuffed and sealed."

"Wonderful. Miss Gold-Berg will do it. Please set her up with that project in the conference room." I offer Ashley my hand. "Deal?"

"Deal." Ashley gives my hand a good shake, then trots off to Low Man's desk. Susan smiles at me. "Well done, Lexi. What about Joshua?"

"Mom! Please!"

"I have something for him to do, too. No worries. He'll be in my office if you need him."

"Wonderful." Susan leaves. Turning on my computer, I beckon to Joshua. Clicking a screen folder name, "VIP," I smile at Joshua and hold a finger to my lips. The folder opens, revealing ten computer games. "You're awesome, Lexi," Joshua says.

I pat Joshua on his bandana and go to my meeting.

Ashley completes her task, and Joshua obliterates my high score at Brick Blasta. "Mom said you could take us to lunch," Ashley informs me. "Can we please go to the Chinese place?" She's not talking about Chinese food. She's referring to Sweet & Sour, a takeout buffet joint where you pay for your food by the pound. "Is that okay with you?" I ask Joshua.

He shrugs. "Whatever." He says that a lot. It makes me sad.

"I want one of these, two of those, and one of that." Ashley is building her salad at Sweet & Sour. Long finished compiling our lunches, Joshua and I lean against the soda machine. This is why Ashley loves the buffet concept. She can select one piece of cucumber or ten or none. To Ashley, it's shopping.

Meanwhile, Joshua's plastic container, emblazoned with "Sweet & Sour Philly" is filled with white rice and sweet and sour chicken. He is a lot more literal than his sister. Joshua opens his container and pops a piece of chicken into his mouth. He's hungry. "Ashley? Lunch is turning into dinner. Let's go."

After lunch, of which Ashley eats less than half of her $12.25 salad, we take the long way back to the office. It's a cool, bright day and the sun is shining. In Philadelphia, the

July sun is like espresso. This February sun is decaffeinated. It feels good on my face, even as those harmful UV rays seep through my cells.

I lead the kids to Rittenhouse Square. We circle once, then park ourselves on a bench. Joshua pulls a Game Boy from his pocket while Ashley admires the well-dressed people who pass, cell phones and Styrofoam coffee cups in opposite hands. "I want to be like this when I grow up," Ashley says.

"What? Stressed out and overcaffeinated? You will."

"No, I want to be, you know." Ashley doesn't have the vocabulary to explain herself, but I understand what she means. Urbane. Cosmopolitan. Sophisticated. Knowledgeable. Eating at the newest restaurants, watching art house movies, and wearing the right shoes. Sitting in the Square on Sunday afternoons, drinking a grande cappuccino while reading the *New York Times* and wearing designer flip-flops. Spending as much on a cell phone as on a pair of shoes. I know what Ashley sees in these people, my peers. It's what I saw two decades ago in yuppies. We are not yuppies, though. What are we? Urbane. Cosmopolitan. Sophisticated. Knowledgeable. I put the adjectives into an anagram. We . . . SUCK?

"I want to be like you, Miss Lexi."

"What? No, you don't."

"Yes, I do."

Looking sideways at Ashley, I ask, "Why?"

"Because." Ashley puts her hand to my hair and wistfully picks up a strand of it. We have discussed hair many times, and I know Ashley's fervent wish that Susan will allow her curls to be straightened. "I wish you were my mom."

"You really don't."

"I do, too."

73

"First of all, I am not old enough to be your mom." But then I realize, I am.

"Secondly, I wouldn't let you do half the things your mom lets you do."

"Like what?"

"Like hang out with me, for one thing."

"Ha, ha. Lexi. Not funny." Ashley looks around Rittenhouse Square. "You are so cool. My mom is so not."

"Hey, your mom used to be cooler than me." Ashley rolls her eyes in disbelief. "Seriously, Ash. When I started working at The Gold Group? Susan was about the age I am now. She was confident, well dressed, really smart, and not afraid of anything. Susan was my idol."

"What happened to her?" Joshua asks. I didn't realize he was listening.

"Nothing." I shrug. "Things just change. And anyway, Ash, I wouldn't let you get your hair straightened, either."

"Why not?"

"Because."

"Because what?"

"Come on, guys. Back to work." Joshua turns off his Game Boy, stands up, offers me his hand, and pulls me off the bench. He is such a sweetie-pie honey face. No matter how often his parents hug him, it isn't enough. With my arm wrapped around Joshua's shoulders, we walk down the path with Ashley trailing behind us.

"Because what, Lexi? Lexi?"

Chest Nuts

Grace has somehow convinced me to visit a trendy bar. I haven't been to such a place for years. Since before I met Ron Anderson. "What do you have to lose?" Grace asked, and I couldn't come up with a reasonable answer except "My dignity." Grace snorted, which I took to mean that I haven't got any dignity left to lose.

And so Grace, Lola, and I are at Chest Nuts, a pun on Chestnut Street, the location of this zinc, chrome, and velvet bar. Ellie is still in Vancouver, and I'm wishing I was, too.

It is Thursday night, which is not the most jumping night of the week, but it's the only night both Grace and Lola could get away from work. Here we are, perched on a maroon velvet settee, surveying the crowd.

Chest Nuts and many other bars fill the streets of Old City, the historic district of Philadelphia. Ten years ago, Betsy Ross's house was the most exciting thing in this neighborhood. Now, Old City is the very definition of cool.

"I feel really old," I shout over the music.

"There are men our age here," Grace shouts, trying to be positive.

"Yeah, but they're looking for younger women," I moan.

We sit on the settee for twenty minutes. The music is too loud to talk over, so we sit and watch other people have fun.

From the corner of my eye, I see a young man approaching our table. I nudge Lola, who is sitting next to me. With a big smile on his face, the guy strides up to us.

"Excuse me," he shouts. "Are you Lola Bravia?"

"Yes." Lola smiles.

"Oh, wow. Your TV show is so great."

Lola's smile gets bigger. *"Muchas gracias,"* she replies.

"Yeah," the guy shouts. "My mom watches it all the time."

"Oh, Lord," I mutter. Grace covers her mouth with her hand to hide her laugh. Lola doesn't miss a beat. "Please tell her I said thank you."

"Yeah, yeah. She'll be psyched that I met you." With that, the young man saunters away. I put my arm around Lola and laugh in her ear. Just to make sure she can hear me.

"Lexi!" Grace shouts over the music. "Don't look, but there's a guy staring right at you. He's really cute. But don't look."

I look. A tall brunette in a tight, beige pullover and black pants looks back at me. Yummy. The brunette squints at me, then raises his hand in a hesitant wave. I wave back.

"Oh my God," Grace squeals. "Don't wave. It's so obvious."

"Pipe down," I tell Grace. Smiling, the brunette walks to our table and crouches down next to me. "Miss James?" he shouts.

"Yes?" I scan his face. He looks a little familiar.

Leaning close to me, he says, "I'm Paul Crowe." He smiles. I smile back at him.

"I was an intern in your office two summers ago."

"Oh." I nod. "Paul. Right. How are you?"

"Great, actually," Paul answers. "It's funny I should see you here because I was going to call the office this week. I'm graduating from Temple and I'm looking for a job in marketing. Would you be willing to write me a recommendation?"

"No problem."

"Really? That would be, like, awesome."

"Call Mike DiBuono in my office. He'll arrange it."

"Thank you so much, Miss James," Paul gushes. "You're, like, amazing."

"Good luck, Paul." I pat him on the shoulder. He bounces away. I turn to Lola and Grace. "We're leaving."

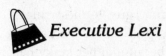 *Executive Lexi*

The Monday morning after a masochistic *thirtysomething* marathon on Lifetime, I get to the office at 9:10 AM. Unfortunately, Monday morning staff meetings start at 9 AM. Oh well.

The eleven-person staff plus Susan, making a cameo appearance, is seated around our conference table. "Here she is," Susan announces with a bright smile when I open the conference room door. Like I'm a child who just came home from her first day of school. The sight of Susan at the conference table does nothing to improve my mood.

Without apologizing for my tardiness, I take my seat at the head of the table, opposite Susan. Low Man sits on my left. "Good morning, everyone. The first matter of business? New business." Low Man kicks me gently under the table. I look at him, irritated. He kicks me again and I look under the table. He's not kicking me. He's shoving something into my leg. It's a rhinestone tiara. Oh, yeah. I almost forgot.

"The first order of business," I say as I get to my feet, holding the tiara behind my back, "is to bestow accolades upon Maria Simons for the successful Bed-In." This is a custom I instituted a few years ago to recognize staff members who do phenomenal work.

Standing behind Maria, I raise the tiara high above her head. "For your excellence in executing the Bed-In, I crown you the PR Princess. Cheryl was the PR Princess for two weeks because of the *New York Times* article. But now you, Maria, have unseated Cheryl. You shall wear this tiara during all staff meetings, until and unless someone does a more spectacular deed, in which case you shall hand over the tiara without crying or dramatics of any kind. Do you agree to these rules?" Maria nods and pretends to get weepy. I situate the tiara on her head, which takes some doing because of her kinky hair. Everyone claps.

Returning to my chair, I smile because it makes me happy to make Maria happy. I look at her, and see that she really is crying.

I adore Maria. Now. At first, I was wary.

Maria came to The Gold Group from a testosterone-laced corporate background. She was a marketing assistant at an investment company. With the economic downturn, the investment company merged with an even stodgier institution, and Maria left before she was laid off. Although she has been at The Gold Group for two years, Maria still wears her skirt and jacket sets and pant suits, which range from black to gray to blue. I finally got her to release her long, black hair from its imprisonment in a tight bun at the nape of her neck. It brings out her green eyes and iced-tea-colored skin. Maria looks softer and more approachable. She is a beautiful woman, the result of a family tree that includes African and Irish blood. But there's no getting around her five-eleven frame and muscular body. The rest of the staff calls her Xena. She likes that.

"Let's get down to business," I tell my staff after Maria's coronation. "Today is the first Monday of a new month— happy March, everyone—so the topic of this meeting is new business."

"I have a great potential client," Maria starts. "Over the

weekend, I had dinner at my girlfriend's parents' house." Maria pauses to adjust the tiara slipping off her head, and I flick my eyes to Susan, whose eyeballs are cast downward and eyebrows are thrust upward. Susan's passive disapproval of Maria's sexual orientation infuriates me.

Maria continues with her new business lead, and Susan listens because Maria usually has strong leads. "Linda's parents are old friends with the Salvo family, which owns Salvo Company, Inc., the biggest hotel and restaurant supplier in the Philadelphia area."

"Salvo has been represented by the Baxter Brothers for years," I say.

"Yes. But Mr. Salvo is retiring and turning the company over to his son Adrian, who was at this dinner party. When I told Adrian that I work for The Gold Group, he said that he would consider leaving Baxter Brothers and getting a fresh approach to the company's public image. He could be tempted, he said. So let's tempt him."

"That account would be worth a million dollars," Susan says excitedly.

"He agreed to a dinner meeting," Maria says. "Lexi, Adrian said he's met you before at a fund-raiser or something. I told him you would, of course, be meeting with him."

"We don't conduct dinner meetings," I remind Maria, and try to remember Adrian Salvo. I can't. We don't do dinner meetings for two reasons. First, they set the precedent that we work around the clock. Second, dinner meetings usually involve alcohol and can lead to a variety of misinterpretations.

"I think you should make an exception," Susan states.

"Why?"

"It's a huge account," she answers.

"I hesitate to violate a long-standing company rule when there may be another solution. Can't Mr. Salvo meet us for lunch? Or can we meet in his office?"

"I guess." Maria shrugs. "He suggested dinner. I hate to give him the impression that we don't want to treat him to dinner."

"She's right," Susan says. Sure. Easy for Susan to say. She's not the one who goes on new business meetings.

"Fine. Maria? You'll attend?" Maria nods vigorously. "Let's bring Low Man. It's about time he got in on the action." Mike smiles, agreeing as if he doesn't know that I want him there as a bodyguard. "Good job, Maria. Great job, actually."

"I'll set it up," Maria says, adjusting her tiara again. She is pleased that I am pleased.

"Other leads?" I ask. And Susan replies, "My sister-in-law needs some help with her travel agency. I told her we'd do a few press releases and maybe a newsletter. Someone needs to be assigned to her account."

Looking wearily at Susan, I ask, "Paid? Or pro bono?"

"What does it matter?"

"It matters because in this office, we track billable hours," I answer dryly. "Pro bono work has to be distributed equally among account executives to make sure everyone remains profitable. I'm the one who distributes the work. So. Paid or pro bono?" Of course, Susan knows all this and I could ask Susan this question privately. But she's ticked me off by supporting the Salvo dinner meeting.

"She's my sister-in-law," Susan says.

Raising my eyebrows, I say, "That's not an answer to my question."

Susan gives me a sugary-sweet I-hate-you smile. "Pro bono," she answers.

"Okay. That's a great project for Low Man on the Totem Pole Mike. Great experience."

No one says anything. This form of warfare is de rigueur. "Mike, get all the information from Susan. Run your ideas by Maria. Susan gets final approval."

"Lexi's approval is fine, Mike," Susan says without looking at me. "I'll be out of the office next week. I'll be available by phone, fax, and e-mail from my home office."

I happen to know that Susan's home office consists of a cubbyhole in her basement. Her real home office is now Joshua's bedroom. Susan is infamous for checking her messages once a day and her e-mail every other day. The rest of us at The Gold Group check our voice mail and e-mail every hour.

"Lexi? Have you assigned the Camp Cool account?" Susan wants to know.

"I'll be handling it myself to keep the pro bono distribution equal."

"Oh." Susan can't decide whether this is good or bad news. The good news is that I am the best in the office. The bad news is that, well, I am me.

Because I don't feel like getting into it with Susan again, I say, "If Camp Cool is so important to Joshua and Ashley's futures, then I want to handle the account myself."

"Wonderful." Susan smiles.

"Wonderful," I repeat. "Meeting adjourned."

The next morning, I am sipping my latte when Low Man brings me a hand-delivered invitation to speak at the University of Pennsylvania's Sorority League Leadership Conference in September. "Pretty paper," Mike says as I read the text.

"Pretty funny," I tell him. "I went to this conference when I was an undergrad. Now they want me to come up with some words of wisdom. Ha."

"You should accept," Mike says. "They'll put your picture in the program. Good PR for The Gold Group. Maybe you'll pick up a hot grad student." Mike winks at me.

"Now there's an incentive. Okay. Please RSVP in the affirmative for me and ask them what the hell they want me to discuss. Want to take a crack at writing the speech? You only have, what? Seven months to do it."

"Sure," Mike answers. "Thanks."

"And will you please get Bob West on the phone? I need to talk to him about doing new shows with Lola."

Bob West at The Cuisine Channel is thrilled to hear from me. I knew he would be. Lola's show was a ratings bonanza for TCC, which means the network made a tidy profit from the commercials. TCC is eager for new episodes.

"There's just one thing," Bob tells me. "We'll need a new crew. None of the old crew will work with Lola again."

"Fine." I'm not surprised. "How long will it take to assemble a new crew?"

"No more than a month." Bob pauses. "Will Lola be okay?"

I give him a different answer. "She's looking forward to this."

"All the same," Bob says carefully, "this time, I'd like to have The Gold Group, not just you, as a producer of the show. That way, your company shares in the risk and the liability. I'm sure Lola will be fine, but if she starts to flip out, she can be reminded that The Gold Group is depending on her as much as the network."

"Why don't you work up a contract and I'll talk to Lola?" I

suggest. We end the conversation cordially, and my mind works.

The Gold Group could have a larger share of the profits from Lola's show. But am I willing to put The Gold Group on the line for Lola? Can I ensure and insure her sanity? On the other hand, this gives me more leverage over her behavior. If she starts to wig out, I will have a contractual obligation to take care of her. This is a good thing. I think. It could devolve into a bad thing. I don't want to become Lola's disciplinarian. But who else can do this for Lola? No one. This is par for the course with me and Lola. She makes me. I make her.

It occurs to me that I should run this Cuisine Channel situation past Susan. I am about to use The Gold Group as collateral. It would be nice of me to discuss it with Susan. There's no answer when I buzz her office, so I walk to the lobby.

"Mike?" I lean over Low Man's desk. "Have you any idea where Susan is?"

Mike rolls his eyes. "I'll give you three guesses."

"She's home? She said she was coming in today."

"Yes, she did," Mike agrees. "But she's at the New Jersey State Aquarium, acting as the chaperone for AGB's field trip."

"AGB?" I squint at Low Man.

"Ashley Gold-Berg, of course," Mike drawls. "That's what she calls herself now. I called Susan at home and Ashley answered the phone, 'Hello, this is AGB.' I thought I had dialed a pharmaceutical company. Of course, the baby diva corrected me. She informed me that 'Ash' is not a suitable nickname, so she wants to be called either Ashley or AGB."

"She has a point. 'Ash' is terrible."

"Well, Veep, if we are reconsidering nicknames, may I formally request the rethinking of Low Man on the Totem Pole?"

"No," I answer, and go back to my office.

Forget it. I'm not waiting for Susan to materialize in the office. I get Lola on the phone and relay the conversation with Bob West. As delicately as possible, I explain that TCC wants Lola to check her Mariah at the door and that The Gold Group will be held in hock if La Diva Lola's nasty side causes production delays. Of course, I don't say it quite like that.

It takes Lola just a minute to think, then say, "*Bueno, amiga. Muchas gracias.*"

"*¿Lola, entiendes la situation?*" She answered too fast. I need to know that she understands what's happening.

"*Sí. Yo entiendo.*" She pauses, then softly says, "*Te amo.*"

"*Y yo te amo más,*" I answer. She gets it.

 ## A Monumental Mistake

On a sunny March Sunday, Lola, Grace, and I sit at table outside Rx. It's not really warm enough to be sitting outside, but we insisted. Grace wears a sweater coat over her scrubs; she's off to work after brunch. I don't know where Lola thinks she's going in her outfit. She's wearing black stretch pants, high-heeled boots, and a poncho with a faux fur collar. My interpretation of brunch chic is jeans, an oversize fisherman's sweater, a baseball hat, and sunglasses.

Lola is telling us about last night's shenanigans at her restaurant while I read the newspaper. "Holy mackerel," I shout.

Grace grabs the Sunday Lifestyle section out of my hands. "Let me see."

Displayed in the middle of the page is a photo of Ron Anderson and Randi Katchman with an accompanying story of their engagement. Duly noted is Ron's "mistake" of a first engagement, and how he narrowly escaped marrying the wrong woman. Grace reads out loud. " 'Fate was waiting for Ron when he went to Tiffany's to return the ring. Randi, who had been hired as a clerk three days earlier, helped Ron with his ring, and with his broken heart. What may seem like a short engagement to some feels like forever to Ron. "I can't wait to begin my life with Randi. I've been waiting all my life to meet the right woman," he said. "Fate stopped me from making a monumental mistake." ' "

"That's me." I raise my hand. "The monumental mistake."

"Maybe this will be a kick in the ass for you to get serious about dating," Grace says.

"It's a kick in the ass all right," Lola says.

"This is supposed to inspire me to date?"

Ignoring my question, Grace says, "It's been six months since you broke off the engagement. You need to get serious about meeting someone. Get back out there. Make yourself available to the right kind of men."

"Should I sit in Rittenhouse Square and wait for the love of my life to find me?"

Lola laughs. "If Prince Charming came up to you in the Square, I'm quite sure you would give him some spare change and tell him to get lost."

"That's true," I agree.

"Still," Lola adds, "Grace is right."

"I don't think you can afford to sit around and wait for love to find you," Grace insists. "I know things aren't perfect with Michael, but I am happy with him."

"How's that proposal coming?" I ask Grace.

"Shut up, Lexi."

"I'm just saying that you two shouldn't be giving me advice on men."

"I've been married already," Lola says. "I'm in a different place."

"A divorced place," I say unkindly. It is unkind, but not untrue. As often as we dissect each other's lives, the COG never confronts Lola about the lack of romance in her life. Lola is over Enrique, her husband. But she is not over the pain of their divorce. She keeps that pain close at hand because it protects her from getting hurt in the future. Lola has constructed her castle so that she does not need a prince. She is the princess. The queen. And the king.

Lola says, "Lexi, I think it's time for you to get back in the game."

"Try that dating service that a friend of mine at the hospital used," Grace says. "She met her husband that way. It's called Modern Dating. 'Matchmaking for successful professionals.' "

"A dating service? Oh, Lord. I don't know," I moan.

"What have you got to lose?" Grace asks.

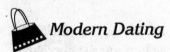 **Modern Dating**

Two days later, I go to the Modern Dating offices after a lunch meeting. A twenty-something, perfectly coifed woman greets me and asks me to fill out the questionnaire, after which a relationship counselor will see me.

Perching on a couch, balancing the clipboarded questionnaire on one knee and my afternoon latte on the other, I review the Modern Dating form. The first questions are about me.

Height: 5'5"   Weight: 135   Age: 33

Should I fudge these answers? I am a PR person. Oh, forget it.

Occupation: Executive Vice President,   Religion: Other
        The Gold Group
Relationship History: Never married   Relationship Goal:

I'll come back to that last one.

The next page is filled with questions about what I am looking for in a man.

Height: Weight: Age:
Occupation: Religion: Smoker/Drinker:
Relationship History: Geographical Area:

This is a test, isn't it? I don't know the answers. My heart starts beating rapidly. I feel like I'm part of a dating game show quiz.

Lexi James, how tall is your soul mate? Five-ten? No, I'm sorry! The answer is six-two. You weren't even close. Let's try another question. Lexi James, what religion is your soul mate? Catholic? Protestant? Methodist? No, I'm sorry! The correct answer is: Episcopalian.

Frantically, I look at the young woman at the desk. She's on the phone. I remove the forms from the clipboard and rip them into little pieces. "I changed my mind," I tell the girl on my way out the door.

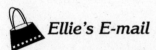 *Ellie's E-mail*

That night, I am sitting in front of my computer in my sweaty gym clothes eating meatballs with chopsticks. I am eating meatballs sans spaghetti because of my no-carb diet. I am eating meatballs because they were all that was left at Rittenhouse Gourmet, the prepared-foods joint around the corner. I am eating my meatballs with chopsticks because I forgot to start the dishwasher before I left for work and my flatware is dirty.

Aha! I have an e-mail from the Fabulous Ellie Archer. The address is a strange one, which she has clarified with the header THIS IS FROM ELLIE so I don't delete it as spam.

Lexi—I met The One. I am in love. I'm staying here an extra week, then we are coming to Phila. I can't wait for you to meet him. Love—Ellie

Huh? I reply immediately, asking a million questions. The e-mail gets bounced back to me. From wherever Ellie e-mailed me, I can't e-mail her.

Immediately, I dial Ellie's cell phone. Voice mail picks up and I leave a message. I call Lola's cell phone. She doesn't pick up. I call Grace, but I get a busy signal. She's probably on line. I forward the e-mail to Lola, Grace and Mia.

This is big news. I need more information. Who is the guy?

How did they meet? What's his name? Since when does Ellie fall in love?

 This is Your Life

The next morning, I straighten my hair and think about Ellie's life. And mine.

While Ellie has had plenty of boyfriends, she has never admitted to being in love. The men in her life and in her bed were more conveniences than relationships. She jettisoned them as soon as they got too serious. As soon as they got in the way of her career. Which is why she is still single.

But now, Ellie is in love? What if the mystery man is The One for Ellie? Will she get married? Something rises in my chest. What is it? All of a sudden, but maybe it's been forever, I feel very alone.

Putting down my brush and blow dryer, I sit on the toilet and start to cry. Stop, I tell myself. Don't do this. Don't be an idiot. Standing up, I look in the mirror.

"Are you depressed?" I ask myself.

"No."

"Are you nuts?"

"No."

"Are you premenstrual?"

"No."

"What the hell is the matter with you?"

"I'm alone."

"You are not alone. You have friends. You have the COG."

"They will get married and leave me. I'll be alone."

"You know what, Lexi? You made your choices. This is your

life, and you may be alone for the rest of it. You'd better get used to it."

 **Control**

"Good morning, my queen," Low Man greets me when I get off the elevator at 9:25 AM.

"Queen?" I spit. "Queen? Is that supposed to mean that I'm old?"

"No," Mike stammers.

Maria hustles up to the reception desk. "Veep, I have information on Salvo Company for you." Maria hands me a file folder.

"Thank you." I turn to walk to my office.

"Lexi, wait. I thought you would want to talk it over with me."

"Maria, how can I talk to you about it if I haven't read it?"

"Fine." Maria walks down the hallway, shoulders rigid. I turn back to Mike. From his half-lowered head, he looks up at me cautiously. "Only disturb me for important calls," I tell him.

"Okay. Do you want to define important?"

I breathe through my nose, practically snorting. "If you're ever going to get out of being Low Man on the Totem Pole, you will have to learn what is important and what is not." Turning on my heel, I walk into my office.

My office door closed, I get to work. First, I check my voice mail and e-mail and respond appropriately. Next, I go through stacks of reports and other crap. I read, double check, and sign everything. Reviewing the contract for Lola's cookbook, I see that Bob West has put everything in order. At noon, I buzz Mike. "Low Man, please come in here. Now."

Mike knocks before he opens my door. "Yes, ma'am?"

I see heads trying to peer into my door. So, the news has spread that I am in bitch mode today. Fine.

"Please redistribute all of that." I gesture toward an enormous pile of paper. "Then please get me a chef's salad and Diet Dr Pepper."

"Yes, ma'am," Mike says as he struggles with the pile of paper on his way out of my office.

"And knock it off with the 'ma'am,' Mike."

Twenty minutes later, Low Man knocks on my door and enters my office with my salad and soda. I hand him a twenty-dollar bill. "It didn't cost that much," he says.

"Keep the change," I tell him as if he were a delivery boy. He frowns. I ignore him.

Opening my salad, I realize that I am not hungry. Diet Dr Pepper in hand, I walk quickly down the hall, up the stairs, and onto the roof.

The March wind blows through my hair and I look over the Philadelphia skyline. This is good. I am in control.

 Dr. Franklin, Session Two

I am in control, but that control is delicate and I don't feel like upsetting it, so I cancel my appointment with Dr. Franklin. To atone for my bitchiness, I buy muffins and croissants for my staff the next morning.

Lady Lexi & the Traditions of Cool

"It's a beautiful day in the neighborhood," Low Man tells me when I get off the elevator after a lunch meeting.

"Is it?"

"No." Before I can ask why, the answer comes running into the lobby, wearing The Answer's jersey. Joshua Gold-Berg gives me a power hug. I find Ashley standing at attention outside my office door. "Good afternoon, Miss Lexi," she says.

"Good afternoon, Miss Ashley." I open my door, and the kids follow me into my office. "What are you guys doing here?"

"We're going to Camp Cool," Ashley says.

"Why? It's March."

"Orientation," Joshua answers.

"Yeah? Have fun."

"You're coming," Ashley says.

"Me? Why do I have to go?"

"To meet about PR stuff. Didn't my mom tell you?" Ashley rolls her eyes.

"Oh, there you are, Lexi." Susan breezes into my office. "Listen, did I tell you about the Camp Cool meeting?"

"Seatbelts!" Susan trills as we strap ourselves into her beige SUV. As soon as Susan's key turns in the ignition, Joshua puts on his headphones and pulls out his Game Boy. Susan begins a monologue about the sterling reputation of Camp Cool. Ashley whips out her cell phone. How do people think with so much noise?

We've been in the car for twenty minutes when I lose patience with AGB's cell phone. It has rung five times and she has called at least that many people. Every conversation is the same.

"Hey. What's up? What are you doing? Nothing. Like, I dunno. Okay. Talk to you later."

"Ashley?" I speak in my quiet, grown-up voice. "If you use that cell phone one more time, I will throw it out the window."

"Honey? Lexi is right. The phone is for emergencies. Turn it off."

"But Mom, if I turn it off, how will I know if there's an emergency?"

"It's for you to call someone if you have an emergency."

"But Mom, what if, like, someone else is having an emergency and needs to get in touch with me?" Ashley waves her cell phone like it's a sixth finger.

"Ashley."

"Mom."

"Ashley."

"Mom." This continues for another five minutes, until Susan realizes she is lost and pulls into a gas station to ask for directions.

"What kind of joint is this?"

"It's a very prestigious camp," Susan whispers.

"Camp? It looks like a campus." Indeed, Camp Cool is three acres of stone buildings, brick paths and perfect landscaping. "Where do you, like, run around and play?"

"Lexi, these children are not here to play. This is a summer prep school."

"So, it's what? Prep camp?"

"Just be quiet. Here comes Mr. Whitman."

"Mrs. Berg?" A man in a suit, tie, and white goatee approaches.

"Yes," Susan coos, and I look at her suspiciously. Susan usually insists on including the Gold in Gold-Berg. "Wonderful to see you Mr. Whitman. This is Miss James."

Miss? Whatever. Extending my hand, I say, "Very nice to meet you. Sir."

"Lexi? You meet with Mr. Whitman. I'll be with the children."

The children? Susan is doing her Mistress of the Manor act. She thinks it impresses people. Nodding grandly, Susan says, "This way, children," and strides toward a group assembling under a veranda, leaving me with Mr. Whitman. "Right this way, Miss James," Mr. Whitman intones.

The walls of Mr. Whitman's office are oak paneled, and the floors are covered with Oriental rugs. Mr. Whitman gestures, which I think he must do often, to a maroon leather chair opposite his mahogany desk. I sit. And cross my ankles. The way my grandmother taught me a real lady sits. I have this ability to chameleon myself to match my surroundings. Chic & Sleek, Jersey Girl, Tough Chick, and Lady Lexi are in my repertoire. It makes clients comfortable if they think I am like them. The real me is a pastiche of all those characters. I think.

"Miss James," Mr. Whitman rumbles.

"Please, call me Lexi."

"Lexi? An unusual name. A derivative of another name?"

"Yes. Alexandra."

"Ah," Mr. Whitman nods his approval. "Alexandra is your Christian name?"

"I don't know how Christian it is. Probably more Greek." I smile. Mr. Whitman doesn't. "Either way, I prefer Lexi."

"But Alexandra is a grand name, with such history. We at Camp Coleridge believe in history and tradition."

"Coleridge? I thought this was Camp Cool."

Mr. Whitman frowns. "An unfortunate nickname, which we highly discourage."

Damn. There goes my whole stinking proposal. This time, I may actually kill Susan. Susan Berg.

Mr. Whitman makes a steeple of his fingers and sits back in his chair. "May I be frank with you, Alexandra?"

"Of course."

"I understand that you have come here for the purpose of outlining a public relations program for Camp Coleridge, and I must tell you that we are not interested in promoting our institution. You see, Alexandra . . ." Mr. Whitman leans forward, putting his steepled fingers on his desk. "Camp Coleridge is a very selective institution. Families have sent their children here for generations. We do accept new enrollments, but limit them to ten every summer. To be accepted at Camp Coleridge, a child must excel in every area of his education. In addition, prospective children and their families must have recommendations from two teachers and two Coleridge alumni. So you see, Alexandra, Camp Coleridge is actually quite opposed to publicity."

Here comes my latent Ivy Leaguism. "I understand perfectly, Mr. Whitman. I had to undergo a similar process to be accepted to the University of Pennsylvania, even though it is the James family alma mater."

Okay, this is not even close to true. My father didn't graduate from college. In fact, he was kicked out for "distributing" pot on campus. Leo James thought it was an inalienable right of every American to be stoned. It was the sixties. Whatever.

The Penn thing strikes the right note with Mr. Whitman, as

I knew it would. "May I offer you a beverage, Alexandra? Tea? Mineral water?"

"No thank you." I smile grandly at Mr. Whitman. "I suppose there has been some confusion on Mrs. Berg's part. Her communication with me indicated Camp Coleridge was interested in public relations."

"Mrs. Berg is mistaken. And quite a bit more." Mr. Whitman puckers his mouth. "You see, Mrs. Berg's children did not have the proper recommendations. In an attempt to circumvent the requirements, Mrs. Berg offered me a trade."

"Public relations for acceptance."

"Yes."

"I imagine, Mr. Whitman, that Mrs. Berg's offer is distasteful to you."

"Indeed it is, Alexandra."

"Yet, here we are. How did this come to pass?"

Mr. Whitman explains. "Mrs. Berg had one recommendation, that of the Hunt family. It seems Mr. Hunt and Mr. Berg are partners in the same law firm. The Hunt family has been with Camp Coleridge since the mid 1880s."

"Oh, the Hunts? A very fine family." Never heard of 'em.

"I'm sure you understand, Alexandra, that the strength of an institution like Camp Coleridge depends on its history and tradition. Our children go on to the finest colleges and universities, and Camp Coleridge is a breeding ground for this country's leaders. We cannot allow just anyone to enroll here. Mrs. Berg," and he says it with a sneer, "is violating hundreds of years of Camp Coleridge tradition. She will no doubt tell her friends that her children are enrolled here, and her friends will of course try to use Mrs. Berg's recommendation to enroll their children. You see, it sets a precedent."

"Yes, sir. I see. But I assure you, sir, that Ashley and Joshua are wonderful children. I hope you won't hold their mother's transgressions against them."

"Your affection for the Berg children is admirable, Alexandra. Of course, we want all of the Coleridge children to excel. Now that the Bergs are part of the Coleridge family, they will be treated like all the rest. I assure you of that."

"Wonderful, Mr. Whitman. Wonderful." I rise gracefully from my chair and extend my hand, turning it so the palm is down. Instead of shaking Mr. Whitman's hand, I squeeze it, just as my grandmother taught me. "Now that our business is concluded, may I go find the children and Mrs. Berg? I would like to see the campus for myself."

"Of course, Alexandra. The boys and girls will have separated by now. The parents are in Longstreth Hall. The girls are in Wright Hall. Just follow the path to your left. And Miss James?"

"Yes, Mr. Whitman?"

"I see from your ring finger that you are neither married nor engaged, but I do hope that once you find a husband and have children, that you will remember us at Camp Coleridge. I'm sure you know many of our alumni."

"Mr. Whitman, I do have children."

"Really?" He adjusts his tie. "You are divorced?"

"No, sir. I live happily with my lover. Yes. Shaniqua and I have three adopted children. Parasol from Paraguay, Chin from China and Leroy from North Philly. And I will keep Camp Coleridge in mind for their futures. Thank you, Mr. Whitman. Good day."

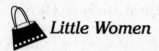 ## Little Women

The heavy oak door to Wright Hall squeaks as I close it behind me. Ringing through the hall is the crisp voice of a woman speaking in Bostonian tones.

"Caroline, you've been at Camp Coleridge for six years. You know the rules." Following the voices, I tiptoe down the polished oak floors. Peeking into the room with the voices, I see book-lined walls, brown leather couches, club chairs with ottomans, and tapestried wing chairs. It looks like a cozy library. "Caroline doesn't like to read because it means she has to wear her glasses," a young voice says. A girl with long, blond hair sticks her tongue out at the girl who spoke, who, in turn, blows the blond a kiss.

"Here are the lists of books we'll be reading this summer. Patricia? Pass these out, please." Moving into what looks like a dining room, I stand in front of an enormous mirror that is angled into the library. Now, instead of looking at the backs of the sofas and chairs, I see the faces of the girls sitting in them. I find Ashley sitting in a wing chair in the back of the room. Patricia approaches Ashley with the book list and Ashley extends her hand to receive it, but Patricia releases the piece of paper and it falls to the floor. With a mighty twirl, Patricia turns her back on Ashley, which allows me to see her face. Patricia rolls her eyes at the other girls and they giggle as Ashley bends to the floor to pick up her book list.

"Settle down, girls," the teacher says. "We'll start the summer with an easy one. You should have all read it by now. *Little Women*."

Whew. I let out a sigh. *Little Women* is one of Ashley's favorite books. She got an A+ on her book report, which I know because Susan brought it to the office to show everyone.

"We're going to do a thorough analysis of *Little Women*. You will be expected to analyze novels in high school and for the rest of your life. Not just reading a book, but looking deep into it for messages and themes. Can anyone name one of *Little Women*'s sociopolitical themes?"

"The Civil War," a girl says.

"Correct. What else? What was the overarching theme of the book? Caroline?"

"Sisters. Mothers."

"Duh," Patricia says. "It's called *Little Women*." Caroline and the other girls giggle.

"What about women? Look at the different sisters and the choices they made. One got married and had children, one traveled around the world and found love, one was very independent and started her own school, and one died. What is the title telling us? What was the place of women in society at that time? Can anyone tell me what a suffragist is?"

Caroline's hand pops into the air. "Someone against slavery."

"No." Caroline looks pissed to be wrong. The teacher looks around the room for another answer. "Ashley? Do you know?"

Quietly, Ashley says, "Suffragists fought for women's right to vote. Abolitionists fought against slavery. Louisa May Alcott was both. So, you were sort of right, Caroline." Ashley offers a small smile, but Caroline glares at her.

"Excellent, Ashley, excellent. Women's rights were a big issue at that time. Of the four sisters, with whom do you think the author most identified?"

Blank faces look at the teacher. Ashley lowers her head. The teacher prompts them. "She was the writer."

I know Ashley knows this. But Ashley doesn't answer. The teacher gives up and answers her own question. "Jo March, of course."

The teacher speaks for ten more minutes, during which time I watch Ashley's head hang. When the group is dismissed and told to meet their parents in Longstreth Hall, Ashley rises but moves backward, letting the other girls leave the room before her. When Caroline passes, she smirks at Ashley. "Nice hair, Ashley." The other girls giggle. Ashley gets tears in her eyes and stands still as the girls tramp loudly down the hall, coming straight at me.

Scooting out the front door, I stand to the side, as if I haven't been eavesdropping. The girls nod politely to me, and I return the nods, although I want to throttle them.

Finally, Ashley emerges, head down, eyelids bulging with tears. "Hey, Ash," I say softly, so as not to startle her.

She wipes at her face, trying to hide her distress. "Hi, Lexi. How was your meeting?"

"Fine. Mr. Whitman was a hoot and a half." Ashley smiles. Lagging behind, Ashley and I follow the gaggle of girls down a cobblestoned path. "How did it go for you, Ash?"

"Okay."

"Are you the only new girl in your grade?"

"Yeah."

"Oh. It's hard to be the new kid. I bet the other girls gave you a hard time."

"Yeah." Ashley hangs her head again, trying to hide her face.

That's it. I can't take it anymore.

Grabbing Ashley's arm, I pull her behind a shed and fold Ashley into a hug. She immediately starts to cry, bursting into big, juicy sobs. I rub her back until she stops. "Ash?"

She snuffles. "Yeah?"

"Sometimes kids are mean to each other. You know that."

"I know. It's just that I've gone to school with the same kids my whole life. I've never been the new kid."

"Being the new kids sucks. For sure. But listen to me." Stepping away from Ashley, I raise her head so she's looking at me. "No matter how mean those girls are, I don't want you to ever, ever play dumb to make them happy. If you know an answer and don't give it, you let them win. The teacher will think you don't know anything, and pretty soon, you'll start to believe that the other kids are smarter than you. Listen, Ashley. Are you listening?"

"Yeah."

"Being dumb is worse than being unpopular. Popularity fades. Smart lasts forever."

Ashley smiles at me.

Driving away from Camp Coleridge, Susan looks at me in the rearview mirror. "Everything settled with Mr. Whitman?"

"Yes," I answer, and leave it at that. I'm too tired to explain.

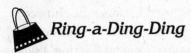

Ring-a-Ding-Ding

Ten minutes after I get home from Camp Cool, my phone rings. "I have big news," Grace says.

Exhausted, I put my hand over my eyes. "What?"

"He asked," Grace shouts.

"Who? What?"

"Michael asked me to marry him. This afternoon."

"Oh my God. Wow." Although Grace predicted Michael would soon propose, I am stunned that he finally did. "Congratulations, Gracie."

"Yeeee!" Grace squeals into the phone.

"Tell me."

"It wasn't romantic or anything because he asked me in the hospital parking lot while we were waiting for the elevator. He got the ring on Saturday, which is exactly when I thought he got it. Remember? Because Mrs. Kelly didn't mention marriage?"

"You were right."

"I know! Anyway, Michael made reservations at some fancy restaurant for tomorrow and he was going to ask then, but you know Michael. He couldn't wait."

He couldn't wait? Right. He waited four years.

"So he just kind of handed the box to me and asked if I would marry him."

"What does the ring look like?"

"The diamond is round. It's a yellow gold band with a pronged setting."

"Didn't you want a square cut and a platinum setting?" Immediately, I regret asking the question. I know exactly what kind of engagement ring Grace wanted because she showed it to me every time we passed a jewelry store. Grace thought, and hoped, that Michael would consult me on the ring. I wish he had.

"Whatever, Lexi. It doesn't matter. What matters is that I'm engaged! I'm calling Lola now. I already told Mia. She's thrilled. When is Ellie getting back?"

"This weekend. Friday or Saturday."

"So, Lex? Since Michael is working tonight and he and I are celebrating tomorrow night, do you think the COG could get together tonight? I know it's last-minute, but you don't have any plans, do you?"

"No," I answer, and ignore the jibe.

 ## The Coordinator of Hoopla

The COG minus Ellie but with Mia assembles at Lola's for a late dinner. Mia's appearance is due to Grace's ultimate happiness. Grace flashes her ring at us. It looks to be about a carat. The round diamond, pronged setting, and yellow gold are not Grace's style. But hey, it's a ring.

"I want to start planning the wedding right away," Grace decrees. Lola claps her hands excitedly. She loves planning parties. "What do you have in mind?" she asks. "Have you thought about it?"

Has Grace thought about her wedding? She's been planning it for years. "Well," Grace begins. "I'd like the ceremony to be at St. Patrick's on Twentieth Street. That's where we go to church. When we go. It's a beautiful place. Old and gothic and everything. Then, for the reception, I'm going to investigate The Rittenhouse Hotel, The Four Seasons, Independence, and the Ritz-Carlton. Lola, will you help me with that part?"

"Of course," Lola answers.

"Great! I can't do anything about the food or music until the site is decided. Oh, but I could work on colors and flowers and decorations. Mia, will you help me with that stuff?"

"Hell, yes." Mia wraps her little arm around Grace's shoulder. As the conversation continues, I smile and watch my friends act like girly girls.

"Ellie has such great fashion sense. Plus she has ins with all those designers from that article she did last year. I'll wait until she gets back and talk to her about dresses."

"What about me?" I ask Grace. "I want to help."

"You do?" Grace seems surprised.

"Of course I do. Why wouldn't I?"

"Well." Grace shrugs. "I just figured that, you wouldn't, you know, want to be involved with, you know. A wedding. Because of yours. Do you want to get involved with the hoopla?"

"Wouldn't you like to put my wedding experience to good use? And what about my work experience? I specialize in hoopla," I tell the COG. "Events are what I do for a living. I am the vice president of hoopla. I am, like, the czarina of hoopla."

"Okay, okay." Grace holds her hands in the air. "You can be the wedding coordinator. The coordinator of hoopla. How's that?"

"Wonderful."

Really? I don't want to deal with the wedding planning. It will be a nightmare, for sure, because Grace will obsess about every detail while she creates her version of a perfect wedding. Mia was very levelheaded about her wedding, but she will have a tough time getting Grace to hype down. Grace will act like Lola did about her television show. She will drive me batty. At the same time, I don't want to be left out of the planning if the rest of the COG are going to participate. I want in.

Dazzle

The first half of April is consumed with preparations for tax day. For two weeks, I am in management overdrive, working with our accounting firm to get everything where it needs to be. Of course, corporate taxes function differently from personal taxes and don't adhere to the April 15 deadline. Still, budgets and P/L statements need to be created, and we have things to do for our employees, and ourselves. Susan happily gets out of my way and lets me deal with the paperwork as I see fit. Our final figures show that last year was profitable, but not by much. The recession forced a lot of companies to cut back on public relations and advertising. Still. A slim profit is better than no profit. Or a loss.

As per our April 15 custom, I buy the staff lunch. It's always an inexpensive lunch because I am extraordinarily conscious of money on tax day. Whatever. It's the thought.

Sitting around the conference table, my staff chitchats and gossips. Maria makes her way toward me, pizza slice in hand.

"Ditching the no-carb diet, are we?" she asks.

"One slice, once a month."

"I've been thinking about dinner," Maria says. Tonight is our first meeting with Adrian Salvo, heir to the throne of Salvo Company. "I have lots of ideas for Salvo. Want to hear them?"

"Nope. And neither will Adrian. I know this account would be a big catch. Trust me, I've been swimming in Gold Group numbers for weeks. We need a big client. But that doesn't mean we go about this pitch any differently than we usually do. We discuss our past successes and make an impression that way. If we start shooting out ideas, Adrian could take those concepts back to Baxter Brothers, or hire an in-house person to execute them for less money."

"Less efficiently," Maria says.

"Of course. But we don't give ideas until we get into the proposal stage, and even then, it's all smoke and mirrors. No specifics until the contract is signed and the check clears. For now, we will dazzle Mr. Salvo with our witty conversation and medals of achievement."

"He is looking for fresh ideas, though," Maria says nervously. "If we don't give him any new ideas, why would he leave Baxter Brothers?"

"We don't have to lay out his new campaign. We just have to point out what's wrong with his current campaign. And that, my princess, is quite an easy feat. Yes?"

"Yes." Maria smiles.

"Remember, confidence is the ultimate aphrodisiac."

"Isn't that what they tell men? To attract women? I didn't know it applied to business."

"It applies to everything."

 ## Fifteen Minutes

Adrian Salvo is eleven minutes late.

Our dinner meeting was scheduled for 5:30 PM. Maria, Low Man on the Totem Pole Mike, and I are seated at a primo table at Lola's. We are quietly waiting for Adrian.

Mike is dressed in navy gabardine pants with flat, notched pockets. Under a single-breasted, navy jacket, Mike wears a china blue, silk tie. Mike's an attractive guy. Kid, really. He's twenty-three and he has a lot of style for someone that age. Mike's short brown hair is always cut just right. His hazel eyes lift at the corners, giving him a clean, bright look.

Adrian Salvo is now twelve minutes late.

Maybe Mike could give Maria some fashion tips. Tonight, she's wearing a black pant suit with a white blouse and black loafers. Maria's hair is pulled back into a tight bun and she's frowning and surveying the restaurant for any sign of Salvo. She looks like a bouncer.

Adrian Salvo is now thirteen minutes late.

Chic & Sleek is who I am this evening. I'm wearing a crisp, white cotton shirt with French cuffs under a black vest. The shirt's collar is slightly open to reveal my pearl choker. My black skirt comes exactly to my knee, and my black pumps have a silver buckle and two-inch heels. I've got my dazzle on.

Adrian Salvo is now fourteen minutes late.

"One more minute and we leave," I tell Mike and Maria.

"Leave?" Mike gulps.

"Being more than fifteen minutes late is a sign of disrespect," I inform them. "You must command respect at the beginning of a client relationship, or you'll never get it back."

"But if we leave," Maria says, "won't he think we disrespected him?"

"If Adrian really wanted to meet us, he would be on time. If he's not serious about the possibility of working with The Gold Group, we are wasting our time. It's better to know that up front." I look at my watch. "Ten seconds."

Mike and Maria look at each other, wanting to contradict me but being wise enough not to. "That's it," I say. "Let's go." I stand up, take hold of my tote, and head toward the door. Mike and Maria remain seated, aghast. Turning back to them,

I say, "Let's go. Adrian Salvo doesn't get one minute of my time." Turning toward the door, I smack into a man who is smiling at me.

"Lexi James waits for no man," he says through his smile.

I raise my left eyebrow. "That's right."

"Please accept my apology," Adrian says, taking my right hand into both of his hands. "Tardiness is my least appealing vice." He shifts his head to one side and purses his lips, frowning like a bad child. "Do you forgive me?"

I find his expression unprofessional, not amusing. "You're forgiven," I tell him curtly, not cutely. Withdrawing my hand, I gesture to the table. "Let's sit down."

 Reservations

"After you," Adrian says. I turn my back to him and walk toward Mike and Maria. I feel Adrian's hand on the small of my back, guiding me forward. Tensing my shoulders, I move away quickly.

"Maria, Maria," Adrian says as if he and Maria are old friends. Which they are not. Nevertheless, Adrian grasps Maria's hands and gives her a peck on each cheek. Maria blushes. Lesbian that she is, Maria is not immune to masculine charm. "This is Mike DiBuono," Maria introduces. The two men shake hands, Adrian giving Mike the wary smile that homophobes give men whom they perceive as potential fags.

The four of us sit down at our round table, Adrian between Mike and Maria, me opposite him. Maria starts talking about The Gold Group's history and client roster. Ten minutes later, a sampling of hors d'oeuvres arrives. "We haven't ordered," Maria tells the waiter.

"Compliments of Miss Lola," the waiter says.

Three days earlier, I called Lola to let her know I would be bringing in a juicy potential client. I don't have to ask for special treatment; Lola insists on making a fuss. It's enormously impressive, and every time Lola does it, I send her thank-you flowers.

"I won't be there, but I wrote instructions in the reservation book," Lola told me.

"*Muchas gracias, amiga.*"

"*De nada, chica,*" Lola answers. "Who's the potential client?"

"Salvo Company."

"Really? Are you meeting with Adrian Salvo?"

"Yeah. Do you know him?" I ask. "I'm sure you know the company. Do you buy from Salvo Company for your restaurant?"

"Yes," Lola answers.

"Wish me luck."

"*Buena suerte.*"

While we eat, Maria continues to put forth the experience of The Gold Group. Mike chimes in appropriately. Adrian listens. I assess Adrian.

If I didn't already know, I could have guessed that he grew up in South Philly. From that neighborhood of black jeans, "how you doin'," and pinkie rings came Adrian Salvo. I peg him at five-eight and over forty years old.

His body looks muscular under his suit jacket, which has three buttons and is black with pinstripes. Adrian is wearing a royal blue shirt with a slate gray tie. There's a lot going on in Adrian's outfit. As he extends his hand to reach his water glass, I see his monogram stitched on the cuff of his shirt. Peaking from the cuff is an enormous silver watch with three small dials on its large face. I see the word "Bvlgari" and know that the watch is wildly expensive.

Adrian speaks with Maria and pretends to ignore me, but he's watching me watch him. This pleases Adrian, that I am looking at him. His thick, black hair is gelled and sculpted into precise waves. Adrian's strong black eyebrows frame his brown eyes.

Adrian Salvo is an attractive man, but something rings false. I think this man has spent too much time in front of a mirror.

"So the Bed-In was your idea?" Adrian smiles at me.

"Yes," I answer, finally coming into the conversation.

"Who did you get in bed with?" Adrian asks with a smirk.

"No one," I tell him. "My staff and I were busy orchestrating the event."

The waiter interrupts with a dessert plate piled high with yummies from Lola's pastry chef. "Wow," Adrian says, suitably impressed. I smile at the waiter and he nods, then disappears.

Mike and Maria spear churros, fried sticks of dough with powdered sugar that are dipped into melted chocolate. Adrian slices into the coconut flan and leans over the table, pointing his spoon toward my mouth. "Try some flan," he smiles.

"No thank you," I answer.

Queen Ellie

"We set up a meeting for next week. We'll review his account then, and if all goes well, he'll be ready to sign the contract." It's Saturday afternoon and I'm sitting at Thai Lake in Chinatown with Grace and Lola. We are awaiting the arrival of Ellie and her mystery love.

"Sounds great," Grace says as she pages through brochures on hotel banquet facilities that Lola brought to her.

"What did you think of Adrian?" Lola asks.

"*Mucho macho,*" I answer, but before I can go into more detail, Grace squeals, "There they are!" and I turn to see Ellie and a tall, handsome man walking toward us.

The first thing I notice is that the man has his arm around Ellie's shoulders. People don't walk like that anymore. They mostly hold hands. As if the man and woman are equals. But this man, he has his arm firmly around Ellie. Intimately. Protectively. That gesture is enough. I know he is different. Different from other men I've known. Different from other men Ellie has known.

Then I notice his jacket. It's tweed. Beneath it is a deep brown vest and beneath that is a beige, open-collared button-down shirt. Most of all, I notice his scarf. It's long and thin and maroon and tossed over one shoulder. I get it.

He's European.

Grace jumps up from the table to squeeze Ellie. Lola follows, and the three of them hug. "Congratulations on your engagement!" Ellie tells Grace. She looks quickly at the ring. "It's fabulous, Gracie. I'm so happy for you."

The man steps back, smiling, letting the girls have their moment. He looks at me and inclines his head slightly, nodding politely to me and smiling. I meet his gaze and nod back. I don't smile.

"Girls, I want you to meet someone," Ellie says, separating herself from Grace and Lola and stepping back to stand at the man's side. "This," Ellie breathes, "is Jean-François Bardet."

Lola immediately offers her hand. *"Enchanté. Je m'appelle Lola."*

Jean-François doesn't shake Lola's hand so much as clasp it for a moment. *"Le plaisir est partage."*

"Hi," Grace bubbles and sticks out her hand. "I'm Grace." He does the same gesture with Grace and I wonder if she will continue to blush or just pass out.

Ellie says, "Jean-François lives in Paris. He's a professor of literature at the Sorbonne. He was on holiday in Vancouver. Skiing." Ellie continues to talk about Jean-François and I struggle to hear her over the disbelief ringing in my head. How could she not tell me about this man? Ellie leans her head to the side, peering around Lola. "Lexi?"

Lola turns to look at me. Raising her eyebrows, she widens her eyes at me. Get up, she mouths. I do.

In perfect English, Jean-François says, "You must be Lexi."

"I am," I confirm, and offer my hand. Jean-François takes it gently, warmly, and I give him a firm shake. Lola and Grace might be gaga over this guy's style and charm, but if he's going to be with my Ellie, I need to find out a thing or two about him.

"Let's sit down," Lola suggests, gesturing to the table and folding into the seat next to me. As they do in Chinatown, a waiter hustles to our table a soon as we are seated. Lola rattles off ten dishes, the same ten we always order. "Oh, I'm sorry," she pauses and looks at Jean-François. "Would you like to order?"

What's that all about? Lola never defers to a man.

"Whatever you order will be fine with me," Jean-François says. Damn skippy.

"So, you met skiing?" Grace squeaks.

"No. I was sitting in a café, going over my notes, minding my own business," Ellie starts. "I had just finished the last interview and I was outlining the article. Then I hear this voice say, 'Excuse me,' and I look up, and Jean-François is standing there, looking down at me." Ellie pauses. The three of us get the visual of Jean-François standing there, looking handsome. Softly, Lola says, "Go on."

"She looked so serious," Jean-François says. "I tell myself, 'She is a writer.' No one except writers look at pieces of paper with such concentration. And besides that"—he pauses to run his hand through Ellie's hair—"she is beautiful."

Grace sighs.

"We had coffee," Ellie continues.

"Then a drink," Jean-François says.

"Then dinner." Ellie smiles. Jean-François smiles back at her. Grace and Lola smile at them.

I'm the only one not smiling. I can't believe that Ellie didn't e-mail me these details.

"We had the weekend in a small town away from the city," Jean-François continues. "We stayed in a . . . *Comment dit-on 'chateau-hotel' en Anglais?*"

"Bed and breakfast," Ellie translates. "It was a darling cottage."

Darling? Since when does Ellie use the word "darling"?

"The proprietors are married fifty years," Jean-François says. "Each room has the name of one of their children. We stay in the room of Marie."

"The owners said they would call it the Marie Antoinette Room for the weekend because Jean-François is French."

"Marie Antoinette? They didn't know she was beheaded?" Grace laughs.

"We didn't bring that up," Ellie says.

"She was a queen," Jean-François says, kissing Ellie's cheek. "Like you."

"So, JF," I interrupt. "How long are you staying in Philadelphia?" Lola punches my arm. Ellie puts her head on Jean-François's shoulder. "What? I'm just asking. Obviously, JF lives in Paris and Ellie lives in Philadelphia. I assume JF isn't moving here."

"No," Jean-François says. "Ellie is moving to Paris." He raises Ellie's hand from beneath the table. She is still wearing her gloves. One glove, actually, on her left hand.

Jean-François pulls off Ellie's glove, and Ellie says, "We are getting married."

For about a minute and a half, we are hypnotized by the emerald-cut sapphire on the fourth finger of Ellie's left hand. The sapphire stands alone in its platinum setting, not a diamond in sight. The ring is unique, chic, and perfect for Ellie. Grace, Lola, and I are speechless.

And then, "It's beautiful," Lola whispers.

"Wow," Grace exhales.

"You are marrying him?" I blurt.

"You are not pleased?" Jean-François asks me.

"Pleased? That one of my best friends is marrying a stranger? You've known each other for, what? Two weeks?"

"We are in love," Ellie says calmly. Too calmly. As if she prepared a defense. As if she knew I would react this way.

"Ellie, you don't even know him."

"I know enough."

"How do you know he's not a terrorist?" I want to know.

"Oh, Lexi." Ellie sighs.

"Shut up," Lola hisses at me.

"I think it's wonderful," Grace gushes.

"Yeah, you would," I tell her. " 'Oh, it's so romantic!' "

"Don't start picking on Grace," Lola warns me.

"Girls!" Ellie yells. We look at her. "I'm getting married!"

With squeals and kisses, Grace and Lola descend on Ellie. Neighboring diners offer congratulations. The owner of Thai Lake comes to shake Jean-François's hand and gives him a Chinese blessing.

Me? I sit stupefied in my seat. Ellie is my best friend. She's moving to Paris. To marry someone she just met. Is this really happening?

 ## Lexi the Terrible

"That," my mother tells me over the phone, "is terrible."

"Yes, it is," I agree. After the Thai Lake fiasco, I am lying on my couch, staring at the ceiling. "And it gets worse. They are staying in Philadelphia for a week, then Ellie is going to Paris with this guy and staying there with him for three weeks. That's almost a month. And she doesn't even know him. At least she speaks French. She lived in Paris for a semester in college. But still. It's terrible."

"I meant," Mom says, "that you are being terrible."

"What?"

"Don't you want Ellie to be happy?"

I don't answer.

"Alexandra? I asked you a question."

"Of course I want Ellie to be happy. Why can't she be happy in Philadelphia?"

 ## Cobblestones

The thought of Ellie moving so far away makes me miserable. It's Saturday night, which means I have nothing better to do than make myself miserable. It's a warm, dry April night, and the air outside my windows beckons to me. I'll go for a walk. I can walk and mope at the same time.

In the same tank top, jeans, and boots that I wore to Thai Lake, I walk down Walnut Street, cross Broad Street, and head east to Old City. To avoid a posse of twenty-somethings, I cross Fifth Street and promptly trip over the cobblestoned street. Cobblestones. Phooey. Bad for high heels and car wheels, the cobblestones were better suited for the colonial era. Smoothed by time, the stones have huddled together to bear the collective weight of horses, carriages, humans, and automobiles. Like lovers. No, not like lovers. Lovers can be temporary. These stones have lain next to one another for centuries, at first ill-fitting and rough around the edges, then reshaped, and molded together by the weight of the world. Like married couples. No, married couples can get divorced. These stones are joined together forever. Like girlfriends.

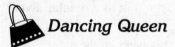 ### Dancing Queen

Contemplating cobblestones, I veer down a side street to avoid a bunch of drunken guys. They turn down the same street, so I head down another side street. And another.

There is probably more trouble ahead of me than behind me, but I don't turn back.

I find myself on Second Street, home of Artists' House. The lights are on in the gallery. Maybe that artist is there. Jack. Mmm. Jack. Should I walk by? Stroll by? A stroll is more casual than a walk. And what if he is there? I'll just be like, "Funny bumping into you here, right outside the gallery where I know you are exhibiting your art." Yeah, right. I should go home. I'm not wearing lipstick. Anyway, Jack has my phone numbers and he hasn't called. It's been over two months since we met. Of course, he's been busy with the exhibit. Or maybe his exhibit is long over and he's long gone.

As I think that thought, the lights go off in the gallery and a person comes out of the building. It's Jack. He rummages in his pocket and removes a key.

Okay. If I walk by now, he'll see me. Do I want him to see me? Maybe I'll just stand here and look in the darkened window of Big Jar Books. What if he walks the other way and doesn't see me? How can I subtly get his attention? Quickly, I whip out my cell phone, dial my own cell number, and strike a nonchalant pose.

"Where are you guys?" I say into my voice mail. "Aren't we

going dancing?" At the sound of a voice, Jack turns and sees me. "No, I didn't get the message," I say. Jack walks toward me. "Really? That's too bad. We'll make it another night." Jack is now standing in front of me. "Okay. Talk to you later. Bye." I hang up the phone.

"Lexi?" Jack smiles and inclines his head shyly.

"Yes," I say politely. Then I squint. "And you are?"

"Jack. Jack McKay. From Artists' House." He points. "We met a few weeks ago."

"Oh, right. Of course. Nice to see you again."

"What are you doing here?" Jack tucks his hair behind his ears. The motion lifts his T-shirt from his stomach, showing me Jack's flat abs covered in light brown hair, and causing me to have a small stroke.

"Huh? Oh, uh, dancing. I am, I mean, I was, because now the plans have changed, but I was going to go dancing with my girlfriends. I didn't get the message. There was a change of plans. So now, I'm not. Going dancing."

Jack smiles. "It's a shame to waste a good buzz."

Buzz? Oh, he thinks I'm drunk. That's okay. I'd rather he think I'm drunk than stupid.

"I'm off to The Wizard. They have dancing there. Want to join me?"

We walk to The Wizard, a club nestled in an alley off Chestnut Street. Jack pays the cover for both of us and we walk into a dimly lit room that is pounding with music. Jack doesn't seem to be meeting anyone, and I wonder why he came here. Then again, Jack appears to be the kind of guy who can walk into a bar by himself and leave with new friends.

Without asking my preference, Jack orders two shots of

tequila and two beers. "Cheers!" he shouts, and we down the shots. Of course, I was not previously inebriated, so the alcohol hits my stomach hard.

It's too loud to talk, which is fine because I'm not in the mood to make conversation. My Ellie-induced gloom lifts slightly, but I'm still hurt that she didn't tell me about her engagement. Hurt, and a little angry. I need to get out my aggression. Finishing my beer, I take Jack's hand and lead him to the dance floor. We start to move.

I quickly decide that I love dancing with Jack. We don't dirty dance. No bumping and grinding. That's boring. Instead, we touch each other in a way that is intimate and rhythmic, but still qualifies as dancing. Jack puts his right hand on my left hip and gently guides my body. I hook my fingers through his belt loop to steady myself and keep him near me. We move independently of each other, losing ourselves in the freedom of the dark and the music.

We dance until 2 AM, when the club closes. Out on the street, Jack hails a cab. Without asking, he gets in the cab with me. "Where to?" the cabbie asks. Jack looks at me and raises an eyebrow. I give my address.

Watching people stream out of clubs, I try to think clearly about what I want to do. I haven't hooked up with a man in seven months. I haven't been with anyone but Ron for almost two years. Am I really taking Jack home? I guess so. Am I wearing good underwear? When was the last time I shaved?

The street, the club, and the cab were dark, but in the bright light of the elevator, I see Jack distinctly. And he can see me. "That was fun," I tell him. He nods, looks at his shoes, and pushes a strand of wavy, dark blond hair behind his ear. The elevator doors open, and Jack follows me to my apartment. As I put my key in the lock, he says, "Hey, Lexi, I just—" The sound of his voice makes me lose my nerve.

Opening the door, I say, "Hang on. I'll be right back," and leave Jack standing in my living room.

Hurrying into my bedroom, I grab my cordless, run into my bathroom, and lock the door. Grace's number is first on speed dial.

"Hello?" Grace whispers groggily.

"Gracie, it's me," I whisper back.

"What's the matter?"

"I have a guy in my apartment and I don't know what to do with him."

"What guy?" Grace whispers again, which means Michael is there, and sleeping.

"The artist. Jack."

"He called you?"

"No. I, uh, bumped into him. On the street. We went dancing. Now what?"

"What do you mean?"

"Should I hook up with him? Or sleep with him? He's really hot."

"Are you nuts? He never called you, Lex. He should take you out on a real date before you hook up with him. A real date. A few real dates."

"So, you're saying that I shouldn't sleep with him."

"Lexi. Please."

"Okay, okay. Sorry I woke you."

I want a second opinion. I want to call Ellie. How can I call her about this when I was such a monster this afternoon? I call Lola.

"The front door is unlocked," she answers.

"What?"

"Lexi?"

"Yeah. Who did you think it was?"

"*Isabel*, my restaurant manager. I forgot to lock the front door of the restaurant, so she's going back to lock it."

"Oh. Whatever. Listen. I'm in my apartment with Jack, that artist. He's really hot and I'm thinking about sleeping with him."

"And?"

"And it would just be sex, but it would be good sex."

"So what are you talking to me for? Go for it."

"Really?"

"I would never tell you to turn down good sex."

Excellent.

When I walk into my living room, Jack is leaning against the front door. He stands up straight and wrinkles his brow. "Is everything all right?"

"Yes. Fine. Thank you."

"You just disappeared and I heard voices so I guessed you were on the phone but I didn't want to leave without saying good night."

What? He's leaving? No. I heard him wrong. "You didn't say good night, did you?"

"That's what I just said. I didn't say good night, so I waited for you to come out of the bathroom. You didn't heave, did you?"

"Heave? No. Why would I?"

"You seemed a bit drunk. That's why I wanted to make sure you got home in one piece."

"Oh. Thank you."

"No problem." Smiling, Jack walks toward me, plants a kiss on my cheek, and turns toward the door. "Good night," he says. "You'll feel better in the morning."

I sincerely doubt that.

 ## Lines

After tossing and turning and not having sex, I sleep most of Sunday, sleep late Monday, and get to the office at 9:45 AM. As soon as I get to my desk, I call Ellie. She answers sleepily. "Did I wake you?" I ask fearfully.

"No," Ellie purrs. "We're just being lazy in bed."

"Good for you," I say, but it sounds fake. Shaking my head, I start again. "Listen, El. I'm calling to apologize for my behavior at Thai Lake. I was really rude to Jean-François. I'm sorry."

"It's okay," Ellie says.

"I was just surprised. Shocked, really. Speechless. In a word? I was flummoxed. I felt like I walked into a meeting unprepared. Which I never do."

"I understand."

"I wish you had called me or e-mailed with the details," I tell her honestly.

"Yeah. I should have. Time went by so fast, and I wanted to spend every minute I had with Jean-François."

She couldn't spare a few minutes to tell her best friend that she was engaged? I know I shouldn't feel this jealousy, but I do. I can't help it. I can, however, stifle it. "Please apologize to Jean-François for me? Tell him that I look forward to learning more about him. In a nonjudgmental sort of way."

"I'll tell him. Thanks for calling, Lexi. I appreciate it."

"I'll see you soon?" I ask. Ellie has already hung up the phone.

As I put down the receiver, Maria's voice calls through my intercom. "Veep?"

"Yes?"

"Adrian Salvo is on line three."

"And?"

"I called to confirm our meeting. He wants to speak with you."

"What about?"

"His account, I imagine."

"Maria, can't you deal with him?"

"Lexi, are you doing something more important than speaking with a million-dollar prospective client?"

"Fine," I grunt. Picking up the receiver, I hit line three and say, "Lexi James."

"Good morning," Adrian purrs.

"Good morning, Adrian." Massive eye roll.

"Maria called to confirm our meeting." He pauses.

"Is something wrong, Adrian?"

"I have a better idea," he says quietly.

"What's that?" I ask, trying to keep my voice even.

"Why don't you and I meet alone? Maria did all the talking at the last meeting. I'd like to hear what you have to say. About us working together."

"I don't have anything different to say from what Maria already shared with you. Are you unhappy with her approach?"

"No, no. It's not that. I'd just like to get to know you better. If we're going to be working so closely together."

Oh, balls. Reaching into my desk, I pull out an index card and, in a professional voice, read: "While I hope that our two companies will work closely together, I feel it would be inappropriate for you and I to spend time alone." There's the straight talk, here's the sugar. "You are a successful businessman, so you know how important my reputation is to me. We would be so thrilled to have your company as a client. I wouldn't want there to be any suggestion of impropriety in our business dealings."

"Okay, Lexi. I get it. I'll see you this afternoon."

"Thank you, Adrian." I put the card back in my desk for future use.

As soon as I hang up the phone, Maria pops into my office. "What'd he say?"

"Nothing."

"Nothing?"

"Nothing, Maria. Nothing."

"Fine." She puts her hands on her hips. "Are you ready to leave?"

"Leave? I just got here."

"We have a potential client meeting in fifteen minutes," Maria says. "It's a ten-minute walk. It's the first day of May. Maybe the spring air will put you in a better mood."

"Just give me one minute."

"Lexi, we have to walk there, meet, then cab to Salvo Company."

"I know what we have to do, Maria. I'll meet you in the lobby in one minute."

Maria mutters and walks away. I don't care what she's mumbling. Closing my door, I stand against it, shut my eyes and see sparkles. The flashing diamond of Grace's ring. The glow of Ellie's sapphire. As the ghost of my engagement past floats through my mind, I feel tired and sad and the same way I did on the day I sat on my toilet and cried. Then I shake my head. "Get it together, Lexi. Get it together."

Opening my eyes, I grab my briefcase and open my door. "Maria!" I bark through the office. "Let's go!"

 ## Zoga

This potential client is a referral from Mrs. Lang, the wife of the owner of Boudoir. It's a place where they practice something called Zoga, and I am meeting with Jane Louis, the owner of the studio. "What is this again?" I ask Maria as we walk through the patchouli scented lobby. Before she can answer me, Jane appears. "Lexi. Maria. Welcome." Jane is barefoot, wearing flared yoga pants and a tank top that shows off her sinewy physique.

Her office consists of three comfy chairs and a long, blond wood table. The room smells like peppermint and grapefruit and it is invigorating. "I know your time is valuable," Jane begins. "Why don't we get down to business? Did Mrs. Lang tell you about Zoga?"

I look at Maria and she shakes her head slightly. "No, Jane. She didn't. Will you explain to us what you do here?"

"Of course. Zoga is a combination of Zen meditation and Indian yoga."

"That sounds like the next big thing," I tell Jane.

She smiles. "Let's hope. We've been so successful with Zoga that we have branched into other areas. You see, other studios offer standard kinds of yoga. I have found that people can benefit from customized yoga routines. For example, we have moga, yoga for mothers, which rebuilds the abdomen, for women who have recently been through pregnancies, and strengthens the lower back and arms, for mothers who pick up their young children. For those young children, we have koga, kid yoga, which consists of safe, easy poses."

"Wonderful," I say sincerely.

"I have also found that the Buddhist overtones of yoga make some people uncomfortable, even though they enjoy the physical aspects of the practice. We have developed classes which include prayers and chants taken from Western religions. For example, we have Choga, which is Christian yoga. One of our most popular classes is a combination of yoga and readings from the Torah. We call that Toga."

Maria covers her smile with her hand.

"We also offer gay yoga. We call it goga."

At that, Maria bursts into laughter. "It's okay to laugh," Jane says. "But I bet that you remember the name of the class and tell your friends about it."

"Jane?" I say. "You're a genius."

"She can't afford our rates," Maria states as we walk back to the office to pick up Low Man and cab to Salvo Company.

"It's not for us to decide what Jane can afford," I answer. "Anyway, maybe we can work a trade deal. Our whole damn staff could use some relaxation therapy."

"Susan will never go for that," Maria says. "We have her sister-in-law's travel agency and her kids' camp to worry about. Susan's hot for a client which can pay big money."

"Yeah? Maybe it's time we started taking good karma as payment."

 Wink

Salvo Company is located at the Food Distribution Center, which is located in South Philly. The FDC is exactly what it sounds like, a series of warehouses with loading docks, refrigerated trucks, swarms of scavenger pigeons, and men garbed in dirty jeans, sweatshirts, flannels, and baseball hats.

There are specific streets for specific foods. The seafood distributors, produce companies, and meat vendors abut each other on different streets. These companies are family businesses, with original ownership going back generations. The great-grandfathers of the current owners started by trolling Broad Street with pushcarts, hawking their goods to housewives. Now, refrigerated trucks crisscross Philadelphia's narrow streets, delivering products directly to restaurants. No one has to go down to the distribution center anymore. That's a good thing.

The FDC action starts in the early morning hours and is long over by midafternoon when we arrive. All that's left is the reek of fish, overripe vegetables, and testosterone.

"Who youse looking for?" a baseball-hatted man with a paunch asks us. Mike, Maria, and I are standing in our sartorial splendor at the first dock of Salvo Company. Maria has her hand over her nose, my Manolos are covered with some spooge, and Mike is trying to look like he's not gay.

"Adrian Salvo," I answer the Neanderthal, who detaches a

walkie-talkie from his belt and barks, "Nicky to A. You there? You got company at Dock One."

From the deep darkness of the warehouse comes a man dressed in work boots, dark denim jeans, a mulberry-colored sweatshirt, and a faded blue baseball hat that simply reads "Salvo." It takes me a whole minute to realize that this man is Adrian Salvo. It's quite a makeover from *The Godfather III* look Adrian sported at Lola's. Maybe it's a make under. But it looks more natural for him to be dressed like this, and he seems very confident as he welcomes us to his domain.

"So that's where we are disappointed with your current PR campaign," Maria finishes after a succinct twenty minutes. She smiles broadly. "We can do better. Here are a few of our strategies that have worked for other clients."

We are seated in a third-floor conference room that is windowless but air-conditioned. The compost smell is diluted, but I still vastly prefer the grapefruit and peppermint aroma of Zoga Jane's office.

There are six of us at a plain white table. Maria is between Mike and me on one side of the table. On the opposite side, Adrian sits across from Maria. He is flanked by Dominic, his sales manager, whose jeans and sweatshirt struggle to hold his belly, and Tony, his product manager, who is sweating through his T-shirt despite the air-conditioning. They are listening attentively to Maria.

I'm not. I'm thinking about how to work Zoga into the client roster. Sitting in front of a million-dollar client, I'm thinking about the one who can't afford me. Yoga, Zoga, moga, goga; they interest me far more than a restaurant purveyor. How can I convince Susan to take Zoga? She might not notice a new client. She would notice Salvo, of course. Maybe if we sign Salvo, I can convince Susan to take Zoga. It would be so easy to get press for Zoga, turn the studio into a great example of our work, and turn Jane into a terrific reference for us. Maybe Jane will want to franchise Zoga to different studios in different cities, like Boudoir. Has she trademarked—

"Lexi?" Maria nudges me.

"Yes?" I blink at her.

"I asked you for the client profiles that are in your briefcase." Maria raises her eyebrows and widens her eyes.

"Oh. Of course." Reaching into my briefcase, I retrieve three spiral-bound profiles showcasing publicity and events for other clients. Standing and smiling, I walk around the long conference table toward Adrian and his corporate capos. I am to give the profiles to the decision maker for him to distribute to his colleagues as he chooses. For me to rise and deliver the packages is a sign of respect to the decision maker, and a sign of corporate submission. The decision maker here is obviously Adrian, and I walk around Tony's enormous bulk to stand behind Adrian and place the packages in front of him. From his chair, Adrian looks up at me and smiles. "Thanks, babe."

Babe? Oh, no, he didn't.

"Lexi?" Maria calls from the other side of the table. "Come back and sit down. Here." She pats the chair I abandoned. Stiffly, I walk back to my seat.

An hour later, the meeting is over. "Thank you so much for this opportunity," Maria says, and I don't miss that cue. From my briefcase, I extract three copies of a contract and lay them on the table in front of Adrian. "We have worked up a standard contract that outlines our responsibilities and requested compensation. Please look them over carefully and let us know if you have any questions or concerns. One copy is for you, one is for your lawyer, and the third is for our records. With the best intentions, I've already signed each copy. We hope to see your signature on them very soon." Whew. I got that out without puking.

Everyone stands up. Mike, Maria, and I head around the table to shake hands. Another sign of respect. I do this at every pitch meeting, but down here in South Philly, signs of respect go a lot further.

Tony and Dominic shake my hand roughly but politely. I don't think they are used to shaking hands with women. I extend my hand to Adrian. He smiles innocently at me and takes my hand in his, shaking it quickly but strongly. "Thank you for coming," Adrian says.

"You're welcome," I reply. "Thank you for your time."

Dominic volunteers to lead us through the warehouse maze, and Mike, Maria, and I follow him to the door of the conference room. I turn around to offer final thanks to Adrian.

Adrian is looking right at me, with leering eyes and smirking mouth. As my gaze meets his, Adrian raises an eyebrow.

He winks.

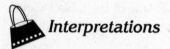 *Interpretations*

"He kissed you on the cheek and left? That's it?" Grace is shoveling saffron rice into her mouth and getting it all over her eggplant-colored scrubs. The COG minus Ellie and Mia is assembled at Lola's restaurant for dinner later that night. We are backtracking to Jack.

"That's it. End of story. He didn't ask for my number or anything. Of course, he already had my number and didn't call, so I don't know why he would ask me for it again." Pointing my fork at Grace, I say, "You know, you should change out of your scrubs before you come to Lola's. It's unhygienic. And unfashionable."

"I was running late. And I was starving. Also? Shut up."

"How did it go with Adrian?" Lola wants to know.

Chewing on a guava-glazed baby back rib, I think about how to explain my interpretation of Adrian's actions. "I think Adrian may be interested in more than a professional relationship."

"What did he do?" Lola asks sharply. She is so protective of me that I hesitate to upset her. She'll probably want to go beat up Adrian.

"When we finished dinner here? He offered me flan on his spoon. Like, to feed it to me."

"Had he already used the spoon?" Lola asks.

"No."

"Is it possible that he was handing you his spoon in a gentlemanly way?" Grace asks. "So you could have the first taste?"

"It's possible," I admit. "I didn't think of it like that."

"Did anything else happen?" Grace asks as she reaches for the salsa fresca.

"He asked for a private meeting."

"Private? Like, a date?" Lola asks.

"He didn't say 'date.' But I gave him my standard speech. I thought that would stifle him. But then, at the meeting today? He called me 'babe.' "

"Please," Lola laughs. "They call every woman 'babe.' The delivery man calls me 'babe' every day."

"Okay. Here's something. He winked at me as I was leaving the meeting."

"What kind of wink?" Lola asks.

"Are there different kinds of winks?"

"Of course," Lola says. "Was it a friendly wink or a sexy wink?"

I think for a moment. "I assumed it was a sexy wink. But I'm not well versed in winks, so maybe I misread it."

"You probably misread it," Grace says. "Adrian sounds like an old-school kind of guy. He probably winks a lot."

"It's nothing," Lola says.

"If Adrian made a move, what would you do?" Grace asks.

"Nothing," I answer. "Not a damn thing."

"Good," Lola says, while Grace asks, "Why not?"

"I never screw around with clients. You know that."

"I know," Grace says. "But you've never had a deal worth this much money on the table."

"I don't want to get a client that way," I say angrily.

"Of course not," Grace agrees. She wipes her mouth on the pumpkin-colored napkin. "I'm just curious how you would handle the situation."

"I would be very delicate about it. I would carefully and politely explain that I don't mix business with pleasure. I'd use stronger words than I already have, but I wouldn't make him feel like I'm rejecting him or insulting his masculinity. I don't want to hurt his feelings. Even though I am, like, not attracted to him. At all."

"You don't find him attractive?" Lola asks.

"No." I shake my head and cut into a slice of avocado. "Not really. I mean, he's not bad. Just not my type."

"Not your type? Right," Grace says. "What could you possibly see in him? He's a successful businessman who runs his family's company. A very respectable company. No, he's not an Ivy League grad and no, he's probably not the most cultured man in the world, but you don't know anything else about him and already you've decided that he's not, what? Good enough for you?"

"It's not a question of Adrian being good enough for me. It's a question of jeopardizing a lucrative business deal. I'm not going to do that."

"Why can't you think of it the other way around?" Grace asks. "The business deal could jeopardize a potential romantic deal."

"I see where you are going with this, and you're wrong."

"Where am I going with it?"

"You're about to say, and Lola, you're about to agree, that I always put business before romance. That is, A, not true. And B, not applicable in this case."

"You're right," Lola says. "It's not applicable in this case. I think you are both making a big deal over nothing."

"I'm tired of talking about work," I tell them. "Gracie? How's Michael?"

"We're fighting. I don't want to talk about it."

I turn to Lola. "Did you get the message from my office today? The cookbook publisher wants to talk to us. We have a conference call scheduled for the day after tomorrow."

"I'm so nervous, *amiga*. I won't sleep for two days." Lola waves her hands in the air. "I don't want to talk about it."

We eat quietly.

Referral

Lola calls me at 10:30 PM that night. "I'm setting you up on a date with John. Drinks. Friday."

"Who's John?"

"A very nice guy. A regular customer of mine. *Muy guapo. Un abogado. Y alto. Y joven.*"

"Is he standing right there?" Why else would Lola switch to Spanish to tell me that this man is handsome, a lawyer, rich, tall, and young?

"Yes. I showed him your picture and he would like to meet you for a drink on Friday. I told him you were probably free, but I should check. So, you'll meet him?"

"Do I have a choice?"

"Not really."

Little Fish

The next morning, I wake up twenty minutes earlier than usual. My appointment at Salon Serge isn't until tomorrow. My hair won't make it that long. The curls are sucking up the May humidity and turning into major frizz. I have to straighten my own hair. By force. I have a system for this.

Wash, condition, pat out water, apply goop, comb out, blow dry until damp. Then the fun starts. Standing in front of my bathroom mirror, I divide my hair, making an equator around my head and clipping the northern end onto the top of my head. Using my huge round brush, I start at one ear with one section of hair. Wrapping my hair around the brush, I pull it tight and blow it dry. Then, I spritz different goop and go over that segment of hair again with the blow dryer. The process gets repeated with small segments of hair until I reach the other ear. Then I attack the northern hemisphere, releasing one section of hair at a time.

I've been straightening my hair for so many years that I have the routine down to twenty minutes. Anyway, letting my curls loose would make me feel unprofessional. I like my hair smooth and sleek. I am the Frizzinator.

"Good morning, Miss Lexi." Doorman John smiles broadly at me.

"Why are you so happy?"

"I gotta have a reason?" John gives me a toothy grin.

Smiling, I leave give John tip money for the grocer's delivery guy.

"Why don't you try something new?" suggests Patrick at Café Oz.

"Morning is no time to try something new. Morning is all about routine. People have the same thing for breakfast for years. Decades. It's just like morning sex."

Patrick laughs. "Please, complete that analogy."

"Morning sex. It's routine. Nothing fancy. But it gets the job done. Like a bran muffin."

"Have a good day, Lexi."

"I have an idea," Low Man tells me when I step out of the elevator.

"Good for you." I keeping walking to my office.

*   *   *

Susan e-mails me from home. I haven't seen or spoken to her in several days.

> *To: Lexi <lexijames@thegoldgroup.com>*
> *From: Susan <susangb@thegoldgroup.com>*
> *Subject: Prospective Clients*
>
> *Lexi—Update me on Salvo, Zoga and any other prospectives.—Susan*
>
> *To: Susan <susangb@thegoldgroup.com>*
> *From: Lexi <lexijames@thegoldgroup.com>*
> *Subject: Re: Prospective Clients*
>
> *Susan,*
>
> *Maria, Mike and I had a good meeting with Salvo and his people. Maria did a great presentation of the proposal we created. Salvo has the contracts. We are awaiting a response. 50/50 odds, considering Salvo's existing tie to Baxter Bros. Zoga cannot afford our normal retainer package, but does have some money to spend. I would like to work with this client. I think we should sign for the money she can afford, and give the according number of hours, even if it's only ten or so a month. Zoga has tremendous PR potential and will therefore be a good source of new leads. I have a good feeling about Jane and her studio.*
>
> *Lexi*

To: Lexi <lexijames@thegoldgroup.com>
From: Susan <susangb@thegoldgroup.com>
Subject: Re: Prospective Clients

Forget Zoga. Sets bad business precedent. Go after money clients. Don't waste your time with little fish. Keep on Salvo.—Susan

 ## Protecting the Elder Council

"There you are!" Esther claps her hands together as if I'm a runaway puppy who's found her way home. "Sit next to me." She pats the wicker love seat.

"Don't I get a hug?" Ruth asks. She puts down her knitting and I bend over her for a hug. Ruth squeezes me so tightly that her Star of David leaves an imprint on my shirt.

"Give me some sugar," Sylvia says with gusto. I raise my eyebrows at her street talk.

"Our new aide Tyrone says that every morning," Ruth explains. "Sylvia thinks she's hip. Next thing you know, she'll be rapping."

Sylvia wags her finger at Ruth. "Tyrone says I have rhythm."

"Fine," Ruth sighs. "Try break dancing."

"Ha! If I danced, I really would break something. My hip, probably. *Kina hora.*"

"*Kina hora,*" Ruth and Esther repeat.

"Lexi, come here," Esther commands. Clearly, the woman has a mission and it involves me. As I sit next to her, Esther takes my hand in hers. "I have a favor to ask you, dear."

Smiling at pretty Esther, I ask, "What can I do for you?"

Esther puts her head close to mine. "Will you buy me condoms?"

"What?"

"Condoms," Esther repeats. "You know. For a penis."

I stare at Esther.

"Her boyfriend died last week," Ruth says.

"And?" Now I'm really confused. She wants condoms for her dead beau?

Sylvia takes over the explaining. "Esther's boyfriend, Emanuel? We called him Manny. Anyway, Manny died. Now Esther is with Maury and she is insisting on using condoms."

Esther shrugs. "I don't know where he's been."

"You know exactly where he's been," Ruth says. She puts down her knitting. I feel a story coming. "Maury was with Miriam, but she broke her hip and moved to the rehab center, so Maury started up with Millie. When Manny died, Maury broke up with Millie and told Esther that he had a big crush on her."

"What is this? Melrose Place?" I'm stunned at the bed hopping. These geriatrics are getting more action than I am.

Esther smiles. "Maury says I have lovely ankles. And he has a wonderful singing voice."

Lovely ankles and a singing voice. Oh, for the days when that was what attracted people to each other.

"Lexi, will you buy them for me?" Esther asks sweetly.

"Why doesn't Manny get them?"

"You mean Maury," Ruth corrects me. "Manny is the one who died."

"I'm sorry. I got confused."

Esther pats my knee. "Don't worry, dear. Manny had a lovely funeral. Maury sang."

"Maury refuses to buy condoms because he thinks it's silly," Sylvia explains. "But he agreed to use them if Esther has them."

"I've never bought condoms," Esther says. "I've used them, of course, but never bought them. We went to Rite Aid yesterday? The three of us? There were so many different kinds. And the writing on the boxes is so small."

I get a visual of the Elder Council in a Rite Aid, standing in front of a display of condoms, adjusting their enormous glasses, trying to read the boxes aloud, arguing about ribbing and lubrication.

"Okay," I agree. "I'll get you a box of condoms, Esther."

Esther smiles. "Make it two boxes."

 ## Wheeling & Dealing

Lola thunders into my office three minutes before the conference call is scheduled to begin. "Lola, where have you been? I asked you to be here twenty minutes ago." I look her up and down. She's wearing a coral silk tank top under a sheer black blouse, black stretch pants, and black boots with three-inch heels. Her favorite braided gold necklace dips into her cleavage. "You look like a hootchie mamma," I tell Lola. She does, however, appear to be relaxed. "Thank God they can't see you over the telephone."

Lola ignores me. "*Vamos*, baby. I'm ready for this call."

We sit on the couch in my office, talking to the publishing people in Manhattan via speaker phone. We come to terms. They accept my proposal that Lola will put her advance toward production of the Spanish edition of the cookbook. They agree that she will instead receive a higher royalty percentage of both books. Things are going well.

Then, "Who will write the book?" the male voice of the VP of acquisitions asks.

Lola and I haven't discussed that.

"Me," Lola says, a bit too strongly. Like, duh.

"*Señorita,*" the man singsongs. Lola rolls her eyes at me. I pinch her arm. "You need a collaborator. Every cookbook is written by the cook and a writer. Your book proposal says that you'll have in-depth explanations of different Latin vegetables and fruits and herbs and whatever. Who's going to write those explanations?"

"Ellie Archer." As soon as I say it, I know it's the right thing. Lola smiles at me and nods her head. She knows I thought of it just that second.

"She's an excellent writer," a female voice says over the phone.

"Ellie wrote a cover story for *Xess* about Lola's divorce and emergence as one of the top female restaurateurs in the country," I explain. "It's appropriate she do this book. A full circle, if you will."

"Has she written a book before?"

"Not a cookbook," I say, giving a different answer. In truth, Ellie's never written any kind of book. But, given her editorial experience, it won't be a problem. I hope.

"She's there in Philadelphia with you?"

"We're all very good friends," I say, again giving a different answer.

"Sounds good," the acquisitions man says. "We'll send the contracts to you."

"Excellent," I say. "I'll look at them and forward them to Lola's lawyer."

"All right then, ladies. We have a deal. Congratulations."

"Thank you," I say. "We're looking forward to working with you."

"*Muchas gracias*," Lola says.

"*De nada*," the man says. "We'll be in touch."

I disconnect the speaker phone. Lola and I sit quietly and look at each other.

We did it.

Lola jumps up from the sofa, grabs my hand, and leads me in a tango around my office. Lola dances all the way out of my office, and onto the elevator.

 ## *Everybody Needs a Little Oh-La-La*

Spinning my chair to look out my wall of windows, I close my eyes as the May sun hits my face. I have done a good job. For Lola. For The Gold Group. Yeah me.

"Where are you going?" Low Man Mike wants to know when I push the elevator button.

"To get a latte. Or maybe a water ice. It's almost summer." Mike smiles and returns to his work. "Hey, Low Man. Want to come with me?"

"I would totally take the account," Low Man says. We are sitting on a bench in Rittenhouse Square and eating water ice out of paper cones. I've just told him about Zoga. "Goga? Love it! Want to do it! Point the way!"

"By the way, Mike, I'm taking the day off tomorrow."

"Ha, ha."

"I'm serious."

"As long as I've been at TGG, you've taken off one day. What's the occasion?"

"I'm spending the afternoon with a charming Frenchman. Then I have a date. With an American. A lawyer."

"Oh-la-la."

"I do believe I've earned a little oh-la-la."

"But of course," Low Man answers.

"You should take off a day, too. Not tomorrow. Or Monday. But soon. You haven't taken a day off in almost a year. You've earned a day off."

Mike leans over and peers into my empty paper cone. "Did they spike your water ice?"

"Very funny. You don't want a day off? Don't take a day off. I just thought you would like a day to do something special. If you can find a Frenchman to spend it with, all the better. Everyone needs a little oh-la-la."

 ## Mes Amies

Ellie's plan is a good one, and it is to let Jean-François charm the Council of Girlfriends the way he charmed her. Lola and Grace are already done deals. They couldn't coo more.

I, on the other hand, require more work. But the fabulous Ellie Archer knew it would be like this. Years of being my friend has taught Ellie a lot about dealing with difficult women.

Today's strategy is to have me show Jean-François historical Philadelphia. The fact that I have taken the day off is testament, I believe, to my friendship with Ellie.

Security keeps changing—not worth it.

* * *

As we walk up Walnut Street, Jean-François says, "Please, tell me about your life. I want to know about it."

I tell him about work. My apartment. We've only gotten to Tenth Street. There are eight more blocks to go. "That's about it," I say.

"And for *l'amour*? What do you do for that?"

"Pray."

He laughs. "Ellie told me you had a fiancé."

"Did she?" Gotta admire the man's straightforwardness.

"You tell to me what happened? If you want."

"I freaked."

"What did you say? 'Freaqued?' What is that?"

"I ended the engagement."

"Ah, *je comprends. Pourquoi?* Why did you end the engagement?"

We cross Twelfth Street. Why? How do I explain it to him? I look up at Jean-François, who is expecting an answer. Smiling shyly, I say, "I would have to tell you a story."

"*Oui.* Tell it to me. *S'il vous plaît.*"

Squinting up at Jean-François, I decide to tell him. Just then, my cell phone rings. I look at the screen and see The Gold Group phone number. You know what? Today is my day off. My one day off. The office will have to deal with itself. With zeal, I punch the cell's on/off switch. Jean-François smiles. "*Très bien*, Lexi. Tell to me the story."

 Supermarket Squeeze

"I was making dinner for my fiancé and his parents in my apartment. I wanted to impress his parents, so I created this fancy menu. I took the day off from work to get ready. I needed a lot of food and there are only small groceries around my apartment, so I borrowed my fiancé's car and drove to a supermarket in the suburbs.

"I had my list and I got a shopping cart and I found everything I needed. Then I got in line. It was a long line. I waited. I didn't have anything else to do, so I looked around at the other women in line. And at the stuff they had in their carts.

"They had loaves of white bread, tins of powdered iced tea, packages of frozen string beans and carrots, jars of spaghetti sauce, bags of potato chips, frozen French bread pizzas, presliced bologna, plastic packages of orange American cheese, twenty-four rolls of toilet paper, bottles of soda, cartons of orange juice, boxes and boxes of cereal, and envelopes of instant mashed potatoes.

"They were shopping for their families.

"And these women? They wore jeans and sweaters, or sweat pants and T-shirts. Their hair was tied back and they wore either too much or too little makeup. Like it didn't matter to them one way or the other. They had rings full of keys with discount cards from ten different stores.

"They had coupons.

"And they had lists, just like me. And I thought, 'I can't end up like this. I can't be one of these women.' I ran out of the supermarket. I just left my cart where it was and ran. And I drove back into the city really fast and I walked around my apartment. Just to remember who I was.

"For dinner, I lied to my fiancé's parents and said that I had to work late and didn't have a chance to cook. I got takeout from Lola's. They loved it. They loved me.

"But I knew. I knew, then, that I couldn't go through with the wedding."

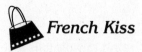

French Kiss

"Crazy, right?" I look at Jean-François.

"Not so crazy." He smiles down at me. "Why did you accept the proposal of your fiancé?"

"I thought I should get married." Trying to be funny, I say, "Everyone was doing it."

"*Oui*. And everyone gets divorced."

"Right."

"Lexi, *mon amie*, you are not required to do the things that the other people do. You do not have to get married because you are of a certain age. You do not have to make children if you do not want them. And? You do not have to go to the supermarket if you do not want to."

"I know. I get my groceries delivered now." I laugh, and Jean-François laughs, too.

"Ah, Lexi. You want something different than what other people want. There is nothing wrong with that. But it makes life difficult for you. *Oui?*"

"Yes," I answer quietly.

"Come," Jean-François says. "We get café au lait and make it better."

We go to La Colombe, a French coffee shop off Rittenhouse Square. Jean-François orders himself an espresso and me a café au lait.

I let him order for me.

*   *   *

Sitting in La Colombe, Jean-François tells me about his parents and his childhood. He talks about teaching and about literature, French and British and American. Jean-François has lived an interesting life. Just like Ellie.

"Ellie says that you are her best friend," Jean-François tells me as we walk through Rittenhouse Square. The afternoon sun shines on us. "Of all the girls, she says that she is closest to you."

"Yes," I agree.

"So, Lexi. It is important to me that you approve of our marriage."

"You don't need my approval, JF."

"But yes. I do." Jean-François stops walking and I turn to face him. "I do not want Ellie to be unhappy for any reason. If you are unhappy that she will be married to me, then Ellie will be unhappy. That, I do not want."

"I appreciate that."

"So." Jean-François continues to walk and puts his arm around my shoulders. "You decide if you like me." He smiles.

"When do I have to decide?"

"Any time that is good for you."

"Okay."

"When you are ready, Lexi."

"Okay, JF."

"For example, now would be a good time."

"Right now?"

"No hurry."

"Good."

"When you know. Not a moment before."

"Okay, JF." I stop walking and turn to face him. "I like you. There. I said it. Happy?"

"Very happy," Jean-François says and puts his hand on my shoulders. "We are friends. You and me. Yes?"

"Yes. We are friends." Jean-François offers me his arm and I loop mine through his.

"*C'est bon,*" I say with a Spanish accent.

"We will work on your French." Jean-François laughs.

"*Oui, monsieur.* Later. Now, I have to go to my doctor."

"You are sick?" Jean-François asks with concern.

"Only in my head."

"Ah, psychiatry." Jean-François nods. "I will see you later?"

"*Oui. Ciao!*" I answer and take two steps.

"No, no!" Jean-François shouts, and I turn around, alarmed. "We must say goodbye the French way. You must give me the French kiss."

"The what?"

"Come here," Jean-François says. He moves me until I stand in front of him. Smiling and holding me still, Jean-François kisses my right cheek, then my left cheek, then my right cheek again. "In France, we give three kisses for friendship. Okay?"

I nod. "Okay."

"*Au revoir,* Lexi," Jean-François says, and walks away, leaving me with tears in my eyes because the gesture was so simple, yet so sincere. Jean-François wants nothing from me. Just my friendship.

As if Jean-François's kisses were soma, I stand in the middle of the brick path of the Square, and I feel calm. Happy. I am so glad that I took the day off to be with him.

The bells of St. Patrick's toll, sending peals of music through the Square. Four bells. Oh, no. It's four o'clock. I'm late for Dr. Franklin.

Dr. Franklin, Session Three

"Tell me about your work," Dr. Franklin says.

I give him the glamour story. The events, the publicity, the schmoozing, the big office and big salary. Incorporating some of Lola's dramatics, I relate the story of my rise to power at The Gold Group. Dr. Franklin sees right through my shtick. "It sounds like there is tension between you and your boss."

"My boss? Susan?" I laugh. "I hardly think of her as my boss. She's got more important things to do than come to the office. Susan has her Dante's inferno of karate, ballet, swimming, piano, doctors, Happy Meals, and Boston Market."

"You don't envy Susan's life?" Dr. Franklin asks.

"Envy? No way."

"Do you think Susan is happy?"

I shrug. "She doesn't seem happy. She always seems to be out of breath."

"Some women are overwhelmed by motherhood, but they adjust."

"I know that. My friend Mia Rose is an awesome mother. She doesn't have Susan's superior attitude about it. It's like this. Susan thinks that anyone who isn't a mother is a lesser being. 'I have to get my kids' is her most common excuse. And she says it with such bravado. 'My kids.' The irony is that I like her kids. I feel bad for them. Susan's running around half cocked all the time, and they don't get her attention."

"You don't envy Susan, but you think she envies you?"

"That's right, Doc." I nod my head wisely.

Dr. Franklin nods with me. "Susan looks down on you to justify her life."

"Yes."

"Or do you look down on Susan to justify your life?"

I look at Dr. Franklin blankly. He waits for an answer.

"Doc, you're supposed to be on my side."

"I am, Lexi." He chuckles. "Is it possible that you are ridiculing Susan's choices to justify your own? From the safety of the lodge, it's easy to criticize someone who wipes out on the slopes. Are you armchair quarterbacking Susan's life?"

"Are you asking me if I am or telling me that I am?"

"I want to know how you see it," Dr. Franklin says.

"This is how I see it, Doc. I see that Susan is trying to lead a double life as a mommy and a career woman and failing at both."

"You think she should make different life choices."

"She can do whatever the hell she wants with her life as long as it doesn't interfere with my life. I have a responsibility to the staff and clients of The Gold Group and Susan's decisions very often sabotage my authority and my plans."

"You have no respect for her."

"And she has no respect for me."

Breaking his dialogue and my rant, Dr. Franklin writes on his yellow pad of paper, then cleans his glasses while my breathing returns to normal. "Wow. I can't believe I said all that. I haven't told anyone that stuff. Not even myself. Talk about a genie in a bottle. More like a bitch in the bottle."

"This is quite a dysfunctional relationship."

"Susan's dysfunctional."

"It take two to dysfunction." Dr. Franklin smiles.

"Yeah, yeah." I exhale loudly. "Now what?"

"That's up to you, Lexi. From what you've told me about your job, it seems that you liked public relations before you became the vice president. Before you went into management, you got a sense of achievement from helping clients with their businesses. Right?"

"Right."

"You became VP because it was the thing to do. You got engaged because it was the thing to do. It seems to me that you spend a lot of time doing what everyone thinks you should do, even though those things aren't what you really want and don't make you happy. You know, Lexi, happy is hard."

"Happy is hard?"

"Yes. To be happy, you have to make hard decisions. If happy was easy, I'd be out of a job." Dr. Franklin pauses again. "Here's what I think about your work situation. I think you have two choices. Either mend the relationship with Susan, or find a new job."

"Both of those things will be very difficult," I tell him, and Dr. Franklin nods his agreement. "Why can't you be one of those shrinks who say, 'I see, that's very interesting,' and then prescribe fun drugs?"

"You don't need drugs, Lexi. If you want to medicate your way through your problems, you'll have to find another psychiatrist."

"I guess this is what you'd call a breakthrough, Doc."

"Yes." Dr. Franklin smiles.

I tilt my head at him. "Should we, like, hug?"

"No." He laughs. "I think we have made a lot of progress today. We should stop here and pick this up next week. In the meantime, think about how you will deal with your work situation. You have some tough decisions to make."

"Yeah," I agree, and drag myself from the couch. At the

door, I turn back. "You know, Doc, I didn't come here to talk about my job. I came here to talk about my romantic life."

"We can talk about that next time," Dr. Franklin says.

 Referral: The Lawyer

With Dr. Franklin's words playing in my head, I walk into a bar on Walnut Street and look around for someone matching Lola's description of John.

"Lexi?" Turning around, I see a nice-looking man wearing khakis, a light blue Oxford, and a navy tie. "Wow. You look even better than your photo," John says.

"Thank you." He is of average looks, but he could be the hottest guy in the world and I still wouldn't be in the right frame of mind for a date. Nevertheless, I agreed to have a drink, and a drink I shall have.

John tells me that he is a lawyer for Project H.O.M.E., a non-profit organization that rehabilitates formerly homeless people by providing them with job training and temporary housing. He loves his job. "Sorry to babble," John apologizes. "Tell me about your job. Public relations, right?"

I look down at my Yuengling.

I start to cry. Sob. Blubber.

My session with Dr. Franklin hits me with whiplash emotion. "I'm so sorry," I cry to John. People in the bar turn to look at me. John pats my shoulder. "There, there," he says awkwardly. His kindness makes me cry harder. "I'm sorry," I repeat. "I just saw my psychiatrist."

John looks alarmed. "You know what? Maybe we should do this another time. When you're less, uh, weepy."

Nodding, I use a cocktail napkin to blow my nose. The napkin can't hold all of my snot and it breaks, leaking boogers onto my hand.

John pushes his chair back from the table and reaches for his wallet. He puts a ten dollar bill onto the table. "You stay and finish your beer, unless it doesn't mix with your medication, and I'll, uh, call you. Later. Bye."

Library Books

The COG plus Jean-François is having a late lunch on Saturday to bid adieu to the fiancés. Mia tried to swap car pool responsibilities, but couldn't, so Grace, Lola and I are waiting for the love birds. They are late, probably due to some Gallic hanky-panky.

"How was your date with the lawyer?" Lola asks.

"We didn't hit if off," I tell her, spinning the answer just a tad. To change the subject, I slide The Cuisine Channel contracts across the table to Lola. She whips out a pen and signs them.

"Don't you want to read them?" I ask her.

"Did you read them?"

"Yes."

"Why do we both have to read them?" Lola replies. I shrug and put the contracts back into my tote.

Breathless, Ellie and Jean-François run into the restaurant. They glow, both of them, and I smile at their light. Ellie is returning to Paris with Jean-François and she will stay there almost a month.

Grace starts babbling to Ellie about wedding stuff. But Ellie has already had her fill of Grace's wedding planning. Trying to alter the subject, Ellie says, "So, Lexi, who will you bring to Grace's wedding?"

"I am so not worried about it."

"Lexi is single," Grace whispers to Jean-François.

"It's not a secret, Grace," I tell her. "Jean-François knows all about the Ron debacle."

"Does he know that you haven't had a real date since then?" Grace turns to Jean-François. "Lexi hasn't moved on with her dating life," she explains to him. "But, before she was with Ron? Lexi used to date a lot. A lot. Not that she was a slut or anything."

I scream, "Grace!"

"What? I said you weren't a slut. Were not." She turns back to Jean-François. "Lexi didn't sleep around. She just dated a lot."

"You did date a lot," Ellie says. Ellie begins a history of my life as a single woman. Lola and Grace add their commentary, and all of a sudden, the COG is doing a *Behind the Music* about my romantic life. I do not find this terribly amusing, and I can't believe Ellie is being so hypocritical. Does her engagement erase her somewhat slutty past?

"I'm reading this great book," I blurt, trying to change the subject. I take out *Click Your Heels Three Times: Discovering the Power Within.*

Ellie takes the book and rubs the plastic covering. "Another library book," she smirks.

"Lexi gets books from the library every week," Lola tells Jean-François.

"Stop picking on me."

Grace, sitting next to me, leans over the table toward Jean-

François. "She's waiting to build her own library until she finds the perfect books."

"What's wrong with that?" I want to know.

"It's sort of like your approach to men," Ellie says.

"Meaning?"

"Oh, come on, Lex." Ellie laughs and puts her head on Jean-François's shoulder. "You go to the library and spend an hour looking for a book that will entertain you. Then you get lost in the book for a week. You lug it around with you. To the Square. To the gym. And to bed."

Ellie continues. "You bond with the book. You feel like you understand it, and maybe it understands you. Maybe it speaks to you like other books haven't. But you know that the book is only yours temporarily. You have to return it to the library at the end of the week. You don't have to make room for it on your shelf. So, when you have time, you dispose of the book and get another one, with which you will bond until it's time to give it back. And on and on."

Ellie and Grace laugh, Jean-François looks confused, and Lola quietly sips her coffee.

Why is Ellie being critical of me? Yes, the COG frequently tease one another. But where does she get off being smug? Now that she's engaged is she holier than me? Is this payback for me questioning her engagement? Is she trying to make herself feel good by making me look bad? Is that sapphire cutting off circulation to her brain? Is she really that secure in her transatlantic romance?

From across the table, Lola looks at me cautiously and gives a slight shake of her head. She knows I am churning with a comeback and she doesn't want me to deliver it.

Tough luck.

"Ellie," I say with a big smile, "I would rather have access to the library than buy a book that I thought looked interesting, but was so different from my own experiences that I couldn't get past the first chapter."

The analogy is clear. There is uncomfortable silence at the table.

Finally, Grace's cell beeps and she reads the page. "It's Michael," she announces. "I'm late for our errands." Grace stands, and we all rise and walk outside. The five of us stand on the pavement looking at one another. No one wants to leave with tension in the air.

"Ellie," I start, and Ellie quickly says, "It's okay, Lex. I understand." She grabs me into a hug, and I wonder just what Ellie thinks she understands.

"I almost forgot," Lola says, and reaches into her bag for a manila envelope, which she hands to Ellie. "The recipes and background material."

"I'll work on it every day," Ellie says. She's promised to write the cookbook while she's in Paris. I have my doubts about how much Ellie will get accomplished, but a contract is a contract and the deadline for a first draft is approaching.

"I'll e-mail." Ellie waves as she sashays away with Jean-François.

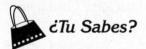

¿Tu Sabes?

"What the hell was that about?" I demand of Lola as we walk through Rittenhouse Square toward her restaurant and my apartment.

"*Ay, chica.* You know, before I got married to Enrique, I had the same little fight with my best friend in Miami. She didn't approve of Enrique."

"I approve of Jean-François. I took the day off on Friday and spent the afternoon with him. I like him."

Lola thinks on that. "I think it's like this. When you get married, your husband is supposed to become your best friend, so you feel like you have to separate yourself from your friends. A little bit. In Ellie's case, she's separating herself a lot. I would guess she is nervous about spending the month in France with Jean-François. I can't really blame her. She made a big decision. Now she's scared. And you? You don't help the situation."

"Because of what I said at the restaurant when she showed up with him? I was shocked. If Ellie had told me before that night, before she appeared in Chinatown with a stranger and said he was her fiancé, maybe I would have reacted differently."

"Maybe. Maybe not. You still would have had the same reaction. Maybe Ellie wanted you to meet him first to change your opinion. Which you did, once you spent time with him. Or maybe Ellie knew that you would be harsh and wanted me and Grace there as buffers. You can be very critical, Lexi." Lola pauses and looks like she has more to say, but doesn't.

"This weekend has totally sucked," I tell her. "I had a grueling session with Dr. Franklin."

"What happened?"

I'm about to tell Lola the Big Realizations I came to about me and Susan, but I think that any hint that anything is wrong at The Gold Group will make her very nervous. Lola has just signed papers committing her to The Cuisine Channel and

The Gold Group. So I say, "Can I tell you later? I have enough to worry about with Ellie."

The late May sun shines through the trees in the Square. Lola puts her arm through mine. "Lexi, everything will be okay. Friendships change. It's part of life. *¿Tu sabes?*"

Lola pulls me toward her restaurant. "Come to the restaurant. I'll give you some paella to take home for dinner."

Lola unlocks the front door of her restaurant and looks at her watch. "The dining room staff isn't here yet, but the kitchen staff should have made a fresh batch of paella because—" Lola stops talking and comes to an abrupt halt in the front of the restaurant. In the middle of the dining room, a man in jeans and a navy blue T-shirt stands with his back to us. Lola's jaw clenches and she reaches into her purse for her pepper spray. "Can I help you?" she shouts.

Startled, the man turns.

It's Jack McKay.

 ## Damn the Paella

"Lola, *buenas tardes*. I came to measure for the sculpture. The one you were interested in at Artists' House? The one I'm about to convince you to buy? The guys in the kitchen let me in. I hope that's all right." Jack pauses. "Hi, Lexi."

"Hi. Jack. Hi."

Lola stares Jack up and down. Turning, she winks at me. Uh oh.

"I'll be right back, Jack. I need to check on things in the kitchen and get Lexi's paella." Lola jogs out of the room.

Wonderful. Haven't I had enough humiliation for one day? Now Lola has given Jack yet another opportunity to reject me.

Jack walks toward me, looking at the floor. He comes to a halt six feet from me, as if deciding that is a safe distance. Putting his hands in his jean pockets, Jack looks at the floor and says, "I didn't call you."

"Yes, Jack. I know that." I open my purse and root around for nothing.

"What I meant to say is that I didn't call you because the gallery has been very busy."

"Don't worry about it. No big deal." Walking around Jack, I shout into the kitchen. "Lola! I'm leaving! *Ciao!*"

"Wait for your paella!"

"I'll get it later!" Turning around, I bump into Jack, who has come up behind me. I stumble backward. Jack grabs my arms and puts me back on my feet. He looks down at me. "You misunderstood what I said."

Standing so close to him and inhaling his soap smell, I can't remember what the hell he said. My panties start to sweat.

"The gallery has been busy. I have to sell my pieces while I can. Still, it was rude not to call you. I apologize. Do you have plans for dinner tonight?"

"No," I squeak, and immediately want to smack myself. I should have lied. What kind of dork doesn't have Saturday night dinner plans?

Jack smiles. "I figured that from the paella."

Damn the paella.

"Will you have dinner with me tonight?" Raising his eyebrows, Jack waits for my answer. He seems unsure of what I will say. His hands are still around my upper arms, and in what I am sure is an unconscious move, Jack slightly tightens his grip on me. Is he nervous? That can't be. What woman would say no to him? Not me. "Yes. I'll have dinner with you."

"Good." Jack seems enormously relieved. "Let's go now. I can talk to Lola later."

"No, stay and talk to her. You have to sell your work while you can. Right?"

Jack shrugs.

"Also? It's only four o'clock. Too early for dinner." I smile at him. "Come to my apartment when you're finished with Lola. You remember where I live?"

"Yes."

"Okay, then. I'll see you in a little while."

"Yes," Jack says again. He moves his hand to my face and lowers his head slowly to mine, giving me plenty of opportunity to stop him. Of course, I don't. I want this kiss. His hands hot on my face, Jack's lips gently brush mine, and I shiver.

"God, I need to make money tonight." "Where did you get those pants?" "Can you work for me tomorrow?" Lola's waiters and waitresses come bounding through the front door, creating an inordinate amount of noise.

Jack steps away from me and clears his throat. "I am going to go find Lola. And talk to her. And then, I'll be over."

I nod. Jack disappears into the kitchen. I stand still, feeling numb and damp.

Then, I run home.

The Bed-In, Part Three

Quickly, I change into my good underwear, rub on deodorant, and brush my teeth. Rooting through my closet for something flattering to wear, I remember that I forgot to pick up my dry cleaning. Balls. I settle for a knee-length black skirt and a beige tank top. Shoes? Which shoes?

The weekend doorman rings to tell me that Jack is in the lobby. "Send him up," I answer. My fingers start tingling and I hop around like a child who has to go to the bathroom. I have that kind of ache between my thighs.

I leave the door unlocked.

Shoes? Shoes? Which shoes? Boots? No, it's the end of May. No boots. Heels? Which heels? How about the ones that tie up and around my calves? Those are funky enough for Jack. I hope.

"Lexi?" It's Jack. Tying the laces around my left calf with the right one finished, I hop to the kitchen, open a cabinet, and pretend to look for something. "In here!" I call as calmly as I can.

Mine is a galley kitchen, with two ten-foot counters running parallel to each other. Since I never cook, my counters are clear of kitchen debris. It's a kitchen built for sex. What else would someone do in here?

Jack walks around the corner into the kitchen. His navy T-shirt has yellow paint drippings that I didn't notice before. I see the curves of his biceps and the definition of his collarbone. He leans against one counter. I lean against the other. "Hi," Jack says as he looks me up and down.

"Hi," I answer. "Did she buy the sculpture?"

Jack stares at my mouth. "Who?"

Laughing, I say, "Lola."

"What about her?"

"Did she buy the sculpture?"

"You look amazing, Lexi."

"Thank you."

We stare at each other.

Should I . . . ?

Hell, yes.

Two steps put me in front of Jack. Because I'm wearing my heels, my mouth reaches his neck. Touching his skin for the first time, I put my palms on Jack's stomach and move my hands upward to feel the muscles in his stomach and chest. Jack pulls his shirt over his head and throws it on the floor. We kiss and kiss and kiss, and with my hand I follow his treasure trail down his stomach to the waistband of his jeans. I unbutton and unzip his pants, pull them down and close my hand around him. Lightly, firmly, then roughly I squeeze him until he is hard.

Releasing him, I take a step backward, intending to get on my knees. But Jack grips my waist and lifts me onto the counter. Leaning forward, I reach under my skirt, pull my panties over my heels, and toss them into the sink. Jack pushes my skirt up to my hips, flips open my legs and raises my knees to his shoulders. He lowers his head and I lean back against the cabinets. Jack moans, and it vibrates through my body.

Just when I'm about to scream, Jack raises his head. "Do you have anything?" he asks.

"Anything?"

"A condom."

"Oh. Crap. No. I haven't, uh, I mean, it's been a long time. Wait! In the bottom drawer of my nightstand. Maybe. Hopefully. Please, God."

Wiping his mouth, Jack walks slowly into the bedroom, leaving me there in a puddle of my own juices and his saliva.

I realize I'm sweating, so I take off my shirt and throw it in the sink, but leave on my bra. And my heels.

A minute later, Jack walks back into the kitchen wearing a condom. He wraps my legs around his thighs and lifts me off the counter, bringing me down on top of him. My palms flat against the counter and my arm muscles flexed, I move up and down on him as he grips my waist and leans backward against the other counter for support.

Closing my eyes, I arch my back and moan, putting my full weight on Jack. He lets me finish, waiting until my contractions cease. Then he stands up straight, lowers me to my feet, and turns me around, moving my hips into his crotch. He pumps into me, and I brace myself against the counter for support. Finally, he groans, and so do I.

Jack releases his hold on me and I turn to face him, leaning against the counter. Jack sags against the opposite counter. He slides off the condom and tosses it into the sink. "My shirt is in there," I tell him, and we peer into the sink to see the condom leaking onto my tank top.

Is it because I haven't had sex in nine months? Is it because I haven't had sex with someone new for almost two years? Is it because casual sex is hotter than committed sex? Is it? Whatever the reason, I devour Jack with no inhibitions.

Sometime after 11 PM, I raise my head from the living room floor and kiss Jack, who is hovering over me. "I can't anymore. I am so sore. I just can't. Don't be mad."

"I'm not mad. I wouldn't be mad at that." He kisses me lightly. "Let's get back into the bathtub. I think the bubbles are still there."

"Okay, but don't start with me again. I need a break. Don't touch me."

"I won't touch you," Jack says as he picks me up from the floor and cradles me in his arms. He carries me to the bathroom. "You're touching me, Jack. Jack? You're touching me." Jack lowers me into the bathtub. "There," he says. "Now I'm not touching you."

I pout. "You're not touching me," I whine.

Jack climbs into the tub and sits behind me. Scooting between his open legs, I lean backward against his chest. "Ahhh," I exhale. "You know? It's funny. I thought you didn't like me after we went dancing at The Wizard."

"I didn't like you after we went dancing at The Wizard."

"What do you mean?"

"Lexi, you were acting strangely. I thought you were drunk, so I wanted to make sure you got into your apartment safely. Then, when we walked through the door, you took off and locked yourself in the bathroom for fifteen minutes." Jack splashes water into my face. "Strange girl. But, I liked you while we were dancing. Once we started talking, everything went to hell. "

"That's great, Jack. Very nice. If my conversation skills were so lacking, why did you ask me to dinner?"

"Because I think you are very, very pretty," Jack answers. "And I was hungry. Still am."

"Oh, balls. I forgot the paella. Sorry."

"I did offer to take you out to dinner," Jack reminds me.

"The restaurants around here are closed," I tell him.

"We could cook something. What do you have in your kitchen?"

"Tomato soup. Tea bags. And several used condoms."

"That's it?" Jack sounds disappointed.

"What do you have in your kitchen?"

"I don't have a kitchen."

"What do you mean?"

"I don't have an apartment." I wait for Jack to give me an explanation. He doesn't. If I want to know something about this man, I have to ask him. "If you don't have an apartment, where do you live?"

"My lease was up a few months ago. I had an exhibit scheduled in San Francisco, so I planned to move there for a while. But in order to make enough money to offset the cost of moving the sculptures out there, I would have to sell more pieces than I have finished. I canceled the exhibition, and I don't really know where I'm going next. For now, I'm staying at friends' houses. I move around based on who has room."

"Oh." So, homeless?

"We could order a pizza," Jack says, getting back to his hunger.

"Sure." A vagabond. That's what he is.

"Tomorrow I'll take you out. For brunch." A vagabond sex god.

"What? No, I can't. I'm having brunch with the COG."

"What's a cog?"

 ### The Legend of Billy Kidman

From a table in the corner of Rx restaurant, Lola waves both of her hands at me. I slide into a chair. "Hold on," Lola says to Grace, who is in the middle of a story. Lola moves her chair closer to mine. "*Dígame.* Tell me everything."

"What's going on?" Grace wants to know.

Lola turns to Grace and quickly says, "Last night, Lexi went to dinner with that artist. Jack McKay." Lola turns back to me. "What restaurant did he take you to?"

Lowering my head, I look at my hands.

Lola explodes. "What? He didn't take you out to dinner? What happened?" Lola gasps and covers her hand with her mouth. "Did he not come over? Jack didn't go to your apartment?" Lola smacks her hand on the table. "I can't believe he did that. I'm not buying that sculpture. I'm going to kill him. Actually, I'll buy the sculpture and then kill him. That way, it'll be worth more."

Grace says, "I told you not to get involved with him."

"When did you tell me that?" I ask.

"When you called me in the middle of the night to ask if you should sleep with him. And I said, 'No, Lexi. Don't sleep with him. He should take you out on a date first.' Remember? I told you to leave it be."

"Sorry, Gracie. I didn't leave it be. In fact, I played with it all night."

Lola thumps me on the back. "Congratulations! You haven't had sex for a long time. How was it? Awesome?"

"Awesome."

"Orgasms?"

"Orgasms."

"Oral?"

"Oral."

"Condoms?"

"Condoms."

"Lexi," Grace interrupts, "did he take you out to dinner or not?"

"No." I go on the defensive. "I attacked him before we could go out to dinner. All of a sudden, it was eleven o'clock and all the restaurants were closed. We ordered pizza. It was great."

Grace exhales loudly and rolls her eyes. "Lexi, that's no way to start a relationship. That's assuming Jack is relationship material. Which it doesn't seem like he is, considering the fact that he has yet to call you and ask you out and take you out. You just keep bumping into him."

"Relax, Grace. Don't get your crucifix in a twist. It was a onetime thing. A one-night stand. Actually? I was laying down most of the time. It was a one-night lay."

Lola claps. "Good one."

"If I do continue to see him? It'll just be a fling. An, easy, orgasm-filled affair."

"A rebound guy?" Lola suggests.

"Yes! Exactly. A rebound guy. Thank you, Lola."

"You're welcome." Lola pats Grace's shoulder. "Don't worry, *amiga*. Lexi's just having fun. I think it's good for her."

Grace shakes her head. "You'll get attached to him."

"I will not."

"You will, too."

"Will not."

"Will, too."

"Hey, hey, hey." Lola holds her hands in the air. "Knock it off. Lexi, you pick on Grace's fiancé all the time. But Gracie, that doesn't give you an excuse for being so hard on Lexi. She's having a tough weekend. Play nice."

"I'm giving Lexi a hard time because she's done this kind of thing before," Grace says.

"What? I have not."

Grace leans over the sugar caddy and sticks her finger in my face. "Billy Kidman."

I gasp. "I can't believe you said that name," I hiss.

"Who is Billy Kidman?" Lola asks.

"Go ahead." Grace folds her arms in front of her chest. "Tell her."

"I dated him in college. It didn't work out."

"Lexi, please. That's, like, under exaggerating." Grace shakes her head at me again. "Billy Kidman was the singer in a band that played at fraternity parties. He looked like George Michael."

Lola looks at me. "George Michael?"

I shrug. "It was the early nineties."

"Anyway," Grace continues. "Billy became Lexi's safety screw. You know how people have safety schools when they apply to college? Lexi had a safety screw so she would always have someone to turn to if a relationship didn't work out. And of course, her other relationships never did work out, exactly because she had a safety screw. As long as Lexi had Billy, she didn't have to work on a long-term, committed relationship with anyone else. What was Billy doing the whole time? Dating someone seriously, as it turned out, and using Lexi for sex on the side. April of our senior year, Billy got engaged to this vanilla Tri Delt. Lexi was left in the dust.

"And that, Lola, is why Lexi should not be encouraged to foster a nonrelationship with a rebound guy. She'll use it as an excuse not to move forward with her life."

"Billy Kidman was a long time ago." My voice is between a whisper and a hiss.

"Yes, it was a long time ago." Lola waves her hands in the air. "*No importa.* It's in the past. *¿Sí?*" Neither Grace nor I answer Lola. We look at our menus.

"Ladies? Ready to order?"

"Challah French toast, please," Lola says.

"I'll have eggs Benedict," Grace says. "And Lexi? She doesn't know what she wants? Do you, Lexi? A sturdy stack of pancakes that will fill you up and get you through the rest of the day? Or unhealthy sausage that will satisfy your immediate needs for food, but leave you empty and wanting more?"

"Ours are turkey sausages," the waiter says. "Pretty healthy as far as sausages go."

I hand the menu to the young man. "I would like the longest, thickest turkey sausage you can find. And eggs. Scrambled. Hard. And the biggest cup of coffee you have. Please." The waiter looks at us strangely and departs.

"You don't know anything about Jack," I tell Grace. "I'm just getting to know him. Isn't that what you want me to do? Date?"

Grace rolls her eyes. "You're not dating Jack. You're screwing him. There's no dating. Where's the dating? Have you had one date?"

"No."

"Right. You go out with me and Lola. And you spend the rest of your nights alone. How's that working for you?"

I gasp, then growl. "Don't you dare Dr. Phil me. I gave you that Dr. Phil line. You can't use it against me."

Grace picks daintily at her eggs Benedict, Lola calmly chews her challah French toast, and I wolf down sausage, eggs, and coffee like a truck driver. To fill the dead air between me and Grace, Lola tells us last night's restaurant adventures.

When the server clears our plates, I look at Grace and pick up the conversation right where I left it. "There could still be a relationship between me and Jack."

"Once you have sex, you can't go back to holding hands," Grace sniffs.

"They only had sex once," Lola says, "or, I should say, they only had sex one night. Maybe it's not too late. But you have to choose, Lexi. Stop the sex now and let a relationship develop. Or just go for the sex."

"Who makes these rules?" I want to know.

"Everybody knows that," Grace says like I'm an idiot.

"Fine. If I have to chose, I'll pick the sex."

"Of course," Grace groans. "Sex is easier than working on a relationship."

"I'm not going to give up great sex on the off chance that a relationship will work."

"Exactly right." Lola smacks her hands together. "I agree."

"You do?" Grace and I ask together.

"Of course. Listen, *chicas*. The man you marry? He may not be so good in bed. So you should take some good sex while you can get it."

Wrinkling my brow, I ask, "Why would I marry a man who isn't good in bed?"

Grace puts her head in her hands. "Because you love him, dummy."

"Well, Grace, o perfect one, I don't know if I like Jack, let alone love him."

"That exactly my point, Lexi. You don't know him. Why don't you have a real date and spend time getting to know him?"

"Fine. I will."

"No, you won't. You'll just keep screwing him. It's easier."

"*Chicas.*"

"I dare you, Lexi. Call Jack right now and ask him to dinner. Tonight."

"Fine. I will." I grab my cell from my purse, then realize I don't have a number to call Jack. Balls. I don't want to tell Grace that Jack is technically homeless, and that I don't know how to reach him. Oh, wait. I'll call the gallery. Sunday afternoon? It should be open.

And it is. Jack picks up the phone. I ask him to dinner. He agrees. "Somewhere between the gallery and my place," I suggest, and stick my tongue out at Grace.

"I'll walk over from Third Street," Jack says. "Meet me on South Street."

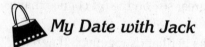

My Date with Jack

At 7:15 PM, Jack is waiting for me at the corner of Third and South streets. Leaning against a lamppost, Jack stares up at the darkening Sunday sky, oblivious to South Street's summer crush of human and vehicular traffic. Jack is wearing a short-sleeved, dark green T-shirt, white cotton pants, and work boots. Around his neck is a beaded necklace, on his wrist is an ornate metal cuff, and his right middle finger sports a chunky silver ring. The boy is wearing more jewelry than I am. Because I didn't know which restaurant Jack would choose, I decided to wear a black linen tank dress and sling backs, thinking I would fit in anywhere.

Except next to Jack. What was I thinking? Standing across the street from Jack, I watch him and feel nervous and ugly and fat. Okay, yes, he slept with me. But I practically threw myself at him. What man would say no to free sex? Free. No flowers, no movie, no dinner. Just sex. Here I am. Do me.

And, okay, yes, he agreed to dinner tonight. But he's, like, a starving artist. And homeless. What homeless, starving artist would say no to a free dinner?

I can't believe I let Grace goad me into this.

"Lexi!" Jack calls to me from across the street.

I wave and smile like a thirteen-year-old at her first rock concert.

"The restaurant is this way." He gestures behind him, down Third Street.

I cross the street and walk up to Jack, lifting my face for him to kiss. He doesn't. Nor does he put his arm around me, or hold my hand. No physical contact. *Nada*. "Let's go," he says. "It's hot out here." Really? Feels pretty chilly to me.

"Here we are." Jack opens his arms wide, and without touching me, corrals me through the door. We step into a small restaurant with saffron-colored walls covered in artwork. I smell the distinct aromas of cumin and cilantro and hear the steel drums of Latin music. "I can't eat here," I whisper. "It's Lola's competition."

"What?" Jack leans down. "I didn't hear you."

"*¡Buenas noches!*" Striding toward us is a short woman with long, brown hair tied back from her face. From the reviews hanging in the window, I see that this woman is the owner. "Jack!" she says. "It's good to see you." Jack leans down and kisses this woman, once on each cheek. Out of loyalty to Lola, I glare at her.

Ignoring my hostility, the woman takes my hand and presses it warmly. "Welcome to Azafran," she says. "I'm Susanna."

She seats us at a table near the back of the restaurant, in front of an empty brick fireplace, the light of votive candles dancing across its mantel. "Listen," Susanna says to Jack. "I have a check for you. I sold the last of your paintings. Do you have more? I'll make room." Susanna gestures at the restaurant's walls, which are filled with what I now realize are local artists' works.

"I have only one left," Jack answers. Susanna puts her hand on Jack's shoulder.

"Whatever you have, I want." Another couple walks in the door, and Susanna excuses herself to greet and seat them.

Jack stares at his menu and splays his legs under the table. His left foot bumps into my right foot. Quickly, he moves his foot and sits up straight. "Sorry," he mumbles.

"No problem," I chirp. Why is he nervous? He's making me nervous. And when I'm nervous, I talk. "You sculpt and you paint?" Jack nods.

"She sells your stuff?" He nods.

"She takes a cut?" He shakes his head.

Good God, man. Speak!

"She lets you exhibit here for free?" He nods.

"Too bad there's no room for your sculptures."

"That's why I'm opening my own gallery," Jack says.

"You are? When? Where?"

"*Buenas noches,*" a redheaded waitress interrupts. After a recitation of the specials, Jack orders for us without asking what I want. When the waitress disappears, he says, "I ordered my favorite things for you to try." Looking directly at me for the first time, Jack raises his left eyebrow. The one with the scar. He smiles.

Well, well. Isn't that sweet? Very unlike Ron. It took him half an hour to order. Ron applied his lawyering to every aspect of life, especially menus. "What looks good?" was his opening offer. My answer didn't matter. Ron wouldn't order until he had argued the merits of every dish. Twenty minutes later, Ron was still negotiating with himself. "What if we get one of this and one of that, but share this and get that with the sauce on the side?"

Jack knew what he wanted, what I should try, and ordered it.

"So, you're opening your own gallery?" I expect a diatribe about artistic vision, freedom of expression, and fulfillment of a dream.

Jack nods.

"Where will it be?"

"I need to find a space," he answers.

"When you open, I can do your public relations. Press releases. An opening event. Ooh, I can see it now. 'Jack McKay, Junk Artist.' " I go on for five minutes, ad libbing a marketing plan.

"I won't need that," Jack says.

"Everyone needs PR. Listen, one great feature article or review can make or break a new business."

"I know. What I meant is that I already know the art critics in town. It's a small circle."

"That's great, but just because you know the critics doesn't mean they will kind to you. Trust me. I'm a professional publicist. It's what I do. You'll need my help. You will."

"The gallery might not be in Philadelphia. It depends where I find a space." Jack sits back in his chair and takes a long drink of water.

"Oh." I get it. No apartment, no lease, no girlfriend, no commitments.

"Excuse me," he says. "I need to use the bathroom." Jack gets up and walks toward the back of the restaurant. En route, he passes Susanna, who is talking to a table of guests. As he scoots by her, Jack plants a kiss on Susanna's cheek. That makes three kisses for Susanna, no kisses for Lexi. Boo.

Jack returns, sits down, then rises again. "Azafran is BYOB. I forgot to bring beer or wine. I'll go to the bar next door and get something. Is beer okay?" I nod, and Jack disappears again.

Exhaling my frustration, I stare into the dark, unlit fireplace. Why is there such awkwardness between us? Our sex was so great.

Arranged on a decorative mountain of ice, an order of ceviche sits on the table between me and Jack. "It's raw fish, cured with citrus," Jack explains.

"I know what ceviche is," I tell him.

"Go ahead then. Dig in."

"You first."

"Fine." Jack dives his fork into the prettily arranged fish. I do the same. Our forks clink, and Jack pulls his away.

Okay. That's enough. "You know, Jack, it's a little late to be worrying about whether or not I have cooties. And for the record, I don't."

"I do not think you have cooties."

"Then why are you acting so weird?"

Jack tilts his head and looks at me. "Because I can't figure you out."

"What's to figure?"

"You really want to know?"

"I asked."

"Okay. Fine. When I saw you at Lola's, you were cold. Like you didn't want to talk to me. Then I got to your apartment and you were hot. Very hot. Very aggressive. So, I thought, 'Maybe she just wants to have sex.' Which was fine by me. Then we spent all those hours together, although we weren't really talking, but I thought maybe there was some kind of something going on there. I asked you to have brunch with me, and you blew me off. Then, you call me out of the blue and ask me to dinner like you want to have a date. Then, on the street, you expected me to kiss you, which I would never do on a first date. Except this isn't really a first date, is it? Except it is, technically." Jack sits back and crosses his arms in front of his chest. "You'll pardon me if I'm a little confused."

"Wow."

"Yeah."

"Okay. First of all, I didn't blow you off for brunch. I had plans with the COG."

"Yeah, what is this cog?"

"My best friends. The Council of Girlfriends."

"Council?"

"Yes. They counsel me on things. Work. Clothes. Men. Whatever. In fact, the whole reason I asked you to dinner is because the COG made me."

"They made you?"

"Yes. They put a lot of pressure on me to do the right thing."

"Who decides what is the right thing?"

"We all do."

"So this is, what? Peer pressure? Didn't you get over that in high school?"

"You misunderstand," I tell Jack.

"Tell me this, Lexi. The night that you were waiting for me outside the gallery? Did the COG make you do that?"

"I wasn't waiting for you. I just happened to end up on that street. I was running away. From. Something."

"Right. That's why you were standing still and talking to your friend on your cell phone."

"Right that minute I was talking to my friend, but I had previously been running away from something. From a bunch of drunks."

"Is that right?"

"Yes. They had knives."

"Knives? A bunch of drunks with knives?"

"And guns."

"Knives and guns? Yikes."

"Yes." I smile. "And swords."

"Swords? Wow." Jack smiles back at me.

"And a pack of wild dogs."

"Okay, Lexi." Jack reaches for my hand and covers it with his, the first intimate gesture of the evening. "Are you really running away from something? Don't give me a snippy answer. I'm not being literal."

"What are you being? Hypothetical?"

Jack laughs out loud. "I'm not going to get a straight answer out of you, am I?"

"I could give you a gay answer."

Shaking his head, Jack digs his fork into the ceviche arrangement. The ice has already melted.

"Listen, Lexi," Jack says when we have devoured the ceviche and the waitress has placed an array of tapas in front of us. "I don't know what you think is going on between us, but I want you to know that I like you. I do. And I'd like to see you again. But right now? I don't have time for a relationship. I'm sorry."

Waving at Jack, I say, "Don't be sorry."

"That doesn't, like, upset you?"

"Not at all."

Jack squints at me. "Why not?"

Swallowing my food, I wipe my mouth and say, "I'm really good at a lot of things, but I'm really bad at relationships."

Jack nods. "Me too."

"I'm worse."

"No," Jack shakes his head. "I'm worse."

"I don't think so. I broke off an engagement."

"I'm divorced."

"Oh. You win."

We smile at each other.

"Do you want to tell me about your divorce?"

"No. Do you want to tell me about your engagement?"

"No."

"Good."

"Good."

"So. How about those Phillies?"

When the redheaded waitress clears our plates, I ask her for the check. Jack insists on paying, even when I remind him that dinner was at my invitation. "*Buenas noches,*" Susanna waves us out of Azafran.

"*Mucho gusto,*" I tell her.

Outside Azafran, we walk toward Bainbridge, South Street's quiet, tree-lined sibling. I look up at Jack. "So? Where do we go from here?"

"Well, I'm going to Chicago. And New York. And San Francisco."

"Really?"

"Yeah. To look for gallery space. Visit some old friends. I need to stretch my legs. I've been in Philadelphia for almost six months."

"Six months? That's a long time for you to be in one place?"
Jack smiles but doesn't answer.

"How will you know when you've found the right space for
the gallery? What are you looking for?"

Now, Jack talks about his artistic vision. He wants to find a
space big enough to exhibit his sculptures the way they should
be displayed. He also wants to exhibit other styles of nontra-
ditional art. "Artists are creating crazy, cool stuff that doesn't
fit into traditional categories, but most gallery owners don't
want to exhibit things that might not sell. I want my gallery to
be open to all kinds of art, to give artists the chance to exhibit
and people the opportunity to buy it."

"Running a gallery will be a lot of responsibility. And
risk."

"Yeah, but it's either that or kowtow to gallery owners for
the rest of my career. Doing things the way they want. This
way, I'll be able do what I want, when I want." Jack shrugs.
"Almost any risk is worth that freedom."

I think about Camp Cool, the travel agency of Susan's
sister-in-law, my own kowtow bow to Adrian Salvo, and the
countless compromises I have made at The Gold Group.

Jack says, "I like talking to you."

"Oh, come on." I wink at him. "You're just using me for sex."

Jack raises his left eyebrow. "I think it's the other way
around. Not that I'm complaining."

"Get that a lot, do you? Women using you for sex? Must be
tough."

"You're different. No woman has ever asked me out to dinner. Usually, women just hang around whatever gallery I'm
exhibiting in and hint that I should ask them out. They think

they are being subtle." Jack points at me. "You, Lexi James, are not subtle. I like that."

Looking down the barrel of Jack's finger, I say, "Thank you."

"Maybe if the timing was different, something would work out between us. Although given our track records, probably not."

"Yeah. You're right."

"I don't know when I'll get back to Philadelphia, or how long I'll be here if I do come back. It depends where I find gallery space. Given my geographical uncertainty, I think we should leave things here. On a good note."

"Okay."

"But I'm glad we had dinner. If I come back, I'll call you."

"Okay."

Jack opens his arms and squishes me into an awkward hug. My nose bumps against the beads on his necklace.

 Hope

In the cab on the way home, I reach for my cell. I feel the need to talk about what has just happened. Although I'm not exactly sure what happened. Things were bad, then they were good, now here I am alone. Jack's leaving and that's the end of his tale, but I feel as though there's a moral to this immoral story that I can't quite grasp.

Who should I call? Grace would first gloat over her accurate assessment of Jack, then tell me that I will eventually find a man who will marry me, impregnate me, and solve all my problems. Lola? No. She wavers between wanting me to get married and wanting me to have great sex. Neither is happening tonight. Mia is probably sleeping and isn't worth waking her. Ellie. Yes. I want to talk to Ellie. But she's with Jean-François on a plane headed for Paris.

Back in my apartment, I head off a flurry of COG phone calls by sending an e-mail.

To: Lola <lola@councilofgirlfriends.com>, Grace <grace@councilofgirlfriends.com>, Ellie <ellie@councilofgirlfriends.com>, Mia <mia@councilofgirlfriends.com>
From: Lexi <lexi@councilofgirlfriends.com>
Subject: My date with Jack . . .

. . . was a bust. I won't be seeing him again. I've been gone from the office since Thursday, so I'll have a busy week ahead. Talk to you all soon.

xoxo
Lexi

Sitting alone in my bedroom, I watch the lights go out in the apartment building across the street. In my head, I replay the conversation with Jack. We are both bad at relationships. We have that in common. We joked about it, but it's not funny. It's painful. I think Jack has felt that pain. Neither of us wants to deal with it. We have that in common, too.

These days, I'm not good at relationships with men or women. Susan and Ellie. And my bickering with Grace. Something needs to change.

There is something else floating around in my head. Something smooth, light, and clean. It's a feeling that started growing last night, but has receded to the point that it's only a pastel figment of thought.

Retreating to my bed, I surround myself with my expensive sheets which I washed this afternoon. Closing my eyes, I inhale deeply through my nose. And I smell it.

Soap. Irish Spring soap.

The smell is not in my bed. It's in my head.

That's when I capture the thought. It is this. For the past twenty-four hours, I had a man in my life. Now he's out of my life. But the idea of him gave me something.

Hope.

 ## Breakfast Cereal

The three-day weekend seems to have lasted forever. I'm emotionally exhausted and have not one qualm about sleeping late.

One good thing about being late to work is avoiding the rush for the elevators. So it is that at 9:24 AM on Monday, I have the elevator all to myself as I swoosh upward to The Gold Group.

Whatever happened to elevator music? When did it get turned off? By whom? Why? I liked elevator music. I mean, I'm standing here by myself and I would like to sing a little song.

The doors open to TGG lobby and Low Man on the Totem Pole leaps from his desk. "Low Man, what happened to elevator music?"

"I don't know. Veep, listen. Susan wants to see you."

"Would you look it up on the Internet for me? I'm curious."

"Lexi," Mike puts his hands on his hips. "Be serious."

"Lexi?" I turn to see Susan Gold-Berg gesturing to me from her office.

"Where were you on Friday?" Susan leans against her desk, and I shut the door to her office.

"I took the day off."

"You turned off your cell phone," Susan says as if she's accusing me of a crime.

I think how often Susan has disappeared from the office for several days without answering her cell, returning voice mails, or answering e-mails. "So?"

"You didn't check your home voice mail, either," Susan says.

"Susan," I moan and sit in a chair opposite her desk. "What's this about?"

"Lexi, you are the executive vice president of this company. You are my second in command. If there is a crisis, the staff needs to reach you. Even if it's your day off. You are responsible for what happens when I'm not here."

"Let's face it, Susan. I'm in charge all the time because you're never here."

"I promoted you to oversee the company while I focus on my family. And I can do that because this, Lexi, is my company."

"People keep reminding me of that."

"What?" Susan squints at me.

Exhaling loudly, I slouch in my chair. "I took one day off and I turned off my cell phone. I took a weekend to myself and didn't check my messages at home. Give me a break. It is your company, right? If there was some big catastrophe, someone could have called you at home." I bend down to dig through my tote for my cell and turn on the damn thing.

"And that's exactly what happened," Susan says quietly.

I sit up straight. "What happened?"

"Friday afternoon, we received a very disgruntled fax from Quaker Insurance. Michelle, who you assigned to the account and who you were supposed to be supervising, kept Quaker Insurance's staff waiting on the copy for their annual report. The writing was very far from finished, and already overdue by three days. The Quaker people were furious. Maria was the most senior person in the office, and she tried to reach you on your cell and at home."

Balls.

"Maria and I came into the office on Saturday and worked on the copy all day. Late Saturday afternoon, Maria drove to Mr. White's home at the Jersey shore to personally deliver the copy. Mr. White's vice president called at 9:10 AM this morning to say that Quaker Insurance will not be renewing its contract when it expires next month." Susan pauses. "And we have another problem. Have you read the *Inquirer's* business section this morning?"

I shake my head.

Susan tosses the *Inquirer* at me. "Independence Hotels has declared bankruptcy," she tells me. "I guess that means they won't be renewing their contract, either."

I look at the newspaper with horror. Susan, however, is very calm. "Maria says Salvo Company is the only new client you've pitched in the past two months. What are our chances of signing them?"

Unable to speak, I shrug.

"Maria thinks we have a less than 50 percent shot at them," Susan says.

I clear my throat. "I don't know."

Susan nods slowly. "Then we won't count on Salvo to make

up our losses. As soon as I got the call from Quaker this morning, I reviewed the quarterly reports you gave me a few weeks ago. We have to lay off two people."

I gasp. I've never fired anyone.

Susan knows this. She moves around her desk to sit in her chair. Leaning across her desk, she says, "You're in management. This is the hard part of being an executive, Lexi."

"Who?" I choke out.

"Who will we fire?" Susan rephrases and shuffles papers on her desk. "We start at the bottom. Mike DiBuono, or Low Man on the Totem Pole as you call him. And Michelle, obviously. She botched the Quaker Insurance account."

Looking at the floor, I say, "That was my responsibility." Susan doesn't answer, so I look up at her and say, "It was all my responsibility."

Tilting her head, Susan looks at me sympathetically. Her anger ebbs as my guilt flows. "Independence Hotels declaring bankruptcy is not your fault. Although you might have been in better touch with them so we had a heads-up on it. But yes, the Quaker Insurance debacle could have been avoided. Easily avoided."

My eyes tear. "There's no other way? We have to fire them?"

"Unfortunately," Susan says. "Don't take it personally, Lexi. This is part of doing business." She looks at me and smiles sadly. "I'll be the bad guy and tell them the news."

"I'll take a pay cut," I offer.

"I'm not blaming you for this," Susan says. "Am I disappointed that you were unavailable on Friday? Yes. Do you deserve time off? Yes. This unfortunate turn of events has made me realize that I have put too much responsibility on your shoulders. I have to be in the office more, and be more involved in running the business. Anyway, a cut in your salary won't save both jobs."

Staring at the floor, I visualize what it would be like to have Susan more involved with TGG. To have her looking over my shoulder, questioning everything I do, undermining my authority. That would drive me nuts. I would go bananas. I would become a breakfast cereal, flaky and brittle, sprinkled with nuts and bananas, cringing every time Susan's mother milk was poured on me. I would drown.

Clearing my throat again, I say, "My entire salary would save both jobs."

Susan shakes her head at me. "You don't have to be a martyr. We may still get the Salvo account. That would make up for Anderson Insurance and half of Independence Hotels. So let's just wait and see how this unfolds."

Susan stands up and grabs her purse. "I have to pick up Ashley for a doctor's appointment, but I'll be back in a little while. Go to your office. Take some time to digest all this. Okay?" Susan takes my hand and pulls me from my chair. "Come on, Lexi. Let's go." Holding my hand, Susan leads me down the hall to my office. "We'll talk when I get back," Susan says, and leaves.

 ## Number Crunches

I stand in the center of my office, perfectly still.

Is this fate? Some higher power convincing me to leave The Gold Group? No. It's the economy, stupid. Recession = bankruptcies + no new clients = Gold Group layoffs.

"Don't be a martyr," Susan said. And yet, when I volunteered to resign, it reminded me of Jack McKay talking about his artistic freedom. "You're in management," Susan said. But like Dr. Franklin pointed out, management is the part of my job that I don't enjoy. "This is the hard part of being an executive, Lexi," Susan said. You know what? Maybe I don't want to be executive Lexi anymore.

My eyes move around my office, and I suddenly feel detached from everything in it. I haven't walked into this room for three days, but it feels like thirty. Was it only Friday that Dr. Franklin said that I should either mend my relationship with Susan or get a new job? I hadn't consciously decided which option to choose. Or maybe I did. Once I said it out loud, the possibility of me leaving TGG became a certainty and it's not half as scary as I thought it would be. Funny, that.

Moving gingerly, as if I'm in someone else's office, I step around my desk and sit in my chair. From my desk, I pull out a pad of paper, a pencil, and a calculator. At the top of the pad, I write: Lexi James Public Relations Company. I squint at the title. Not very catchy. But it's a start.

An hour later, there's a knock on my door. "Lexi?" It's Maria. Without waiting for a response, Maria opens the door and peers into my office. "How are you holding up?" Maria asks. She smiles sadly, as if entering a wake. I guess she is. The wake for my career at The Gold Group.

"I'm okay," I tell Maria, and erase the excitement that has built up inside of me.

Maria looks at my desk and sees a calculator and an adding machine. "That's what I thought you would be doing," she says.

"What do you think I'm doing?"

"Going over the numbers. Not trusting that Susan's calculations are correct. Trying to find a way to resolve this without firing anyone." Maria opens the door all the way and I see that she's holding her own calculator and pile of paper. "I'm doing the same thing. Shall we compare numbers?" She smiles at me, grateful for a cohort.

"Of course, of course," I answer warmly.

In the time it takes Maria to shut the door and cross the office to my desk, I realize that she has been emboldened by her weekend jam session with Susan. Why else would she take the initiative to review our corporate numbers? How did she get them? Susan must have given them to her. What's going on between them?

As Maria sits across from me, I gather my papers and throw them into a pile on the floor behind me. "My head is a blur and even the numbers I know are right are coming out wrong. Let's work with what you have."

Three hours later, Low Man buzzes my intercom. "Veep? Mommy just called to say she won't be coming back here today and you should call her at home if you need her."

"Thank you." Did I really think Susan would support me through this? I did. Whatever. The disappointment must show on my face, because Maria says, "It doesn't matter if Susan is here or not. We've been over these numbers a zillion times and it always comes out the same. The only way we can keep Michelle and Mike is if Salvo signs with us."

"Yeah," I agree dispassionately. "There's no point in beating ourselves over the head with the budget. Let's get some lunch. My treat."

"Your treat? Deal."

*   *   *

After work, I go to the gym, pound the elliptical stair climber, and think. At home, I use the Internet to research other, smaller PR companies in the Philadelphia area. I think. And then I think some more.

 ## The Word of the Day

"Do you know the word of the day?" Low Man asks when I get off the elevator the next afternoon after a lunch meeting which I nodded my way through.

"I didn't know we had a word of the day."

"It's a new policy I instituted to enhance our staff's vocabulary."

"Oh. Great." Looking for a memo I need, I rifle through Low Man's outbox, which has a sticker declaring it an "I'm Out" box. Finding the memo, I turn to walk to my office.

"Veep! You didn't ask me about the word of the day."

Groaning, I ask, "What is the word of the day, Low Man?"

"The word of the day is"—he pauses for dramatic effect—"kohlrabi."

"Why?"

"Go into your office and find out."

Maria sits on my couch. A giant wicker basket sits on my desk. The basket is gorgeous, filled with colorful fruits and vegetables. They are arranged like flowers. Bok choy, kohlrabi, and kale act as a deep green backdrop for heirloom tomatoes splattered with red, white, and yellow patterns. Golden mangoes sit next to purple eggplant. Edible pansies with baby arugula petals are scattered through the basket.

I know what this stuff is because Maria has done her produce homework and she points out the various items as we
stare at the basket. Eventually, I spot the ivory envelope
wedged between a mango and a tomato. This produce bouquet is obviously from Salvo Company, and I assume the envelope contains news that we have notched the account. Like
the good queen I am, I hand the envelope to Maria. She's done
most of the work on Salvo. Trying to be delicate, Maria carefully opens the envelopes and removes a letter.

Smiling, Maria reads the letter. Then, she frowns. "Oh," she
says and looks at me. "We didn't get the account. Adrian's father has decided he wants to stay with Baxter Brothers."

"Why?"

Maria reads more. "Loyalty," she spits, then turns back to
the letter. "Adrian thanks us for our effort. He hopes we enjoy
the basket and accept his appreciation."

"That's gallant," I admit.

"Whatever," Maria sneers. She throws her long body onto
my couch and crosses her legs angrily. "Asshole."

"Hey, don't take it personally." Sitting down next to Maria,
I lightly punch her arm. Remembering that Maria is the
pitcher of her lesbian league softball team, I offer an analogy.

"This was the first big account you pitched, so I understand
your disappointment. But, we pitch a lot of potentials and
don't sign all of them. Sometimes we strike out. Sometimes we
hit a home run. Sometimes we're stranded at second base until
the client makes up his mind. The most important thing is to
be a good sport about the game."

Maria shrugs, but I think she appreciates my attempt at
sports talk. "I had a feeling that we wouldn't get the account,"
she admits.

"Why?"

"Honestly, I think we did a great presentation. But Salvo leaving Baxter Brothers is a huge thing. And then, I thought there was something weird going on between you and Adrian."

"Weird? Like how?"

"At the first dinner meeting, you didn't seem to like him at all, even though he was clearly smitten with you. Then, at the warehouse, you seemed to like him until he winked at you and you looked mad. But you didn't say anything to him. Or me. I couldn't figure it out."

"There was no weirdness," I tell Maria.

"Okay," she answers. "I guess it's my inability to understand heterosexuals."

"I guess."

"So, Lexi. This is it. No Salvo. Mike and Michelle have to be laid off."

Carefully, I say, "It's really up to Susan to make that decision final. Who knows? She may have found a different solution. Let's keep the layoffs quiet until Susan tells us otherwise."

"Of course," Maria says.

Maria leaves, and it's my turn to spread out on my couch. Salvo declined. There's no money to save jobs, which means that I will give up mine.

The word of the day is goodbye.

 ### *Mistress of the Universe, Redux*

The reality of me leaving The Gold Group begins to hit me. I have an overwhelming need to be away from everyone. "I'll be working at home for the rest of the day," I tell Low Man, and don't give him a chance to ask me questions.

I make it to my apartment without getting emotional. Doorman John is helping Mrs. Fraleigh unload her car, and he doesn't see me sneak into the building. Thank God for Mrs. Fraleigh's diversion. Thank God John can't say, "Is everything okay?" because that would send me over the edge and I have to hold it together, hold it in, until no one can see me.

As soon as I unlock my apartment door, I start to cry. I sit down on the floor in my business suit and I cry. I have dedicated more than ten years of my life to The Gold Group. The idea of running my own business was exhilarating until it became reality. Lately, everything about reality seems to terrify me. I cry. I don't stop for a long time.

Hours later, I wake up curled on my floor with my head resting on my arm. Alexandra James, Mistress of the Universe, curled up in the dust and grime of her apartment floor.

 ## Take Me to the River

Tearing off my dusty clothes, I put on shorts, a sports bra, a tank top, and a baseball hat. Grabbing my keys, I storm out of my apartment. The elevator takes too long to arrive, so I jog down the stairs. I have to get out of here and into new air.

Doorman John is gone for the day. There's no one to ask me where I am going, which is a good thing, because I don't really know.

Swinging onto Eighteenth Street, I turn onto Locust Street and head east. I walk fast, pumping my arms. Passing two-hundred-year-old brownstones, I glance into their windows.

Through the curtains, I see families and lovers and dogs and televisions and dinners and laughing and talking.

When I reach Broad Street, I turn my back to City Hall and walk south to Pine Street. Clutches of people wait for SEPTA buses, and I dodge around them and their briefcases, bags, and thousand-yard stares. This might be an ordinary day for them. They have no idea that my life has changed forever.

Striding east on Pine Street, I hit Antique Row. All the shops are closed, but I pass store after store of old furniture, mirrors, paintings, and junk. Small cafés share the street with the antique shops. There are people in Last Drop and Taco House, and they, too, are laughing and loving and living.

Turning again, I reach South Street where it crosses Tenth Street. One side of the street is bombed-out housing. The other side of the street has a sparkling new Whole Foods. Black kids play handball against the sides of the dilapidated houses. White folks hustle out of Whole Foods with organic foods piled in recycled brown bags. This corner, right here, is the reality of Philadelphia.

Farther down on South Street, the shops and restaurants are newer and funkier and the people are white and black, and either tourists or teenagers. My pace slows because the street is jammed with bodies. I let myself be carried down the street, jostled by elbows and knees, sort of swimming through the crowd and not caring where it takes me.

It takes me to Front Street, which should actually be called First Street, but isn't. The Quakers named the streets in this city. They used the word "first" only when it applied to God. If there is a God, he doesn't live on this street.

Looking up, I see the South Street footbridge, which connects Front Street with Penn's Landing, which connects Philadelphia to the Delaware River.

Now I start running.

Shoving people out of my way, I jog across Front Street and up the incline of the South Street bridge and I zigzag around the raised pylons of the bridge where gaggles of teenagers smoke cigarettes and joints and sip beer and vodka from brown paper bags, and I dash down the bridge and into a parking lot and I zip around the traffic on Delaware Avenue and I reach the Penn's Landing promenade and I run through the benches and trees and onto the cement walkway that overlooks the river.

And then, I stop.

I stop. Panting, I look north to the Benjamin Franklin Bridge, lit up in the summer night sky. I look east at Camden's developed waterfront, which looks pretty from this distance. I look south at the Battleship *New Jersey*. I look around me, up and down the walkway, and I don't see anyone else. And so, I scream.

Fists balled, neck flexed, I open my mouth and scream. Inhaling and exhaling, I scream as loud as I can.

I scream at Susan because she put me in charge of her company. I scream at Adrian Salvo for his loyalty to the Baxter Brothers. I scream at Dr. Franklin for asking me tough questions.

And then, I stop.

And then, I laugh.

Part of my life has ended. Another part has begun. What has ended ends here. At the black, wet river. Into the river, I throw my anger and my disappointment and my self-doubt. Into the river, I throw my fear.

I will be okay. I know this.

Turning my back on the Delaware River, I walk down Penn's Landing to Chestnut Street and cross the footbridge to Front Street. Here is the beginning of Old City, the literal genesis of the city of Philadelphia, where Ben and Betsy and Billy Penn forged a more perfect union.

And so will I.

Walking slowly up Chestnut Street, I smile at the chic restaurants and clubs. Beautiful people crowd the streets and I walk around them, not through them. Turning south at Fifth Street, I walk to Locust Street and through the Society Hill neighborhood, with its old trinity houses, narrow alleys, and colonial street lights. When I hit Washington Square, the sister of Rittenhouse Square, I walk through the brick pathways to Walnut Street. Picking up my pace, I pass the Walnut Street Theater with a line of patrons waiting to enter. Wills Eye Hospital is glowing with healing light, as are the buildings of Thomas Jefferson Hospital. At Twelfth Street, I hit the gayborhood, filled with cafés, boutiques, and discos. Then I'm back on Broad Street, and I wonder for the umpteenth time why we don't just call it Fourteenth Street.

Leaning against a street light, I look up and down Broad Street and see the street alive with white lights declaring this the Avenue of the Arts. Restaurants are hustling and bustling. The Kimmel Center for the Performing Arts, the new hope of Philadelphia's cultural community, a giant space ship of light and sound, sits at one end of Broad Street. On the other end of the street is the enormous mansion of the Union League, the bastion of old, white, male, Philadelphia with its grand staircase and prestigious flags. This, too, is the reality of Philadelphia.

Crossing Broad Street, I walk the last few blocks to my

apartment building. In the lobby, I wait patiently for the elevator and when I board it, I look in the mirrored walls and see that I am sweaty and pink and gross. But I want someone to hug me.

I call my mother.

 ## *Chee•tos for the Soul*

She cannot see me so entirely disheveled because it will panic her. While Mom drives over from Jersey, I shower and put myself back into working order.

"This reminds me of the time when you were at Penn," Mom says upon entering my apartment, "and you got really sick and I drove over with some incense and chimes and you felt better the next day."

"I had a hard time living that down," I tell her.

Mom shrugs.

We sit on my sofa and Mom hands me a small wicker basket. What has she brought me now? A candle and tofu? I remove the white linen napkin to find Chee•tos and a Diet Dr Pepper. This is infinitely better than the enormous gourmet basket I received earlier today. I hug my mommy and dive into my goodie basket.

"So what's going on?" Mom asks as I devour the Chee•tos. I lick my fingers. "I'm leaving The Gold Group," I say calmly. I tell her the entire story. Mom listens to me without interrupting. As I explain what little planning I have done for my own company, I get excited about it. "I'm a little afraid," I finish, "but I think it will be a great experience for me to run my own business."

Nodding, Mom pushes her lips together, holding in her comments.

"What's wrong, Mom?"

She shakes her head and smiles falsely. "Nothing."

"You can tell me."

She exhales loudly. "It's a risk, Lexi. An unnecessary risk." I don't say anything, so Mom continues. "The economy is bad. What if you don't find clients? You have a very nice lifestyle. Why jeopardize that?"

I blink a few times, shocked at my mother's lack of support. "I think I can do it, Mom."

"It's not just the money."

"Oh, good." I sag into the couch. "There's more."

"I'm worried about you taking such a big step at this point in your life. Look how long it took Susan to build The Gold Group. Do you really want to dedicate the next few years of your life to work?"

"You mean, instead of getting married and having kids."

Mom smiles wistfully. "I know things didn't work out with Ron, but what if you meet someone else? It would be so difficult for you to get married and have kids and run your own business. That's your big criticism of Susan."

I look at my mother with great tenderness. "Mom, I know that you want grandchildren. It's not going to happen, at least not right now."

"It's not that I want grandchildren. I mean, I do." Mom nods vigorously so I don't think she's letting me off the hook. "But I want you to have children for yourself. Having a child is a wonderful experience," Mom says with tears in her eyes. "You've been such a joy for me. I want you to be happy, Lexi."

"This will make me happy, Mom. At least for now. If I meet

196

someone and want to have children with him, I'll adjust. You and Dad didn't have a conventional relationship and you figured it out. Eventually."

"What did your father say about this?"

"I haven't told him yet."

"You told me first?" Mom asks with undisguised pleasure.

"Mom," I admonish her.

"Sorry," she says quickly.

"I called you because I was looking for comfort. I didn't expect to be the one doing the comforting." I think about my baseball speech to Maria this afternoon, and I wonder why I am consoling people about my own problems. I'm giving the love when I should be feeling the love.

"Sorry," Mom repeats.

"Do you feel better?"

"I guess so." Mom sighs. "Maybe one day you'll marry a nice Jewish boy."

I roll my eyes. "Mom? I'm not Jewish."

"You're half Jewish," she protests.

"Not really."

Mom points to herself. "I'm Jewish."

"Not really."

Mom looks offended, so I smile and give her a hug. "If you were really a Jewish mother," I whisper into her ear, "you would've brought me chicken soup instead of Chee•tos."

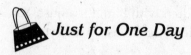

Just for One Day

By 10:45 AM, I have rehearsed my resignation speech three times and I'm ready to deliver it to Susan. Only she's not in her office. I walk to Low Man's desk in the lobby.

"How are we?" he greets me.

"Wonderful. Have you any idea where Susan is?"

Mike bats his eyelashes at me. "I'll give you three guesses."

"She's home? She said she was coming in today."

"Yes, Veep. She did."

"Listen, I'm leaving and I'll be gone the rest of the day."

"What? Where are you going? You can't leave. Who will be in charge of us?"

"You're in charge, Low Man." I smile at him. "Just for one day."

I go to the bank, the office supply store, City Hall, a printer, the post office, and a used furniture shop, and I pay a surprise visit to The Gold Group's law firm to pick up a copy of my contract and noncompete agreement. I'm ready. I feel prepared. Time to call the COG.

The COG Support System

"So that's the story," I finish. The COG is gathered in my apartment later that night. Lola, Grace and Mia are seated at my dining room table, which is now littered with the remnants of food that Lola brought from the restaurant. Ellie is with us via speakerphone, despite the fact that it is almost 1 AM in Paris. This is an emergency session of the COG.

At the other end of the table is the manuscript of Lola's cookbook. Lola has just received it from Ellie, who worked on it more industriously than I thought she would. The manuscript sits there, waiting to be addressed.

"The good news is that my lawyer and I reviewed my noncompete agreement from The Gold Group, and there is nothing contractual to stop me from opening my own PR shop. The noncompete says I couldn't work for another firm. It doesn't say I can't start my own firm."

No one says anything, so I keep talking. "I don't want a firm, though. I want something small. Really small. Like, just me. What I enjoyed about public relations was the work I did in the beginning of my career. Back then, I was involved on a daily basis with my clients. The publicity and the events were geared toward helping their businesses. I made a difference in their lives. That was rewarding. Not financially rewarding. Spiritually rewarding."

"So, you're not hiring anyone?" Mia asks.

Shaking my head, I say, "I couldn't pay anyone."

"You could pay me in hugs."

"What?"

"Sorry. That's what I tell my kids. Listen, I was going to start working at The Gold Group in September."

"Oh God, Mia. I forgot. I'm sorry."

"I don't want to work there if you won't be there. Remember, you said I couldn't work for any PR firm except yours?"

"Yes. I did say that."

"And I was going to work for work, not for money. So you

don't have to pay me. Oh, oh, oh! You can trade me." Mia looks smug.

"Trade you what? What do you need that I can offer?"

"Just yourself." Mia smiles. "Auntie Lex. The ultimate babysitter. So Michael and I can have some time alone."

"You've got a deal, Mia Rose." I get up from the table and hug her until she squeals with delight. Unfortunately, the rest of the COG doesn't seem enthused.

"Lexi, don't you want to take some time off?" Grace asks. "Regroup?"

"No. I'm fine. I'm really excited about this."

"How do we get started?" Mia asks. Grace shoots Mia an irritated look. Mia ignores her. For once, they are in disagreement about my future.

"I made a business plan. It's simple. I'll do the PR work. We," I gesture to Mia, "will do the work. No secretary. No office, even. I'll work out of my apartment. For now."

"How will you get clients?" Grace asks.

"Word of mouth. And there are other clients I've met with over the past year who couldn't afford The Gold Group. But now they can afford me."

"I guess you have it all figured out," Grace says. "You work fast."

"I'm excited," I answer. "Finally, I'm excited about something."

Ellie and Lola haven't said a word. Of course, they don't want to ask selfish questions. Grace, however, has no such qualms. "What about Lola's book and TV show?"

I breathe deeply. "Those contracts are with The Gold Group."

"What does that mean?" Grace asks.

"It means that those projects continue without me."

"We will renegotiate," Lola says, smacking her hands together. *"No importa.* I won't do the book or the show without you."

This is what I wanted to hear. I wanted Lola to be loyal. However, her loyalty is not reality.

"The book is a done deal," I explain. "The cookbook will be published. The Gold Group will get its cut of the royalties. You waived your advance to get the book published in Spanish and English, and that was a big concession for the publisher. You can't risk them welshing on that.

"As for the show, the network made it clear that my name was not enough to get their comfort level to the point where they are willing to produce more episodes. The network wanted The Gold Group behind that project. That was the condition we agreed to. There is no reason to think that my name will be enough now, if it wasn't then."

"No me gusta para nada," Lola says angrily.

"It doesn't matter if you don't like it," I tell her. "That's the way it is."

We sit quietly for a few minutes.

"Your support is overwhelming," I mumble.

"It's a lot to absorb," Grace says. "I'm worried that you'll work even longer hours and focus more completely on your career, and not have time for anything else. I mean, you've sacrificed so much for your work. Do you really want to start all over again? At this stage of your life? I thought you wanted other things."

"I want a lot of things. Right now, I want this thing."

Grace nods as if she understands, but I know she doesn't. "Do you have enough money saved?"

"Yes. One of the advantages of not having kids? Not spending money on them."

Before I detail my plan, Lola smacks her hand on my table and sits up straight. "Listen, *amiga*. If you're going to start your own business, you need to start big. You can't run it out of your apartment. You need a fancy office. A secretary. And we'll have a big party at the restaurant. A big party. *¿Cómo se dice?* A launch party. *¿Sí?*"

I smile indulgently at Lola. She didn't listen to the description of my financial status. She was already envisioning things as she thinks they should be. "I appreciate the offer, but I don't want a launch party. Like I said, I don't want to do anything big. I want to stay small for now. See what happens."

"So, what? You're going to answer your own phone and schedule your own appointments? You can't do that," Lola decrees, shaking her head.

"Why not?"

"People like us don't answer their own phones."

"She'll be fine," Ellie says, giving her opinion for the first time. "If this is what Lexi wants, she'll make it happen. I think it's great. You'll be very successful, Lex." Her words are congratulatory, but her tone is flat.

"Ellie," I ask quietly, "are you mad at me?"

"If you believe that running your own business will make you happy, then I'm all for it. We have to respect each other's decisions. Don't we?"

Ouch. She's right. I get it.

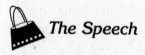 **The Speech**

The office is nearly silent when I get off the elevator at 9:15 AM the next morning. Low Man on the Totem Pole looks at me glumly from his desk and doesn't offer a morning witticism. "Why is it so quiet?" I ask him. "Did you kill everyone?"

"Mommy is in a bad mood," Mike answers.

I wait until 10 AM to buzz Susan's intercom. "Yes?" she barks.

"It's Lexi. I would like to come in and speak with you."

"Come on, then," she says.

We're off to a great start.

Perched on the chair across from Susan's desk, I smile and begin my speech. "I've given this a lot of thought, Susan, and I believe that now is the time for me to resign from The Gold Group. I appreciate how much—"

"No," Susan snaps.

I blink a few times. "Excuse me?"

Sighing loudly, Susan shuffles through a stack of papers on her desk. "I said no. I won't accept your resignation."

"Do you have a choice?"

"We are facing a difficult time, so now is exactly the wrong time to quit." Susan slams her hand on top of her desk, making me jump and ease into my seat, away from her desk. "You're the executive vice president of this company. You're not going anywhere."

"Susan, I don't think you understand. I want to leave."

"And go where? You have a noncompete agreement. You can't work for another PR agency within fifty miles of Philadelphia."

This speech is not going the way I planned. I want to rewind my TelePrompTer and start again. No can do. Oh well. Here goes. "I'm going to start my own company."

Susan looks at me with disdain. "Really? Well good luck to

you." She turns away from me, toward her computer, and starts typing on the keyboard.

"Susan," I try again, "I was hoping that you would be happy for me."

Staring at her computer, Susan says, "Why would I be happy for you? You are abandoning me when I need you the most. You leaving will make my life very complicated. But I don't suppose you care about that."

"I'll stay through next month. The Quaker Insurance fee will cover my salary, and Mike and Michelle's, for the next six weeks."

"I'm firing Michelle."

"I'm sorry to hear that. I guess it's your decision to make."

"Yes, it is." From her computer, Susan looks at me sideways. The anger on her face takes me by surprise. "Will you compile exit reports on all the clients, and finish the next Gold Group quarterly reports so I have a firm handle on the business?"

"Yes, of course."

Susan spins around to her filing cabinet, putting her back to me. I sit still, not sure if I should leave, and not sure if I should ask my last question. Susan looks at me over her shoulder. "Is there something else, Lexi?"

"Yes." Inhale. Exhale. "I'd like to tell the staff that—"

She cuts me off and whips around to face me. "I'll tell the staff when I think it's appropriate. Morale will be low when Michelle leaves. You'll make things worse. Just wait." Susan turns away from me again.

"Okay," I say to her back. What Susan tells the staff doesn't matter. They will ask me for my version, and believe me. And, hopefully, wish me well.

I stand up. Should I say something nice to Susan? Thank her

for the years I spent at The Gold Group? She's too angry right now, I decide. I'll think of my parting words later. I have time.

 ## Guilt

The days proceed quickly. More quickly than ever before. During the day, I prepare for my departure from The Gold Group. Reports, files, and summaries. At night, I prepare for my company. Plans, goals, and budgets. I fall asleep exhausted. My brain hurts.

Because Susan has yet to fire Michelle or tell the staff about my departure, I feel as if I'm living a double life. I don't care for it. It feels like lying.

Mom calls me at the office, which is highly unusual. Picking up the receiver, I ask, "Who died?"

"No one," Mom says. "But you never told your father about your new business plan."

"Balls. I can't believe I forgot to tell him."

"I saw him at the Collingswood May Fair. Which you also forgot to attend. Anyway, I asked Leo what he thought about your business which he knows nothing about," Mom explains. "Needless to say, he was hurt that you hadn't told him. He is your father."

"Yes, he is. I'll call Dad right now. Thanks, Mom."

"James Furniture," a deep voice says over the phone.

"Daddy?" I squeak.

"Yes," my father says with uncharacteristic brusqueness.

Cutting to the chase, I apologize for not telling him my

news sooner. "Mom totally flipped when I told her the news, and I didn't want you to worry. I wanted to have all the details worked out so you would think I had everything under control."

I know it's bad form to play my parents against each other. Tough. Divorced kid's prerogative. Actually? I get more leeway since my parents were never married.

Dad and I chat about the particulars of my venture, and he gives me good advice about accountants and lawyers. Which is, in a nutshell, to listen to their advice but make my own business decisions. "You have to trust your gut," Dad tells me. He's right, and he's clearly forgiven me for delivering the news late. Fences mended, we hang up. I still feel guilty. Tired and guilty. More tired than guilty. More tired than anything.

 ## Ellie Returns

On a hot June Friday, I wait for Ellie at the baggage claim area of Philadelphia International Airport. We can no longer meet our traveling friends at the gate, so baggage claim has to suffice. It's less romantic, but so is the world. Still, it's nice when someone is there to welcome you home.

Ellie has been gone for almost a month and I've missed her desperately. We've e-mailed, but it's not the same. I crane my neck to catch sight of her the minute she descends from the escalator. Finally, I see her and I put my arms in the air to get her attention. Then, I'm struck by how beautiful she looks.

Ellie is smiling, and she's not smiling at me because she hasn't seen me yet. She's just smiling. At nothing. At everything.

Lowering my arms to my sides, I stare at Ellie. She looks

like a different person. She is different, and I realize that I don't know this version of Ellie. She is experiencing something without me. Ellie has let herself fall in love.

There is a part of her life, now, in which I am not involved.

Again, I feel the distance between me and Ellie. This makes me sad.

"*Bonjour! Comment ça va?*" Ellie asks as she gives me the three-kiss friendship kiss, then takes a step back.

There it is, that distance now literal. I can't bear it. Dropping my purse to the floor, I wrap Ellie in a giant hug. She lets me hold on to her and whispers in my ear. "Have you worked very hard?" Her English is slipping.

"Yes," I answer and pull away, letting her think that my emotion is stress-related. Ellie smiles sadly and puts her arm around me. "It all will be good," she says. We walk to the baggage carousel.

Ellie looks down at me. "Am I talking funny?"

"A little," I tell her. "Welcome to America."

"It sounds like you're going through a divorce," Ellie says as we load her luggage into Lola's Jaguar. In telling Ellie about the last few weeks at The Gold Group, I've described my recent sensations of loss and freedom. "You were at TGG for, what? A decade? And it's not a clean break because you continue to work there. It's like you're legally separated but still living in the same house. That your staff feels the tension is not a surprise. Sounds like kids reacting to their parents' divorce."

"So in this scenario, I'm married to Susan?"

Ellie laughs and we get into the car. Before I turn the ignition, I look at Ellie. "I felt like we left things on a bad note. That day we had brunch? Before you left for Paris? That whole library book analogy? And then when we were talking on the day I told the COG about my new business, I thought you were upset with me. About the book thing. Not the library book thing. The cookbook thing. That I can't be a part of it."

Ellie nods and thinks quietly. "It's funny, Lex. When you told the whole COG about your business plan, I thought, 'This is a huge thing. Why didn't she tell me first?' Now I know how you felt when I showed up in Chinatown with Jean-François and told everyone that we were engaged. It's that feeling of being left out of your girlfriend's life." Ellie smiles at me. "It sucks."

I smile back at Ellie. "I wasn't trying to get back at you. That didn't even occur to me."

"I know," Ellie says. "It's just the way things sometimes happen."

We are quiet again, then I say, "I really do like Jean-François. And you look beautiful. Must be love."

"Or it could be all the cheese and wine and bread I ate."

"Well, then this will be a real change of pace." From my purse, I pull a package of Kandy Kakes, the peanut butter and chocolate Tastykakes. Ellie laughs with delight. *"Merci beaucoup. Et toi?"* I hold up my Butterscotch Krimpets.

"Voilà!"

 ## Mademoiselle Archer

The entire COG will momentarily assemble for dinner in my apartment. Ellie changes out of her sweater and skirt and into shorts and a button-down Oxford that reaches her knees, and obviously belongs to Jean-François. Ellie hugs herself, and I think she must miss him already. That touches me deeply. "Do you want to call Jean-François and tell him you arrived safely?" Ellie smiles her appreciation. "If you want privacy, use the phone in my room."

"I won't be long," she promises. I make a mental note to get an international calling plan.

Grace stumbles into my apartment and hurls herself at my couch. Grace's green scrub top is hospital-issue and clashes with her plum scrub pants. That means someone vomited or bled on Grace's own top and she had to change. "Do not ask me about my day," Grace moans.

"No problem," I answer. Grace releases her tote bag and it falls to the floor, spilling bridal magazines.

"Aunt Gracie!" Simon Rose bursts through the door and makes a running jump toward Grace, diving onto her belly. Climbing over Grace's organs and ribs, Simon moves upward until his face is directly above hers. "You smell funny," he tells her seriously.

"Come here, Baby Sy!" Squatting, I hold open my arms. Grace groans as Simon uses her body as a springboard to jump into my hug. "Kisses," I insist. We rub noses.

"*¿Dónde está Tia Lola?*" Simon asks.

"*Tu español es muy bueno.*" Mia now takes Simon to Chicos y Chicas, a Spanish class for preschoolers.

"*Muchas gracias. ¿Dónde está Tia Lola?*"

"*No sé. ¿Dónde está tu madre?*"

Simon shrugs. He scales down my body until his feet touch the floor. "Who else is here?" Simon runs into my room, barging through the door. "Aunt Ellie!" I hear Ellie squeal as Simon jumps on top of her.

Lola rushes into my apartment with a loud, cheery, "*¡Hola!*"

In her hands are silver containers of food. Our dinner. At Lola's voice, Simon rushes out of the bedroom and runs to Lola. "*¡Tía Lola, Tía Lola!*"

"Ah, ah, ah," Lola raises her palm and Simon skids to a halt. "*Cuidado, Simon. Caliente. Muy caliente.*" Lola brings the food to me in the kitchen, then returns to Simon, who is standing exactly where Lola left him. She kneels down and picks up Simon. "*¡Besos! ¡Quiero muchos besos!*" Simon and Lola kiss each others cheek's, back and forth, back and forth, and count, "*Uno, dos, tres, cuatro, cinco, seis.*"

At *seis*, Mia appears at my door. "Simon, if you want to take the steps, you have to wait for me and not run ahead."

"I'm busy, Mommy," Simon answers.

"Lola!" I call. "Did you bring the forks? If not, we have to use chopsticks."

Glowing, Ellie comes out of my bedroom. I watch her as she leans against the doorjamb and smiles. Is she smiling at the commotion in my apartment? Or is she smiling at something else? Something I can't see?

"Give me the salsa," Grace says to Lola. We're sitting at my dining room table devouring Lola's food. With forks. Which Mia washed.

"Say please, Aunt Gracie," Simon singsongs.

"Please," Grace mumbles.

"Say *por favor*. Say that, Aunt Gracie."

"Lola?" Grace whines. Lola passes her the salsa.

"I don't remember the arrondissements," Mia tells Ellie. "What is it near?"

Ellie is telling us about Jean-François's apartment. Flat. Jean-François's flat. "The Sorbonne, where Jean-François teaches, is in the fifth arrondissement." Ellie makes a circle of plantain chips. "You understand?" We nod. "The flat is in the sixteenth arrondissement." Moving northwest, Ellie makes another pile of plantains. She puts a shrimp on the eastern edge of the second plantain arrondissement. "*Voilà*. That is our flat."

Our flat. Language shifts aside, Ellie considers the flat to be theirs.

"Do you like the flat?" Lola asks with a mouth full of frijoles.

"It's gorgeous. It is small, but not too small. The neighborhood is very nice. Jean-François decided to live in a small apartment in a nice neighborhood instead of a giant apartment in a district that is not so good.

"The best part is the bedroom. The walls? They're painted warm yellow. The trim is wood. Beautiful French doors go to a little balcony."

"What do they call French doors in France?" I want to know.

"Doors," Ellie answers. Lola throws a stalk of sugarcane at me.

"*¡Tia Lola!*" Simon is horrified.

"*Lo siento mucho,*" she apologizes.

"The windows of the balcony door? They're covered in sheer fabric which lets in beautiful, diffused sunlight which reaches all the way to the bed. Jean-François has a mahogany sleigh bed." Abruptly, Ellie stops talking.

In my experience, when a woman stops talking to her girlfriends about the sex she is having with a man, it means she is in love with him. They are no longer having sex. They are making love. Women don't gossip about making love because sharing it with friends betrays its intimacy.

"Do you like sleeping in a sleigh bed?" Grace asks Ellie.

Ellie smiles. "I like waking up in it."

*   *   *

After dinner, we clear my dining room table. Mia sets up Simon with crayons and a coloring book. Café con leches in hand, we reassemble at my table. Grace begins her wedding pow-wow. "Okay, people. The date is set for the last Saturday in September. That means we have a little more than three months. The clock is ticking."

She spreads out her magazines, each dogeared to a dress, floral arrangement, or favor. Grace has swatches of fabric, cassette tapes and CDs of bands and disc jockeys, menus and proposals. "What does your fiancé want?" I ask. Grace sets her face into a mighty fake smile. "Michael said to narrow every decision down to two options and then he'll give me his opinion. He is so busy at work. You know how it is."

Two hours later, Simon has fallen asleep on the floor and we all want to join him. But it is Ellie whom Grace chides for not paying close attention. "You're going to have to do this, too," Grace warns her. Ellie smiles, and I know she's not thinking about napkin colors. She's thinking about that sleigh bed.

 ## Saturday Afternoon with the Parents

My mother has reached the age where she makes lists, then makes lists of her lists. She leaves notes for herself, then leaves herself notes about where to find the notes. So it goes.

She may misplace notes, but Gloria Northstein never loses a coupon or sale notice. Despite the fact that my mother and stepfather have more than enough money to pay for whatever they want, Mom will never pay retail for anything. Not appliances, not clothes, not toothpaste, not grapefruit. Mom will have a coupon, a credit card discount, a raincheck, or something. She will drive twenty minutes to the wholesale fruit market to pay ten cents less for the four grapefruit she eats every week.

Why? From what I understand, Mom believes that paying a discounted price for something cheats "the man" out of his profits. That brings her joy. It's a sixties thing. Whatever.

When Mom picks me up on Saturday morning, she hands me a pile of coupons and store circulars. Of course, I don't need anything, and if I really needed something, I could buy it myself. But that wouldn't be any fun. It's the middle of June and stores have just started discounting their summer stock. Bargains abound.

"Which?" Mom asks. This is code for: based on the information you are now holding in your hand, which mall has the most stores offering the best coupons and discounts?

"Cherry Hill," I answer. Macy's issued a coupon for 15 percent off clothing and shoes, with an additional 10 percent discount for store credit card holders. We have a winner.

While she drives, I look at my mom. I remember when I thought she was the prettiest mom in town. She is still pretty, but she has mellowed into being attractive. Mom has big brown eyes, great eyelashes, and fabulous eyebrow arches. She has never cut off her long, wavy hair. She won't admit to it, but I know she colors her hair to get it to its natural amber shade. She still wears those long, medallion earrings from the seventies. And she's never lost her passion for turquoise. Her collection includes turquoise earrings, turquoise rings, and an especially intricate turquoise belt that Mom sometimes wears over her flowing skirts and dresses. I happen to know that my mother owns a pair of jeans, but she never wears them in public. It's always skirts and dresses. To honor the mother goddess. Or something like that.

"What's the matter?" she asks, glancing at me. Looking at Mom's profile, I smile.

"Yer purty," I drawl.

"Beauty comes from within, Lexi."

"Just say thank you, Mom."

"Thank you." Mom smiles. Then, she smacks her hand to her forehead. "Lexi," she says, "look on the backseat for a yellow pad of paper."

I look. "I don't see it."

"Look harder."

Look harder? The backseat is empty, but I turn around and stare at it. I know Mom is stalling, trying to remember where she put this pad of paper. "Oh, Lexi," Mom says suddenly. "Look in the bag on the floor. The brown paper bag. On the floor. Under the seat. There should be a yellow piece of paper."

I look. "Eureka."

"What does it say?" She can remember where the piece of paper is, but not what it says.

I unfold the piece of paper. In big block letters, it reads IN-TAKE ON SATURDAY. I hold up the paper for Mom to see.

"Crap," she says. "I had a feeling I was supposed to be somewhere other than here. Sorry." Mom turns the car around at the next intersection.

Mom manages the Magic Hanger, a consignment shop that sells used clothing at low prices to underprivileged women and their children. This not only suits my mother's discount discipline, but it jives with her theory of reincarnation. Even clothes, she says, deserve a second chance at life.

After helping Mom sort clothes for a while, I get bored. Mom gives me leave to call my father. His furniture shop is a few miles from the Magic Hanger.

"James Furniture," Dad answers in his smoky baritone.

"Hi, Daddy," I squeal. Mom rolls her eyes.

"Alexandra the Great," he says, and I am happy to be restored to my place of honor in his heart. "Whatcha doin'?"

"I'm at the Magic Hanger," I answer. "Wanna drive me home?"

My father laughs. "If your mother drives you over here, I'll drive you home."

Mom agrees. See? It's like car pool. Some things never change.

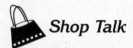 ## Shop Talk

James Furniture is on Hadden Avenue in Collingswood, a quaint town that is the polar opposite of the condominiumed, strip-malled Cherry Hill. Dad's shop is a storefront displaying the furniture and a full workshop in the back. The shop smells of wood, shellac, and testosterone.

The shop's simple name belies the high-end furniture and its hefty prices. The shop has been open for almost thirty years, and Dad has focused so much love and attention on it that James Furniture is like a younger sister to me. As such, we have a sibling rivalry.

James Furniture, like me, is quite successful. Like me, she brings great joy to my father. She is a high-maintenance endeavor; to bring out her best, she requires an expert touch, the proper tools, and genuine appreciation for her medium. Like me.

*   *   *

"Hello girls," Dad greets me and Mom as we enter the shop. Mom blushes. I watch.

My father is a handsome man. Somewhere around six feet tall, Dad has straight, light brown hair, bright blue eyes accented with crow's feet, and the full mouth I inherited. Dad calls himself a manual laborer, and has a muscular lankiness and blistered hands, but he is also an artist and has a confident individuality.

Dad returns Mom's blush with a special smile. Although I really don't want to know about it, I understand that my parents had a white-hot passion for each other. At the dinner following his second wedding, my father, champagne bottle in hand, waltzed me around the dance floor. "She's a nice lady," I told him, referring to his new wife.

"Yeah," Dad answered and took a chug of champagne. "But I'll never love another woman like I loved your mother." He was telling me this hours after he married another woman who was not my mother. Shocked and saddened, I couldn't think of anything to say.

"Why?" was the only word that came out of my mouth. What I meant was: why did you marry your first wife? why did you marry your second wife? why did you let Mom go?

Misinterpreting the question, or dodging it entirely, Dad answered, "Because she gave me you." And I knew he was lying through his twice married teeth.

Mom is the one who got all mature and wanted a stable life. Mom made her choice and got the husband and house she wanted. But still. Mom must remember that physical connection. If she didn't, she wouldn't blush.

Truly, I hate to think about my parents' relationship with

each other and what it means to me. When I was a little girl, I wanted my parents to be normal. Divorced. Like other kids' parents. Because then I would know the rules of the relationship. The rules of any relationship.

Dad hustles me into his shiny red pickup truck. It's an antique, lovingly restored by my father. Tossing my torso into the cab, I swing my legs around until they fit under the dashboard. I'm tall enough to get into the truck like a normal person, but I've been launching myself into Dad's truck like that since I was a little girl. I like it. It makes Dad laugh.

"We have to hustle," Dad says as he drives down Haddon Avenue. "Mary Ann's sister and her husband are visiting and I'm cooking dinner, and I have to shower and change." Dad looks down at his faded jeans flecked with mahogany varnish. He shakes his head, disapproving of his appearance. But he's wearing the same thing he's worn my entire life. Beat-up jeans and a T-shirt.

One autumn of my childhood, when I was maybe six or seven years old, my father was between wives and girlfriends, so he and I spent a lot of time alone. Dad would pick me up from school and take me to the shop, where I could accomplish some very, very, very important chore that only I could do for him. Like stamp "Paid" on the invoices. Then we would go to his house and cook dinner together. Not just macaroni and cheese, but real meals with salad and a main course and dessert. After that, we would fall asleep in the hammock in Dad's backyard. I would rest my head against Dad's soft T-shirt, smoothed by many, many washings, and I would close my eyes to listen to the birds and squirrels, and drift off. When I woke up in the morning, I'd be in my room and I would know that Dad carried me upstairs and put me safely in my bed.

". . . and a wasabi dipping sauce to go with the grilled tuna." I realize Dad is describing the dinner he intends to cook for his in-laws.

"Sounds a little fancy for the shrew from Shreveport." My father's wife's sister has disapproved of Dad since the day she met him. That hasn't stopped her from staying in my Dad's house or eating his food. "Why are you so nice to her?"

"Sometimes, when you are married, it's easier to do something you don't want to do than not do it."

"What? That made no sense."

"You'll understand someday, Lexi."

"Yeah? When?"

I know he's about to say "when you get married," but he stops himself. Because at the rate I'm going, I may never get married. Instead he says, "Someday. Someday, Lexi."

 ## Dress Shopping: The Bride

"Twirl."

At the clerk's command, Grace twirls. Standing on the dais, arms outstretched, on her tiptoes, smiling widely, Grace spins slowly in front of three mirrors. White layers of organza float around Grace's knees. "It's dreamy," she tells the saleswoman, who is nodding with a smile ironed onto her face and hope in her raised eyebrows. Grace looks at me. I know she wants to ask, "Is this the one?" But she dare not.

On the floor of the dressing room, I am sitting with my legs crossed, breathing deeply and trying not to throttle the bride. This is the twenty-third dress Grace has modeled today.

We are at Maria Romia, a posh boutique just off Rittenhouse Square. We started the day at Suky Rosan, another posh boutique in a posh Philadelphia suburb. "We'll go there first," Grace told me this morning, and I was hoping that by "first," she meant first and last. What she really meant was that we'd spend two hours at Suky Rosan, try on every dress available, critique every little bit of each one, then move to Nordstrom's and go through the same process, then make a ten-minute pit stop at David's Bridal, then go to Saks Fifth Avenue, and finally arrive here at Maria Romia. My efforts to remain alert but calm have included three café lattes, a pack of Bubble Yum, and a gallon of water with lemon, which is what these bridal salons serve.

Now I am on the edge of a bridal breakdown.

I should have known that Grace would be unable to make a painless decision about such an important matter. "It has to be the perfect dress," Grace informed every sales clerk, and every clerk lied and said, "You'll find it here."

But they don't know my Gracie. From where I sit on the floor, I see Grace frown into the mirrors. No dress will be perfect. Because Grace can't see herself as anything approaching perfection, no dress will make her so. It's up to us, her friends, to tell her which dress is the perfect one.

But it's only me here with Grace. Ellie flew back to Paris. Lola is working at the restaurant. Mia has a Simon and David filled day.

"Do you think it's too *Ally McBeal*?" Grace asks me. The strapless bias-cut dress was too Hollywood. The dress with the draped neckline was too *Dynasty*. The spaghetti-strapped crepe sheath was too *Saturday Night Fever*. The dress which

Grace is currently modeling is an empire-waisted gown with beaded lace detailing and a skirt that ends above the knee.

"I think a long skirt is more appropriate for you," I answer honestly. The clerk exhales with quiet frustration. Grace frowns with gusto and spins around to inspect her backside in the mirror. "No," she declares. Grace walks to the rack of thirteen dresses she previously discarded, and I realize she may try each of them on again. That cannot happen. I must end this nightmare. I've negotiated million-dollar deals. I can negotiate this dress business to a satisfactory conclusion. How?

I think I've had too much caffeine to be tactful. "Gracie?"

She turns to look at me. "Oh, sweetie," she coos and rushes to me. Bending over me in her white lace froth, Grace says, "You look so unhappy. Are you thinking about your wedding dress?"

Staring up at her, I say, "I am now."

The truth is, I never bought a wedding dress. My mom and the COG offered to go shopping with me, but I declined. I went to one store, tried on three dresses, and put one on hold. I never went back for the dress. The engagement was broken the next week.

If I had done serious shopping for my wedding dress, I would've wanted Mia with me. Or Ellie. Or Lola. Anybody but me. That's right, I wouldn't want me to help me buy my wedding dress. I'd be my last choice as a dress consultant. This whole "dress of my dreams" thing seems silly to me. I have yet to have a dream about a wedding dress. Only nightmares.

My cell phone ringing interrupts my internal monologue and I see Mia's cell phone number appear in my ID display. "Mia," I whisper, "save me."

"Not going well?" Mia asks seriously.

"No" is all I can muster.

"What's happening?"

"She doesn't like any of the dresses."

"Don't whisper about me," Grace says from the other side of the room. "I hate that."

"She doesn't like anything?" Mia asks. "Not one dress? How many has she tried?"

"Eleven here." I keep whispering. "Twenty-three total. And she went shopping with her mom yesterday and tried on eighteen other dresses. How many freaking kinds of wedding dresses are there? She's probably tried on dresses twice without realizing it."

"Put Grace on the phone," Mia commands.

Holding out my cell, I stand and walk toward Grace. "Mia wants to talk to you," I tell her, as if we've misbehaved, gotten caught, and are about to be reprimanded. Grace takes my phone and says cheerfully, "Hi, sweetie." While Grace listens, I retreat to a chaise longue.

"Forty-one," Grace says. She listens.

"I don't have a feeling about any of them," Grace says. She listens.

"Yes, I've seen dresses like that, but I haven't tried them on because I didn't think that they would—" She listens.

"Really?" Grace sounds pleased and surprised. She listens.

"I think you're right, Mia," she says resolutely. She listens.

"You are absolutely right." Grace nods. She listens.

"Okay. Thank you so much for calling." She listens.

"I love you, too," Grace says and hangs up the phone. Tossing my cell to me, she says, "Stay here. I'll be right back." Out into the boutique she swishes. The clerk looks at me. I shrug.

One minute later, Grace returns with a dress and the clerk hustles into the dressing room to help her get into it.

Several grunts and groans later, Grace emerges from the dressing room, ascends the dais, and stares at herself in the mirrors. The gown is an A-line, spaghetti-strapped, ivory lace dress with a satin ribbon at the waist. Shyly, Grace smiles at her reflection. "Wow," she says.

"I second that wow. It's perfect, Grace."

The clerk, smiling at long last, says, "This is called a princess dress."

Grace beams. "That's what Mia called it. A princess dress." Grace twirls one final time.

 ## *Referral: The Doctor*

That Mia? She's a freaking genius.

Leaving Grace at Maria Romia to pay for her princess dress, I walk through Rittenhouse Square, find an empty bench, and collapse. It's a gorgeously hot day, and the square is filled with people eating, reading, kissing, sleeping, and talking. A dread-locked white boy sits on the grass playing acoustic guitar. Delighted to be in the fresh air, I close my eyes and tilt my face to the sun.

My cell phone rings. It's Grace, and I think about not answering. Have I not fulfilled my Coordinator of Hoopla duties for the day? What on earth could she possibly need me to do now?

"I forgot to tell you about Mark," Grace says.

"Who is Mark?"

"He's a doctor. He's smart. He's cute. He's single." Grace is speed talking, which means that I'm not going to like what she says.

"The four of us were going to have dinner tonight. Me and Michael and you and Mark. Except Michael forgot to tell me that we are having a Kelly family dinner and I forgot to tell Michael that we had plans with you and Mark. So I called Mark and explained the situation, and he agreed that you two should have dinner without us, and he's picking you up at 6 PM."

"Grace!"

"Everybody at the hospital tries to set him up with their friends, and Mark never agrees. He's a cardiologist and he's very selective. With women and with patients. It's very hard to get an appointment with him. Mark only agreed to this because I talked you up so much. I gave you a great referral." Grace chuckles at her joke.

"You could have asked me first."

"Lexi, don't start with me. I'm planning a wedding." From now until September, that is Grace's Get Out of Hot Water pass.

"Call Dr. Mark back and tell him that I can't make it," I command.

"No," Grace barks. "It's five o'clock and it would be rude to cancel now."

Dr. Mark picks me up at 6 PM on the dot. I meet him in the lobby of my building. He's better-looking than I imagined, with brown hair clipped close to his head and warm brown eyes. Dr. Mark is two heads taller than me and looks fit. He's wearing summery beige pants and a pale blue button-down shirt open at the collar.

In his Audi, we drive over the Ben Bridge to Cinnaminson, New Jersey, and Dr. Mark parks in front of Fuji Mountain, one of the best Japanese restaurants in the area. The wild creations of sushi, sashimi, tempura, and vegetables keep us eating for hours. We talk about work, and in an attempt to seem stable, I gloss over my impending departure from The Gold Group.

Dr. Mark refuses my offer to split the bill, or leave the tip. We drive back to my building with the windows rolled down to let in the cool breeze, singing along to the radio station that plays hits from the eighties.

Walking me to the door of my building, Dr. Mark suggests another date. I agree. He leans forward to kiss me and I turn my head to give Dr. Mark my cheek.

Upstairs, I call Grace and tell her about the date. She commends me for not screwing Dr. Mark. "You see? There's hope for you after all." Hope? That's not the name of this feeling. I turn on my computer and find Ellie on line, which makes me happy. I instant message her.

lexi:	Deadline, insomnia, or jet lag?
ellie:	A tragic combo of all three. I called earlier. Where were you?
lexi:	A date. Gracie set me up with someone.
ellie:	How did it go?
lexi:	I performed well.
ellie:	Performed? Explain.
lexi:	I felt like I was acting. Like a different version of myself. A mature, sophisticated version of myself.
ellie:	Hmmmm . . .

lexi: It's not bad that I acted mature and sophisticated. Those are good things to be. Maybe dating Dr. Mark will bring out those qualities.

ellie: You don't need him to bring out those qualities!!

lexi: Sometimes I wonder . . .

ellie: You shouldn't feel like you're acting when you're with someone. You should be yourself. Oui?

lexi: Oui.

 ## Passing of the Throne

"You're early," Low Man tells me Monday morning.

I look at my watch. "It's nine o'clock, Mike." He smirks at me. "Hardy har, Low Man."

Heading into the conference room, I take my seat at the head of the table. Low Man follows me in and joins the rest of the staff as we settle in for our monthly Monday morning staff meeting. Susan rushes in, face flushed, hair askew. She heaves a pile of manila folders onto the table and sits in her chair at the opposite end of the table. Susan looks around the table. "Everyone is here. Good. Let's get started."

"The first order of business," Susan and I say at the same time. Surprised, I look at her. Annoyed, she looks back at me.

"The first order of business," Susan continues, "is the announcement that Lexi is leaving The Gold Group at the end of this month."

Everyone gasps, including me. I had no idea that Susan was going to tell the staff today. Ignoring the shocked reaction, Susan keeps talking. "Lexi has decided to start her own little company." The staff starts whispering. Susan raises her voice. "I have appointed Maria Simons as The Gold Group's new vice president. Congratulations, Maria." Susan claps loudly and everyone, including me, joins her. Through my shock, I note that Maria's title is vice president, whereas mine is— was—executive vice president. Susan is playing power games with Maria already. That's not my problem. Not anymore. I am genuinely happy for Maria. She deserves the promotion.

"Thank you," Maria acknowledges the applause. She does not look surprised, which means she knew this announcement was coming. Maria smiles down the table at me. "I'll do my best to follow the example Lexi set."

"Thank you, Maria," I say warmly.

Susan doesn't like that one bit. "As our new vice president, Maria is going to lead this meeting," she snaps. "Maria? Why don't you take Lexi's seat so you can see everyone?" All heads swivel toward me, waiting for a reaction.

"I'm fine here," Maria answers.

I swallow hard and tell myself that Susan is acting immature and I should be the grown-up in this situation. In my cool professional voice, I say, "Susan's right, Maria. You should sit here." I smile at Maria. "Better view." Gathering my papers, I stand up and hold out the chair for her. Maria gets up and approaches the chair as if it is a throne she will ascend. Which it is.

Holding my head high, I walk around the table and take the seat Maria abandoned. "Go ahead," I encourage Maria.

"Since this is the first Monday of the month," Maria starts in a shaky voice, "the first order of business, or the second, is new business."

"No," Susan interrupts again. "You and I can discuss new

business privately." Susan inclines her head toward me. She clearly doesn't want to discuss business leads in front of me, and she has let everyone know that. Ouch.

Sensing that the staff is appalled at Susan's behavior gives me strength. With my face frozen into a smile, I look at Susan. "I can step out of the room, if you like."

"Not necessary," Susan answers without looking at me. "Maria, continue with the redistribution of the clients that will take place when Lexi is gone."

And so the meeting continues.

Maria adjourns the meeting, and I walk quickly to my office and shut the door. Standing in the middle of what was my haven from the rest of the world, I begin to feel the emotions that I blocked during the meeting. Anger. Sadness. Fear.

"Veep?" Low Man calls through the intercom. "Mark is on line four."

"Mark who?"

"He said it was a personal call."

"Thank you."

Who is Mark? When I answer the phone, my voice reaches for a professional coolness, but there is too much emotion in it. "Are you okay?" Dr. Mark asks.

"Fine. What's up?"

"Are you free for dinner tonight?"

Running my hand through my hair, I exhale a little too loudly. "Bad day?" Dr. Mark asks. Should I tell him what's really wrong? The only alternative is to lie. I have a feeling that Dr. Mark will not be enthused about my exodus from TGG and the genesis of my company. And I'm right.

"That's going to take a lot of energy," he says. "And time."
There's that word again. "With my schedule, it's already difficult to find time for a relationship." I let Dr. Mark say his piece
in peace. He goes on and on about the demands of his medical
practice. Sure, he's saving lives, but I'm trying to save my own
life. While Dr. Mark talks, and I pull up Brick Blasta on my
computer. I am determined to beat Joshua Gold-Berg's high
score before I leave The Gold Group. "What's all that beep-
ing?" Dr. Mark asks.

"Must be on your end." I put the game on mute.

Dr. Mark winds up speech."You starting your own company, I mean, that won't leave you with a lot of free time."

"You don't have to make excuses or apologies, Mark. We're
just in different places in our lives." Ding, ding! I got within
fifteen points of Joshua's score.

"Why don't you call me when get some free time?" Dr.
Mark asks.

"Okay" is my flat comment.

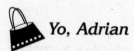 ## Yo, Adrian

The next day, Maria and I go to Independence Hotel for a
meeting with the accountants who have taken control of the
hotel's books. Maria can't do the meeting without me, because
we have to review four years' worth of bills for retainers and
expenses incurred by The Gold Group on behalf of the hotel.
The past is my domain, but the future is Maria's. So, when talk
turns to future procedures, I excuse myself. "I'll be back," I
whisper to Maria.

Walking through the nearly abandoned hotel is eerie. There

is a skeleton staff still working to accommodate the smattering of guests. Wandering into the restaurant, I find it dark, empty of customers and servers. It's rather depressing. I walk to the enormous windows and look out into the garden, which is still intact.

"Hey," a voice says from behind me. Startled, I turn to see Adrian Salvo. "Sorry," he says. "I didn't mean to scare you."

"Don't worry about it. What are you doing here?"

"I have an appointment with the accountants. You, too?"

I nod and imagine the owners of Independence Hotels shaking in their shoes at the thought of owing money to Adrian Salvo. Maybe he's not connected, but I wouldn't want to take that risk.

Subtly, I give Adrian the once-over. He's left his *Rocky I* look at the warehouse and brought his *Rocky III* look. Navy suit, crisp white shirt with twinkling cuff links, maroon tie with white stripes, a diamond pinkie ring, a Rolex on one wrist and a gold rope bracelet on the other.

"How you been?" Adrian asks me.

"Fine. Great. You?"

"Can't complain." Adrian bobs his head. "Listen, I'm sorry that we didn't sign with The Gold Group. I liked what you said, but Pop wanted to stick with the Baxter Brothers. You know how it is."

"I understand."

"You get my produce arrangement?"

"Yes. I should have thanked you for it earlier."

"You can thank me now." Adrian comes to a stop in front of me and smiles with his mouth closed. "Maybe it's better that we're not working together."

"Why?"

"A girl like you? I bet you don't get involved with your clients." Adrian shrugs. "I'm not a client." He smiles. "You can take me up on that dinner offer. How about tonight?"

"I'm flattered, but I'll have to decline."

Adrian raises his right eyebrow. "You wanna just cut to the chase?"

"Sorry?"

"Come on. I know women. You've been checking me out since we met." Adrian looks at me like he's expecting a response, but I'm speechless. "There's a lot of empty hotel rooms upstairs. I don't have to meet with the accountants for, like, twenty minutes."

"Twenty minutes?"

"Yeah. You're right. That's not enough time. Women your age? Takes a little longer to get the juices flowing."

If possible, I am more speechless.

"Don't worry." Adrian keeps talking. "I'll take good care of you." He winks.

It's the wink that snaps my brain back into working order. "I knew this was going to happen. My friends thought I was making a big deal out of nothing."

"Hey, babe. Not for nothing." Adrian looks at his crotch. "But this ain't nothing."

Shaking my head at Adrian, I say, "And Lola said I was exaggerating."

"Lola?" Adrian releases his hold on himself. "Lola Bravia? You know her?"

"Yes. She's one of my best friends."

Looking at me with pity, Adrian says, "You should both be grateful to me."

"Grateful? What for?"

"How many invitations do single women your age get? Me? I like a challenge. The problem is, you get attached. It's so good, you can't get enough."

"Adrian?"

"Yeah, babe?"

"I cannot imagine the kind of woman who would sleep with you, but let me assure that I am not one of them. You wouldn't know what to do with a woman like me. I'm out of your league."

Adrian looks at the floor, then lifts his head slightly and looks at me with a nasty squint. "Yo, Lexi. Your friend Lola?" He grabs his crotch. "She can't get enough of this. So you tell me. What kind of woman is she?"

"Lexi?" I turn to see Maria standing in the middle of the empty restaurant. Her mouth is hanging open. Adrian quickly releases his crotch and puts both hands on his waist. I am too shocked by Adrian's accusation to say anything, but I walk toward Maria. Adrian grabs my arm. "We're not done here," he says.

"I'll see you back at the office," Maria says, and runs off. I turn back to Adrian.

"Looks like you don't know your friend Lola very well." Adrian shakes his head at me.

"I don't believe you."

"Really? Well, I'm over her house almost every night. She leaves the door open for me."

That time I called Lola late at night and she answered by saying, "The door is unlocked." Did she think it was Adrian calling?

"And it's not just at night. Sometimes she wants a little pick-me-up during the day. She was all nervous about this big meeting about her cookbook, right? She was all stressed out. I told her I couldn't do anything because I was working at the warehouse. So what does she do? Comes down there in black stretch pants, gold jewelry, see-through top. We did it in my office. It made her late to her meeting, but she said it was worth it."

That meeting was with me. I had no idea she was late because she made a booty call at the nasty Food Distribution Center. My head starts to spin, and I feel vomit rising in my throat. "You're a pig, Adrian."

"Yeah?" Adrian smirks. "You know what pigs eat? Scraps of food that no one else wants. Just like Lola." Turning his back to me, Adrian walks toward the door.

"Yo, Adrian." He turns around. I slap him across the face.

 ## Who's Screwing Who

"Yo, Veep." Low Man greets me when I stride off the elevator.

"No more 'yo,' Low Man. I am banning 'yo' from this office. Spread the word."

"Will do." Low Man salutes me.

I cannot believe that Lola didn't tell me about Adrian. Is it true? Could he be lying?

Maria is waiting for me in my office. "You should have told me," she spits.

"Told you what?" Carefully, I sit in my chair so as not to fall over.

"That you are screwing Adrian Salvo."

"What?"

Maria springs from my couch and marches to my desk. Glaring at me, she hovers over my desk. "I asked if anything was going on between you two. You said no. And then, there you are in the hotel together." Maria's voice rises as she continues. "Is that where you had your rendezvous? The Independence? Guess you'll have to find a new spot."

"Maria."

"You lied to me, Lexi." Now she's shouting.

"Calm down. I did not lie to you. There's nothing going on between me and Adrian. You misunderstood the situation." I swallow hard, finding the words difficult to say. "It seems that Adrian and Lola are a couple."

"Adrian and Lola?"

"Yes." I close my eyes and inhale through my nose. "Although I don't see how this is any of your business."

"It is my business. It is exactly my business, Lexi."

I can't focus on Maria's words. Lola's hootchie mamma outfit swims in my head.

"Did you do anything to compromise The Gold Group getting the Salvo account?"

With my eyes closed, I quietly ask, "Why would I compromise the Salvo account?"

"To have it for yourself. For your new company."

I open my eyes and glare at Maria. "I can't believe you said that."

"Salvo would have been a huge coup for me. And Susan."

"Oh, I see. Now it's 'me and Susan.' "

"It would've been a coup for you, too, Lexi. We worked hard to get that account. Maybe we didn't get the account because old man Salvo is loyal to the Baxter Brothers. Or maybe you made a deal with Adrian to decline The Gold Group so he could sign with your new company. You get the client and Lola gets the Italian Stallion." Maria pauses to swallow.

In my calm PR voice, I say, "Maria, please. Why are you acting like this?"

"You're leaving. I'm staying. This is my shot. How often does a lesbian of mixed races get named vice president of anything? Do you think Susan wanted to make me her VP? No. She didn't. But she didn't have a choice. There's no one else nearly as qualified, and Susan doesn't have time to do an executive search. Or maybe she's doing a search behind my back and she only appointed me VP temporarily. Either way, I'm taking this opportunity and running with it. And I'm damn well going to make sure you don't take our best clients with you."

"Wow," I say, and watch Maria as she breathes heavily and tries to catch her breath. "I wish you knew that I want the best for your future. And I'm sorry that you feel this way about me. However, your various hypotheses don't hold up because of the simple fact that I did not know Lola and Adrian were sleeping together."

This shocks Maria even more. "I thought she was your best friend. A member of the BOG."

"COG."

"Whatever." Maria folds her arms in front of her chest. "You didn't know about the affair?"

"Affair?" I lean back in my chair. "That's a rather fancy name for what may be something as mundane as a few screws in the socket. It could be, and probably is, no big deal."

"But you didn't know about it?"

"That's between me and Lola and quite frankly, Maria, I'm losing patience with you."

Maria storms out of my office.

Spinning around in my chair, I look out my wall of· windows. That's when I see the reflection of Susan standing behind me.

 ## The End, Part One

Using one of her best offensive tactics, Susan begins in midconversation. "And what do you think Bob West and The Cuisine Channel will think of Lola's affair?"

"I don't know if she is having an affair with Adrian. I'm not going to take his word for it. Even if it is true, why would Bob West care who Lola is screwing?"

"It doesn't matter if it's true or not. People always care who women are screwing, Lexi. The more successful and powerful the woman, the more rumors fly about the details of her sex life. Don't you know that? And how will potential advertisers feel about Lola if there are rumors that she is less than a role model?"

She's right. "How would Bob West find out?"

"The same way you did." Susan sits the chair opposite my desk. "Which raises the question. Why didn't you know about this?" Before I can say anything, Susan puts her hand in the air. "Wait. I don't really care to know the details of your friendship with Lola. But I do know the details of the deal you made with The Cuisine Channel. You leveraged my company against Lola's stability and her reputation." Susan puts her palms flat on my desk. "If The Cuisine Channel sues us, I'll sue you. Your company will be history before its first chapter is written."

"You'd like that, wouldn't you Susan?" She glares at me,

but I keep talking. "Is that why you are blowing this whole thing out of proportion?"

Susan slowly stands up. Looking into her eyes, I see rage. "Lexi, I am so disappointed in you." Susan breaks eye contact and begins to pace around the room. "Do you know how hard I worked to build a good, solid reputation for The Gold Group? Do you know how hard it was for me, as a woman, to build a business? And to have that business respected?"

This speech isn't about me and Lola, or Lola and Adrian. It's about me and Susan. I don't interrupt. I had this coming.

"When you walked in here, The Gold Group was already a success. I showed you how to run a business. I gave you the opportunity and the tools to succeed."

I clear my throat. "You were a great mentor, Susan."

Susan laughs sarcastically. "Don't use that condescending tone of voice with me. I know what you think of me now. You think I'm just a mom." Susan perches on the edge of my couch. "Just a mom, who runs herself ragged caring for two kids and a husband. That's what you think, right?"

I don't answer her. Susan looks at the wall opposite the couch. Staring at Lola's face on a framed cover of *Xess*, Susan smiles wistfully. "You know, Lexi, I never told you this, but I heard rumors about the ending of Lola's first marriage."

"I'm not interested in rumors."

Susan nods, but continues. "I heard that Lola's husband did not cheat on her. I heard that Lola manufactured the adultery claim to force him to give her control of the restaurant. I heard that Lola paid a waitress to claim they had sex. Of course, the waitress never had to testify to that, because Enrique gave in to Lola's demands. And why did he do that? Not because Lola hired a great lawyer." Susan turns to look at me. "But because she hired a PR person to ruin his reputation. Tell me, Lexi, what kind of person hires a publicist to deal with a divorce?"

"A lot of people in the public eye hire publicists for divorces."

Susan nods. Then, "But Lola was not yet in the public eye. She owned the restaurant and got some good press. But she didn't have the TV show yet. Now she does. She has the TV show and the cookbook. Thanks to you. How does she repay you? By putting her reputation on the line with some sordid affair and lying by omission."

The bile comes back into my throat, but I swallow it and refuse to let Susan win this round of mind games. "That's a whole lot of innuendo, Susan. The only thing we know for sure is that Lola is a Gold Group client, and Adrian Salvo is not. Our obligation, and our interest, is to protect Lola's reputation."

"When does filming start?" Susan asks, catching me off guard.

"In two weeks."

"Maybe it's not too late to back out of this deal. You may have been willing to ensure Lola's stability. I am not."

"Susan." I breathe deeply, stand up and walk around my desk. Standing in front of Susan, I say, "If The Gold Group detaches itself, The Cuisine Channel will cancel the series. I don't have the collateral to do the deal myself. Please don't back out of this." I look into her eyes. "Please. Susan, I can fix this situation with Lola."

"I don't need you to fix the situation. I can do it myself."

"How?" She doesn't answer me. "Susan?"

Susan tightens her face. "Are you pitching Salvo as a client for your new company? You have some kind of deal working with him and Lola?"

Firmly, I say, "No."

Sadly, Susan says, "I don't believe you, Lexi."

All out of words, I shrug.

"I don't think you have The Gold Group's best interest at heart." Susan looks at me coldly, as if I am a stranger, not someone who has cared for her company and her children. "I can't trust you anymore, Lexi."

My face falls. That hurts me more than anything else she has said in the past several weeks. Or past several years. Or ever.

Susan stands against the door to my office. "I will honor the deal between us, Lola, and The Cuisine Channel."

"Thank you, Susan."

"But I won't honor any agreement between you and me. Today is your last day at The Gold Group."

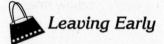 ## Leaving Early

Moving like a robot, it takes me half an hour to collect my personal items. I didn't have many personal things here. They fit into my gym bag. A box of tampons, two cans of Diet Dr Pepper, a spare pair of nylons, a tube of lipstick, a framed letter of thanks from the Jewish Geriatric Home, the framed cover of *Xess* with Lola's triumphant smile.

Everything else in my office, even my cherished rug, belongs to The Gold Group.

Leaving my keys on the desk—Maria's desk now—I turn off the lights and shut the door. Susan has obviously not told the staff about my early departure. No one gives me a second glance as I walk to the lobby, and I can't bear to say goodbye like this. In disgrace.

"Leaving early?" Low Man asks.

"Yes," I answer. "I'm leaving early."

But I don't leave the building. I kept the key that gives me access to the roof. It's mine. I paid for it fair and square.

Two hours after I leave my office, I'm still sitting on the roof in the hazy, warm air. Staring across the city, I ask myself the same questions over and over.

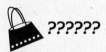 *??????*

Does Grace know? Ellie? Mia? Did Lola tell any of the COG about Adrian? What if none of it is true? What if all of it is?

What am I going to say to Lola? How do I tell her that I know about her affair, and so does Susan Gold-Berg? What's Susan going to do to "fix" this situation? Has she already called Lola? Does Lola know that I know?

What about me? How long will it take me to sign my first client? How will I do that?

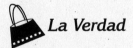 *La Verdad*

Later that night, I stand in the back alley of Lola's restaurant and knock on the kitchen door. A tiny woman answers. "*¿Cómo?*"

"*Por favor, necesito Lola. Me llamo Lexi.*"

"*Sí.*" The woman shuts the door. It opens a minute later. Lola comes out dressed in clogs, black stretch pants, a chef's coat with the name "Paco" and an apron tied around her waist. The white coat and apron are covered with green, red, and black smears. She doesn't look surprised to see me.

"You're busy?" I ask. "You're cooking?"

"I'm working on the food for TV. Trying to figure out the timing of the dishes." Lola crosses her arms in front of her chest and doesn't ask what I'm doing at her back door.

"Can you take a walk with me?" I ask.

"Not really." She looks irritated. She must have talked to Susan.

"I thought we could talk," I say quietly.

"You have something to say? Say it."

After the day I have had because of her, Lola's attitude sends me over the edge. "Fine. Are you sleeping with Adrian Salvo?"

Lola raises her chin. "Yes."

"How long has it been going on?"

Holding my gaze, Lola answers, "Almost four months. It started after Valentine's Day. He was here going over invoices and asked what I had done for Valentine's Day. I told him that I hadn't done anything except work. He took me out for a drink. And then, well." She stops.

"That was two weeks before I met with him. But we already had the meeting set. And you knew that. I told you that."

Lola shrugs. "That was a coincidence."

"Why didn't you tell me about it? "

Now, Lola walks away from me. She leans against an alley wall and looks down at her clogs. She doesn't answer me.

"Don't you want to know how I found out?"

"I already know how. Adrian came over this afternoon. He told me everything."

"Everything? Really? I doubt that."

"Lexi, I tried to tell you that Adrian wasn't attracted to you. You kept saying that he was hitting on you, and I kept saying that you were wrong. Now look what it's come to. I'm sure you were embarrassed when Adrian rejected you, but you didn't have to hit him."

"Wait. What?" Walking to Lola, I stand in front of her and try to control my anger. "That is not what happened. Adrian hit on me. I rejected him. Then he started saying really bad things about you. That's why I hit him." Should I tell her what Adrian said? No. There's no reason to humiliate her.

"You misunderstood him. Adrian wouldn't say bad things about me."

Whispering, I say, "You don't believe me?"

Lola raises her eyes to mine. "I think you misunderstood the situation." Lola looks at me so steadily that I know she believes Adrian. She wants to believe him.

"Lola." I take a deep breath. "Why didn't you tell me about any of this? Before?"

She looks at her clogs again. "I thought it would be awkward for you and Adrian. I didn't want to influence the business you had with each other."

"Lola?" She looks up at me. "That's crap. But let's go with that theory for the moment. You didn't tell me for my own good. Did you tell any of the COG?"

Her face caves in a little bit. "No."

"Why not? Don't we tell each other everything? You having a boyfriend is big news. Why wouldn't you want to share that? If you didn't want to tell me—for my own good—why not tell Ellie? Or Grace?"

"I was waiting. To see if it developed into something. Something real. Until then, I wanted it to be a secret."

"Lola, don't you know when you keep something secret from your girlfriends, that something is usually bad?"

Lola sags against the wall. "But you spoke so badly of Adrian after you met him. I thought, maybe you would like him and then I would tell everyone. But you made fun of him and you thought he was hitting on you, and I know that's just his old fashioned machismo, which is not that different from how Latino men act, and I know that, but you don't, and then his father decided not to sign with The Gold Group, and I thought maybe I could have done something to get him to sign with you, but I didn't, and I thought you would be mad about that, especially because you resigned because of that very thing, so things kept piling up and I kept not telling you. And then it was too late."

Leaning against the opposite alley wall, I do a slo-mo replay of Lola's speech. "That all makes sense to me."

Relieved, Lola exhales loudly. "You know how you didn't like Jean-François at first, but then you changed your mind after you spent time with him? I thought that would happen with you and Adrian."

"Right. Except Adrian is a scumbag."

"He is not."

"Lola? He is."

Lola looks at the ground and kicks at a cigarette butt. "I guess it's ironic. I'm about to film new episodes of my TV show. My cookbook will be out soon. Two things I worked for and fought to make happen."

"Yeah." Nodding, I put my hands on my hips. "That's right. You have a lot going for you."

"And I've never felt so alone." Lola turns her face to me, and there are no tears in her eyes. Just sincere sadness. "I used to think that I had all the time in the world to find another husband."

"Another husband? You want another husband?"

"You think I want to be alone for the rest of my life?"

Of course she doesn't. No one wants to be alone. That goes without saying, but for some reason, I never thought it applied to Lola.

"I'm almost forty, Lexi. How many more men are going to be interested in me?" When I open my mouth to protest her statement, Lola holds her palm up to me. "Stop. You don't know what it's like to be divorced and be my age and alone." Now, the tears come.

"You're not alone, Lola."

"You know what, Lexi? Adrian might not be perfect, but he makes me feel less lonely."

"I didn't know you felt that way, Lola." Now it's my turn to look at the ground and process what Lola has told me. I feel very far away from her, and at the same time, too close. This alley feels claustrophobic and dark and dirty and wrong, just wrong.

"Lola?"

"Yes?"

"Susan Gold-Berg will probably call you tomorrow. She inadvertently found out about your relationship with Adrian. You need to reassure her that the relationship won't interfere with production of the TV show."

"Can't you reassure her?"

"No. Today was my last day at TGG."

"Today? I thought you had another month."

"I changed my mind and decided to leave early," I tell Lola.

"Oh? Okay." Awkwardly, we stand in the alley without speaking.

Finally, I ask, "Are you going to keep seeing Adrian?"

"Yes," Lola answers. "Listen, I'm sorry that I didn't tell you about him. I thought I was doing the right thing. But, I'm not going to tell the other girls. Not for a while."

"I don't understand that."

Gently, Lola says, "You don't have to."

Independence

"I can't believe you don't want to go out with him again." Grace is haranguing me about Dr. Mark. She has no idea that, forty-eight hours ago, I had a lifequake. Grace can't see the damage, but I'm still feeling the aftershocks.

We are at the Rose family Fourth of July bash. Every year, Mia Rose transforms her back yard into a patriotic wonderland. This year is no different. The stone path leading from the house to the pool is decorated with tiki torches. Each of five round tables has a red checked tablecloth and a centerpiece created from enormous sticks of red, white and blue rock candy. Manning the grill is a rented chef, who is issuing ribs, chicken, seafood kabobs, and burgers with any kind of cheese. Enormous bowls of cole, potato, and other salads sit on an iced buffet. A bartender in an Uncle Sam hat serves lemonade and iced tea to the kids and cocktails or beer to the adults. Springsteen, Mellencamp, Ethridge, and Crow play from speakers attached to the back of the house.

In the middle of this fabulousness is Mia Rose, whose goal is to have nothing to do at her party but spend time with her guests.

*　　*　　*

"Where's Lola?" was the first thing Mia said when Grace, Michael, and I arrived without her.

Grace answered. "She left me a message saying that she couldn't come."

Mia looked at me. "Where is she?" I shrugged in response. "You don't know?" Mia looked at me strangely. "What's going on? Is something wrong?" I shook my head and Mia dropped the subject.

Sitting on the low brick wall ringing the back of the Rose yard, I watch the adults partying and the kids playing in the pool and I feel the absence of Lola and Ellie. The three of us always came to Mia's party together as each others' dates. Not this year.

Grace is still talking. "You should have talked him into seeing you again. He's such a great guy. What's the matter with you, Lexi? Lexi?"

"What?"

"Are you listening to me?"

"No."

Grace folds her arms over her chest. "Are you going to sit all the way over here and be antisocial all night?"

"Yes."

"Fine." Grace walks over to Michael and interrupts his conversation to wrap her arms around his waist. Michael flings his arm over Grace and absentmindedly winds his hand through her hair.

I sit by myself, at the edge of the party.

The Elder Council Floor Show

Monday morning, I wake up late, my brain churning. Four days have passed without a word from Lola. I still haven't told anyone that I've left The Gold Group. My parents and the COG were plenty concerned about my business venture. I don't want them to get extra jittery. Still, I need to talk about what happened. I decide to visit the Elder Council.

"Lexi? Girls, look who it is. What a treat!"

"What are you doing here? What is she doing here?"

"*Oy.* You got fired. Did she get fired?"

"You look terrible. She looks terrible."

"No, I did not get fired. Well, sort of. I resigned. Then I got fired. But I have a bigger problem. Something happened. Something bad."

"*Bubbeleh*, come sit and tell us your problem." Ruth pats the chair next to her. "We'll help. Come. Tell."

"Okay." I collapse into the chair. "One of my best friends? Her name is Lola."

Esther nudges Sylvia and asks, "Can she merengue?"

"Yes."

"And do the cha cha?" Sylvia asks.

"Yes. She's Latina. She knows all those dances. Anyway, she has this boyfriend."

Ruth winks at Esther. "Does he wear a diamond?"

"Yeah, actually. He has a diamond pinkie ring."

"Let me guess," Sylvia says. "Something happened, and then the punches flew."

"Yes. How do you know all this?"

Esther sings, "Her name was Lola. She was a show girl. Ya dah dah dah dah dah." Esther, Sylvia and Ruth stand. Esther puts her hands on Ruth's waist. Ruth grabs Sylvia's hips. Sylvia leans on her walker. They dance a geriatric samba line.

Ruth sings, "His name was Rico. He wore a diamond. La da di da di da di da." The other residents in the room start to clap along. Sylvia sings, "And then the punches flew, and chairs were smashed in two. There was blah blah blah blah blah and a single gunshot, but just who shot who?" The whole room sings, "At the Copa! Copacabana! Copa! Copacabana!"

"We had an entertainer here yesterday," Sylvia tells me after the Elder Council floor show.

"Lovely young man," Ruth adds.

"He had a keyboard," Esther says.

"Bravo, ladies. Now can we talk about my problem?"

"Of course, *shayna*. Tell us." Ruth waves me on, and I tell them about Lola and Adrian.

"Let me tell you something," Sylvia says after my story. "There is one issue on which girlfriends don't listen to girlfriends. Clothes, hairstyle, career, family? Girlfriends take their girlfriends' advice about all of that. But when it comes to men? We don't listen to each other. And do you know why? Because we don't want to hear the truth." Sylvia nods wisely, then points at Esther. "Ask her. She never listens to us."

Esther shakes her head. "I don't."

"And we're always right," Ruth says in a singsong voice.

Esther nods her head. "They are."

"But what you have to do," Ruth tells me, "is be there for your girlfriend when the *mishigas* hits the fan. You have to care more about your girlfriend than you care about being right. Because, if things get bad with Rico . . ."

"Adrian."

"If things get bad with him, Lola will need your support. All you can do is wait it out."

A bell sounds. "Lunchtime," Esther announces.

"Lexi, we're having pickled herring. Want to stay?" Sylvia asks.

"Do I have to?"

"What do you have against pickled herring? It's good for you," Ruth says.

They may be wrong about pickled herring, but they are right about girlfriends.

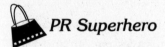 *PR Superhero*

Slightly nauseated by the thought of pickled herring, I walk back to Rittenhouse Square. It's already a steamy July day, but I wander around the Square's bricked paths, enjoying being outdoors. For the first time ever, I don't have to be any-where in particular. It's a strange feeling. Sort of like playing hooky. Which I never did in school, so this is really a novel experience.

Within ten minutes, I'm bored.

Café Oz's lights sparkle at me from the other side of the Square. There's something for me to do. Get coffee. Caffeine is never a bad idea.

It's 12:30 PM and Café Oz is almost empty. In the morning and evening hours, the joint jumps. Not now. Patrick slumps against the windows, looking out at all the people walking by and not coming into Café Oz. When he sees me, Patrick waves and looks excited to have a customer.

"Hey, Lexi!" he greets me a little too enthusiastically. "What are you doing here in the middle of the day? Did you take the day off from work?"

"Sort of," is my short answer. "One grande latte, please."

"Only if you drink it here. Please? Keep me company."

"Okay." I have nothing better to do. While Patrick does his latte magic, I notice, for the first time, that the tables in the café are set for service. "You serve food here?" I ask Patrick.

"Trying to. We started lunch here a month ago. It hasn't caught on. Yet. Most people come in for their morning coffee, leave, and don't come back. Like you. Or they come in to study or hang out at night. But I have faith. Business will pick up. Eventually."

I ask, "Who owns this place?"

"I do," Patrick answers.

"Really? I had no idea." Patrick carries my latte to a table overlooking the Square. I sit across from him and eagerly sip my coffee.

"My last name is Oskowitz," Patrick explains. "Hence, the Oz."

"Oh. I assumed it was Oz as in 'Wizard of.' "

"I think the Oz will look good in the ads."

"What ads?"

"The ones I'm thinking about running. They will cost me money, but there's not much else I can do to drum up business."

"Sure there is," I tell Patrick.

"Like what?"

"Did you issue a press release? You know, 'Café Oz Now Serving Lunch.' Some newspapers might mention it in their food sections. It's a start. And all it costs is copying and postage. Hey, how about all those businesses on the Square? Deliver complimentary lunches to them, include a menu and a coupon, and you'll be putting that advertising money to better use. You know what else? Signage would help. A lot. Then there's more intensive media stuff to do. Press releases about your food, your entrepreneurship, blah, blah, blah." I sip my latte.

Patrick stares at me. "How do you know all that?"

"Ah, well. You see me as a caffeine-dependent business executive, but my other identity is as a publicist and promotions person. I am a PR superhero. Able to leap declining profits in a single quarter. Faster than word of mouth. More powerful than a single ad." I stop talking and laugh. Mia and I used to do that shtick all the time, but I haven't thought of it in years.

"Wow. I'm impressed. Do you work for a big firm?"

"I did. I left. I'm starting my own firm. Well, firm might be too big a word for it. 'Business' might even be overdoing it, considering I have no clients."

"I'm sure I can't afford your rates, considering I can't afford anything, but if I could, I'd hire you."

"Oh, I understand the lack of capital concept. One of my best friends offered to work with me, and I'm paying her in hugs."

Patrick smiles. "I could pay you in lattes."

Raising my eyebrows, I smile back at him. "That's not a bad offer. Do you know how much money I spend in here? These four-dollar lattes add up pretty quickly."

"And now I can not only caffeinate you, but feed you. You could have lunch here every day." Patrick and I look at each other, somewhat surprised at the turn our relationship has taken. This isn't how I pictured getting my first client, but it actually makes a lot of sense. I'm inspired to help Patrick. My lethargy has left the building. I offer my hand to Patrick. "Deal?"

Patrick shakes my hand. "Deal."

 ## Offers They Can't Refuse

The next morning, I wake up with energy. Me? Energy in the morning? Yippee.

Impatient to get my day started, I stare in the mirror and try to think of a quick hair solution. It's 110 percent humidity and it will be all summer. No longer will I have the day long shelter of Executive Tower's air-conditioning. Now that I have to pay for my air conditioning, I will use it sparingly.

So, hair? Why straighten in it this humidity? I'll leave it curly and worry about more important things.

I have a plan.

Dressed in a honey-colored tank dress with my animal print scarf around my neck, I arrive at Zoga for my 9 AM meeting with Jane. In her karmarific office, I explain my situation and offer Jane my PR services for a two-month trial period, in exchange for two month's worth of Zoga classes. It's an offer she can't refuse. I put the contract in front of Jane. She signs it. Done.

At 10:30 AM, I walk into Salon Serge, site of my biweekly cut and color. Serge is waiting for me and I make him an offer similar to Jane's, exchanging my public relations services for my cut and colors. The blowouts I'll pay for when I want or need them. Serge hesitates, not sure he needs new clients. Laying out his future, I talk to Serge about developing his own line of products. "I oversaw the promotion of QT cosmetics," I tell him, and he recognizes the initials of the now-rich Philadelphia makeup artist. When I say the magic letters QVC, he signs on the dotted line.

Feeling fabulous, I walk home past Lola's and peek in the windows. I don't see her, but I go inside. "*Buenos tardes, Isabel. ¿Dónde está Lola?*"

"*Ella está en Miami*," Isabel the day manager answers. "*Por una semana.*"

"*¿Por qué?*"

"*No sé exactamente. ¿Vacación?*"

That's unlikely. Lola wouldn't take a week-long vacation in Miami right before filming starts. Maybe she's taking refuge with her parents, hiding from Susan. Or me. Or both.

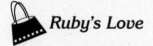 **Ruby's Love**

At 9:15 AM the next morning, Doorman John summons me to the lobby. Although I've been awake and working for hours, I have yet to shower or dress, but I pad downstairs in my jammie bottoms and a tank top. Doorman John has three daughters. He's seen plenty of pajamas.

Greeting me with a grin, John gestures toward the storage area, where sit boxes of pens, pencils, yellow pads, folders, and a gray filing cabinet. "I take one day off," John says, "and come back to find all this. You gonna tell me what's going on?"

I put my arm around Doorman John. "I'm going to be in the building a lot more often."

"Good." John nods. Then he frowns. "You get fired?"

"No. Well, yes. I resigned and then I was fired." The more I say that, the better it sounds. I give John the highlights of the story, including my three new clients. "Here's where you come in, John. I'll need your help with messengers and deliveries. I wouldn't ask you to do that for nothing, so I'll give you a monthly compensation for your time and energy. Do we have a deal?" I offer John my hand to shake.

John smiles but doesn't shake my hand. "All this time, Miss Lexi, and I didn't know you were in public relations."

Lowering my hand, I say, "Yes. That's what I do." I refrain from the superhero speech, feeling goofy enough standing in the lobby in my jammies.

"Well, now. My wife has been looking for some help. She works as a secretary, but she's been dreaming about starting her own business."

"What kind of business?"

"My wife," John smiles, "makes the best cookies in the entire world."

"Is that right?"

"That is the honest truth," John says proudly. "They're called Ruby's Love. That's my wife's name. Ruby. Now, let me tell you about the different kinds of Ruby's Love. We got chocolate chocolate chip, oatmeal raisin, and almond sugar cookies. She sells them to stores in West Philly where we live. But she wants to branch out into Center City. A little publicity and some guidance from you? I bet she'd be a big hit."

"John, I would be honored to help your wife."

"All right." John smacks his palms together. "How about

we do it like this? I'll act like your secretary down here. Free of charge. You help my wife. Free of charge. Plus, you get a box of cookies every week. When your business makes a profit and Ruby's Love makes a profit, we'll talk about money."

"That's the best deal I've heard all week." I smile and offer my hand to John. This time, he shakes it.

"So what's your company called?" John asks.

"Lexi James Public Relations."

"Oh."

"What?"

"Nothin'."

"John? You don't like it?"

"Honestly, Miss Lexi? It doesn't flow."

"Flow?"

"Yeah. It doesn't flow. It doesn't have rhythm. It's not catchy."

"Oh. Well. It is informative. Says what it is. No bull."

"Now there's a good name, Lexi. No Bull Public Relations."

"John, please."

"I'm serious. You need a name people will remember. Come on, girl. You're the PR person. Go on and PR yourself."

At 2:28 PM exactly, I pick up my phone and take a deep breath. The timing of this little maneuver is critical.

Yesterday, I e-mailed Maria asking for the professional courtesy of telling me when The Gold Group planned to release a statement about my departure. Maria e-mailed me back with a very brief "Tomorrow afternoon."

It's 2:30 PM. Perfect. The Gold Group will have sent out the press release announcing my departure and Maria's new position. If she was even there today, Susan will have left the office to retrieve her kids from Camp Coleridge. With the newspaper's 3 PM deadline for tomorrow's issue, there won't be enough time to get Susan to answer her cell, and Maria won't be confident enough to make a statement on her own.

"Vince Getty, *Philadelphia Inquirer*." Vince is the *Inquirer*'s gossip columnist. Forget about the business section. Everyone reads the gossip page.

I've worked with Vince for years. Thanks to me giving him scoops on my clients, Vince owes me. I mean to collect. "Hello, Vince," I say in my smooth PR voice. "This is Lexi James."

"Really?" he says. "I was just wondering how to get in touch with you. I don't have your home phone number."

"Well, Vince, you are the first reporter I'm giving it to," I say and tell him the numbers.

"So, Lexi," Vince says nonchalantly. "I have this statement from The Gold Group."

"I'm sure you do. Would you like to know what's really going on?"

"Of course," he answers, then asks every gossip reporter's first question. "Who else have you told?"

"You're the first and only. As long as it runs tomorrow as the top story in your column. Do we have a deal?"

"Deal," Vince agrees. "I'm listening."

 ## Take Me to the River, Again

These boots were made for walking. Really? They are sneakers and they were made for cross training. That's not the point.

I'm walking down Eighteenth Street toward the Benjamin

Franklin Parkway. I'm not just walking. I'm speed walking. No, trotting. No, striding.

At The Four Seasons Hotel, I turn left onto the Parkway and hug the perimeter of Logan Circle, a fountain composed of statues of languishing American Indians. Lit brightly in the dark, water spews into cascading arcs.

On my right is the Free Library, the first one in America. In front of it is a monument to William Shakespeare. "All the world is a stage," it reads. Yes? Then perhaps this is the end of my first act and the beginning of my second.

On my left is the Franklin Institute and I see the enormous statue of dear old Ben. I blow him a kiss.

Pumping my arms and feeling a trickle of sweat down my back, I pass the apartment buildings that line the Parkway. Also lining the Parkway are the flags of every country in the world, displayed from poles in alphabetical order.

Ahead of me is the Philadelphia Museum of Art, lit like a palace, its famous steps sweeping from the sidewalk to the promenade. Cutting through Eakins Oval, a circular green spot with a statue of George Washington on horseback, I reach the bottom of the Art Museum's steps.

Taking them two at a time, I jump up the marble steps, huffing and puffing until I reach the top. Then I look east.

City Hall stands at the end of the Parkway. From his perch on top of City Hall, William Penn surveys his city. I wave to Billy.

I see Liberty Place One and Liberty Place Two, their upper floors lit like colored glass.

If I stop moving, my muscles will cramp. I jog in place, and I think. I think that I am, for the first time in a long time, proud of myself.

With the Art Museum behind me, I raise my fists in the air.

Read All About It

The next morning, I hop out of bed at 7 AM, brush my teeth, don my flip-flops, and charge downstairs in my pajamas with a ten-dollar bill clenched in my fist. At the newsstand across the street, I buy ten copies of the *Philadelphia Inquirer* and burst back into the lobby of my building.

"Page two," I tell John, thrusting the People section at him.

Introducing LexiCo!
by Vince Getty

Ta da!, says Lexi James, the now former VP of The Gold Group, who late yesterday called me to chat about a press release from TGG announcing her departure. With great enthusiasm, Lexi said that she has formed her own boutique firm—LexiCo—which will be HQed in her Rittenhouse Square home. (Call her. She's listed!) Lexi left her high-powered position last week, acting on a change of heart about her business. "I want to work for smaller companies where I can make a real difference," she said. Lexi already has new clients. In just a few days, she has signed Ruby's Love cookies, Salon Serge, Café Oz, and an interesting place called Zoga. "All of these businesses are within five blocks of my home," Lexi said. "I'll be promoting my community." Lexi also has made pro bono work a priority and will do PR for the Magic Hanger, a used clothing store which makes designer duds available to needy women. The

Magic Hanger is located in Cherry Hill, where Lexi
was raised. "There's no place like home," Lexi said.
"It's full circle for me." Susan Gold-Berg, prez of
TGG, was not available for comment.

"Your phone will be ringing all day," John says.

"That's the idea." Dashing upstairs, I hook up my new
phone, which has caller ID and voice mail. Clearing my throat
and using my PR voice, I create a message.

"Hello, this is Lexi James. I'm on the other line, but if you
leave a message, I'll call you back as soon as I can. Thanks for
calling and have a great day."

Barf. But the saccharine is necessary.

After changing into yoga clothes, I run downstairs and
wave to John as I head to my morning Zoga class. Anyone
who calls will think that I'm on the other line, just too impos-
sibly busy—already—to speak with them.

Hee, hee.

"Lexi? It's Grace. I can't believe you didn't tell me the news
about your company. I mean, jeez. I have to read about your
life in the newspaper? Call me. I want to hear everything.
Bye."

"Lexi? Are you there? It's Mom. If you're there, pick up.
Honey? No? Okay. I read the newspaper this morning and I'm
a little confused. I thought you were supposed to be at The
Gold Group for another month. Maybe I got the dates mixed
up. Please call me. It's Mom."

"Good morning, Ms. James. It's your humble employee Mia
Rose. I am so excited for you! And me! I can't wait to start
working together in September. Hold on a minute. David,

don't do that to your brother. Okay, I'm back. Congratulations, Lexi. I'm really proud of you. Bye!"

"Lexi, it's Dad. Congratulations, honey. Call me when you can."

"*Bon jour,* Lexi. It's Ellie and Jean-François. I got the *Inquirer* over the Internet. We want to say congratulations on LexiCo. Love the name. Love the clients. Good for you, girlfriend. I thought you were staying at The Gold Group longer. Anyway, congratulations!"

Lola doesn't call.

 **Runaway**

On one of the hottest nights of July, the night doorman rings my apartment. "Miss James? There's a woman down here to see you. Name of Mia."

"Send her up, please." Mia? What's she doing here? It's almost 9:30 PM.

At Mia's knock, I open the door with a smile. Which immediately falls into a frown. Mamma Mia is a molto mess. Her hair is in a messy ponytail. She's wearing khaki shorts, a white top, and a baby blue, zip-up sweatshirt. The sweatshirt confuses me until I remember that Mia's Michael air-conditions his house into the Ice Age.

"Lexi!" Mia sobs.

"Mia? What happened?" I pull her into my apartment. Mia covers my face with her hands. Wrapping my arm around her tiny shoulders, I lead Mia to my couch and reach for a box of tissues. Mia stops weeping and wipes at her face.

I try again. "What's the matter?"

"I'm pregnant." She starts to cry again.

"Oh my God! How far along are you?"

"Just over a month." Tears fall over Mia's face.

"Oh, Mia. Mia? Stop crying, sweetie. Is this one of those hormone things? It'll pass."

Taking big gulps of air, Mia says, "We stopped having sex."

"Who? You and Michael?"

Mia nods.

"But you're pregnant. What about the vasectomy? Oh my God. Mia? Did you have an affair? Are you pregnant with your lover's child? Who is he? Why didn't you tell me? Good Lord. Nobody tells me anything anymore."

"Lexi, shut up. I did not have an affair. The baby is Michael's. Where there's a sperm, there's a way."

"Oh. Then why did you say that you stopped having sex with him?"

Moping her face dry, Mia turns towards me on the couch. "We didn't have sex for two months. Two months. Do you know how long that is?"

"Well. Yeah. It's two months."

"We used to make love, like, every day. Then it became every other day. After we had David? We only had sex first thing in the morning because we were both exhausted at night. Once Simon was born? We only did it on the weekends. Do you see the trend here?"

"Seems like a downward trend."

"Yes. Then it got worse. We just stopped trying to find time. If it happened in the morning, that was great. But rare. All of a sudden, I realized two months had passed without us having sex. That's unbelievable to me. I sleep next to that man every night and wake up next to him every morning. We had to go out of our way not to have sex. You know what I mean? Like, I'm there. He's there. But whatever used to be there? Is gone."

"It's not gone."

"We went, like, two weeks without even kissing. What kind of marriage is that?"

"You're asking me about marriage?"

"I'll tell you what kind of marriage that is. It's a bad marriage. When the husband and wife don't even kiss each other hello or goodbye or good night. That's what Oprah and Dr. Phil say all the time. A marriage depends on intimacy and the husband and wife have to maintain that intimacy or it disappears." Mia resumes her crying jag.

"How do you get from no sex to you being pregnant?"

"When I realized that two months had passed, I freaked. I had the boys sleep at their grandparents' house. I went to Boudoir and bought some sexy lingerie. And then I didn't even bother to put it on. I jumped Michael the minute he got home. We made love for hours and ate pizza in bed and took a bubble bath and promised not to let so much time pass without being intimate."

"That sounds great, Mia."

"Yeah. It was." She looks out my window at the lights of the city.

"So? What's with the hysterics?"

Mia stares into the dark night. "I ran away."

"Pardon?"

"I ran away. From home. This afternoon, I went to the gyne and found out for sure that I'm pregnant. The rest of the day, I was in a daze. After dinner, Michael played catch with Simon and David. Then they camped out on the couch to watch the

Phillies game. I told Michael that I was going to Wawa to get milk. I drove to Wawa. I kept going. Driving and driving." Mia looks at me. "I passed six Wawas between my house and here."

"That's a lot of Wawas."

"I didn't stop at any of them. I didn't want to go back home. I got to the bridge and realized that I didn't have my wallet. I didn't have money for the toll. So I went through EZ Pass without stopping." Mia's eyes widen. "I broke the law."

Patting her knee, I say, "Extenuating circumstances."

"I was going to sit in a coffee shop and think, but I didn't have any money and they don't let you just sit there without buying something. You know?"

"Right."

"I didn't want to call Grace. I thought you would understand me acting crazy." Mia doesn't say this meanly. It's just a fact that her emergency COG member is Grace. Not in this situation. Grace wouldn't understand.

"What did Michael say when you told him about the baby?"

"I didn't tell him."

I frown at Mia. "Why not?" She looks out the window, avoiding my gaze. "Mia? Are you considering an abortion?" Still, she doesn't answer me. We sit quietly for a few moments.

Then Mia asks, "Can I stay here tonight?"

"Of course, sweetie." Wrapping my arms around Mia, I hug her tightly. We stay like that for a while, and my brain starts to think. Pulling away from Mia, I look at her and say, "No. You can't stay here. You have to go home."

Mia's eyes get big. "Why?"

"Because you have a husband. Who loves you. He's probably worried sick about you. Going out for milk? Milk, Mia? The symbolism is rich, but come on. Milk doesn't take an hour and a half to buy. Michael has probably called the police by now."

"Fine." Mia pushes herself off the couch and stands with her arms crossed in front of her chest. "I'll go to a hotel."

"Really? With no money and no ID? Good luck."

Mia looks at me sideways, then lunges toward my coffee table and swipes my wallet out of my purse. Clutching it to her chest, she stares at me defiantly. This makes me laugh. Mamma Mia Rose, the one who got it right, stands in my living room in her shorts and ponytail and pouts and I laugh so hard that my face hurts. "Now you're a thief? A pregnant runaway thief?"

"It's not funny," Mia wails. And then she smiles. Rolling her eyes at my peals of laughter, Mia tosses herself onto the couch next to me. She pulls her hair out of its ponytail and smooths it down the sides of her face, then tucks it behind her ears and pulls at her bangs.

"Mia Rose, I know why you came here. To me." Pausing, I look at Mia and smile. "You thought I would let you run away. Because that's what you think I did. Run away. From Ron. From marriage. From everything. That's why you came to me instead of Grace. Yes?"

Mia shrugs. "Maybe I thought that in the back of my mind. But I don't think of you like that, Lex. I think you made the decision that was right for you at the time."

"And you'll do the same thing, Mia. You'll make the decision that is right for you and your family. And you don't have to make this decision on your own. You have a husband who loves you. You have two fantastic sons."

"Yeah." Mia rests her head on the back of the sofa. "I had a plan," she tells me. "Want to hear it?"

"Sure."

"It went like this. Go to college. Work for a few years. Get married. To a nice Jewish guy. Have two kids. Stop working and stay home with the kids. Be a good wife and mom. Go back to work when the kids go to school." Mia stops and looks at me. "That was it. My whole plan. Michael agreed with it. We wanted to give our kids the right kind of start in life, which to us, meant having a mom who stayed at home and didn't work. I didn't want to be one of those moms who pop out a kid and toss it into day care. Now that I was going to start working again? I realized how excited I was to get back into the professional world. And now? I'm pregnant. That wasn't in the plan and I'm not sure what to do about it."

"Okay, first of all? You'll be working for me." Waving my arms around my already cramped living room, I say, "All of this is waiting for you. And I already told you that we would work out a flexible schedule. You could even bring the baby to work with you."

"Really?" Mia's face brightens and I think about the reality of trying to work with a crying, poopy baby in the apartment.

"If you choose to have the baby, we'll work something out." Putting my arms around Mia, I hug her tightly. "You'll figure it out. With Michael." Rising from the couch, I get my phone and bring it to Mia. "Call your husband and tell him that you are on your way home."

Mia takes the phone. She smiles at me. "You're a good friend, Lexi."

Such a simple statement it is, but so sincere that it brings joy

264

to my heart, especially with the specter of Lola still in my mind. "Thank you, Mia."

Mia gives me her Mommy Look, which is when she looks at her boys and makes them think that she already knows what they have done wrong so they might as well confess. "What's going on with you and Lola?"

I would love to tell Mia, to share the burden of the story's implications and to get her advice. But Lola said that she didn't want the COG to know about Adrian. Of course, I could tell Mia, swear her to secrecy, and Lola would never find out. But that wouldn't be the right thing for me to do. So I simply say, "Nothing."

She doesn't believe me, but Mia shrugs and says, "Okay."

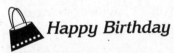 ## Happy Birthday

LexiCo is one month old, and I'm as exhausted as a new mother.

Like a new mom, I've found that it's the little things about LexiCo which amaze me the most. For example, mailing one letter can take three hours. First, I have to find the correct address and correct spelling of the addressee's name. The database program for my home computer sits on my desk and mocks me because I haven't had time to install it.

Once I have the address, I write the letter. I edit. Spell check. Double check spell check. Print the letter, assuming I have paper and ink in the printer. If not, I run down the street to the office supply store. And it's July, so running anywhere in the day's heat is no fun.

When the letter is printed, I address the envelope myself.

The database program howls with laughter at my terrible penmanship, chortling that my life would be easier if I could find time and energy to open the box and read the installation instructions.

Then? The stamp. I am used to automatic stamping machines, suchs as the one in The Gold Group's mailing room. Here? I am the machine. Stamping one letter is no big whoop. Doing a 120-piece mailing like I did earlier this week for Salon Serge? Just the stamping took an hour and a half. Mail gets picked up from my building's box once a day. If I miss that pickup, I have to go to the post office, sort local and nonlocal mail and stuff envelopes, two by two, into the slots.

And that's what it takes for me to mail a letter.

Why don't I hire someone or get an intern? No time to go about doing that, and I'm not wild about having a stranger in my apartment. So for now, I have to do everything myself.

"So who are you going to bring to the wedding?" Grace asks me.

"Don't start with me." Sitting at my dining room table, Grace and I are working on a mailing for Zoga. It's Grace's day off and she wanted to review wedding details, so I told her that I would help her if she helped me with the mailing. "Hand me that stack of envelopes, please?"

Pouting, Grace hands me the last twenty envelopes. "Don't snap at me, Lexi."

"Sorry."

"I was afraid that when you started LexiCo you would give up on dating. Didn't I say this would happen?"

"Yes, you did."

Grace makes crisp folds in the press releases and stacks

them in a neat pile. "It would be fun for you to have a date at the wedding. I guess you'll have to dance with Lola. You two will be the only single people there."

As casually as I can, I say, "Lola's not bringing a date?"

"Who would she bring?"

Looking down at the envelope I am addressing, I say, "No one, I guess."

By lunchtime, we're done with the mailing and I thank Grace profusely for her help. She runs to Café Oz to get salads for our lunch, and returns with everything we need. Except forks. "There are chopsticks in the top drawer of the kitchen," I tell her as I finish checking my e-mail.

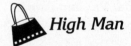 **High Man**

I'm sitting at Café Oz with my eyes half closed, proofing a press release and waiting for my caffe latte. I've graduated from grande to molto grande.

Propping my chin on my fist, I look out Café Oz's windows at the sidewalks sweating in the August heat. I love sitting here in the middle of the day and looking into Rittenhouse Square. Even though it has been a month since I left The Gold Group, I can't shake the feeling that I'm playing hooky because I'm not locked in an office building.

"Lexi?"

I look up at Low Man on the Totem Pole Mike DiBuono. "Hey," I say with a big smile. "How are you?" He looks quite trim and summery in his flat-pocketed, beige pants and bright blue button-down shirt. Low Man's shoes are excellent brown sandal loafer-type things. He makes me feel quite unhip in my tank top, shorts, and flip-flops. Whatever. I gesture to the chair across from me and he sits. "What are you doing out of lock up?" I ask.

"It's lunchtime," he answers. "I've been reading so much about Café Oz's new lunch menu that I decided to try it out. This place must have a great PR person." Low Man gives me a big smile. A server deposits my molto grande latte on the table and I thank her for my caffeine.

"That's your lunch?" Low Man asks.

I sip my latte and wipe away the resulting milk mustache. "It's how I get my calcium." Low Man chuckles. "It's funny I should see you today," I tell him. "Yesterday I was thinking how strange it is to see people every day for years, to be part of their lives and have them be part of your life, and then all of a sudden, be cut off from them." He nods. "You know who I was thinking about yesterday?"

Low Man starts to guess. "Maria? Michelle? Me? Certainly not Susan."

"Not Susan. Her kids."

Low Man raises his eyebrows in surprise so I explain. "I knew Joshua and Ashley from the time they were babies. I saw them grow up and, I don't know, I felt some sort of auntly affection toward them. How are they?"

"Fine. They are spending the summer at Camp Coleridge. Seems to be going well."

"Good. I'm glad to know that. Thanks."

Low Man nods at the papers in front of me. "What are you working on?"

"Proofing a press release."

"Who wrote it?" he asks.

"My best employee. Me."

"Honey, you can't proof your own work," he admonishes me. "Allow me." He holds out his hand to receive the red marker in my hand. I look at Low Man cautiously. I give him the pen.

A few minutes later, Low Man moves the two pieces of paper toward me. "Not your best work," he says. "You must be tired. You look tired. You look like hell, actually."

"Thanks. You're still Low Man at The Gold Group? Right? No promotion?"

"I know everything that goes on at The Gold Group."

"Good for you."

"So, Lexi. How many clients do you have?"

"Five."

"All on retainer, or part trade?"

"That's none of your business."

"I'd like to make it my business." Low Man smiles at me.

"What do you mean?"

"Listen, Lexi. I've been trying to get up the nerve to call you, but God works in mysterious ways and here you are sitting right in front of me, so I'll just tell you what I've been thinking."

"Do tell."

"You haven't notched a money client," Low Man says. "If you had, I would've read about it in the papers. Or heard it on the grapevine."

"And?" I cross my arms in front of my chest, feeling protective of LexiCo.

"You need to get a money client. For the actual money and for the prestige."

"Thanks for the business lesson, Low Man."

"I'm guessing that you haven't signed a money client because you don't have the time or energy or opportunity. You are doing all the work yourself. All the writing, all the phone calls, and all the administrative chores. I'm guessing that you don't have time to follow up on leads or pursue new ones. I know that you haven't been in touch with your old contacts and leads. If LexiCo is going to succeed, you need another body and another mind to share the work."

He's right. "In September, my friend Mia is going to work with me part-time. Until she has her baby. And then, I don't know what's going to happen. Mia will be a huge help. But, yes, I could concentrate on new business if I had someone working with me full-time." Why am I telling Low Man all of this? I guess I trust him. "Anyway, I can't afford to hire someone."

"See? That's the catch-22. You can't get a money client without someone to share the work, but you can't hire someone to share the work until you sign a money client."

"This is illuminating."

"Lexi," Low Man leans toward me, over my molto grande latte. "I can help you get the money client. Some of the accounts TGG is pitching are leads you developed which are now coming to fruition. And a few accounts are up for renewal. I think it's only fair that you get a shot at pitching those accounts."

"You're going to give me this information? Why? What's in it for you?"

"A new job. An opportunity to get in on the ground floor of what I know will be a successful company." He smiles at me. "I want to stop being Low Man on the Totem Pole."

"Good Lord." I grin at him. "You're devious."

He shrugs his shoulders.

Thinking about his comments, I take a sip of my latte. "I don't want to poach clients from TGG. I feel strongly about that."

"That's very ethical of you, Lexi. Although you never had a problem poaching clients from other agencies while you were at TGG. After all, that is how you met Adrian Salvo."

The name makes me wince. "Things have changed. I don't want to get a reputation for stealing clients. That's not how I want to build my success."

"I understand. But I'm not suggesting theft." Low Man looks around Café Oz, taking note of the line forming at the door as a hostess hurries to seat customers. In a low, yet high voice, he says, "Since you left, many clients have been on shaky ground with TGG. Those clients up for renewal? Many of them are interviewing other agencies. Your noncompete prevents you from stealing TGG clients, but it doesn't prevent you from pitching clients who are up for grabs. All I'm suggesting is that you get in the game. You deserve a shot at those accounts." He pauses, then, with seriousness, says, "Keep taking the high ground, but don't sacrifice opportunities. You can do both."

Having said his piece, Low Man leans back in his chair and nods at me, secure in the soundness of his statements and relieved to have gotten them off his chest. I admire his audacity and appreciate that he must have put quite a bit of thought into the future of LexiCo. He gives me information, I go after the big clients, I sign a client, I hire Low Man. Sounds like a win-win. And I thought I was the deal maker.

"You've got a deal, Low Man." Then I correct myself. "You've got a deal, Mike."

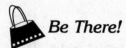

Be There!

I am writing a press release about Café Oz's summer iced-coffee drinks when my computer beeps to tell me I have a new e-mail.

> To: Lola <lola@councilofgirlfriends.com>, Ellie <ellie@council ofgirlfriends.com>, Mia <mia@councilofgirlfriends.com>, Lexi <lexi@councilofgirlfriends.com>
> From: Grace <grace@councilofgirlfriends.com>
> Subject: Bridesmaid Dresses
>
> That's it! No more rescheduling. Meet me at Bridal Heaven at noon on Saturday. NO EXCUSES! Except for Ellie. Ellie and I decided that since we're almost the same size, I'll try on her dress and she'll get it altered when she comes home in a week or so. But the rest of you I'll see on Saturday. BE THERE!
>
> I love you!
> Gracie

Dr. Franklin, Session Four

"I'm nervous about seeing Lola on Saturday." I have just finished telling Dr. Franklin the Lola-Adrian-Susan-Lexi story, which I refer to in my mind as the Copacabana Affair. "And then Mia called to tell me that she is going to have the baby, but she doesn't want anyone to know she's pregnant until the first trimester is over, so I have to keep that secret as well. I don't like this. I feel like a secret agent. Like the woman on *Alias*. Without the wigs."

Dr. Franklin nods but doesn't comment. That irritates me. "What have you got to say about all of this?" I ask him.

"What I have to say is that you need to come in for regular sessions if you want me to be of help to you. I'm not here to give you quick solutions. If you want my help, you need to come in once a week, or once every two weeks. Can you make that kind of commitment?"

Without hestiation, I answer, "Yes."

Dress Shopping: The Bridesmaids

"Please tell me you're kidding," I beg Grace.

Mia, Grace, and I are at Bridal Heaven on Walnut Street and I'm staring at my reflection in the full-length mirror. Still in her street clothes, Mia tries not to laugh at me. Grace's Idea of the Moment is to have the COG wear green dresses. Kelly green. As in Michael Kelly.

This particular abomination is a kelly green dress with long sleeves made of lace that button at my wrists. The scooped neckline does indeed scoop; the girls are almost totally exposed. The tight skirt comes to just above my knee.

"I look like a leprechaun hooker."

"¡*Dios mio!*" Lola sweeps into the dressing area. She is fifteen minutes late and I was beginning to worry that she wouldn't come at all. But here she is, hand over her mouth, staring at me in horror. Lola turns to Grace. "I can't believe you made Lexi try that on." Lola looks at me and points to the curtained dressing room. "Go change. *Por favor.*"

"Maybe it is a little much," Grace admits.

It takes some writhing to get out of the dress. Just when I've freed myself, Lola talks to me from the other side of the curtain. "Lexi? Here are two more dresses for you to try. I think the colors will look great on you." Lola thrusts two dresses through the curtain. One is midnight blue, the other is a pale rose. "Do you need help getting into them?" Lola asks.

"I don't think so." But I am surprised and pleased that she offered to help.

"*Bueno*. Let me know. I'll be out here."

When I emerge from the dressing room in the midnight blue dress, Lola claps her hands. "Look, Gracie. See how pretty Lexi looks?" She's acting as if nothing happened between us. Should I act like that, too?

"It's not green," Grace complains.

"Forget the green," Mia tells her.

"Here, Lexi, let me fix this for you." Lola adjust the dress's straps, then smooths the fabric over my butt and yanks the hem down in the back. As she moves around me, I follow Lola with my eyes, waiting for her to give me a wink, a pinch, or a punch. Nothing happens.

An hour later, I've dutifully tried on a rack of dresses. They blur in my mind, but Lola and Mia, neither of whom has tried on a dress, discuss the pluses and minuses of each one with Grace. "How did I get to be the mannequin?" I ask, but I'm not complaining. I'm too focused on Lola's behavior. That it is normal.

As I'm changing out of a dress, Mia pushes aside the curtain of the dressing room, and comes in without asking. Drawing the curtain behind her, Mia says, "I'm going to throw up."

"So you come into the dressing room? There's, like, a thousand dollars' worth of satin in here." Quickly, I clear the clothes from the chair in the room. Mia sits and takes a deep breath. Frantically, I look around the dressing room for a receptacle of some kind. There is nothing, not a trashcan or a cup in sight. My eyes land on the leprechaun hooker dress. That wouldn't be any great fashion loss. Grabbing the kelly green dress, I drape it between my arms to catch Mia's vomit. Preparing for her to blow chunks, I close my eyes and look away.

"Never mind." Mia springs to her feet. "It passed." She walks out of the dressing room.

Lola and Mia make Grace make a decision about the dresses. She narrows her choices to five, each a variation of the other. "I think they are similar enough, but different enough," Lola says as we look at ourselves in the mirror with Grace wearing what will be Ellie's dress. "I don't think one dress would look great on all of us," I say. "We have such different shapes."

"But these dresses complement each other," Mia says. "They look good together."

"Fine," Grace waves at the mirror. "Sold." As we continue to preen in the mirror, Grace removes a package from her purse. She gives a small box to each of us. "This is an early bridesmaid gift." Inside the boxes are hair clips covered in Swarovski crystals and pearls. Each is slightly different, but all are beautiful. "Maybe everyone will wear them in their hair at the wedding?" Grace suggests. "Even if you don't, I wanted to give you something to remember today. It's a special day. Us being here together. I wish Ellie were here." Grace wipes a tear from her eye. "And you've all been very patient with me. Even you, Lex. And, I'm sure, being the Coordinator of Hoopla, that you're working hard on my bridal shower. That will be a really special day, too."

I nod.

Grace and Mia walk into the dressing room to change. Lola looks at me with big eyes. "Did you start planning the shower?"

"No. I've been so busy. Oh boy."

Lola smacks her hand together. "We can have the shower at my restaurant. We'll serve appetizers and that big salad Grace likes. I'll have my kitchen make a cake. *No problema*."

"You'll help me?"

"Of course," she answers, then modifies, "it's for Gracie. What are you doing Tuesday morning? Why don't you come to the restaurant and we'll work on the shower. I bet we can plan the whole thing in an hour."

"Okay."

"*Bueno*," Lola says, and turns to go to the dressing room.

"Lola? Wait." I grab her arm, then release it. I swallow hard. "Are we okay? You and me? Is everything okay?"

She nods and smiles. The smile is polite. Not warm. "Everything is okay. We started filming the new episodes last week."

"Oh. Good. So everything worked out with Susan?'

"Yes." That's all she says.

Lola moves toward the dressing room and I follow her. Mia and Grace are using the only two rooms, so Lola and I stand on the other side of the curtains and wait. "Lex?" Grace calls.

"Yeah?"

"Did you tell the girls about your Dr. Mark mistake?"

"You just told me that you don't have time to date," Mia says.

"I don't. Grace thought I should find a date for the wedding," I answer.

"Did you?" Mia asks.

"No," Grace and I say at the same time. Mia and Grace emerge from the rooms at the same time. "Lola and Lexi will be the only two single people at the wedding," Grace says. She turns to Lola. "Unless you have someone you want to bring?"

"No," Lola says. "I'm coming alone." Lola shifts her gaze to me and gives me the same polite smile. She walks into her dressing room. I walk into mine.

 ## Surprise

It doesn't mean that she's not seeing Adrian, I tell myself as I walk to Lola's for our shower meeting. It means that she's not bringing him to the wedding. Whether Lola broke it off with Adrian or not doesn't change the fact that she lied to me. Do I want to know if Lola is still seeing Adrian? Do I want to know what happened between Lola and Susan? Yes, on both counts. But I can't ask. Not after what has happened.

Lola's doesn't open for lunch until 11:30 AM, so it is with surprise that, as I approach the restaurant at 11 AM, I see the front door propped open. A van with blinking hazard lights sits at the curb. Which is strange, because deliveries are made through the kitchen in the back. Is Lola's being robbed in broad daylight? My muscles, freshly pumped from Zoga, tighten, and I hold my yoga mat in front of me like a sword. I'm sweaty and unshowered and ready for a fight.

Peeking through the window, I see Lola talking to a man

wearing a white T-shirt and jeans smeared with gook. I'm about to knock on the window and wave when the man turns.

It's Jack McKay.

For the love of Buddah!

Leaping out of the window, I smack my shoulder against the brick wall of the restaurant and stifle my yelp of pain. Lola says, "I thought she was coming at ten-thirty, but maybe I got the time wrong. We might have said eleven o'clock. Why don't you wait? She'll be here any minute." Grabbing at my pony-tail, I untie it and try to smooth my curls into some kind of order. Then Jack mumbles something and walks out of the restaurant. Ducking behind a shrub, with which my frizz blends in nicely, I watch Jack get into the van and drive down the street. When the van has turned the corner, I stand up, put my hair back into its ponytail, and walk into Lola's.

"You just missed Jack McKay," Lola says. Picking a booth, I slide myself onto the cushy seat and unpack bridal magazines. Lola sits down across from me. "He installed the sculpture this morning." I raise my eyes to the metal sculpture of inter-twined whisks, spatulas, measuring cups, knives, forks, spoons, pots, and pans. The silver and brass gleam under a spotlight. "Jack said he can install colored spotlights. If I want. Later."

"It looks great."

"Thanks." Lola gives me the same polite smile she offered in the dressing room of Bridal Heaven. Returning the smile in kind, I move a pile of magazines towards her. "I brought these so we could get some ideas. Not that you don't have any ideas to start. I mean, you're the party expert, so if you have ideas already, I mean, that would be great."

Lola takes a magazine. "I haven't really thought about it. I've been busy with, you know. The TV show."

"Oh, right. Right." I don't ask about filming. I don't ask about anything. If she wants to tell me, she will.

Lola flips pages and lands on a layout of bridal shower party favors. "Which one do you like?" she asks in a false falsetto, moving the magazine toward me.

"I don't know. Which do you like?"

Lola shrugs. "You've known Grace a lot longer than I have. You know what she'd want."

"Yeah, but you're the one who knows about hostessing."

Instead of looking at each other, we stare at the magazine pages. "How about that?" I point at plastic boxes of pink, scented candles.

"Or that," Lola says and points at small bags holding various shades of pink nail polish.

"That's much cuter," I say.

"No." Lola shakes her head. "The candles are better."

"No, really," I insist. "I think the pink polishes are the better idea."

Lola shrugs her shoulders. "Okay. I mean, if that's what you think."

"Yeah. I do. But, I guess we could just, you know, keep skimming these magazines and see if anything else jumps out at us." Lola nods and opens another magazine. Casually, she says, "Jack was waiting for you. He asked about you and I mentioned that I was meeting you. I wasn't talking to him about you, or anything like that."

"Okay."

"He asked me to tell you the news about his gallery."

"Yeah?"

"He found a gallery space in Philadelphia. One of those gigantic old warehouses in the Northern Liberties area. He wanted you to know that. I'm not trying to butt in or anything like that. I said, 'Jack, her telephone works. ¿*Tu sabes?*' But then I thought maybe that was the wrong thing to say because maybe you don't want to hear from him. I didn't know."

"It's fine. Thanks for telling me."

"Okay. You're welcome."

Lola returns her attention to the bridal magazines and I stare at the top of her head. We're sitting here and we're talking to each other like casual acquaintances. The borders of our relationship have changed. The trust is gone. I used to feel safe telling Lola anything because I thought she was telling me everything. That sense of security has been breached.

Lola looks up and sees me watching her. "What?"

"Nothing," I answer.

This, then, is the new normal of our friendship.

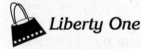 **Liberty One**

I thought it would be more cloak-and-dagger, but Low Man simply faxes me a list of The Gold Group's prospective clients, and clients up for renewal. Reviewing the lists is a walk down memory lane. Literally. With the client files at TGG and out of my grasp, I have to tap my memory to recall the particulars of the accounts.

The details of Liberty Bank's account come to mind easily. There was no heavy lifting with Liberty Bank. It was promotion of banking incentive programs and publicity for the bank's charitable works. I can do that. Easy.

*   *   *

"George Larrabie, please," I ask the receptionist when I call the bank's headquarters. "This is Lexi James calling."

George picks up the phone promptly. "Lexi? Good to hear from you."

In my PR voice, I say, "Thank you, George. I know bank presidents are always busy, so I'll get to the point of my call. I understand that Liberty Bank's contract with The Gold Group is up for renewal. Would you consider hiring my new firm to handle your public relations needs? If you give me the opportunity, I'd like to make a presentation to you and your board."

There is silence at the other end of the phone. Then, George says, "Of course, of course. I'll connect you with my secretary to make an appointment. End of the week work for you?"

"Thank you, George. That would be wonderful." End of the week? That's in three days.

Balls.

 **Press 3**

"You have . . . one . . . new message. First new message."

"Lexi? It's Jack McKay. Hi. Hello. I'm back. In Philadelphia. I got a cell phone. Finally. I forget the number, but it probably showed up on your caller ID. Call me back. I'd like to see you. Okay. Bye."

"To save this message, press 2. To delete this message, press 3. To . . ."

"The message has been deleted."

"Goodbye."

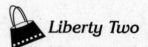 **Liberty Two**

Seventy-two hours later, I'm sitting in the anteroom of George Larrabie's office. In my hands are color charts and detailed action plans, all in nifty navy folders emblazoned with silver "LexiCo" stickers. May the goddess bless Kinko's.

In the mirror over the secretary's desk, I catch sight of my reflection. Not great, but not bad. I'm wearing my navy jacket and skirt and my white blouse with navy pinstripes. Tied around my neck is a navy scarf with white polka dots. I haven't worn heels in almost a month and my pumps are pinching me, and not in a good way.

It's not my clothes that are the problem. It's my face. My curls are spoiled by their freedom from the blow dryer and refuse to obey my command to stay tied into a bun. The circles under my eyes are giving me that adorable drug addict look. Whipping out my daybook, I make a huge note: BUY UNDEREYE CONCEALER.

"Lexi, it's wonderful to see you," George welcomes me, and shows me into his office.

"Thank you," I answer, grateful for his hospitality. George sits behind his massive oak desk and gestures to a chair in front of it. I sit. I'm confused. Aren't I presenting to his board?

I smile and wait for George to do something. He looks uncomfortable. Oh. I get it. I'm not presenting to the board because there's no way I'm going to get the Liberty Bank account. Why waste anyone else's time?

Leaning back in his chair, George says, "Well, Lexi." I brace myself. "The Liberty Bank account is yours."

"What?"

George smiles and nods. "Did you bring a contract for me to sign?"

Holding my hands up like stop signs, I say, "Wait a minute. Don't you want me to make a presentation?"

"No need."

"No need?" What's going on here?

"I know you'll do good work," George says. "You've always handled situations with the utmost discretion."

Discretion? Huh?

George smiles tightly and his eyes move quickly to a photograph on his desk. A guilty, sad look crosses his face.

I've seen that look. At the Ritz-Carlton. In the lobby, near the reception desk. George was with a woman. A woman who, I bet, is not the woman in the picture on his desk.

I get it. George thinks I'm blackmailing him. He thinks I'll rat him out unless he gives me the PR account. George probably thinks I've been biding my time, waiting for the perfect opportunity to use what I know.

I could do that. The Liberty Bank account carries a three-thousand-dollar monthly retainer. I need that money. I could take the account, keep my mouth shut, and do really good work for Liberty Bank.

I would have done it for The Gold Group without a second thought. I would have renewed the Liberty Bank account and never realized or questioned why George Larrabie was giving me what I wanted. But now I know what this is all about. What I did for The Gold Group, I won't do for LexiCo.

Inhaling deeply, I look kindly at George. "I don't want your account this way," I say smoothly. "If you allow me to compete fairly with The Gold Group and other agencies, I will thank you for the opportunity. Beyond that, I'm not asking you for special treatment. I don't want you to give me the Liberty Bank account. I want to earn it."

George runs his hand through his thick gray hair. "If you make a presentation to the board, I can't guarantee they will vote to hire you."

"I understand." George and I look at each other silently. George looks, what? Scared? Disgusted? Yes, he looks like he's disgusted with me. After all, George thinks I came here to manipulate him into giving me the Liberty Bank account. Perhaps in George's world, adultery is accepted but blackmail is unseemly. I feel dirty, even though I've done nothing wrong.

I clear my throat. "George, with all due respect, I don't want this account. I apologize for wasting your time. You can continue to rely on my discretion."

Standing up, I smooth my skirt and offer my hand. George jumps to his feet, shakes my hand and says, "I appreciate your integrity. Good luck, Lexi."

"Thank you, George." I smile back. "Good luck to you, too."

Not until I'm back in my apartment do I feel better. I am free to make my own decisions. Free to follow my conscience. Free to be poor. I laugh out loud. Boy, is Low Man going to be disappointed. I really do want to hire him. I'll get a money client. But I'll get it my way.

Unexpected Celebrations

That night, I'm at my desk in my jammie bottoms and a sports bra, eating Chee•tos and using the Internet to look up information about the other companies on Low Man's list. The phone rings.

"Lexi James," I answer.

"Are you working? It's almost midnight."

"Who is this?"

"Jack McKay."

"Oh. Hi." As if he can see me through the telephone, I run my fingers through my hair and wipe the Chee•to residue from my mouth.

"Congratulations on your new business. LexiCo is a catchy name."

"Thanks. Congratulations to you, too. What's your gallery called?"

"Nothing, yet. I have a couple weeks to think of a name. We're not opening until the middle of September. But your company is up and running, right?"

"Yes." Smiling, I lean back in my chair. "And it was a pretty big day for LexiCo."

"Did you snag a big client?"

"Nope. I let one go."

"That's a good thing?"

"Yes. Because I got to make the decision. I did the right thing."

"Congratulations."

"Thank you."

"So, what made you decide to go out on your own? Last

time I saw you, you were warning me about risk and responsibility and all that good stuff. What changed?"

"It's a long story."

"I want to hear it," Jack insists. "You know what? I'm coming over."

"What?" I jump up from my chair. "No."

"Yes. We'll celebrate your moral victory."

"I'm not dressed."

Jack pauses, then asks, "Is someone there with you?" He doesn't wait for an answer. "I would still like to see you. We can talk about business."

"You're in Northern Liberties. That's on the other side of town," I protest.

"The gallery is in Northern Liberties. I'm in an apartment three blocks from yours."

"You are? Whose?"

Jack avoids the question. "Listen, this is cause for celebration. Don't worry. I'm not going to come up to your apartment and sexually harass you. Unless you want me to. No, really, Lexi. I won't come upstairs. Meet me in the lobby in four minutes." He hangs up.

There's not much I can do to improve my appearance in four minutes. I pull a tank top over my sports bra and exchange jammie bottoms for a pair of cargo shorts. Once again, my hair revolts and refuses to be arranged into a ponytail. Whatever. I let it go loose. Face? Whatever makeup is left over from my morning meeting at Liberty Bank has either vanished or smeared around my eyes. Which looks accidentally sexy. No time to fix it. My purple flip-flops wait for me by the door.

When I exit the elevator, Jack walks through the lobby door.

He's wearing faded jeans, a mustard-colored T-shirt, and work boots. A canvas bag is slung across his broad shoulders. "Perfect timing." He smiles, and before I can react, Jack grabs my hand. "Love the curls," he says and pulls me out the door.

With my flip-flops flapping in the quiet midnight, Jack drags me across the street into Rittenhouse Square and down a brick path to a bench lit from above by a street lamp. "Sit," he tells me, and unzips his canvas bag. "I always say you should keep a bottle of champagne in the refrigerator for unexpected celebrations like this." From the bag, Jack removes a bottle of ginger ale. He shakes the bottle, then unscrews the cap. The bubbles spray onto the pavement. "Unfortunately, this will have to do."

"I appreciate the effort."

Jack turns toward me on the bench and crosses his legs Indian-style. Leaning forward on his elbows and looking not unlike a COG member, Jack says, "Tell me everything."

"Why are you so interested?"

Jack tilts his head and raises his left eyebrow. "Things didn't work out with us romantically, but I do like you as a person and we are in similar situations now. You're starting your business. I'm starting mine. It's a lot of hard work and it's risky and a little scary, quite frankly, and a lot of people don't understand that." Nodding in agreement, I think of my friends' lack of support when I told them that I wanted to start my own company. "The COG was less than thrilled about my entrepreneurship."

"See? Further evidence that the COG isn't always right."

"Yeah."

"Have you become less COG dependent since I've been away?"

Looking at the ground, I consider his question. "Things have changed."

"Enough about the COG. Tell me about LexiCo." It takes me an hour to tell Jack the entire story. He listens to every word, not yawning once and asking a lot of questions. When I'm finished, I insist that Jack tell me about his gallery. We talk about sole proprietorships, incorporating, bank accounts, lines of credit, and most importantly, the importance of following one's gut.

Finally, Jack walks me back to my building. Outside the lobby door, he offers me his hand to shake. I take it and give it a shake. "I'm glad we can be friends, Lexi."

"Me too. Thanks for listening."

"Thanks for listening to me."

Suddenly, I have tears in my eyes. It's been a long, emotional day. And I haven't told anyone about it, except Jack. But Jack can't deal with tears. He starts to walk backward down the street. "Let me know if there's anything you need. I'm around."

"Yeah, about that. Where exactly are you staying?"

From halfway down the block, Jack shouts, "Just call my cell. Good night!"

Upstairs, I toss myself into bed, and although my body feels heavy with sleep, my shoulders feel lighter for having shared my day. With Jack McKay. Interesting. He's the last person I would think to confide in. As I fall asleep, I realize that I didn't even smell him.

A COG Shower

"Act surprised," I tell Ellie. Having just picked her up in Grace's very practical but uncool Honda Accord, we are driving toward the nonsurprise bridal shower.

"Grace knows, too," Ellie says. "She's the one who told me."

"Whatever, El. Act surprised. Make your mom happy." Flipping open my cell phone, I hit the first speed dial.

"What does my mother have to do with it? You and Lola planned it."

"Then make us happy and look surprised. *¿Ça va?*"

"*Ça va.*"

"Gracie? It's Lexi. Can you hear me? Good. I'll be at your apartment in five minutes to pick you up. You'll never guess where we're going."

Although she knows about the shower, Grace is not prepared for the wave of love that envelops her and Ellie when they walk into Lola's. "It's overwhelming," Grace tells me later as she sobs in the bathroom. Like everything about Lola's, the bathroom is posh. With comfy chairs, fresh flowers, and thick towels, the room is dedicated to the comfort of the women who use it.

We are sitting on the long, marble counter and I'm rubbing Grace's back. "All of these people are here for me," she says softly.

"Not really. Half of them are here for Ellie."

"You know what I mean." Grace blows her nose. "Kammie

came from Manhattan just for the shower. Isn't she awesome? All of these women. All of this . . . estrogen."

"In the restaurant?"

"In my body. I'm getting my period tomorrow so I'm a little premenstrual."

"I hadn't noticed." Mia and Lola come rushing into the bathroom. Mia pokes at my shoulder. "What did you say to her?"

"Ouch! I didn't say anything. Quit poking me."

"I'm a little emotional," Grace understates. "It's not Lexi's fault." Ellie bangs open the bathroom door. "What's going on in here? Why is Grace crying? Lexi? What did you do?"

Exasperated, I throw my hands into the air.

"She didn't do anything," Mia explains. "Gracie is just overwhelmed."

"Yes," Ellie sighs and collapses into a chair. "It's been a long time since I've seen most of these people. How many more times can I tell the story of how I met Jean-François?"

"We should've written it on cards and distributed to people as they came in," I say seriously. "We could have said, 'Ellie is marrying a Frenchman. Here's the story. She'll take questions at the end of the shower.' " Ellie laughs.

Mia sits on another chair. "We could just hang in here for a while." She pauses. "I need to be near a toilet anyway."

"Why?" Lola asks. "Did you eat something bad?"

"No." Mia puts her hands over her mouth, much as Simon does when he doesn't want someone to talk. Smiling behind her fingers, Mia blurts, "I'm pregnant."

"What?" Grace jumps from the counter and envelops Mia in a hug. "How pregnant are you? Why didn't you tell me?"

"Two months," Mia answers. "I really shouldn't tell anyone until I'm finished with my first trimester. Oh, well."

"This calls for a celebration," Lola declares and hurries out of the bathrooom.

Ellie hugs Mia. "Michael is happy?"

"Thrilled," Mia says with a big smile. It's my turn to hug Mia Rose, and when I do, she whispers in my ear, "Thank you, Lexi." Just then, Lola bursts back into the bathroom and locks the door behind her. Turning, she shows us a tray of mini Veuve Clicquot bottles made more festive with colored straws. "Champagne!" Lola cries and gives a mini bottle to everyone but Mia, to whom she hands a bottle of sparkling water.

"Ellie, you have to set a date," Grace admonishes after she brings the COG up-to-date on her wedding plans. We're still languishing in the bathroom. Because the restaurant is closed for the shower and all the guests are women, Lola has directed toilet traffic to the men's room.

"I will set the date," Ellie promises. "When we get back from vacation."

"Where are you going now?" Lola wants to know.

"Well, it's August in France," Ellie says.

"It's August here, too," I tell her.

Ellie smacks herself in the head. "Sorry. Champagne. Jet lag. What I mean is Europeans typically take vacation in August. Jean-François was teaching summer classes at the university so we couldn't leave Paris. But he doesn't have to be at the university until the beginning of October, so we'll take our vacation in September. He arrives in a week or so. We'll drive across America. I've traveled all over Europe, but of this country, I've seen the East Coast and California and nothing in between. We'll be back here for Grace's wedding. That's the plan. We take a few weeks. We drive. We go."

"Your English is getting progressively worse," I tell Ellie. "You might need a translator."

"As soon as you get back, you need to set a date," says one-track-mind Grace. "You can't be engaged forever." Ellie nods, but I think she wouldn't mind being engaged forever, or at least until Grace's bridal fever abates.

"Speaking of travel," I say, "guess who's back in town? Jack McKay. I saw him a few nights ago." I give them a very brief description of my celebration with Jack.

"Did you sleep with him?" Grace wants to know.

"No."

"Still"—Grace shakes her head—"I can tell that you're getting attached to him."

"I am not," I protest. "I haven't seen him for months."

"I understand why you like Jack," Ellie says. "Bad boy with a heart of gold."

"Billy Kidman," Grace declares.

"Don't start with me," I warn her. Turning to Ellie, I say, "I don't think that Jack is much of a bad boy and I'm not sure his heart is gold. Maybe a metal alloy of some kind."

"*Oui*, but he sounds like trouble. He didn't call you when he came back to Philadelphia. He tells you that he doesn't want a committed relationship. What's the point of getting involved with a man like that?"

"Thank you!" Grace shouts.

Spinning around, I point my finger into Grace's face. "One more word out of you and I'm going into the restaurant to tell your mother that you're planning on moving in with Michael. Before the wedding."

Grace gasps. "You wouldn't."

"Oh, but I would."

"Girls," Mia moans. "Stop it."

Grace pouts and sticks her straw in her mouth. Appealing to the COG, I ask, "Can't Jack and I just be friends?"

In unison, they shout, "No!"

Mia gets to her feet. "I have to pee again, but before I do, let me say this. Lexi, you need to be careful about Jack. Ellie is right that his life is very unsettled. I think you need someone a lot more stable than that. Lola? You know him better than any of us. What do you think of him?"

Lola, who has remained almost silent for the past half hour, looks at the floor. "Lexi can make up her own mind."

"Since when?" Grace asks, and everyone laughs except Lola. For a quick second, Lola turns her eyes to meet mine and she gives me a small, sad smile.

 ## The Whoosh of Success

"Lexi! Hurry up! The reporter from the *Times* is waiting."

"Okay, okay!" Getting off the toilet, I pull up my pants, button them, and run into the living room. I pick up the telephone and nod at Mike DiBuono, former Low Man on the Totem Pole, current vice president of LexiCo.

Mike came through for me. He clued me in to five companies looking for public relations that The Gold Group had declined to pitch because Maria and/or Susan decided the potential clients couldn't afford the retainer.

"That's stupid," I told Mike at our second meeting over dinner at Sang Kee. I'm introducing Mike to my spay sha soup. "They could take the small clients and give them to the new hirees, with Maria overseeing their work. Susan doesn't want to waste time with the little fish, does she? But then, if you lose one big money client, you're in deep doo doo. You need to diversify."

Mike nodded and sipped his soup. "Greed ain't what it used to be."

I called each company and requested an opportunity to make a proposal. Of those five accounts, I nailed two. As I promised, I hired Mike as vice president of LexiCo. Mike didn't have a noncompete with The Gold Group because he was a mere junior account executive. Now he's the VP. He makes me call him Veep.

Okay, so he's the vice president of not a whole lot, but Mike has lifted my work load by half, which leaves me time to pursue new clients. Although he is doing account work, Mike knows a lot about administrative work. I'm fascinated by his knowledge of postage, collating, database entry, and more. Mike is in my apartment by 8 AM at the latest. I'm always working when we walks in, but sometimes I'm still in my jammies. Mike stays as late as he needs to, and he has a key to my apartment so he can lock up if I have to leave before he does.

It's either funny or sad that the first man I've given my house keys to is a gay man.

"Did you flush the toilet?" Mike asks, his hand covering the phone.

"Of course not." We can't flush the toilet and talk on the phone at the same time because the toilet makes a loud whooshing noise that lasts for a few minutes and is discernible to whoever is on the phone. Such are the drawbacks of working in my apartment.

When I finish my conversation with the *Times* reporter, I

have a guarantee that she will include photos of Zoga Jane with the story on the studio. "Thank you so much," I tell the reporter just in time to hear the other line beep in my ear. That call waiting beep drives me nuts. I need to get a new phone system. "Good afternoon, LexiCo," I chirp. I listen. "I'm just fine thanks, and you?" I listen. "Yes, he's right here. Just a minute." I hand the phone across the dining room table to Mike. "It's the producer at Channel 6. He wants to talk to you about tomorrow's shoot at Café Oz with Ruby's Love cookies." Mike takes the phone and I get up from the table. "Wait, Mike, what do you want for lunch? I'll go get it."

"Club sandwich, nonfat mayo, nonfat cheese, nonfat turkey, and a Diet Coke. Thanks."

"No problem. Oh, one more thing? Don't forget to flush the toilet when you're off the phone." I smile at Mike and leave.

 ## Overruling the COG

Later that week, as I'm about to turn off my computer and my brain, my phone rings. It's Jack calling. He sounds nervous. He offers a greeting, then launches his plea. "Will you go with me to a fund-raiser on Saturday night? It's the Big Ben Benefit for the Franklin Institute. I had a date but now I don't, and I have to go because one of the cochairs has bought a lot of my art. I realize this is last minute, but this could be a good event for both of us. We'll meet people who have money to spend on art and PR."

My brain is a few sentences back. "You had a date, but now you don't?"

"Yeah."

"Explain."

"You see, I was dating this girl but she got mad at me because one night I left her apartment at midnight and didn't come back until after two in the morning and I couldn't adequately explain where I went."

"You called me from another woman's apartment?"

"I thought she was asleep. She's a sound sleeper. Or so I thought."

"Jack," I say with reproach.

"So, in effect," he continues, "this is all your fault and you should feel horribly guilty and come to my aid and be my friend and my date."

"I do feel guilty," I tell him honestly. However, the COG just advised me to stay away from Jack. You know what? "I'll go."

"Good. I'll pick you up at seven o'clock."

The Big Ben Benefit is a snazzy affair. What to wear? It's August, which is an unusual time for a black-tie fund-raiser. However, there are no other functions this weekend, so Big Ben has no competition except the Jersey shore.

Something slinky, then? I own five little black dresses, in varying degrees of littleness. My favorite is a spaghetti-strapped, A-line dress that flows into soft ruffles at my ankles. My black mules with stiletto heels match perfectly. Yes, stiletto mules and a long dress make walking a challenge. So what?

Now, for the hair. Looking at my reflection in the mirror, I sigh at the sight of my hair. It has grown long. Way past my shoulders. I decide to postpone the hair arranging and tackle the face.

Once upon a time, mascara and lipstick were all I needed. No longer. Now I don't go anywhere without my concealer. Wiping large swaths of it under my eyes, I look like a football player with beige instead of black eye markings. As I blend, I look closely at the crow's feet stretching from the corners of my eyes.

Wrinkle, wrinkle, little line. How I wonder what you are. Up above my cheeks so high. Like a time line of my eye.

The rest of my cosmetics applied, I return to the conundrum posed by my hair. Straight? Curly? Up? Down? Curly and down, I decide, and that's my final answer. It's just plain easier to let my hair be its natural self.

My phone rings at 6:56 PM and the night doorman tells me that Jack McKay is waiting in the lobby. "Ask him to come upstairs," I answer.

 ## The Big Bouquet

At Jack's knock, I open my door. He's wearing a kilt. And a white shirt, black bow tie, and black tuxedo jacket. "Interesting choice," I tell him.

"Thank you." Jack grins like a kid. "I like to make an impression. It's my family's plaid from Scotland. The clan McKay. I'm quite proud of it, to tell you the truth." Jack is holding something in both hands behind his back. I hear rustling and peer behind him. "Oh this? I was going to bring you flowers to thank you for coming with me."

"Jack, that is so sweet." I reach out my hands to accept the bouquet.

"But I didn't."

"Oh." I put my hands down at my sides.

"I thought it might be too datelike. And since this isn't a date, I thought that might be inappropriate. I didn't want to make you uncomfortable, so I didn't bring a bouquet of flowers. But I drew you a picture of them." From behind his back, Jack brings an ivory sheet of paper with a pastel chalk drawing of wild flowers.

Accepting the drawing, I admire it. "Thank you." That really was very sweet of him. "I'll get it framed."

"Framed?" Jack laughs. "It's just a cheap drawing. Throw it away when you're tired of looking at it. It's not worth getting it framed."

Ten minutes later, we're waiting in my hall for the elevator. Instead of looking at each other, we stare at the doors until they open. Jack waves me into the elevator, then stands on the opposite side of the car. We stare at the descending numbers. "By the way," he says without looking at me, "you look stunning."

"Thank you," I answer graciously.

Standing at the bottom of the white marble staircase leading up to the Franklin Institute, I hitch up my dress with one hand, hold my purse in the other hand, and move tentatively up the first step. Wobble wobble. There go my stiletto heels. Watching me wobble, Jack stands two arm lengths away from me and tries not to laugh. When I glare at him, he offers me his arm. "Friends don't let friends fall on their ass," he says.

 ## The Big Ben Benefit

The Franklin Institute is a gorgeous monument to dear old Ben's scientific experiments. Its thirty-odd steps lead to marble columns and a loggia worthy of a Founding Father. The

Franklin Institute glitters in sunshine or starlight. It stands on manicured lawns that act as the gateway to the Benjamin Franklin Parkway, home of the Philadelphia Museum of Art, the Rodin Museum, the Free Library, and other parts of Philadelphia's cultural center.

The Franklin Institute is also a fine place to have a party, and the Big Ben Benefit is its annual gala fund-raiser. White lights lead to the main atrium, which vibrates with music from the live band. Bouquets of red and yellow flowers burst from every table. Butlers swish through with trays of finger foods. Surrounding the party scene are scientific exhibits, so Philadelphians can feel smart while they get sloshed.

Jack and I move around the room. Despite his attention-getting appearance, Jack really is shy when the cochair of the event introduces him to other partygoers. The cochair and his wife gush about Jack's Junk Art, and Jack receives their compliments with gracious modesty. When the wife encourages Jack to tell her friends about his gallery, I excuse myself to get us libations.

Drinks in hand, I look around for Jack and see that he has been introduced to a new group of people. Good for him. When I catch his eye, he winks at me. I raise his beer in the air and he shakes his head slightly, so I park myself at a cocktail table and observe the crowd.

"Lexi?"

Turning, I see Maria Simons. She looks like a big stick of butter. Butter, not butta. Maria's rectangular frame is swathed in yellow satin. The color looks good against Maria's light brown skin, but the shape of the dress is all kinds of wrong, drawing attention to her muscular shoulders and thick thighs.

If Maria still worked for me, I would have made her go home to change.

"I wasn't sure if that was you," Maria says. "Your hair is so different." She offers a smile. "You look great, though." Hesitantly, she asks, "How are you?"

"Fabulous," I say with gusto. "You?"

Maria rolls her eyes. "Things could be better. I guess you heard what happened with Lola's TV show." I smile and nod as if I know what she's talking about, and Maria starts to vent. "When The Cuisine Channel told me that one of the show's sponsors dropped out, I freaked. Everybody freaked. Thank goodness Bob West found a replacement sponsor so quickly. But I can't believe we have to reshoot the first seventeen episodes with Real Chef pans instead of Cook Rite pans. We were supposed to wrap next week, you know? Now we're looking at two more weeks of filming. Did Lola tell you that the TCC wants to do a slice-and-dice?"

"No."

"They decided last week. Instead of retaping seventeen entire episodes, TCC wants to edit around any shots that show the Cook Rite pans. The director has to film new footage which can be edited into previously taped footage. To do that, Lola will have to watch herself on monitors and attempt to recreate what she was doing and saying and cooking. As Lola has made perfectly clear, she is a cook, not an actress. She and the director are yelling and screaming at each other. It's total chaos, and it's only going to delay things more."

Playing with the label on my beer bottle, I say, "That sounds like a bad situation."

"Lola wants to put filming on hold, take a few days off, and come up with a better solution. She's worried that the slice-

and-dice is going to compromise the quality of the shows. Susan wants to plow through and get it finished. So does TCC, obviously." Maria pauses, and I feel as though she's waiting for me to comment. When I don't say anything, Maria says, "I think Lola is right."

"So do I."

Maria looks relieved at my answer, although I don't know why. My opinion isn't going to help her in any way. Sighing loudly, Maria says, "I wish I could convince Susan to change her mind." She looks at me with comic jealousy. "You had such freedom to do what you wanted."

What happened to the paranoid freak who accused me of sabotaging The Gold Group? And does she really think Susan will give her autonomy after a month's tenure? Yes, she has my throne, but only because I abdicated. Leaning close to me, Maria says, "Come on, Lexi. Tell me the secret. How did you get that freedom?"

With my PR smile plastered on my face, I answer, "I earned it."

"There you are." Jack arrives at the cocktail table and picks up a beer bottle. He realizes it is empty, and reaches for the other one. That, too, is empty. What can I say? Maria's melodrama made me thirsty. Looking at Maria, Jack smiles and waits to be introduced. "Good luck," I tell Maria. Taking Jack's hand, I lead him back to the bar where I get another beer.

"They gave me their addresses to put them on the gallery's mailing list," Jack says. "As if I have one of those." We are strolling around the room, not arm in arm and not hand in hand.

"Get a database program for your computer," I tell him. "Then you can do regular mailings to people who have ex-

pressed interest in the gallery. Openings, holiday stuff, whatever."

Jack shrugs. "I guess I should buy a computer." We sit at a
table so I can rest my stilettos.

"Yes. And you should get a Web site." A friend of Jack's is
already working on his Web site, and Jack tells me about it.
From behind me, I hear a familiar voice. I'm pretty sure I know
who it belongs to, but I don't want to turn and look. Philadelphia is such a small town. A village, really. The same sorts of
people go to the same sorts of events, and I'm amazed that I
haven't seen him before tonight. Then I hear, "She's here with
a guy who's wearing a kilt?" It's got to be him. Diving into my
handbag, I remove my lipstick mirror and hold it over my
shoulder. There he is. Ron Anderson. I watch his mouth move
as he says, "I guess she couldn't find a normal guy to date.
She's really hit rock bottom. I feel bad for her."

Sucking air through my mouth, I snap my bag closed,
stand, and walk away from the table, in the opposite direction of Ron's voice. Jack follows me. "What's the matter?"
Holding my chin in the air to let the tears flow backward
into my ducts, I stride toward the entryway. "Where are you
going? Lexi? Lexi?" With my back to Jack, I blink my eyes
clear and, for the second time that night, plaster my PR
smile onto my face. Turning to Jack, I say, "Have you ever
seen the heart?"

"The what?"

"No? It's amazing. One of the best things about the Franklin
Institute. All the schools come here on field trips to see it. I've
seen it twice. We could probably sneak upstairs and look at it."

"Are we allowed to go upstairs?" Jack asks.

"Probably not."

"Good. Let's do it." Jack grins.

"I'm not sure which way to go."

"There's a sign over there," Jack says from behind me. He puts his hand on the small of my back and gently guides me through the crowd. His palm presses against the curve above my hip; the tips of his fingers reach my spine. It has been three months since our Bed-In, but Jack's touch gives me goose bumps. And makes me feel less lonely.

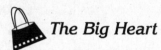 The Big Heart

"That is amazing," Jack says as we look up at the heart.

"Too bad it's dark in here," I say. "Think we'd get in trouble if we turned on the lights?"

"What are they going to do? Give us detention?" With that, Jack walks away to find the controls and fearlessly break several rules.

Standing by myself, I look up at the heart in the darkness.

"Ready?" Jack calls. I hear him hit a series of buttons. The lights come on and before me is the giant heart.

The heart is several stories tall. It is an anatomically correct heart, complete with veins and arteries and all that stuff. There are passageways for visitors to walk through and observe the inner, intimate workings of the human heart. It even beats. Da-dum. Da-dum.

"Cool," Jack says. "Let's go in."

Following Jack, I step up a walkway and run my hand along the blue veins that lead through the heart's chambers. It looks like a giant cave, lit from inside. The walls glow dark red, deep blue and purple. The beat vibrates the walls. Da-dum. Da-dum.

"Way cool," Jack says as we walk through one of the heart's chambers. Holding the hem of my dress, I laugh and say, "Someone should make one of these out of a penis."

Jack turns around and smiles at me. "Something on your mind, Ms. James?"

"No. No. It's just that this is, you know, a big throbbing heart."

Jack cocks his left eyebrow.

"I just mean that, you know, here we are. I'm wearing a dress. You're wearing a dress."

Putting his hand on the blood red wall, Jack leans over me. "This whole friends thing is working out really well. Don't you think?" He takes a step closer to me and bows his head to look into my eyes.

But my eyes drift to Jack's left brow. I am hypnotized by the scar there. It's a white line through Jack's brown eyebrow. How did he get that scar? Did it hurt? Does it still? Inclining my head, I stare at the scar. I want to touch it. Slowly, as if the scar might still hurt, I reach my hand toward Jack's face.

Mistaking my intent, Jack takes my hand and kisses my palm. I draw away from him as if he's burned me. "We should go back to the party," I tell him.

Jack takes a few steps backward and leans against one of the cavelike walls of the heart. He looks irritated that I have spurned him. "What were you running away from at the party?"

"My ex-fiancé."

Jack's face immediately smooths into compassion. "Oh, Lexi. I'm sorry." My eyes start to tear again and I press my lips together. Jack hops down two steps and, in one smooth move, wraps me into a hug and winds his hands through my hair to cradle my head.

And then I don't feel like crying. I just stand there and appreciate Jack's embrace. Inhaling, I try to catch his soap smell, but it's smothered by his clothes.

After a few minutes, Jack moves me backward and looks at me like he wants to kiss me. Pushing him gently, I tell him that this is a bad idea. "I'm just trying to be smart about it."

"I know," he answers, but he doesn't let go of me so I keep talking.

"We both admitted that we aren't good at relationships, and the way this is going, I mean, it seems like it's getting relationshipish and I don't think either of us has the time or, or, or the desire to start something serious right now, what with our businesses just starting, and so I think we should stick to the friendship thing, because that way neither of us will get hurt or hurt the other person." Finished, I smile at Jack and take a step backward.

Jack nods and takes a step forward. "You're right." I take a step backward. He takes a step forward. I take a step backward and bump into the wall of the heart. "But I'm going to kiss you anyway." With my back against the wall, Jack leans into me and raises my chin with his finger. I look up into his blue eyes and move my eyes down to his mouth.

It's just a kiss, I tell myself.

Jack kisses me.

I kiss Jack.

It is a slow kiss. Jack touches his lips to mine, gently at first, then with more pressure. He moves his head slowly, moving his mouth over mine. Jack puts one hand on the back of my neck, his thumb on my jaw. Moving forward with only the slight pressure of his hand, I lean into his body. Slowly, Jack puts his other hand on the small of my back. He moves the thumb of that hand slowly over my spine.

Oh my goodness.

Jack slips his tongue into my mouth very slowly.

I can't move my limbs. All my energy is focused on my mouth. Limp against Jack, I let him move me backward again, into the wall of the heart. He takes his mouth from mine, and I have an instantaneous feeling of loss. I want his mouth on mine again.

But now Jack is standing at arm's length from me. I wonder quickly if he means to leave me here in a puddle.

No. He puts his hands on my shoulders and slowly, slowly, slides the straps of my dress down my arms. Jack gives me plenty of time to stop him.

I don't.

In a quick movement, Jack turns me around so my back is to him and my front is pressed against the throbbing wall. He unzips my dress and it falls to my feet. Jack spins me around and, looking into my eyes, puts my hands on the opening fold of his kilt. "Yes?" he asks.

"Yes," I whisper.

Many heartbeats later, Jack covers me with his kilt. We are lying on the floor of the heart. "I think we just made an enormous mistake."

Jack continues to stare up at the bloodred ceiling of the chamber and doesn't respond. "Jack? Did you hear what I said?"

Smiling, he says, "You lost me after enormous."

Groaning, I ask, "Can you stop being a guy?"

"What do you want me to be?"

Tossing his kilt off me, I reach for my dress. "We better get dressed before we get caught."

Jack hands me my purse. "Do you have a tissue in there?" I open my bag and fish out a tissue. Jack wraps the used condom in the tissue.

"Funny how you had that condom handy," I comment.

"Jacket pocket," he says, answering a different question. "And why do you think we made an enormous mistake? I mean, here we are. In the heart of hearts." Jack nudges me. "Get it?"

"I get it. And two of my most recent mistakes are downstairs partying—Ron and Maria." I'm not looking to add to their roster.

"Relax," Jack says. "Let's dance."

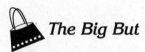

The Big But

After the benefit, outside my building, I thank Jack for a fun night. He looks serious, as if he's been working on a speech during the cab ride. To preempt him, I suggest we end the night. "Let's not ruin the night by talking, okay?"

"I have something to say to you, Lexi."

Here we go. Another "let's be friends" speech. With my hands on my hips, I say, "Let's have it."

Jack leans against the brick wall of my building. "I'm about to say something, and I'm either really right or I'm really wrong."

"Not good odds."

"Can you be serious for a minute?" Jack tucks his hair behind his ears. The street light hits his face and I see wrinkles around his eyes and mouth, and quite a few creases on his forehead. Just that minute, I realize that he is older than I am.

"I'm sorry. Go ahead."

"Here's the thing. I think there is, without a doubt, something between us. A combination of friendship and passion. It scares both of us, I know. We've both made mistakes in the past. But here's what I'm wondering. Should we try to work this out? Maybe we should put our fears and pasts behind us, and try to figure out how to"—Jack waves his hands in the air as if conjuring a magic spell—"make this a relationship. What do you think?"

After a few seconds, I say, "I don't know."

Jack squints at me. "What do you mean?"

"What do you mean, 'What do you mean'?"

Cocking his eyebrow at me, Jack says, "I mean, I don't understand your answer."

"This is a really bad time to be having this conversation."

"When we met seven months ago, that was a bad time. Now is a bad time, too. Well, maybe we should just go with the bad timing and turn it into good timing. I mean, I think we should just make the decision that we want to try. Admit that we could really screw things up, or something great could happen. I think we just have to"—Jack waves his hands again, then blurts—"commit to it."

Truly, I am touched by Jack's words and the emotion behind them. I feel, I don't know, honored? He wants to make a commitment. To me. But I don't know if I can do it. Even if Jack was Captain Fantastic, I don't think I have the, what? "Tools," I say out loud. "I don't think that I have the tools to make a relationship work. But I'm working on it. And I thought I was making progress in the emotional maturity department, but then I saw my ex-fiancé and all that guilt and fear of failure came back."

"You have to get over that," Jack tells me.

"Oh? Okay. No problem."

"Or maybe you're just using that as an excuse not to move forward with your life and take another risk." Jack is getting upset, and I don't blame him.

"Maybe you're right," I admit. "But."

With a wry smile on his face, Jack kicks the pavement and says, "I'm not going to stand here and beg you to be with me. I feel like a girl."

That makes me smile, but Jack's not kidding. He's getting progressively pissed. Taking a step closer to him, I put my hands on the flap of his kilt. "Can I think about this?"

Jack stares at the pavement and shrugs. "Yeah. Whatever." He looks up at me and I give him a quick kiss on the cheek.

"I'll call you," I tell him.

 ## The COG's Assault

Thwack.

A rolled up *Sunday Inquirer* smacks against my head and jolts me awake. "What the hell?" I sit up to see Mia, Ellie, and Grace standing around my bed. "That really hurt," I whine. "You could have given me a concussion."

Ellie points at Grace and says, "She's a nurse."

"What happened to 'First, do no harm'?" I mumble and rub my head.

"That's for doctors," Grace answers.

With my hand on my head, I look at the COG. "I want my house keys back."

"Don't you want to know why we're here?" Mia asks.

Lowering my head gingerly onto my pillow, I pull my covers up to my chin. "No. I don't want to know." Curling into a ball, I put a pillow over my head. Grace tears the pillow from my grasp. "You aren't curious?"

"Given that you broke into my apartment and assaulted me with a deadly weapon, I'm guessing that you're here to yell at me about something. I'm too tired to be yelled at. Come back later. Call first." I roll over and close my eyes.

There's a pause, then Ellie, Mia, and Grace cannonball themselves onto my bed. Mia rolls me onto my back. "Here's what happened," Grace begins. "While we were waiting for you at brunch, we started going through the Sunday paper. And guess what we saw?" Grace puts a newspaper broadsheet over my face. Groaning, I grab the newspaper from my head and hold it away from my face so I can focus on it. In the middle of the page, there is a picture of me and Jack with a caption which reads, "Patrons dance at last night's Big Ben Benefit."

 ## Read All About It, Part Two

It's a black-and-white photo of me and Jack. We are dancing. Jack has one arm wrapped completely around my waist with his fingers touching the inside of my hip. His other arm is by his side, giving full view to my body, flat against his. One of my hands is on his chest. The other hand is on the back of his neck. Our faces are inches apart.

I look at the COG with total guilt.

"You might as well tell us the whole story," Mia says. I spin the story and tell them that Jack invited me to the benefit at the last minute and I agreed because I've been really stressed about LexiCo and needed to have some fun. I try for sympathy. They don't buy it. "You needed some sex," Ellie states.

"Billy Kidman," Grace belches.

"How do you know we had sex?"

"Please!" Grace shouts.

"Look at the two of you in this picture," Ellie says.

"But, wait," Mia says. "Jack isn't here. Where did you have sex? Did he finally show you his apartment?"

"Um, no. No apartment." The COG raise six eyebrows at me.

"You're lucky you didn't get caught," Ellie says disapprovingly.

"That is so unhygienic," Grace admonishes.

"What's with the kilt?" Mia asks.

"So what happens now?" Ellie asks.

"I don't know. What's in the bag?" I reach for the plastic bag from the bakery down the street. "Did you bring me breakfast in bed?"

Mia slaps my hand away. "Answer the question."

"Jack suggested that we try to work on a relationship." Grace opens her mouth to criticize and I jump on top of her and put my hand over her mouth. "But I don't think that's the right thing to do. I need to find someone stable and all of that. Is that what you were going to say, Gracie?" With my hand still over her mouth, Grace nods. "The thing with Jack is too complicated and I'm not going to pursue it. Happy?" Grace nods, and I release her. She punches me in the arm with her left hand. "Ouch!" Her diamond leaves an indent on my bicep.

"Girls," Mia says. "Stop it."

Rubbing my arm, I realize that one of the COG is absent. "Where's Lola?"

"She waited at the restaurant but said she didn't have time to come over here and roust you out of bed," Ellie says.

Grace says, "She didn't want to come over because you have such horribly bad morning breath."

"Shut up," I laugh. But it's not funny that Lola doesn't feel comfortable in my home.

Mia opens the bakery bag and removes plastic containers of flavored cream cheese. "I'll get knives," she says, and wanders into the kitchen.

"We'll have to use chopsticks," I holler.

 ## The Elder Council on Shtupping

Later that afternoon, the Elder COG is waiting for me in the sun-drenched, over-air-conditioned activities room. Of course, they read the newspaper. Or at least they look at the pictures.

"Oh, Lexi," Ruth starts. "What a beautiful photo of you and that man. Ach, the dancing. The dancing!"

"Who is he?" Sylvia croaks. "Tell us everything."

I absolutely do not tell them everything. I edit. "Jack is a friend. He needed a date. We had a good time."

"It looks like you're more than friends," Esther says wickedly.

"*Mazel tov, shayna*," Ruth says and clasps her hands together. "Maybe it is love, yes?"

"Lexi?" Sylvia interrupts. "Is he a good *shtup*? Because that's really important."

"Sylvia!" I look at the other women, expecting them to admonish Sylvia for her brusqueness. But they don't. They want to know, too.

"You can tell us, dear." Esther pats my knee.

"We can help," Ruth says. "Three old ladies. We've got a lot of experience." Ruth nods her head sagaciously. While I am processing the thought of the Elder Council having sex advice to share with me, Sylvia gets impatient. "He looks like a good dancer," she says.

"So?" The Elder Council throw their hands in the air and tsk at me.

"This generation," Ruth moans.

"What they don't know," Esther sighs.

Sylvia clarifies. "If he can dance, he can *shtup*."

"Sylvia!" I cover my ears, but I've already heard her.

"It's true, *bubbeleh*," Sylvia says, patting my shoulder. "Why do you think we went to all those dances when we were young? To see how a man moves his body. To see how he moves your body. Back then, we didn't get into bed with each other until we were married. Well, Esther did, but most of us of didn't."

Shrugging, Esther says, "I was a slut."

"So anyway," Sylvia continues, "what's this Jack like in the sack?"

Trying to be coy, I ask, "How do you know that I had sex with him?"

"*Shana*," Ruth says. "In that picture, you look like you just got out of the backseat of a car."

I'm not about to tell them that there was no car, and we had just gotten out of the throbbing heart. "Anyone for gin rummy?"

Baby Sy's First Day of School

"Don't cry. It'll be okay. Oh, honey. Don't cry." It's Simon Rose's first day of school, and who's doing the crying? His mother.

Mia Rose is distraught. Baby Sy's first day of school is Mia's first day of work, and she didn't come to my apartment alone. She brought her prenatal mood swings.

"It's because of the pregnancy," I whisper to Mike, who is looking at Mia with undisguised horror. Mia was long gone from The Gold Group when Mike began his tenure. This is, unfortunately, the first time they have met. "She's almost through her first trimester."

"So we have six more months of this?"

"No," I insist in a hushed voice. "I don't know. I hope not. She wasn't like this with her other two pregnancies." Mike and I wince as Mia blows her nose into a tissue. "She'll be fine," I say unconvincingly. "She'll be fine."

Within the hour, Mia is back to her nonweepy self, and by lunchtime, Mia and Mike are best friends. While Mike brings her up to speed on computer advances of the past six years, Mia teaches him the finer points of writing, editing, and proof-reading.

Just before Mia leaves to get home before her sons, I stride into my apartment with a huge smile on my face. "How did it go?" Mia and Mike ask at the same time. Before I answer, I look around the apartment at the gray metal filing cabinet I bought on the first day of LexiCo, and the twin it has since sprouted. The pretty walnut wood of my dining room table is hidden by piles of papers. Mia sits on my couch and uses an end table for a desk so she can write on the LexiCo laptop. Mike sits at the desk, tucking his elbows between the printer and scanner so he can access the desktop computer's keyboard. My living room closets, once neatly organized, now stand open, belching office supplies onto the floor.

"How did it go?" Mia repeats.

Holding up my hand, I show her a pair of silver keys. "We move in ten days."

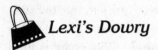

Lexi's Dowry

"I'm looking for something more modern," Grace told the realtor. "We're planning on having children right away and I don't want to spend time fixing up a house." Grace and Michael are looking for a house to buy. Actually, Grace is doing the looking. As with the wedding planning, Michael told Grace to narrow her choices before he toured homes.

I agreed to accompany Grace on a nighttime tour of available houses near Rittenhouse Square. The Philadelphia real estate market has been booming for several years, with houses selling high and fast. I wanted to see what all the fuss was about. We had already looked at three houses, none of which Grace liked. Now she was dismissing the fourth house.

But of course, we had spent an hour here before Grace made up her mind. In that time, I started to mentally move in. My couch would go there, that space could be used for storage, my dining room table would fit perfectly right here, and all that space there would be for LexiCo.

"Can I look around one more time?" I asked the realtor, and

she agreed. As I walked through the house, I fell in love with it. "I want to buy this," I told the realtor. She looked at the ring finger on my left hand, saw it was vacant, and offered me a polite smile. Before she questioned my marital status, I told her that I could afford the house on my own.

Which was not exactly true.

"I want to use my wedding money to buy the house," I told my mother over the phone. When I was engaged to Ron Anderson, my parents told me that they had, together, saved money to pay for my wedding. This was news to me, but welcome news. Obviously, that money was never spent, and it had accrued into a nice chunk o' change. More than enough for a big, fat down payment on a house.

"I may never have a wedding," I told Mom, "but I want this house." She wanted to know my father's opinion. "He understands that it makes business sense. LexiCo has already outgrown my apartment, so I'll have to rent office space, and it makes a lot more sense for me to buy a house and turn a floor into office space. I'll get a tax credits, which equals out to . . ." Hurling numbers at my mother, I could feel her resistance crumbling.

"Your dad said it was okay?" I mumble something in the affirmative. "If it's okay with your father," she finally said, "it's okay with me."

With a huge smile on my face, I hung up with Mom and redialed the phone. "Dad? I want to use my wedding money to buy a house."

And I did. Settlement was today, which seems fast but my realtor assured me it was average timing for the frenzied Philadelphia real estate market.

*   *   *

The keys I dangle in front of Mia and Mike belong to the house. They, and my parents, have seen the house, and everyone loves it.

LexiCo and I will be leaving Rittenhouse Square. Will I be sad to leave the Square, my posh apartment, and my whooshing toilet? Yes. But, look. This is me, moving forward. Moving south, actually. The house is a brownstone that sits six blocks south of the Square.

The brownstone has a narrow foyer that leads to a large living room with bay windows and a fireplace. Behind the living room sits a large, modern kitchen. Which will come in handy one day, if I decide to cook something. The second floor has three bedrooms and a bathroom. Those rooms will be offices; mine, Mike's, and Mia's. Mike is ecstatic to have an office, even though it has a mirrored ceiling, left over from the previous, kinky owner. The third floor has a big bedroom, master bathroom and a tiny terrace. That's all for me.

"Just because we spent your wedding money doesn't mean you can't get married," Mom said when she looked at the house.

Dad smiled, put his arm around me and said, "You might not get a big wedding, but this house? Now, it's your dowry."

 The Elder Council at Brunch

Not surprisingly, the COG has canceled brunch. Grace is frantic with wedding plans. Lola is filming the TV show. Mia has her boys, and Ellie is somewhere in Texas with Jean-François.

"I want a fish plate," Sylvia says. On this Sunday, I am

brunching with the Elder Council at Café Oz. "There is no fish plate," Patrick patiently tells Sylvia. "We have a lox, cream cheese, and bagel dish. Would you like that?"

Sylvia fiddles with the giant white, plastic necklace she wears over her purple velour sweat suit. Sylvia enjoys torturing Patrick. "I really want chopped herring and whitefish salad," she moans. "Is the lox Nova?"

"Of course it is." Patrick smiles.

"*Danken gut*," Sylvia sighs. "The Nova, please, and an onion bagel." Sylvia hands Patrick her menu. Smiling at me, he leaves to deliver our orders.

"You are such a pain in the *tuchus*," Esther tells Sylvia. "You should behave when Lexi takes us out to eat."

"At least I'm not dressed like a hooker," Sylvia answers.

"You're just jealous that I have style," Esther huffs. I doubt that Sylvia is jealous of Esther's style. Queen Esther is not dressed for a casual Sunday brunch. She's dressed for high tea with the Queen of England. Esther wears a long, lacy dress, white gloves, a gigantic hat, and pearl earrings. She doesn't get out much.

Ruth pats my hand. "How are you, *shayna*?"

I look closely at her. "Ruth? Did you color your hair?"

"A touchup," she answers, patting her bob, which is the same shade as a navel orange.

"She's getting ready for Halloween," Sylvia grunts.

Ruth ignores Sylvia. "How's the house coming along?"

"I move in Wednesday. I can't wait."

"You should have much happiness in that house," Ruth says. "*Kina hora*."

"*Kina hora*," Sylvia and Esther repeat.

Patrick brings our drinks. Latte for me and decaf coffee for everyone else. "We need the juice, *bubbeleh*," Ruth tells Patrick, and he brings three tall glasses of orange juice. The ladies reach into their purses, and each places a plastic container on the table. With a simultaneous pop, the containers open to reveal the Elder Council's morning pills.

"I forgot my blue one," Esther moans.

"You can have mine," Sylvia tells her, passing a shiny blue capsule.

"You need it," Esther protests.

"You need it more," Sylvia says.

"Wait a minute." Ruth dives into her purse and pulls out a spare pill container. "Esther, can you substitute two of my pink pills for a blue?"

"No," Esther says. "The pinks don't mix with my green pills."

"I can take two pinks," Sylvia says. "They go fine with my white pills."

"And they don't counteract the red pills?" Ruth asks.

"Oh, yeah. Here." Sylvia offers a pill to Esther. "Take my blue and give me your yellows in exchange for my reds so I can take the pinks."

"That works," Esther agrees.

The Elder Council exchanges their rainbow of pills and I turn on my cell phone in case I have to call 911. In the ten minutes it takes for the ladies to swallow their pills, Patrick brings our food. Sylvia makes a careful sandwich out of her food, spreading the cream cheese, layering the lox, then the tomato, and topping it with an onion. "That is so fattening," Esther scolds.

"*Zash til,*" Sylvia says with her mouth full. "Who cares?"

"What's this?" Ruth asks me, pointing at her cornflakes. Before I can answer, Ruth calls, "Patrick!" and waves her hands in alarm.

Patrick hustles to our table. "What's wrong, Miss Ruth?"

"What is that?" Ruth points to the offending slice of fruit.

"It's a mango. Try it. It's good."

Ruth shakes her head. "I don't know from mango."

"Mine's delicious," Esther coos and winks at Patrick. "You're such a good cook."

"It's cottage cheese," Sylvia says, spraying the table with tomato.

"Shut up," Esther whines as Patrick walks away to get Ruth new cornflakes.

"Girls," Ruth moans. "Stop it."

Watching this, I smile and realize that the Elder Council of Girlfriends and the younger Council of Girlfriends aren't that different. May our friendships survive as long as theirs.

Kina hora. Kina hora.

 Chapter One

Moving sucks. End of story. Mike, Mia, and I unpack only what is necessary for us to work and I leave the rest of my life in boxes.

On Saturday, the mailman drops the first bundled bunch of envelopes through my mail slot, and I see that most of the items have been delayed because they were addressed to my previous address and it takes time to receive forwarded mail. Flipping through the bundle, I see a postcard invitation to tonight's opening of Gallery X. Reading the postcard, I realize it is Jack McKay's gallery, named X to defy artistic description.

Sitting in my living room's bay window and thinking about Jack, I feel bad that I never called him. But I think that I was

right about the bad timing. Buying this house was a big commitment for me. True, it was a financial commitment and not
an emotional one. But, still. A new chapter of my life is beginning. Here it is. Chapter one. Now, I think. Now is the time to
work on a relationship with Jack.

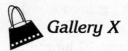 ## Gallery X

It's a humid September night. The cab stinks and I hold my
nose as we cruise downtown. I hope my dress doesn't absorb
the cab's stench. I'm wearing a flirty, flowered sundress with
straps that cross my back. I feel good. I just hope I smell good.

There is a crowd outside the building, and I'm happy to see
that the gallery has such a following. Pushing through the
people, I walk inside. The warehouse space is bedecked with
white twinkle lights. From the ceiling hang framed paintings
created with oil, watercolor, and acrylic paints. Via a pulley
system, the paintings can be lowered for prospective buyers.
Photograph arrangements hang on the walls at eye level.
Sculptures begin on the floor and reach upward, forming a
maze through the warehouse.

Walking through the maze, I pretend to look at the art. I'm
really looking for Jack.

Then I see him. He's talking with people. Gesturing. Laughing. And, his arm. His arm is around a woman.

Moving stealthily, I circle the sculptures to look at the
woman. She is short and thin. About my age. Her curly blond
hair touches her shoulders. She's wearing gray pants and an
expensive-looking blouse. She is pretty.

Jack kisses her. On the mouth. I gasp, and a squeal comes

out of me. Jack turns and sees me. First he squints at me, then he raises his eyebrows in surprise. Raising his hand, Jack waves me over.

Turning on my heel, I head for the door.

"Lexi," I hear him call. "Wait." I turn and wait for Jack to catch up with me. He's wearing faded jeans, boots, two silver rings, and a blue T-shirt with a white "X" painted over his heart. "I'm surprised to see you here," he says.

"Great gallery," I mutter. "Congratulations." I turn to the door.

"Thanks," Jack says to my back.

Spinning around to face him, I say, "I thought we could talk."

"Now? It's my opening night. I can't talk now."

"Oh, right. You have your new girlfriend to keep you busy."

"Jealous?" Jack smiles.

"Does that make you happy?"

Jack stops smiling. "No."

"Well, I can see that you've moved on to blonder pastures."

Calmly, Jack says, "Lexi, you didn't call me for a month."

"I shouldn't have come," I tell him. Turning away, I walk to the door. Jack doesn't stop me. Outside, I pause and hope that Jack will run out after me. He doesn't.

 ## Dr. Franklin, Session Eighteen

Tossing myself on his couch, I exhale loudly. "Strange as this is to believe, I made a big mistake."

"Go on," Dr. Franklin says.

"I went to Gallery X to see Jack."

"What happened?"

"There was a blond chickadee attached to him."

Dr. Franklin clears his throat. "You thought Jack would welcome you with open arms?"

"Yes."

"Even though you never gave him an answer about the future of your relationship, and he probably assumed that you weren't interested."

"Yes."

"Did you tell Jack that you were going to the gallery?"

"No."

"When you saw Jack, did you tell him how you felt?"

"No."

"What did you do? Leave?"

"Yes."

"I see." Dr. Franklin nods. "So, Lexi, you thought that Jack would be waiting for you, and you would walk into the gallery and everything would be perfect. Do I have that right?"

"Well." I roll my eyes. "It sounds stupid when you say it like that."

"It couldn't be as simple as that, Lexi. Nothing ever is." Dr. Franklin smiles at me, and he does that so rarely that it startles me.

"What?"

"It's a good thing that you went to see Jack."

"Right." I nod. "Because humiliation keeps me humble."

"The point, Lexi, is that you're open to the possibility of a committed relationship." We sit quietly for a few moments.

Then I say, "I guess I missed my chance with Jack."

Dr. Franklin smiles. "Maybe not."

"Doc, he didn't want to talk to me."

"That was bad timing. Try again. He put himself on the line and told you how he felt. Now it's your turn."

 ## The COG's Best Laid Plans

Grace is already waving her arms around. I see this through the window.

We the COG are finally gathering for brunch. Ellie is back from her American road trip, Mia has her husband watching their sons, Grace has the day off from the hospital, and Lola . . . I don't know what exactly is up with Lola, but she's sitting at the table with the other girls. After a one-month recess, the COG has convened, and Grace is already waving her arms around.

As I walk toward the table, Grace covers her face, leans into Mia, and begins to sob. "What's going on?" I ask, sliding into a chair.

Mia shakes her head at me. Grace sobs harder. No one tells me anything. We wait.

After a few minutes, Grace swallows her snot and wipes her face. She looks at me through her leaking mascara, and I wince and wait for the news.

"Michael Kelly is an asshole," Grace says. I look at Lola, Mia, and Ellie.

I shrug. "Okay."

"Can you believe," Grace says direly, pulling away from Lola and slamming her hands on the Formica table, "that Michael wants to elope?"

"Elope?" I choke. "The wedding is next week."

Grace starts to cry again.

"What made him? When did? I mean, why? Why does Michael want to elope?"

"Michael said that the wedding is making Grace crazy," Mia explains. "He says it's too much pressure on both of them and that the whole thing has lost its meaning, so he wants to go away and get married quietly."

I find that difficult to contest. Looking at the faces of the other women, I think we all agree with Michael. All but Grace.

Gently, I ask, "Did he say where he wants to go to elope?"

"Las Vegas," Grace spits.

"That could be great, Gracie. You could stay in a fabulous hotel. Go to the spa, eat great food. See a show, gamble. And you could get married by Elvis."

Grace yelps and puts her head down on the table. Mia and Lola rub her back.

Watching my Gracie cry, I think. Hard. "Grace?"

"Lexi," Mia says, "don't help."

"No, I have a legitimate question. Grace? You have to make a choice. Do you want to be married to Michael, or do you want to have a big wedding? You can't have both."

The COG raise their collective eyebrows, surprised at my sudden wisdom. And they all know the answer. Grace picks up her head and wipes at her eyes. "I want to be married to Michael," she says firmly.

"Okay, then." Reaching across the table, I hold Grace's hands. "There's no sense in crying about this. You're getting what you want, but not the way you want it."

Grace nods. "You're right. But what about all the arrangements? All that money?"

"Hey, Gracie. If there's one thing I know how to do, it's get money back from wedding vendors."

The COG laughs at this and, sensing a break in the drama, a waiter comes to take our order.

"Let's talk about something else." Mia sighs. "I'm still pregnant, and that's all I have to say. Lola? How's the TV show?"

"We're filming the last episode on Thursday. *Gracias a dios.* Then the cookbook comes out and I'll have to deal with that." Lola doesn't offer details of the cookbook, and I don't ask. If I really wanted to know, I could ask Ellie. But I don't really want to know.

"What's going on with your house?" Grace asks me, wiping her nose.

"Still not unpacked," I report. "This morning, Mom brought over a bunch of plants and whatnot. She burned rosemary and waved it through every room. To get rid of the bad spirits. Just to be on the safe side. We don't want to irritate the goddess."

Our food arrives. Stuffing eggs into my mouth, I say, "So, El? How was the road trip?"

"Great, great," Ellie says quietly. She clears her throat. "I got some news yesterday."

"What?" Grace asks.

"I'm pregnant," Ellie answers.

Grace spits her juice back into her glass. "Pregnant?" she squeaks.

"Yes," Ellie says and smiles shyly. "I went to the doctor yesterday. I'm almost two months pregnant. It's sooner than Jean-François and I planned, but we're very excited." She looks at us, and we stare back at her.

I am the first to reach out and hug Ellie. "Congratulations," I shout.

Lola, Mia, and Grace come from around the table and join

in our hug. I separate from the bunch and look at Ellie. She is beaming. She is happy.

"Wait a minute," I tell the COG. "I have an idea."

Walking home from brunch, I smile and hug myself. The COG loves my idea. Flushed with success and a sense of possibility, I reach for my cell and call Gallery X. "Is Jack McKay there?"

 ## The Ceremony

My mother futzes with the bow on the back of my dress. I let her. I know the bow is fine, but if Mom wants to futz, she can futz.

Dad sticks his head into my room. "Everyone's ready," he says. I take Mom's hand and Dad's arm. We walk out of the room and down the steps. I hear the violinists and cellist playing. "You look beautiful," Dad says. Leaning down, he kisses my cheek, then takes Mom's arm and escorts her into the garden.

The garden in the back of my house looks beautiful at dusk. Flats of flowers and a few bushes have been hurriedly planted around the garden. From the trees hang red and orange Chinese lanterns, lit with votives. Rows of white plastic chairs adorned with white tulle are divided by a white satin swath of fabric. At the end of the aisle is a lattice wall, festooned with green leaves, orange, red, and yellow flowers, and white tulle bows. The minister stands in his robe, smiling at the guests. To the minister's right are four men in tuxedos. To the minister's left are Lola, Mia, and Grace in strapless gowns.

Standing in the doorway, I turn my head. "Are you

ready?" I ask Ellie. A tear leaks from Ellie's left eye and she nods. "Are you nuts?" I hiss. "Don't cry. That makeup took two hours."

"Okay, okay," Ellie says, pulling herself together.

"Breathe," I say soothingly. "Just breathe."

This is Jean-François and Ellie's wedding.

The flowers, music, dresses, and food were already ordered and paid for. We just needed a bride and groom.

The wedding was to take place at the Kellys' home, but since that wouldn't work for this wedding, we needed a new location. I couldn't think of a better way to christen my new house. We simply stowed the boxes in the basement and let the wedding decorator do whatever he wanted.

The dresses? Grace and Ellie are the same height and almost the same weight, especially with Ellie's morning sickness. The wedding dress got a few emergency alterations, and Grace wore Ellie's bridesmaid gown, which had fit her months ago in Bridal Heaven.

Jean-François's family and their friends sucked up the steep, last-minute air fares and flew to Philadelphia. Ellie's family trained from Manhattan.

The party will be in honor of both newlyweds, the Bardets and the Kellys. Their parents are ecstatic about splitting the bills.

If Grace has any remorse about missing her trip down the aisle, she has the presence of mind and strength of character not to show it. Peering down the aisle, I see Grace glance at the ring on her finger and smile. Ellie has the princess dress, but Grace got married by the King.

*   *   *

"Auntie Lex, now?" David asks.

"No, I go first. You follow me," I tell the Rose boys.

"Wait," Ellie says, and grabs my hand. "Stay with me. Let the boys go. I want you right in front of me. Okay?"

"Okay." Now my eyes tear. "I'll stay right here."

"Now, Auntie Lex?" Simon asks.

"Now."

David and Simon, dressed in tiny suits, walk down the aisle blowing bubbles. Simon is blowing more air than bubbles. "Like this, Baby Sy," David whispers loudly. They stop in the middle of the aisle, and David directs his brother's air stream toward the wand. Bubbles float toward the darkening sky.

Then it's my turn. Giving a big smile to the fabulous Ellie Archer, I breathe deeply and walk down the aisle.

At the end of the aisle, I take my place next to Grace. We make quite a fetching row of bridesmaids. The dresses are similar but of different pastel colors that complement our different complexions. Grace wears pale pink, Lola wears pale orange, Mia and her unborn child are swathed in light green, and I wear pale blue. We are a rainbow.

Turning, I watch Ellie walk toward us. Behind her veil, she smiles widely. Looking at Jean-François, I see that he has tears in his eyes. Jean-François's three brothers, standing with him, nudge one another and smile at Ellie. The French folks in attendance have never seen an American wedding, and I am happy that this is a magical experience for them.

Ellie has chosen to walk herself down the aisle, and although my parents would kill me if I did that, it suits Ellie's lifelong independence. She comes to a stop beside Jean-François, and he raises her veil.

And then, Jean-François leans in to kiss Ellie. "Not yet," the minister says. Ellie ignores him and receives Jean-François's kiss. Everyone giggles.

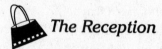

The Reception

Dinner is served on the ground floor of my house. White-clothed tables are arranged against the walls, which are adorned with white twinkle lights. Somehow, everyone fits. We had to forgo formal seating and a formal dinner presentation, so people mix and mingle at the tables and help themselves to the buffet set up in my kitchen. Lola did not do the catering, but she is nonetheless directing the cooks in my kitchen. She is here without a date. Even if she had intended to bring Adrian to the Kellys', she would not bring him to my home. Then again, I don't know if they are still dating.

The garden's chairs and aisle have been replaced with a small band for formal dancing. There is a DJ on the second floor, in what will be Mike's office. The mirrored ceiling came in handy after all.

Many of Ellie and Jean-François's friends and family couldn't come to Philadelphia on such short notice. Since it's my house, I have filled it with people who are important to me.

In the garden, my parents are dancing. With each other. I wonder what their spouses think of that? Looking to my left, I see Mom's husband dancing with Dad's wife. Whatever.

Inside, Doorman John sits at a table with his wife, Ruby. She is a beautiful woman, and John never seems to let go of her hand. Near the windows, Zoga Jane is flirting with Café Oz Patrick.

"You've got to see this." Mike grabs my hand and pulls me up the stairs. Looking into the DJ room, I gasp. The Elder Council of Girlfriends is doing the electric slide with Jean-François's brothers.

Should I worry about the ladies' various heart conditions? As if reading my mind, Ruth waves at me and yells, "*Zorg za nisht!* Don't worry!" Okay. I won't worry. They'll be talking about this for years, both the *bubbes* and the brothers.

 **The Gift**

Hearing the doorbell ring, I walk back down the stairs and open the door.

"Lexi?"

"Jack?"

"What are you doing here?" we ask simultaneously.

"I'm here for the wedding," Jack says. "Jean-François invited me."

"Jean-François? How do you know him?"

"Ah, Jack! *Comment ça va?*" Jean-François comes from the living room to give Jack a huge Gallic hug.

"*Trés bien. Ça va?*" Jack answers.

Hands on my hips, I pout. "Excuse me?"

Jean-François puts his arm around me. "Jack, this is Lexi James."

"He knows my name."

"Ah." Jean-François grins. "You know each other?"

"Yes," I answer.

Jack points at me and Jean-François. "How do you know each other?"

"Jean-François just married Ellie. My friend Ellie? She's a member of the COG."

"Oh," Jack nods. "The COG."

"Yes." Jean-François rolls his eyes and smiles affectionately. "The COG."

"Hey!"

"Sorry," Jean-François says with a smile. "Pardon me for a moment." He turns to help his mother descend the staircase.

"How do you know Jean-François?" I ask Jack.

"He came into my gallery last week," Jack explains. "He bought a painting that he said would be perfect for a friend of his. We got to talking and Jean-François told me about the wedding. Since some of his friends couldn't come, Jean-François invited me. Here I am."

"You missed the ceremony," I tell Jack meanly.

"I told Jean-François that I would be late because I had to close the gallery," Jack says. He looks me up and down. "What's your problem?"

"I called you. At the gallery."

"You did?"

"Yeah. I left a message. You never called me back."

"I didn't get the message," Jack says. "It's been so hectic and everyone's answering the phone. The message probably got misplaced. I'm sorry about that." Jack tilts his head and peers at me. "What were you calling about?"

As he walks toward us, Jean-François calls, "Jack, where is the painting?" Jean-François claps his hands together in anticipation. "Lexi, you will love it."

"The painting is for Lexi?" Jack asks and laughs.

"Yes, of course it is for Lexi," Jean-François answers. "I tell you it is for a special friend." He looks down at me. "It is, how you say? A warm house gift."

"Housewarming," I correct him.

Jean-François continues, "And it is a thank you gift for having our wedding in your home."

"This is your house?" Jack asks.

I nod.

"Jack? The painting?"

From behind the front door, Jack brings forth a two-foot-by-four-foot structure covered in brown paper. He rests it on a table next to the door. With a sweeping gesture, Jean-François pulls the wrapping from the painting. *"Voilà!"* he shouts. "It is of Rittenhouse Square. Where you and I became friends, Lexi. *D'accord?*"

"Yes." I nod. The painting is a gorgeous oil landscape of the Square. The picture shows a bright, sunny day with the Square in full bloom. But there are only two people in the picture. They sit on a bench, kissing. Taking a step closer to the painting, I squint at the kissers. The woman has brown, curly hair and she's wearing purple flip-flops. A bottle of ginger ale sits on the bench. The scene reminds me of the night Jack and I talked—talked, not kissed—in Rittenhouse Square. Pointing at the painting, I look at Jack. "Is that me?"

"Yes," he answers.

"That woman is Lexi?" Jean-François asks, leaning down to peer at the painting.

"Yes," Jack repeats.

"You told me that the man is you," Jean-François says. Standing up, Jean-François wags his finger from me to Jack. "You are lovers? I did not know this."

"We're not," I tell him. "I mean, we were. But we're not

now." Looking up at Jean-François, I smile and say, "Jack has a new girlfriend."

"Lexi didn't call me for a month," Jack tells Jean-François.

Into the foyer comes the COG, Elder COG, and my parents.

"What's all the hubbub?" Sylvia asks.

"What is Jack doing here?" Lola asks.

"Is that the painting?" Ellie asks.

Before I can begin to explain, Jean-François takes over. "This is the painting I buy for Lexi for a thank-you and warm house present from me and Ellie. This is Jack, the painter, and he painted him and Lexi kissing in Rittenhouse Square, because they were lovers, but he did not know that the painting was for Lexi and I did not know it was Lexi in the painting when I bought it." Jean-François spreads his arms over everyone's head. "*Voilà!*"

No one speaks for a moment. Then, the foyer erupts with sound.

"Did you know he painted you?" Grace asks me.

"Is that Lexi in the painting?" Esther asks. "I don't have my glasses."

"You were my daughter's lover?" Dad asks Jack.

"When were you two lovers?" Mom asks me.

"Is he Jewish?" Ruth asks.

Grabbing Jack's hand, I pull him through the house into the backyard. The band has taken a break, so it's just the two of us standing under the white lights. Shutting the door behind me, I turn to face Jack. We start talking at the same time.

"She's not my girlfriend," he says.

"I wanted another chance," I say. We smile at each other.

"If you give me another chance, I'll give you another chance," he says.

"We should just start over," I say.

"How do we do that?" Jack asks.

"Wait," I tell him. "Stand here." Jack obeys, and I cross to the other side of the yard. Casually, I stroll through the yard and make a wide circle around Jack. He stands with his hands in his pockets and looks at me as if I'm crazy. Then, as if suddenly noticing him, I look him up and down, smile shyly, and meander toward Jack. Extending my hand, I say, "Hello. I'm Lexi James."

Jack raises his left eyebrow and takes my hand. "I'm Jack McKay."

 ## The End, Part Two

"What a romantic day," Grace mumbles with her mouth full of cake.

The party is over. Jean-François is escorting his family to their hotel. Doctor Michael has to do a late night round before he leaves tomorrow on his honeymoon with Grace. Lawyer Michael is driving the Elder Council to their Home. As getting the ladies in and out of the car could take a while, the Rose family decided to wait here for Michael to return.

The COG has gathered in my bedroom, the only clean space available. David and Baby Sy, stripped to their undies, are fast asleep on a pile of fluffy towels. We girls have changed into what I have unpacked: T-shirts, yoga pants, and jammie bottoms. Lola accepted one of my T-shirts, and then it turned out that it was hers, anyway. I am enormously pleased that she is with us. It might be a start, or not, but I'll take it for what it is right now.

The wedding dress hangs from the back of my bathroom door, and the bridesmaid dresses hang from hooks around the bedroom. The dresses watch us like an audience of our alter egos, our former selves, or, at least, our other selves.

Ellie, Grace, Mia, Lola, and I are huddled on my bed with the remainder of the wedding cake between us. We are savaging it with forks. Plastic ones. My old forks? They sat in my dishwasher so long that they rusted and I threw them away. With gusto.

"What did you say?" Lola asks Grace.

"What a romantic day," Grace repeats. "It was a wonderful party, Lexi. Perfection. Everyone had a great time."

"Yeah." I sigh. "At least for one night, everybody was happy. Even me."

"I'm going to throw up," Ellie says.

"Don't get critical when Lexi gets mushy," Mia chides.

"No, really. I'm going to hurl." Ellie launches herself off the bed and into my bathroom.

"Should we help her?" I ask the COG.

"She needs help throwing up?" Lola asks. "You're the nurse, Grace. Go help her vomit."

"I'm okay," Ellie says, stumbling into the room. "The nausea passed." Ellie lies down on my bed and stares at the ceiling. "This part of pregnancy sucks."

"Want some cake?" I ask, and wave a forkful of chocolate chip cake with white chocolate icing under her nose. Nauseated she may be, but good cake is good cake. Ellie opens her mouth, and I airplane the cake onto her tongue.

With her mouth full, Ellie says, "I don't know how I'm going to get through the flight without vomiting. Jean-François and I leave for Paris in three days."

"I'm leaving on my book tour next week," Lola says. "I leave Monday. Twelve cities. I'll be gone almost a month." Lola points her fork at Grace. "Where are you and Michael going on your honeymoon?"

"St. Thomas," Grace mumbles. She swallows her cake and smiles. "Two weeks in paradise. I can't wait." Grace turns to me. "What's going to happen with you and Jack?"

Smiling at my friends, I say, "I'm not really sure. We're starting over. We'll take it slow. Figure it out. Work on it. I've got time. There's no rush."

"How did you leave it with him?" Ellie asks.

"I asked him if he wanted to go steady." The COG giggles.

"I have some news," Mia says.

"Let me guess," I say. "You have to pee. What with Ellie throwing up and you peeing, I better call a plumber."

Mia hurls a chunk of cake at my head and it lands on my pillow. "Hey, now," I yell. "These are expensive sheets. Three hundred and fifty thread count, don't you know."

"Tell us your news, Mia," Grace says.

"Michael and I found out the gender of the baby," Mia says.

"What is it?" the COG screams in unison.

"It's a girl," Mia whispers.

Grace and Lola cover Mia with kisses and hugs. Ellie puts her hands on Mia's belly. And me? I wipe a tear from my eye and realize that she'll be here soon. The first member of the next generation of the Council of Girlfriends.

Epilogue

Sorority League Leadership Conference
Irvine Auditorium, University of Pennsylvania
September 2003

"What I have learned is that life is all about choices. I've made a lot of mine. Yours are still to come. And you'll have a lot of choices to make. Which job, where to live, who to love, when and if to have kids. Sometimes you will make the right choice and sometimes you will make the wrong choice. But you have the freedom, the liberty, and the independence to do what you think is right for yourself.

"Generations of women before you, and before me, have fought for our right to determine our own lives. That's a privilege a lot of other women in the world do not have.

"What I'm saying is that you have choices to make. That means you can choose to do this, and choose not to do that. Just because we can do everything doesn't mean we should.

"Whatever you decide to do, do it well. You have a lot of choices. Make them wisely."

Want More?

Turn the page to enter
Avon's Little Black Book —

the dish, the scoop and the
cherry on top from
MELISSA JACOBS

More About Me

Once upon a time, I was a PR consultant. Successful, I was. But just because you're good at something doesn't mean it's what you were put on the planet to do. Still, I wasn't unhappy. Just unfulfilled.

What did you want to be when you grew up? I wanted to be a writer. For always. As a child, I told stories to my parents, my grandparents, my brother. My dolls had complete life stories. Inanimate objects had personalities.

Storytelling became writing via my first diary. It was a hardback book with a long-stemmed red rose on the cover. My mother gave me the diary so I could write about my feelings. My father had just died. I was eight.

That rose-covered journal became a conduit to my creativity, and to my father. Now I know that my father dreamed of being a writer. Then I believed that my father could read what I wrote, so I described my life in great detail. Colors, textures, tastes, smells. Little did I know that I was writing in what would become my favored form: first-person narrative.

Fast-forward twenty years. As a PR consultant, I lived medium, if not large. The morning after a tragic first date, I e-mailed the story to my friend Leigh. She laughed, she cried, she published it in her magazine, *Cuizine*. Greg, Martha, and Bob let me write for *Inside* and the *Jewish Exponent*. Maury gave me assignments for *SJ* magazine.

During the first third of 2001, I was Dr. Jekyll and Ms. Hyde, doing PR during the day and writing at night. I dabbled in fiction, conducting weird experiments with rhythm, points of view, and characters.

On September 12, 2001, I decided to give up PR and dedicate myself to being a full-time writer. Life is short. Dream big.

Of course, it wasn't that easy. I had contracts, leases, and obligations. It took almost a year to deconstruct my life. By June 2002, I was writing full-time. In September, I ran out of money. I had to choose. Return to PR to afford my swanky lifestyle? Or keep writing and do the starving artist thing?

If not for Mom, I would've had to go back to PR. If my father inspired my dream of writing, my mother made it come true.

Mom let me move into the basement of her condominium. She acted like it was perfectly normal for her single, thirty-something daughter to be living and working in her dank, dark basement. It was there that the Council of Girlfriends was born. While I wrote, Mom kept me sane. Relatively speaking.

When I completed *LJ&TCOG,* I researched literary agents and found my Yoda, Betsy Amster. She made me a better writer. Then she made me an author. In December 2003, Miss Betsy notched a deal with Avon Books.

Who is the first person I told? My mommy.

In February 2004, I went to the NYC HQ of HarperCollins, of which Avon Books is a division. On a cold, windy day, I hustled down East Fifty-third Street to meet the Avon Ladies: my editor, La Princesa Selina; executive editor and Boss Babe Lucia; and the wittily wise PR Pam. Late and somewhat disheveled, I scanned the street, looking for the right building. Then I saw it. The big, red sign. HarperCollins Publishers. I laughed out loud.

You see? Dreams do come true.

The Author Interview:
Lexi James and Melissa Jacobs

LEXI: You're late.

MELISSA: Very sorry. But I'm only twelve minutes late. I have another three to spare before you get huffy.

LEXI: I don't get huffy. I simply believe that punctuality is important.

MELISSA: You're right. It is.

LEXI: Okay, then. Let's get started. I invited you to my home to discuss the novel and how you wrote it.

MELISSA: I like what you've done with your house. I see you found another leopard print rug. And the couch is fabulous.

LEXI: My mother helped me find both things. That woman knows how to get bargains.

MELISSA: So does my mom. But that's where the similarities between our mothers end.

LEXI: Let's start there. With similarities. Readers are going to think that you and I are the same person.

MELISSA: We're not.

LEXI: No. I'm a much better dresser.

MELISSA: Oh, please. You do not dress better than I do. We simply have different styles.

LEXI: Right. And, um, how would you describe your style? Jersey girl chic?

MELISSA: Listen, I sit in front of a computer all day and talk to myself. When I have to, I can look very presentable. Also, you're taller than I am. You can wear different styles.

LEXI: Yeah, you are short.

MELISSA: Petite.

LEXI: Fine. Petite. So, I'm a taller, thinner, more stylish version of you.

MELISSA: Yes. But, I'm smarter than you are.

LEXI: I'm younger.

MELISSA: I'm funnier.

LEXI: I'm richer.

MELISSA: Not for long.

LEXI: Thank goodness for the book deal. Were you down to your last few shekels?

MELISSA: I was. When my advance check came, I had $131.71 in my checking account.

LEXI: When you stopped working and moved in with your mother, did your friends think you were crazy?

MELISSA: I raised crazy to a new level. But my friends know that I take a lot of risks.

LEXI: I don't.

MELISSA: I know. You should've left The Gold Group long before you did.

LEXI: I know that. Now.

MELISSA: Right. And see? Your risk turned out well.

LEXI: As did yours. But you couldn't have known that you would get an agent, let alone a publishing deal.

MELISSA: It all could've gone horribly wrong.

LEXI: What would you have done if Miss Betsy hadn't taken you under her halo?

MELISSA: I don't know. I didn't have a Plan B.

LEXI: Let's move on. What was it like to go from glamour girl to starving artist?

MELISSA: When was I a glamour girl?

LEXI: Just go with it.

MELISSA: Fine. At first, it was difficult. I was very used to having disposable income. There was a time when I wouldn't have thought twice about spending fourteen dollars on a one-pound bag of baby arugula or forty-five dollars for an ounce of hair goop. Not having money

made me think about what I needed, and what I didn't.
My life became very simple, and there is a beauty in
that.

LEXI: How very Zen.

MELISSA: Don't mock. This is a dream come true for me.

LEXI: Being poverty-stricken was a dream come true?

MELISSA: No, dork. Having a novel published is a dream
come true. Nothing comes without sacrifice, right?

LEXI: Tell them about your unwilling sacrifice to the Shoe
God.

MELISSA: It's a tragic story. While I was writing, my mom's
basement was attacked by mold. All of my shoes, thirty-
eight pairs, were ruined. I was left with a pair of sneakers and black flipflops. The Shoe God took away the last
vestige of my old life. She stripped my last shred of
vanity.

LEXI: I weep for your shoes.

MELISSA: They died a horrible death. But did I really need
thirty-eight pairs of shoes?

LEXI: Yes.

MELISSA: No. And right after that, Miss Betsy agreed to be
my agent. It was karmarific. I gave some yin and got
some yang.

LEXI: Your shoe sacrifice notwithstanding, I'm glad that you
took the risk and wrote the novel. Otherwise, the world
wouldn't know about the Council of Girlfriends.

MELISSA: How are the girls?

LEXI: Wonderful. They send their regards. Let's talk about the
COG. Are there parallels between my girlfriends and
your girlfriends?

MELISSA: No. I know Latino food pretty well, which is why
Lola is a Latina restaurateur. Lola also has my ambition.
My cynicism. My incomprehensible taste in men.

LEXI: I don't want to talk about Adrian.

MELISSA: Me, either. How's Jack?

LEXI: Fabulous.

MELISSA: You should thank me very much for introducing you.

LEXI: You have my eternal gratitude. Is there a Jack in your life?

MELISSA: I've never met a man like Jack. I'd like to.

LEXI: I don't think that you would be happy with someone like Jack.

MELISSA: Why not?

LEXI: You are a lot like Jack. You need a levelheaded person to keep your feet on the ground. You're creative types. Dreamers.

MELISSA: Thank you.

LEXI: I don't mean that as a compliment.

MELISSA: Oh.

LEXI: Let's get back to the COG. Do you have a Gracie in your life? A relentless romantic?

MELISSA: At one time in my life, I was a relentless romantic.

LEXI: What about Mamma Mia?

MELISSA: Everyone has friends who live in the suburbs with their husbands and children. Had I taken the Husband and Children exit, I would have been a lot like Mia.

LEXI: The Fabulous Ellie Archer?

MELISSA: Had my life gone a different way, I might have ended up as Ellie.

LEXI: So what you're saying is that each of the COG is a part of you.

MELISSA: I think every woman wonders what her life would be like if she had done this or that, married that man or taken that job.

LEXI: So it's all about choices.

MELISSA: Amen.

Girlfriends' Guide to Philadelphia

Bring your girlfriends to Philadelphia!

Why did I set *LJ&TCOG* here? Because Philadelphia itself is a character, its moods shifting with its neighborhoods. Historic, trendy, posh, macho, outdoorsy. What about Philadelphia's reputation for being rude, overweight, gauche? That description could fit many cities, not to mention some of my dates.

But I digress. What can you and your COG do in Philadelphia? History. Shopping. Museums. Exercising. Theater. Dining. Art. Philadelphia has something for everyone. Take it from me. Philadelphia loves you back!

Let's start where the United States started: Old City. This neighborhood is exactly what it sounds like. Old. Historic. The Liberty Bell, National Constitution Center, Betsy Ross's House. All that good stuff is in Old City. You don't have to be a history geek like me to appreciate the historical significance of Old City. You'll feel proud to be an American and lucky to be living in these times instead of those. For starters, the shoe options were really limited back then.

My favorite historical Philadelphian? Ben Franklin. Philadelphia is saturated with Ben's name and image. He was a writer, a philosopher, an inventor, and quite the wit. At my alma mater, the University of Pennsylvania, it's Ben 24/7. Him being the founder and all. Pay your respects to Ben by pitching a penny onto his grave at Fourth and Arch Streets. Why a penny? You know what Ben said, "A penny

saved is a penny earned." In case you haven't read the big
Ben biography, the fence surrounding his grave has a Cliff
Notes version of his life.

End of history lesson. Let the partying begin. Girlfriends
Kammie, Monica, and I have determined that Old City is the
place to go for nightlife if you are under thirty. There are lots
of clubs in which to boogie oogie oogie. Or try the bars in
Northern Liberties, the next neighborhood to the north. I
don't know much about Northern Liberties. I flunked my hip-
ster test and they don't let me in.

For outdoor dancing on the waterfront, venture onto
Delaware Ave, also known as Christopher Columbus Boule-
vard. If you go, go with a sense of humor. Kammie and I
spent some time at a club last summer and it was like being
in an episode on Animal Planet. "Observe the mating rituals
of the modern American male . . ."

Before you go to Delaware Ave or elsewhere, review your
secret girlfriend lingo. You know, the code words you use to
tell your friends to rescue you immediately, give you five
more minutes to decide, or beat it so you can mack on the
hottie.

I've been girlfriends with Monica and Kammie for so long
that we don't really need code words. An eyebrow is suffi-
cient. Unfortunately, the eyebrow usually says: Help!

Back to the tour. South and west of Old City is the Society
Hill neighborhood. It's a quaint area filled with three-level
brick houses called trinities. Why are the houses called trini-
ties? Because, in Yore, the three floors were enough to fit the
Father, the Son and the Holy Spirit. I don't know what the
Jews did.

Along Society Hill's brick sidewalks sit lovingly decorated
homes, their doors and shutters painted in traditional colonial
colors, their window boxes overflowing with flowers and
greenery. Private gardens hide down cobblestoned alleys.
Brass and blue plaques note buildings' historical significance.

In the midst of Society Hill is Washington West Square. Wash West, as we call it, is a quieter version of Rittenhouse Square, the much discussed park in *LJ&TCOG*. Surrounding Wash West are luxe apartment buildings, coffee shops, boutiques, and theaters. Wash West is also a good place to break up with someone. It's private, but public. The landscaped serenity of Wash West soothes a broken heart. Trust me. I know.

Farther west, on the 1100 block of Walnut Street, is Caribou Café, my favorite French restaurant. On the next block is Aoi, a bare-bones Japanese restaurant that offers all-you-can-eat sushi for $19.95. If you have more money, try El Vez, a fun Mexican restaurant, at Thirteenth and Sansom. Around the corner is Capogiro, an authentic gelateria. Girlfriend Monica and I gelato'ed our way through Italy, and Capogiro gets our yum of approval.

If you and your girlfriends are looking for inexpensive food in a casual, fun setting, head north to Chinatown. Sang Kee is one of my favorite spots, which is why Lexi goes there to get her "fie dolla" soup. Vietnam is another fab restaurant, especially the upstairs dining room. Great for dates, too. You can linger, or get fed and get out.

Back to Broad Street. Broad Street is Fourteenth Street. Why do we call it Broad? Because it's wide? Because this is where colonial hookers trolled? I don't know.

The fantabulous Ritz-Carlton Philadelphia reclines majestically at the corner of Broad and Chestnut. Yes, the opening scene of *LJ&TCOG* takes place there. The lobby is where Girlfriend Monica and I treat ourselves to drinks after arduous shopping. Also? Great bathrooms.

In addition to being Fourteenth Street, Broad Street is also the Avenue of the Arts. Theater, dance, music. Cultured girlfriends will find plenty of performances. Even those on the starving-artist budget can find reasonably priced tickets.

At the other end of Broad Street is our sports complex. I hope that I have presented Philadelphia as a sophisticated town. But what of the much publicized bad behavior of Philadelphia sports fans? We have roughly the same reputation as British soccer fans.

My brother Dave is a fan of all seasons. And he suffers for it. Still, he roots for the Eagles, Flyers, Phillies, and Sixers. As long as the athletes work hard, dripping with blood, sweat, and tears, Philadelphians cheer for them. No matter what the odds of winning. I think it's the Balboa Factor. We don't like hot dogs. We like underdogs.

Watching my brother live and die with every sports season, I have come to believe that being a Philadelphia fan is a lot like going on a blind date. You think, "I'll be casual. I won't get too excited, or too invested in the outcome." But you do. You wear lipstick and clean underwear. Just in case. Because, as the late, great Tug McGraw said, "You gotta believe."

Enough about sports. Let's get to the shopping.

West of Broad Street is the Rittenhouse area. Welcome to my neighborhood. Okay, I currently live in Mom's basement. But I lived in the Rittenhouse area for most of my decade in Philadelphia.

My first apartment was near the corner of Sixteenth and Locust. Tiny, it was. But full of sunshine. My second apartment was a fourth-floor walk-up two blocks away, at the corner of Sixteenth and Pine. Oh, the memories that apartment holds. It is where I started my PR consultancy, fell in love, fell out of love, straightened my hair for the first time, was burglarized, and spent a lot of time on the roof of the building, staring at the Philadelphia skyline and wondering what would become of my life.

Shopping. I promised shopping.

The neighborhood above Broad Street is a mecca of independent boutiques and high-end national retailers. Everything is here, from Anthropologie to Zegna. Walnut Street has the three Bs: Burberry's, Brooks Brothers, and Banana Republic.

In my opinion, Philadelphians dress rather conservatively, albeit fashionably. Someone suggested to me that artsy-sexy Jack McKay would wear leather pants. But I've never seen a straight man wear leather pants in Philadelphia. And I'm not suggesting they start.

Brides? Head to Maria Romia, the boutique in which Grace finds her princess bridal gown. If you're not a bride but still want to feel like a princess, get pampered at one of the umpteeen spas in the neighborhood. Girlfriend Ilene and I have spent many hours oohing and aahing at Adolf Bieker, the spa inside the Rittenhouse Hotel. If you are on the starving-artist budget, get the same level of pamper at Four Sisters. The clean, comfortable salon is near the corner of Twentieth and Walnut. Manicure and pedicure for twenty-five dollars? Sold!

Some of Philadelphia's best restaurants are in the Rittenhouse neighborhood. If you're on the starving-artist budget, check out the bar menus at the posh places. The ambiance is free. Or go to a casual spot like The Black Sheep, the best Irish pub in Philadelphia. I also like Boathouse, the wood-paneled bar in the Rittenhouse Hotel.

Along Eighteenth Street are Rouge, Devon, and Bleu, the holy trinity of the Rittenhouse singles scene. All three are good restaurants and have excellent sidewalk seating. Girlfriends over thirty will enjoy this scene. These joints are jumping with fun and flirting.

Need somewhere to spend some quiet girlfriend time? Go to Tuscany Café. There are other, swanker coffee shops, but I prefer Tuscany. I like the matte yellow walls, the blue spotlights descending toward the dark wood tables. Quiet art sits on the walls near the large windows topped with stained glass. My favorite table is along the back of the café. If you go into Tuscany, you'll see the table. The window it faces has a stained glass design of a red and blue coat of arms floating in navy and violet swirls. That table is where I started writing *LJ&TCOG*.

*   *   *

In the middle of all this glamour is Rittenhouse Square. It's one of my favorite places on the planet. I hope that I have done it descriptive justice in *LJ&TCOG*.

Stroll the Square. If it's winter, you'll see lighted orbs hanging from the trees, shining cherry red, tangerine, and aqua through the cold air. Every Christmas, a magnificently decorated tree sits in the middle of the square, acting as a festive focal point for the neighborhood.

If it's spring or summer, you'll see men, women, and children walking, playing, eating, playing guitar or chess, or reading. Perhaps you can envision Jack and Lexi chatting on a bench. Or me, sitting by the fountain and dreaming about becoming a novelist.

There is much more of Philadelphia to explore, but I'll leave you here, amid the flowers and grass, the statuary and benches.

Thank you for reading my book.

Melissa Jacobs
May 2004

Where did Jack take Lexi for their first official date? Azafran. What was their first course? Ceviche! You, too, can savor the flavors of ceviche. Make this dish for a romantic dinner for two, or as fun food for your Council of Girlfriends. *¡Buen provecho!*

Susanna's Ceviche

SERVES 6

> 2 *lbs. scallops, grouper, or mixture*
> ½ *large Spanish onion, diced*
> ¼ *cup chopped cilantro*
> ¼ *cup chopped parsley*
> 1 *or 2 diced jalapeños, depending on desired spiciness*
> 1 *cup juice (lemon, grapefruit, lime, orange, or mixture)*
> *Salt and pepper to taste*

Clean and dry the seafood. Cut into one-inch pieces.

In a large mixing bowl, combine all ingredients. Toss seafood, making sure it is well covered with ingredients. Refrigerate for two hours, tossing every half hour.

Serve very chilled in martini glasses, coconut shells, or in small dishes on a mountain of ice.

Susanna Goihman, chef and owner
Azafran
617 South Third Street, Philadelphia
215-928-4019

MELISSA JACOBS

MELISSA JACOBS ran her own success-ful public relations company for five years, then fired herself. "I learned that money can buy shoes but not happiness." She said good-bye to Philadelphia, embraced her inner Jersey girl, and is now pursuing her dream of being a novelist.